Karma

Threads of Hindu–Muslim unity; shared goals of the welfare of
these two communities; and the non-violent struggle of the
untouchables, peasants, and the city's poor for their rights
are deftly interwoven in Premchand's novel. It is startling
to note how topical these issues are even in the India
of our times and yet how divorced from out urban
lives. So light is his touch that his protagonists
seem to be at times at odds with themselves,
but for that very reason,
more human.

Lalit Srivastava is Professor Emeritus,
Department of Biological Sciences at
Simon Fraser University, Canada.

Karmabhumi

PREMCHAND

❧

Translated by LALIT SRIVASTAVA

OXFORD
UNIVERSITY PRESS

OXFORD
UNIVERSITY PRESS

YMCA Library Building, Jai Singh Road, New Delhi 110 001

Oxford University Press is a department of the University of Oxford. It furthers the
University's objective of excellence in research, scholarship, and education
by publishing worldwide in

Oxford New York

Auckland Cape Town Dar es Salaam Hong Kong Karachi Kuala Lumpur
Madrid Melbourne Mexico City Nairobi New Delhi Shanghai Taipei Toronto

With offices in

Argentina Austria Brazil Chile Czech Republic France Greece Guatemala
Hungary Italy Japan Poland Portugal Singapore South Korea Switzerland
Thailand Turkey Ukraine Vietnam

Oxford is a registered trademark of Oxford University Press
in the UK and in certain other countries

Published in India by Oxford University Press, New Delhi

ISBN-13: 978-0-19-569666-0
ISBN-10: 0-19-569666-2

Typeset in Bembo 10.5/12.5 by Sai Graphic Design, New Delhi 110 055
Printed at Ram Printograph, Delhi 110 051
Published by Oxford University Press
YMCA Library Building, Jai Singh Road, New Delhi 110 001

CONTENTS

INTRODUCTION

※⟨⟩⟨⟩⟨⟩⟨⟩⟨⟩⟨⟩※

Dhanpat Rai, widely known as Premchand, was born on 31 July 1880 in a village called Lamhi about four miles from Benaras. His parents were poor, and after primary education in the village and matriculation from Mission School in Benaras, he started earning his living as a tutor in 1899. Unable to obtain admission to university because of deficiencies in mathematics, he taught in various small schools before being selected for teacher's training and being appointed as sub-inspector of schools. Soon after his matriculation, Rai started writing stories and articles with a nationalistic flavour. One collection of his short stories published in 1907 caught the then British government's attention. The book was banned as it was considered seditious and all the remaining copies destroyed. But Rai continued to write, and in 1916 adopted the pen name 'Premchand'. A prolific writer despite a short lifespan, ill health, and financial problems, he wrote many famous novels like *Sevasadan, Nirmala, Gaban, Kayakalp, Karmabhumi, Rangbhumi, Premashram*, and *Godan*, and nearly three hundred short stories. He also edited several magazines such as *Maryada, Madhuri, Hans*, and *Jagran*, and for a short time in 1934, worked in Bombay as a scriptwriter for films. He presided over the first conference of the Progressive Writers' Union in 1936, and died the same year in Benaras.

Some of Premchand's works have been translated into English: *Godan* (The Gift of a Cow), *Nirmala, Gaban* (The Stolen Jewels), and *Sevasadan* (House of Service), and at least four collections of his short stories are available in English. This novel, *Karmabhumi*, which I translate as *The Field of Action*, is set in Uttar Pradesh (UP, formerly the United Provinces of Agra and Oudh) where he was born and grew up and where most of his other novels are also situated. However, this novel covers a wider social fabric than many of the other novels. It was written in the 1930s, and to see the novel in its historical and local perspective it is essential to understand Hindu–Muslim relations, the Hindu caste system, the abject misery of peasants and the poor in villages and cities, and the impact of Mahatma Gandhi and his satyagrah movement on the Indian national scene.

The first Muslim invasion of India took place in AD 712, but it was not until 1192 that Muslim sovereignty was established in northern India and later extended to southern India. From then until 1857, when it was succeeded by the British crown, Delhi was ruled by Muslim princes, although some Hindu princes also held sway in many parts of western and southern India. The contact with Arab Muslims, and then Turkish and Persian Muslims, led to the evolution of two languages in India—Hindi and Urdu. Urdu was not a language that was distinct from Hindi. It had evolved from Hindi and shared with it the same basic grammatical system as well as much of the vocabulary, but it had an Arabic alphabet. Hindi had a Sanskrit base and was written from left to right like all Indo-European languages, while Urdu had an Arabic and Persian base and was written from right to left. Many Hindus wrote with distinction in Urdu, and there were Muslim scholars of Hindi literature and Hindu thought. Present-day Uttar Pradesh, with Lucknow as its capital and Delhi at its western edge, became the seat of Muslim culture where both Urdu and Hindi flourished. Through most of the eighteenth and nineteenth centuries, Urdu was the official language, and all educated people, whether Muslim or Hindu, learned it as their first language. This situation remained unchanged until the late nineteenth and early years of the twentieth centuries when English gradually replaced Urdu as the official language. Premchand grew up with both languages, wrote in both, and achieved a place of honour in the literature of both languages. When I was growing up in Uttar Pradesh in the 1930s and 1940s, we spoke a mixture of the two languages known as Hindustani; my Muslim friends would use more Urdu words, we would use more Hindi words, but everyone understood each other. Hindustani is the language in *Karmabhumi* and many of the distinctive idioms which Premchand uses are derived from it.

By the beginning of the twentieth century, the two religions, Islam and Hinduism, had coexisted in India for more than a thousand years. Except for occasional outbursts of violence, the two religious communities lived together in harmony. They not only tolerated each other but, indeed, there were numerous instances of friendship (such as that between Amarkant, the main Hindu character of *Karmabhumi*, and Salim, the chief Muslim character) and strong social bonds, excluding marriage, between the two communities. Hindus were the first to take advantage of English education: they became clerks in the government, entered the Indian Civil Service, and provided the bulk of businessmen and professional people such as lawyers, doctors, and teachers. This was the beginning of the Hindu middle class. By contrast, the great majority of Muslims were either landlords or peasants. The former disdained learning a foreign language or entering a trade, whereas the peasants were the same as their Hindu counterparts, with the result that there were few professional people and hardly any middle class among the Muslims. As a result, some Muslims feared that in an independent India they might be relegated to second-class status. This view is expressed by Mr Ghaznavi in a dialogue with Salim, but he qualifies it with the conviction that Hindus would never treat Muslims so. (Nevertheless, this fear was the basis for the demand for Pakistan by Muhammad Ali Jinnah, leader of the Muslim League, and led to the division of the country in 1947.)

During the decade before *Karmabhumi*'s publication, Premchand had been very much influenced by Gandhiji's satyagrah movement, and his writings, stories, and essays clearly reflected his sympathies with India's poor and the fight for India's freedom. India of the early 1900s consisted of a great mass of poor and illiterate people who were exploited by the privileged few. Peasants in the villages were cheated by moneylenders and landlords and the poor of all castes in the cities were exploited by the rich nd powerful. The untouchable classes were treated as pariahs by their own upper-caste Hindu brethren.

Since Vedic times (1500–800 BC), the caste system had been one of the pillars of Hindu society. Caste was at first based on profession: teachers and those devoted to learning and worship were Brahmans, those devoted to warfare and affairs of state were Kshatriyas, those devoted to trade and business were Vaishyas, and those devoted to farming and menial tasks were Shudras. Within each group there were smaller groups or subcastes. A small subgroup of Shudras, the untouchables, were those employed in gathering night soil and were leatherworkers. Although initially there was vertical mobility between the castes, with time the boundaries became rigid and caste became hereditary. As the caste system became rigid, opposition against it grew. However, it has shown remarkable resilience through the ages. It survived not only the powerful impact of Buddhism and many centuries of Muslim rule and the spread of Islam, but also the strenuous efforts of innumerable Hindu reformers who raised their voices against it, specially against its worst aspects—untouchability and the exclusion of a large section from the main fabric of Hindu society. The untouchables could not enter the temples or homes of caste Hindus, even their shadow could not be allowed to fall on a caste Hindu. Into this rigid and caste-bound society in early 1900s—still living like a feudal society in the Middle Ages—came Gandhi with a vision of change, a change that would galvanize the tradition-bound Hindu and Muslim populations into social and political action. The magic of Gandhiji's satyagrah movement was that it encompassed three goals—India's independence from British rule, the removal of untouchability, and the alleviation of poverty, expressed poetically as the wiping of every tear from every poor person—in one single movement.

Premchand has structured *Karmabhumi* to give importance to the two social issues of the Gandhian movement; the political issue of independence, although very real, is mentioned only in passing. It is social reform that is highlighted in the temple incident, the poor villagers' protest for relief from land tax, and the march of the poor people in the city demanding land for their individual homes. All of these protests are subject to suppression, but the leaders of the movement oppose these suppressive forces in a typically Gandhian manner with non-violent protest and willingness to suffer the consequences of their actions without rancour towards their oppressors. In this movement, women participate equally with the men and the movement gains momentum as it draws students, teachers, farmers, and labourers in its fold. Premchand has been called the first great artist of the progressive Indian social revolution.[1]

The novel is also an expression of Indian philosophic thought. The Hindi title, *Karmabhumi*, does not lend itself to an easy translation in English. In Hindi, the word 'karma' has many meanings—act, work, deed, occupation, business, fate, destiny; and 'bhumi' means earth, ground, field. I have loosely translated it as *The Field of Action* which ties in with the Urdu title of the book, *Maidaane-amal*.[2] The main theme of *Karmabhumi*—the uplifting of the downtrodden poor including the untouchables, and the inherent right of people to better their lives irrespective of their birth or station in life—is expressed through the Hindu philosophy of karma and its Gandhian interpretation of non-violent protest with its principle that ends do not justify the means.

[1] As cited in Permanand Shrivastava, 'Bhoomika' to Premchand's *Karmabhumi*, Hindi text, p. 6.

[2] Premchand translated the book in Urdu under the title *Maidaane-amal*, which was published by Jamia Millia, p. 5.

The theory of karma says that you must do what your duty requires you to do without regard to consequences. This theory is expounded in the Bhagvad Gita by Lord Krishna on the eve of the epic battle of Mahabharata between the Pandavas and their cousins, the Kauravas. Arjuna, the great Pandava warrior, seeing his cousins, relatives, teachers, and friends, arrayed in battle against him, throws down his great Gaandeeva bow, and says to Lord Krishna, his charioteer, that he cannot fight his friends and relatives. Krishna then explains to Arjuna that it is his duty to fight, irrespective of the consequences, that it is his dharma as a warrior to perform this action, this karma.

In Premchand's novel, human life is also portrayed as a field of action in which the character and destinies of individuals are formed and revealed through their actions. Some of these actions, which might seem melodramatic in ordinary realistic fiction, gain resonance in *Karmabhumi*, placed as they are within this symbolic and philosophical framework. It is in this context that we interpret pivotal points in the narrative such as when Amarkant concludes that he must leave his home, when the young mother Munni leaves husband and child to go into exile, when the untouchables are attacked by the police for attempting to enter the temple and Sukhada joins the battle to support them, when the village poor revolt against a rich landlord, and when the district officer Salim, having become convinced of the oppressive governmental policy, resigns from the Indian Civil Service. In each case the character (or group) concerned is depicted as coming to a point of moral awakening where he, she, or they must act on their convictions. The climax of the book comes on an actual field where the dispossessed and poor of the city are assembled. As each speaker—Lala Samarkant, Renuka Devi, and Dr Shantikumar—gives his/her reasons why the struggle for land for the poor must continue, they are stopped by the police and taken to prison. Finally the shy and affectionate Naina, Amarkant's young half-sister, is moved to speak. Her words are stopped by a bullet but her death on the field of action leads to eventual victory for the greater cause of gaining land for the poor.

In *Karmabhumi*, the marital life of Amarkant and Sukhada is played out against the backdrop of the larger canvas of class conflict and peoples' movement. The marriage fails due to differences between the two personalities, but they come together towards the end with each realizing the other's worth. In the process, Premchand expounds his ideas on education, on marriage and rights of women, his sympathies for the poor and dispossessed, his dislike of cant and superficialities of religion, and of priests who prey upon the gullibility of the devout, the powers of self sacrifice and mass movement, and his dreams of an independent India.

Premchand is an educator *par excellence* and devoted to learning as shown by the fact that he himself obtained his B.A. degree studying privately at the age of thirty-nine. Throughout *Karmabhumi* there is strong emphasis on the role of schools and education: indeed the first chapter of the book depicts a classroom where the wrong kind of education prevails, a so-called 'Western education', where the emphasis is on money rather than on idealism or learning. Later in the text the author offers an alternative: his perspective on a more idealistic Indian education as developed in Dr Shantikumar's school.

Amarkant is portrayed as an intelligent and idealistic, but weak, young man. To learn to act in a more independent manner he must first overcome the dominance of his father and then of his wife. Premchand develops his psychology in some detail. Amarkant's mother had died when he was very young; his stepmother, while she lived, berated him on every occasion; and his father Lala Samarkant, a rich moneylender, constantly scolded his son for spending his money on idealistic pursuits. Deprived of love in his formative years, Amarkant grew up to hate his father's business and his sham adherence to the superficial formalities of the Hindu religion. Throughout the text, Premchand uses the word 'dharma' in a variety of ways to make his readers reflect upon the differences between 'real' and 'superficial' religious acts.

Amarkant is married at the age of eighteen to Sukhada, a beautiful girl from a wealthy family, whose mother is the only surviving family member. Sukhada is portrayed as an intelligent girl, proud of her good looks and heritage and, in the first two years of their marriage, fond of a comfortable life. Though steeped in the Hindu tradition of respect and affection for her husband, she nonetheless dominates Amarkant with her analytical mind and common sense. Persuaded by her, he grudgingly begins to involve himself in his father's business. There he learns that individual human beings are a mixture of good and evil. To his dismay he learns from a thief, Kaale Khan, that his father is not above accepting stolen goods to sell them at a profit; but he also learns from an old Muslim woman, Pathanin, the widow of his father's former watchman, that his father has been supporting her for many years at the same salary that her husband used to receive. Amarkant takes Pathanin back to her hovel where he meets her granddaughter, Sakina, who captures his imagination by her modesty and courtesy. Struck by the family's extreme poverty, Amarkant tries to help them by finding customers for Sakina's sewing among his wealthy friends, especially the Muslim Salim. Denied love at home and feeling stifled by his father and wife, Amarkant feels he must leave home in order to develop and nurture his soul. Drawn to Sakina, he rashly offers to marry her, but until told by his father that there is no place in his house for Sakina as a wife, Amarkant leaves the house and embarks on his wanderings from village to village.

Accustomed to a life of comfort and luxury, Amarkant's wife Sukhada cannot understand his reasons for helping the poor and his apparent desire to live as a labourer. She is angry and humiliated when he leaves her for Sakina. But her attitudes toward life and its meaning undergo a sea change when she sees the police firing upon the untouchables in order to keep them from entering a temple. When Lala Samarkant, her father-in-law, refuses to stop the police, she takes matters into her own hands and jumps into the fray herself. Instantaneously she becomes the leader of the city's poor and deprived. Now that she sees the conditions of the poor with her own eyes, she, who had never suffered a hardship in her life, begins to understand what her husband was trying to do. Even though she does not forgive him (when she meets her husband in Lucknow prison) for leaving her for Sakina, she now understands his motivation and holds him in high regard.

Amarkant's character also evolves over his years of exile. During this period Munni, a Hindu villager who had been raped by a British soldier and who had killed two Englishmen in revenge, helps him. She was willing to die but the court had released her on grounds of insanity. Leaving her family and ancestral village behind, she had gone to Haridwar and ended up in a village of untouchables. After several months of wandering, Amarkant arrives at this village. Just as Sakina'a acceptance had restored his pride, so Munni's presence in the village acts as a balm on his sense of dignity when he begins to take part in village affairs and soon becomes its leader. The climax of his stay in the village comes with the farmers' movement against the levying of land tax. At first he tries to reach a settlement with Mahant, the landlord. But after receiving news of Sukhada's arrest in a letter from Naina, and impelled by the desire to gain recognition as his wife had had, he deviates from the path of non-violent protest in favour of direct confrontation. He is arrested by Salim, who is the District Officer, and sent to prison. This deviation from the Gandhian path results in loss of life of the poor villagers.When he receives this tragic news in prison, he realizes that the Gandhian path was much the better one. In conclusion, a number of individuals help Amarkant to reach a higher moral consciousness: first his wife, then Sakina, Munni, the villagers, Salim, and finally Kaale Khan, who in his death in Lucknow prison (where Amarkant has been sent) exemplifies his staunch belief in a personal God.

Premchand excels in delineating characters. Amarkant takes a long time to mature. In the beginning, he is shown as being idealistic with little common sense—witness his dialogues with Shantikumar about the running of the free school and with Salim about his intended marriage to Sakina. He is also weak and vacillating. Although he talks of sacrifice and living as a labourer, he is easily drawn into luxurious living by his mother-in-law. He finds himself on the road to sacrifice only as a revolt against what he perceives as Sukhada's love for comfort and indulgence. He waxes hot and cold on the same issue—witness his behavior in leading the farmers' movement against collection of land tax. However, near the end he matures and displays an ability to compromise without sacrificing his principles.

Sukhada, by contrast, knows her strengths, acts consistently, and is fearless in expressing herself; but she also discovers her weaknesses when she goes to see Sakina. She finds that Sakina, unlike what she had imagined, is not a wily woman with seductive glances; instead, she has modesty, grace and an ability to love—qualities that enable women to rule the hearts of men. Although Sukhada becomes aware of the qualities she lacks, she is still very angry with Amarkant. She says to Shantikumar, a university professor, that the punishment for such men is that their wives retaliate in kind, but in the next breath, with her grounding in Hindu cultural values, says that that path is not for her.

Lala Samarkant is a self-made man, proud and jealous of his achievements, who tries to make money in business by any means, fair or foul, but who nonetheless observes all the duties and ceremonies of religion without understanding the substance or rationale behind them. The departure of Amarkant serves as a pivotal point in his life, leading him first into despair and the building of a temple, and finally to introspection which makes him realize the truth behind his son's struggle for the poor and downtrodden.

Similarly, other characters in the novel—Salim, Sakina, Munni, Shantikumar, Naina—are all drawn with immaculate vividness and are true to life. This is not to say that the characters don't have weaknesses.

They all do, just as real-life characters always do. Premchand had written
in an essay, 'Novel', several years before composing *Karmabhumi* that 'to
portray characters excellently and ideally, it is not essential that they be
blameless. Even the greatest men have some weakness or another. To make
characters come alive, there is no harm in emphasizing those weaknesses.'[3]

Social conflict is spread throughout *Karmabhumi* and Premchand explores
conflict resolution by both violent and non-violent means. Of the two,
Premchand clearly favours non-violent resistance as Mahatma Gandhi had
preached and practised. But to be successful, non-violent resistance requires
an opponent who has a basic sense of decency and fair play. It is debatable
whether Gandhi would have succeeded against the fascist regime of Nazi
Germany or communist regime of Stalin's USSR! That Premchand is aware
of this and is ambivalent on the issue is clear in the dialogue between
Amarkant and Salim in Part 5, Chapter 8, where Amarkant eloquently
pleads to Salim for non-violent resistance who remains unconvinced of the
efficacy of the method.

Near the end of the story almost everyone has either been sent to the
prison or arrives there for a meeting. Having resolved her doubts about
Amarkant's character in talks with Munni and Sakina, Sukhada now sees
herself and her husband in a new light. It seems to her that her severity and
harshness have been replaced by grace and tenderness, that her emptiness
has been filled with honey, that her incompleteness as a woman has been
satisfied by the love of her husband. With the coming together of Sukhada
and Amarkant, it appears that a new country is being born out of the old
one, a country which is more awakened and more alive. Premchand
concludes his novel with a message from the Governor of UP, appropriately
conveyed by Lala Dhaniram, that everyone arrested in the people's movement is to be released and that a people's committee is to be set up to look
into the reform of land tax, thus ensuring success of the movement.

[3] Ibid., p. 11.

TRANSLAT' R'S NOTE

The translation of a novel from one language into another is a hazardous task. It is especially so when a Hindi novel is translated into English because the two languages differ from each other not only in grammar and construction, but also because many words and expressions have no counterparts in the other language. For instance, in Hindi, verbs are declined according to the subject; also, sentences often do not state the subject or the object, the context tells who or what is intended. A literal translation, therefore, is often baffling and sometimes unintelligible. Although it is necessary to have it as a first step, it has to be converted to everyday English, which involves a more or less free and colloquial translation. The present translation is the result of such an attempt. I have tried not to deviate too far from the intent, spirit, and flavour of the original, and many Hindi names and words have been retained for the Indian reader familiar with the setting of the novel in its particular Indian context. For western readers and Indian readers with a similar background, a glossary of Hindustani words used in the book has been provided.

The format of the text has been slightly changed. In the Hindi text of *Karmabhumi*, long dialogues occur between characreters with no indication of who is speaking. This is possible in Hindi because the grammar makes it clear who is saying what. However, in an English translation where verbs and adjectives do not follow the subjective noun, such dialogues are confusing. Hence in some places I have inserted the name of the speaker, for example, 'Amar rejoined', or 'Naina replied', for clarity. Other changes include grouping of very short sentences, and certain forms of speech. For instance, in Hindi one often says *do-char din* which literally translated means 'two-four days'. These forms have been changed to 'three or four days'.

As noted by almost every translator of Premchand's novels or short stories, there are some inconsistencies in the Hindi text of *Karmabhumi*. Premchand was a very prolific writer and he probably did not have the time or the inclination to re-read and correct some of the ambiguities/errors that inevitably creep into a novel of the size of *Karmabhumi.*These inconsistencies have been corrected in the translation. For instance, in Part 1, Chapter 7, Pathanin says to Amarkant that she has sons, daughters-in-law, and grandchildren, and the implication is that they are all living but they don't take care of her. Later in the same chapter she says that they are all dead. In this translation, I have amended the first reference to imply that they are all dead. Similarly, a reference to Amarkant having been relieved of the task of selling caps has been changed to selling handkerchiefs to correspond with the description.

Among the Hindi words that have no counterpart in English and one which occurs repeatedly in *Karmabhumi* is 'dharma'. Dharma has several meanings, depending on the context: religion, duty, code of action, morality, moral principles, obligation, righteousness. The concept of duty or code of action or dharma is not an inflexible entity, but is commensurate with one's station or place in life. For example, a soldier's dharma is to fight a battle with honour and bravery; he is not to concern himself with the consequences of success or failure. When a specific meaning is clear I have translated dharma into that meaning; otherwise, I have left it as 'dharma'.

Certain aspects of Indian, especially Hindu, culture and tradition need to be explained for non-Indian readers. In Hindu thought, this world and all it represents, animate and inanimate, is part of the *Brahman*, the absolute Godhead. We, the individual *atmans*, can achieve *nirvana*, the freedom from the cycle of birth and rebirth, by fusing our spirits with the Brahman. Brahman is inconceivable and unknowable, but the world he created, his *maya*, is knowable. The attachments that we make to our relatives and friends (love, affection, etc.) are considered *moh*. Maya and moh have various meanings depending on the context, but generally connote something that is unreal or insubstantive and transitory, in contrast to the spiritual world and the love for God, which are real and of eternal value. Nonetheless, it would be simplistic to think that maya and moh are totally unreal; they are 'real' to people (who themselves are part of maya), but that reality is temporal and has no lasting value.

In Hindu society, sons, daughters, and daughters-in-law show respect to their elders, when meeting them after a while, by touching their feet. Similarly, if seated, they get up if an elder enters the room; a wife, if sitting, stands up when the husband enters the room.

Auspicious occasions are often celebrated with showering rice and *batasha*s (small semi-spherical cakes, very light and fluffy, made of rice flour and sugar) on the general populace; sometimes coins may be showered as well. People collect these things, called loot, for their use. On the birth of a child, servants are offered gifts, sometimes jewellery to female servants.

Karmabhumi gives graphic accounts of women's place in society. Not only do they participate equally with men in the struggle for the removal of untouchability and upliftment of the poor, they are also very conscious of their rights and duties vis-à-vis men. In Part 3, Chapter 6 for instance, Sukhada, an educated Hindu woman, expresses her conception of her conjugal rights and duties to Dr Shantikumar, a university professor. Yet she is deeply grounded in Hindu cultural values and, contrary to western conception, she is no vassal or chattel of man.

Another instance of grounding in Hindu values is shown by Munni, an uneducated village woman. Western readers may think that Munni is exaggerating her situation when she pleads for death during her trial on a charge of murder, and, on acquittal, when she begs her audience for respect and oblivion for herself in exile. She considers herself defiled and thus unfit for living as wife and mother. She realizes in her own mind that even though she is being hailed as a *sati* by the general population and her husband is ready to take her back, yet this accolade is transient and the stigma of impurity will remain with her for ever. Later, the same feeling of having been defiled and thus unfit for being a wife and mother keeps her from going back to her husband and child when they come searching for her in Haridwar.

In Hindu society, a daughter is thought to belong to her (future) husband's family. For this reason she is considered a guest in her own familial house, held in trust until her wedding when she is passed on to her husband or her husband's parents. Girls were considered to be of marriageable age after reaching puberty and many were indeed married when they were between fourteen and seventeen years of age. Also, marriages used to be arranged between families of similar background and caste, but with little direct input from the bride or the groom. For these reasons, a period of several years (up to three or four) would elapse during which the new bride and groom would get to know and adjust to each other, develop mentally and physically, and gradually assume the responsibilities of parenthood and running their own household. During this period, the bride would often go back to her parent's house (*maika*), sometimes for months, only to return to her husband's or father-in-law's house (*sasural*). With time, both the frequency and duration of visits to the maika would reduce and eventually become normal visits to a parent's home.

At the time of writing of *Karmabhumi*, Hindus were allowed several wives, although the general practice was for only one (which has since 1947 become the law). Hence the idea of a marriage between Amarkant and Sakina was legally possible, even though, as Salim said, it would have led to much turmoil, possibly even bloodshed.

Acknowledgements

Several people helped me in this translation by providing the meaning or interpretation of a particular word or phrase in the Hindi text. People from India include Mala Sharma of Noida, Alka Srivastava of Greater Noida, Vinaya Sinha of Delhi, and Premanand Srivastava of Gorakhpur. Those from North America include Indra Aggarwal and Yamuna Kachru, both from Urbana, Illinois; Vidyut Aklujkar of Vancouver, K.D. Srivastava of Vancouver, Amir Pirbhai of West Vancouver, and Sirish Sinha of Toronto. Shirin Punja of North Vancouver read the entire translation and provided valuable comments about its readability and coherence. The help of all the above is greatfully acknowledged. I would particularly like to thank Tanya Brown for typing much of the manuscript and providing her valuable insight into modern colloquial English. I am also very grateful to Sandra Djwa, my wife and a Professor of English, without whose input, encouragement, and knowledge of English literature and usage this book could not have been translated. I thank the editorial team at Oxford University Press, Delhi for help in producing the final copy of the text, and in seeing this endeavour to completion.

PREMCHAND'S APPEAL

❦

There are many people who read a novel from the perspective of history. It is my submission to such people that just as the characters in this book are fictitious, so are the places in it imaginary. It is very possible that there exist people with names such as Lala Samarkant and Amarkant, Sukhada and Naina, Salim and Sakina; but the difference between imaginary and real characters is the same as is between the world created by God and that created by His creatures. Similarly, in this book, Kashi (Benares) and Haridwar are imaginary places. And it is quite possible that you may not find the incidents and scenes depicted in this novel in these two places of pilgrimage in the United Provinces. It was difficult to invent names of characters and places without any basis in reality. So, then, why not Amarnath and Kashi? Instead of Amarkant, it could have been Tamarkant, and instead of Kashi it could have been Tasi, or Dumdal, or Dampu; but we have heard such weird names in this world that it would not be surprising if people or places with those names also exist. Just as some of us name our impoverished hut 'Garden of Peace (Serenity)' or 'Saint's Abode' and our wretched son Ramchandra or Harishchandra, we have given names to our characters and places that are indeed most beautiful and sacred. Is that in any way improper?

5 September 1932

Karmabhumi

PART ONE

CHAPTER 1

Even land taxes are probably not collected as ruthlessly as school fees are collected in our schools and colleges. On a set day each month it is essential that fees be paid. If you don't pay your fees, either your name is struck off the roll, or you pay a daily fine until the fees are deposited. In some places it is also the rule that the fees are doubled on a set day and if, on a later specified date, the doubled fees are not paid, your name is struck off. Such was the rule in Queens' College in Kashi. If on the seventh day of the month your fees were unpaid, then by the twenty-first you had to pay twice the amount, otherwise your name was struck off. Such strict rules could have no purpose other than to force the children of the poor to give up school. The same heartless bureaucratic rule that pervades other government departments also pervades our educational institutions. It shows mercy to no one. You must arrange for the fees from whatever source you can: borrow money, pawn ornaments, sell household pots and pans, steal—but fees you must pay, or else pay double fees, if you don't want your name struck off. Some leniency might be exercised in the collection of land or wealth tax, but no such indulgence is shown in our educational institutions where a kind of martial law prevails. Money rules in our law courts; money also rules in our schools, only it is a more harsh and pitiless rule. There is a fine if you are late; a fine if you don't show up in the classroom; a fine if you have not learned the lesson; a fine if you cannot buy books; a fine if there is any offence. They are not institutions for education; they are institutions for fines! This is the ideal of our much touted Western education. It is no surprise that students graduating from these institutions are ready to cut the throats of the poor or sell their souls for money!

It is fee collection day today. Heaps of money are piled on the desks of the teacher. The clink of coins can be heard from all sides; even in the jewellery market there is less jingling of rupees. Teachers sit in classrooms like *chaprasis* in a *tahsil* office. As the name of each boy is called, he comes up to the teacher, pays the fees, and returns to his seat. It is the month of

March and the fees for March, April, May, and June, as well as the examination fee are being collected. Every boy in the tenth grade has to pay forty rupees!

The teacher called out the name of the twentieth boy on the list, 'Amarkant!'

Amarkant was absent.

The teacher asked, 'Hasn't Amarkant come today?'

One boy replied, 'He was here. Perhaps he has gone outside.'

'Did he bring his fees?'

No one answered.

The teacher's face showed a tinge of regret. Amarkant was one of the better boys in class. He said, 'Perhaps he has gone to get the fees. If he is not here within the hour, he will have to pay double the fees. I can't help it! Next boy— Gobardhandas!'

Suddenly a boy spoke up, 'If you permit, Sir, I will go out and look for him.'

The teacher smiled and said, 'You must want to go home. All right, go, but come back within ten minutes. It is not my job to run after you boys to collect the school fees.'

The boy said politely, 'I will be back right away. I swear, I will not go out of the school yard.'

This boy was one of the well-to-do boys in the class. He was a great sportsman and a great conversationalist but if he disappeared after answering the roll call he would not show up till evening. He paid double fees in fines every month. He was a tall, slim, and refined young man with a fair complexion, who lived for sports. His name was Mohammad Salim.

Salim and Amarkant sat next to each other in class. Salim received special help from Amarkant in composition and arithmetic. Indeed, he copied from Amarkant's papers and the two had become friends. Moreover, Salim was a poet, and Amarkant would listen to his *ghazals* with great eagerness. This was another reason for their friendship.

Salim stepped out of the classroom looking here and there, but saw no sign of Amarkanat. And then he saw him standing behind a tree. 'Amarkant!' he called, 'You idiot! Come pay your fees. Panditji is getting annoyed.'

Amarkant wiped his eyes with the skirt of his *achkan* and, walking towards Salim, asked, 'What, has my number come up already?'

Salim looked at Amar's face and saw his reddened eyes. It was unlikely that Salim had ever wept in his life. Astonished, he said, 'Oh, you have been crying. What's the matter?'

Amarkant was a rather short young man, thin and delicate, and of dark complexion. He was about twenty years old, but hadn't sprouted any whiskers yet and looked like a boy of fourteen or fifteen. The usual expression on his face was of pained resolve, akin to despair, which seemed to suggest that he had no one left in the world. At the same time, his face had such warmth and compassion that, having seen him once, it was difficult to forget him.

He smiled and said, 'Nothing at all. Who's crying?'

'You are, who else! Tell me truthfully, what the matter is.'

Amarkant's eyes brimmed over. Try as he would, he could not stop the tears. Salim understood. Taking his hand, he said, 'Are you crying because of the fees? My good fellow, why didn't you tell me? You still consider me a stranger. You are being very foolish and ought to be shot. Such formality among friends! Come on, let's get back to class. I'll pay the fees. You've been crying for an hour over such a little thing. Say, it was lucky that I came, otherwise, your highness's name would've been struck off today.'

Although comforted, Amarkant felt weighed down by this kindness. He said, 'Will Panditji agree?'

Salim straightened up and said a little sharply, 'It is not up to Panditji. It is a government regulation. But you are very naughty. Its fortunate that I am carrying money, otherwise you would have done really well at the exams! Look, I have just composed a ghazal, which you must applaud:

That you remembered my devotion,
It is good, today at least you remembered.

Amarkant was in no mood to listen to a love song; but unless he listened nothing would be accomplished. He said, 'How delicately put! You have said it very well. I would give my life for such clarity in language.'

Salim said, 'That is my speciality dear brother ! A ghazal is not simply a resonance of words. Listen to the second couplet:

Again in my chest rose a pain,
As I recalled your demeanour.'

Amarkant was again obliged to heap praise. 'Irrefutable. How can you think of such couplets?'

Salim laughed, 'In the same way as you can figure out problems in arithmetic and write compositions or give speeches at the Association. Come on, let's have some *paan*.'

The two friends got roll of betel leaf each and then proceeded towards the classroom. Amarkant said, 'Panditji will scold us thoroughly.'

'He'll just collect the fees.'

'And if he asks me where I have been?'

'Say you forgot to bring the fees.'

'I won't be able to say that. I'll tell the truth.'

'Then you'll get a thrashing from me.'

In the evening when school was over and the two friends walked homewards, Amarkant said, 'The favour you did me today ...'

Salim put his hand on Amar's mouth and said, 'Stop, don't say another word. Never refer to this incident, even in your sleep.'

Amar asked, 'Are you coming to the meeting today?'

'What's the topic of discussion? I don't seem to remember.'

'Oh, it's the same thing, "Western Civilization".'

'Give me a few points, otherwise I will have nothing to say.'

'What can I tell you! We all know the negative features of western civilization. Just elaborate on them.'

'You may know them. I can't think even one.'

'Well,' said Amarkant, 'one is our kind of education. Wherever you look, it is the same shopkeeper mentality. There is a shop for litigation, a shop for knowledge, a shop for health. A lot can be said on this point alone.'

'Alright, I'll come.'

CHAPTER 2

Amarkant's father, Lala Samarkant, was a very industrious man. His father had left him only a hut at his death, but Samarkant had amassed a fortune in six figures through his own efforts. To begin with, he had a small agency for selling turmeric on a commission basis. Soon he added brown sugar and rice agencies, and the scope of his business expanded continuously for three years. Now he had closed the agencies and was involved only in borrowing and lending money. He would cheerfully lend to anyone who could not get a loan from a moneylender, and he would also collect his money. He was surprised when others lost money in such deals. There were not many people with his work ethic either. He would go and bathe in the Ganges while it was still dark and, before sunrise, he would already have visited the Vishwanathji temple and arrived at his shop. There he would instruct the clerk about the day's tasks, then go out to collect the monies owed to him, and return in the early afternoon. After lunch, he would return to the shop and stay there until midnight. He was also a big man. He had only one meal in the day, but he ate it with relish. He would exercise with clubs, rotating them 200 to 250 times.

Amarkant's mother had died in his childhood and, at the instigation of his friends, Samarkant had married again. The seven-year-old child had welcomed his new mother with much affection, but he soon learned that his stepmother would not tolerate his obstinacy and mischief in the same forgiving manner as his mother had. As an only son, he had been his mother's darling and so had grown to be an obstinate and naughty boy; whatever he wanted, he had to have. But his stepmother admonished him for every little thing and matters had reached such a pass that he hated her. In order to spite her, he would do everything she forbade him to do. He also became stubborn towards his father until no ties of affection remained between father and son. Whatever Lalaji did, his son would reject: he loved cream, his son disliked it; he would assiduously pray and read scriptures, his son considered it hypocrisy; his greed knew no bounds, his son despised money.

But sometimes good comes of bad. Normally, a son follows in his father's footsteps. A moneylender's son is a moneylender, a scholar's son a scholar, a lawyer's son a lawyer, a farmer's son a farmer; but, in this case, revulsion caused the son of a moneylender to become his adversary. Whatever the father esteemed, the son renounced; and whatever he opposed, the son adopted. He witnessed on a daily basis the dealings and intrigues of money-lending, and he hated it. It could be attributed to a previous incarnation, but clearly Amarkant's character was moulded to a large extent by his animosity towards his father.

The saving grace was that Amar did not have a stepbrother; otherwise, he might have left the house. Samarkant valued his wealth more than his son; wealth was not being amassed for his son's comfort, rather his son was needed to keep the wealth in the family. The stepmother, of course, wished that Amar be thrown out, thus clearing the way for her darling daughter, Naina; but on this point Samarkant was immovable. The irony was that Naina was very fond of her stepbrother, and if Amarkant had a soft spot for anyone in the family, it was for Naina. In looks, Naina resembled her stepbrother so much that she might have been his real sister. This resemblance further endeared her to Amarkant. In his affection for Naina he used to forget his bad treatment at the hands of his father and stepmother. There was no other child in the household and although her mother knew that Naina needed a companion, she could not consider Amarkant a suitable playmate and wished that her daughter would stay away from him. But Naina, although a child, did not obey this wicked dictat. The affection between brother and sister grew to such an extent that finally the stepmother's nature overcame that of the mother. She disowned Naina as well, and departed this world wishing for a son.

Naina was now the only female in the house. Samarkant realized the difficulty of marrying Naina off while still a child. He himself could not marry again as he was aware of the problems of marrying at old age. Thus he considered it necessary for Amarkant to get married, and there was no one to oppose this proposition!

At that time Amarkant had been almost eighteen but in build and mental development he was still a weak lad, for how could a plant grow or flourish without direct sunlight? The years in which he might have grown or broadened his horizons were spent in bad company and with no self-discipline. He had been in school for ten years, but had only managed to reach grade eight! However, these things were considered to be unimportant for marriage. What was important was money, especially in the business community. Negotiations were started with a rich family in Lucknow. Samarkant was most eager because, except for a widowed mother, there were no close relatives in the girl's family, and there was unlimited wealth. One gets such a girl only with great good fortune. But her mother had her brought up like a son, in luxury instead of denial; as a result she was severe instead of polite and sharp instead of tender. Moreover, she was not used to denying or limiting herself in any way. Consequently this young woman with masculine qualities was wedded to a young man with feminine traits who lacked manly virtues. If the two were to exchange clothes, they could have supplanted each other, for a suppressed masculinity is indeed femininity.

Although they had been married two years there was no bonding between them. Each went his or her own way. They lived in separate worlds, in thought and in deed, and it seemed as if two animals belonging to different habitats had been caged together. But in these last two years Amarkant had developed a capacity for self-control and hard work. The laxity, inertia, and self-effacement that had been the hallmarks of his character were being replaced by earnestness. He had also developed a liking for his studies. Although Lalaji now wanted to engage him in household affairs—he was able to read telegrams and urgent messages which was sufficient ability in Lalaji's eyes—Amarkant was like a traveller who had spent his day resting and now wanted to walk at twice the pace to reach his destination.

CHAPTER 3

As always after returning from school, Amarkant went to his little den and sat down in front of his spinning wheel. In that palatial home, where a wedding party could have been comfortably accommodated, he had chosen this small room for himself. He had made himself a promise to spin thread for two hours every day and had fulfilled that promise for several months despite his father's opposition.

Although large, the house was not designed as much for the comfort of its occupants as for the safekeeping of possessions. There were many large rooms on the ground floor, very suitable for storage but with little provision for ventilation or sunlight, the reasoning being that if air or light could make their way in, so could thieves. The house was built to be theft-proof. The upper two floors were airy and open. The kitchen was on the ground floor, the sitting and sleeping quarters were on the upper floors. Two rooms on the ground floor faced the street, one was Lalaji's sitting room and the other was for his clerk. Beyond the rooms, was a cow-shed. Lalaji, a staunch Hindu, was a great worshipper of cows.

Amarkant was busy spinning thread when his younger sister, Naina, came and said, 'What happened, *Bhaiya*, did you deposit your fees or not? I have twenty rupees that you can take. I will borrow more from someone tomorrow.'

Amar kept spinning the wheel and said, 'The fees had to be deposited today. My name has been struck off. What would I need the money for now?'

Naina resembled her brother so much in colouring and features that if Amarkant were to put on a sari, it would be difficult to tell the two apart. Instead of a weak boy there would be an attractive girl.

Amar was joking, but Naina turned pale. She said, 'Why didn't you tell them that you would deposit the fees in a day or two and that they should not strike off your name?'

Amar, enjoying her discomfort, said, 'I did tell them, but they wouldn't listen.'

Naina said crossly, 'Then, why didn't you take my bracelets when I offered them to you?'

Amar said, laughing, 'And what would you have said if *Dada* had asked what had happened to them?'

'I would've said something, but I wouldn't have told Dada.'

Amar pulled a face and said, 'I wouldn't like to do anything on the sly, Naina! Alright, I have deposited the fees; now be happy.'

Naina was not convinced. She said, 'Have you really deposited the fees? Where did you get the money?'

'Yes, Naina, honestly, I have deposited the fees.'

'Where did you get the money?'

'From a friend.'

'How could you have begged him?'

'I didn't have to beg. He gave it to me.'

'He must be a real gentleman.'

'Yes, he is very gentlemanly, Naina. When the fees were being collected, I felt ashamed and went outside. I don't know why I started crying. I must have felt bereft that I didn't even have forty rupees. A little later, this friend came to fetch me. He understood right away why my eyes were red and immediately went and deposited the fees. But tell me, where did you find these twenty rupees?'

'I am not going to tell you.'

Naina tried to run away. This twelve-year-old girl was simple and modest, but at the same time, clever; however, she was very open, and it was difficult for her to hide her anxieties.

Amar quickly grabbed her arm and said, 'I won't let you go unless you tell me. I won't tell anyone, honest.'

'Naina said, shamefaced, 'I got them from Dada.'

Amar said in a detached manner, 'You shouldn't have asked him, Naina. If he can rebuff me so heartlessly, I don't want to ask him for a penny. I had thought that you had them lying about somewhere. Had I known that you would ask him, I would have said flatly that I didn't need the money. What did Dada say?'

With tears in her eyes Naina said, 'Nothing really, except to say that you don't do anything, but need money all the time, sometimes for fees, sometimes books, sometimes donations. Then he asked the clerk to give me twenty rupees, and told me that I owed him that amount.'

Amar said angrily, 'You return the money. I don't want it.'

Naina started sobbing, for Amarkant had flung the money and it lay scattered in the little room. No one tried to pick them up. Suddenly, Lala Samarkant stood at the door. Naina stopped crying and Amarkant started preparing himself for the onslaught that was to follow. Lalaji was a big stout man, looking the archetypal Seth with bald head, pendulous cheeks, and a large stomach. His face had the sharpness that comes from self-restraint but it was deeply marked by selfishness. He said harshly, 'You've been spinning the wheel all this time. How much thread have you woven? Is it worth three or four rupees?'

Amarkant said proudly, 'We don't spin the wheel for money.'

'Then why do you spin it?'

'It is a means to self-purification.'

For Samarkant, this was heaping insult on injury. He said, 'That is news to me. Now, undoubtedly, you are going to be a very wise man, but, in addition to that accomplishment there are also some household chores that need to be done. Who will do these chores? All day you are at school, when you come home you sit at the spinning wheel, in the evening you have other activities, and at night your women's school opens. I am not a work horse. I am caught in this worldly web because of you people, but I am not going to take anything with me upon my death. You should help me a little. You claim to be very virtuous. But what virtue is there in the old father killing himself with work and the young son not even caring?'

Amarkant replied impertinently, 'I have told you repeatedly not to do anything for me. I don't need the money. You are getting old and should spend your time in hymns and prayer.'

Samarkant said sharply, 'Lala, you will have to beg if there is no money. You won't be sitting here spinning the wheel so contentedly. Instead of helping me, like a weakling you have the temerity to say that you don't need the money. Who doesn't need money? Even ascetics would give their lives for money. Money is obtained only with a lot of hard work and industry. Even big people don't hold money in contempt. Who are you to say such a thing!'

Amar continued to argue perversely. 'The world may run after its money, I don't want it. A poor labourer can live his life without sacrificing his principles and his soul. I want at least the opportunity to try to live my life this way.'

Lalaji had no time for such useless discussion. He said, defeated, '*Achcha baba*, have your fill of such a life; but please don't bother me every day for money. I don't want to squander my hard-earned money on your foibles.'

Lalaji left. Naina wanted to cry alone somewhere, but felt unable to move. Amarkant felt forlornly that life was such a burden.

At that moment, the maidservant came from upstairs and said, 'Bhaiya, *Bahuji* would like to see you.'

Losing his temper Amarkant said, 'Go and tell her I am not free. She comes here saying, "Bahuji is calling you".'

But when the maidservant started to go away, he felt ashamed of his sharpness and said, 'I am sorry, Sillo, forget I said anything. Tell her I am coming soon. What is your mistress doing?'

Sillo's full name was Kaushalya. She had lost an eye and her husband and son to a smallpox epidemic and had not been altogether right in her head ever since. She would laugh at serious things and cry when things were comical. Everyone in the household, including the servants, berated her. Only Amarkant considered her a human being. Regaining her composure, she said, 'She was writing something. Lalaji was shouting at you, so she sent me to fetch you.'

As if dusting himself off after a fall, Amar put on a happy face and went to see his wife. Sukhada was standing at the door of her room, and said, 'It is becoming more and more rare to see you. When you return from school, you sit at your spinning wheel! Why don't you send me to my mother's house? When you need me, you can send for me. This time I have been here for six months. My term of duty is over, now I should be released.'

So saying, she put some sweet and salty snacks on a plate, set it on a table, and taking him by the hand led him to a chair. Of all the rooms in the house, this room was the largest and most airy and well furnished. There was a carpet on the floor with several cushioned and plain chairs symmetrically arranged on it. In the middle was a small, round, engraved table. Bound volumes of books filled glass shelves. Several types of games were also arranged on the shelves. In one corner, a harmonium stood on a table. Paintings by Dhurandar, Ravi Verma, and several other artists decorated the walls along with some older prints. The room reflected good taste and wealth.

Amarkant had been married to Sukhada for two years. In this period, Sukhada had stayed at her father-in-law's twice, each time for a month, before returning to her mother's house. This time she had been with her husband for six months, but her affection for him was still more or less superficial. Deep inside, the two were still very much apart. Sukhada had never lacked anything, she had not suffered any hardship in life, and she was afraid to stray from her routine life into the unknown. Living in comfort and luxury was the thing dearest to her heart. She had been trying to interest Amarkant in the affairs of the household. Sometimes she would implore him calmly, at other times she would express her displeasure or lose her temper. In the absence of a mother-in-law, she had assumed the role of mistress of the house. Lala Samarkant was the master outside the house, but inside the home control rested in Sukhada's hands. However, Amarkant would shrug off her displeasure with a laugh and not try to influence her in any way. Her love of luxury frightened him in the way that a scarecrow frightens birds in a cultivated field. Although the field was green and rich in grain, the scarecrow with both arms spread out, stood still and stared at the birds. Thus it came about that he would hide his hopes and fears, victories and losses from Sukhada just as he would hide his defects. Sometimes, if he was late coming home, Sukhada couldn't resist being sarcastic, 'What, you home? Who is there to interest you here! How will you find the joys of the big world here at home!' Such reproof, like the farmer's cry, 'Away, away', simply increased Amar's fear of the scarecrow. Occasionally, he would try to cajole her and explain his principles earnestly, but to Sukhada they represented weakness and she would toss them aside impatiently. She respected her husband's self-sacrificial nature, but she couldn't understand its significance and therefore pitied him. If he had asked for her sympathy or cooperation, then perhaps she would not have disregarded him. But since he held back within himself, so to say keeping his own counsel, he would make her cry. In turn, she would hold back and not tell him her inner feelings. The two would still talk and laugh together and discuss literature and history, but they were poles apart in deeper matters. It was a mixing not of milk and water, but of sand and water that separated the moment they came together.

Amar either did not hear the tenderness behind her complaint, or if he did, could not understand its essence. He was still smarting from Lalaji's onslaught. He said, 'I agree with Dada that it would be best if I abandoned my studies and started thinking about making a living.'

Sukhada said, irritated, 'Yes, I hear that studying too much makes one insane.'

Amar, preparing for a fight, said, 'You have no reason to blame me. I don't shirk studying, but I can't study under these circumstances. I alone know how ashamed I was at school today. It is much better to go hungry than to study, killing your soul.'

Sukhada argued, 'My understanding is that a man can tend the shop for an hour or two and still find time to study. It wouldn't be so bad if the time you spend on the spinning wheel and your other activities were spent in the shop. Also, if you never tell anyone anything, how can they know what you are feeling? Even now, I have about a thousand rupees. It is my money that I can spend any way I please. You haven't even mentioned your problems to me. I may be bad, but I am not your enemy. My blood was boiling listening to Lalaji today. What a commotion, all for forty rupees! Whatever money you need, you should take from me. If your self-esteem is hurt by taking it from me, then take it from my mother. She will then consider her life justified. She has only this one wish left, that you ask her for something. Let's both go to Lucknow. You can study there in peace. Mother would even pay for your studies in England, and you can get a good degree there.'

Sukhada had made this proposal without any ulterior motive. Perhaps for the first time she had spoken of her feelings to her husband. But Amarkant took it amiss. He said, 'I will not live off my in-laws for the sake of a degree. If I can study while earning money through my own labour, then I will study; otherwise, I will seek some employment. Up to now, I have been enamoured of college for no good reason. Anyone who wants to learn can learn a lot of things outside school. I don't boast, but I don't think anyone in the college has read as many books on literature and history as I have read in the last two or three years.'

Sukhada, wanting to put an end to this unpleasant discussion, said, 'Alright, have something to eat. Your meeting is today, you probably will not be back before nine o'clock. I will go for a movie. But if you want to take me, I'll go with you.'

Amar said indifferently, 'You may go, I have no time for a movie.'

'Films can also benefit one in many ways.'

'So, I am not stopping you from going.'

'Why don't you come?'

'A man who does not earn anything has no right to go to a movie theatre. I can have only what I have earned through my own labour.'

The two sat in silence for a while. When Amarkant had finished eating, Sukhada persuaded lovingly, 'Do start tending to the shop beginning tomorrow evening. No doubt an industrious man overcomes difficulties, but to unnecessarily create difficulties for oneself is not wise.'

Amarkant understood what lay behind this solicitude, but he did not say anything. A person devoted to luxury is so afraid of dangers! She wants me to suck the blood of the poor, to cut their throats. I cannot do it.

Sukhada could perhaps have won him over by supporting his viewpoint. By trying to dissuade him, she was only reinforcing him in his views. Amarkant could have brought her around to his way of thinking by sympathizing with her; instead, he had frightened her by his posture of dreary self-sacrifice.

CHAPTER 4

Amarkant stood first in the provincial Matriculation examination, but because he was overage he could not get a scholarship to study further. Instead of being sorry he was relieved in a way because he wanted to get on with his resolve of earning himself a living. He started working as a correspondence clerk for many of the big houses. As he was the son of a rich man, he had no problem getting work. The compatriots of Lala Samarkant were envious of him, probably because of his business practices, and were keenly awaiting a showdown between the father and the son. At first, Lalaji was angry at the implied insult of his son being in the service of his rivals. But when Amar suggested that he was doing that work only to gain some business experience, he stopped protesting, thinking that at least Amar would learn something. Sukhada was not content to give up so easily, and one day the two quarrelled on this issue.

Sukhada said, 'Aren't you embarrassed to go around flattering other people's egos for five or ten rupees?'

Amar said calmly, 'There is no disgrace in working for a living. To be dependent on others is shameful.'

'Then are all these sons of rich people shameless?'

'Yes, they are; it is not surprising either. I wouldn't take money from Lalaji now even if he gave it to me happily. I kept hurting him while I was unaware of my own abilities. Now that I know that I can earn for myself, why should I beg anyone for money.'

Sukhada said relentlessly, 'So, if you consider it insulting to accept money from your father, then how can I stay dependent on him. I should also find a job either as a teacher in some school or as a seamstress.'

Amarkant was trapped. He said, 'No, it is not necessary for you to do so.'

'Why not? I also eat, am clothed, have jewellery made, buy books, and subscribe to magazines, all at the expense of someone else. Indeed, it may also mean that I have no right to your earnings. I should earn money with my own labour.'

Amarkant found a way out of the trap. He said, 'If Dadaji or your mother become annoyed or I become sarcastic, then undoubtedly it would be necessary for you to earn your living.'

'You may not say it, but I can still sense it. I used to think I had some rights as a wife. I would have fought to get whatever I wanted from you. But now I know that I have no rights, that you can ignore me at will. Isn't that true or is there something else?'

Amar said, defeated, 'Then what should I do? Tell me. Should I keep fighting Dada for money each month?'

Sukhada said, 'Yes, that is exactly what I wish you would do. Stop working for others, and look after the affairs of your own house. Whatever time you now spend on those jobs, spend it here.'

'I hate this business of borrowing and lending and considerations of profit and interest.'

Sukhada smiled, 'That is wonderful reasoning! Abandon the patient, and he will get better on his own. The patient will not get better; instead, he will die. At least while you sit in the shop you won't allow such hateful business to be conducted. It is also possible that, seeing your enthusiasm, Lalaji might entrust the entire business to you. Then you can follow your own inclinations. You don't have to take on the whole responsibility if you don't want to, but you could certainly influence Lalaji somewhat. He is doing what people all over the world are doing. You can't change his thinking and policies by remaining aloof. I must tell you that I will leave you and go to my mother's house if you go on in this way. I cannot abide the manner in which you want to spend your life. You have been battered in childhood and are used to hardships. But for me it is a new experience.'

Amarkant felt defeated. Given time he could have thought of several rejoinders, but at the moment he couldn't think of any—indeed, he thought her argument justified. Until now, his desire for independence, which had its germ in the indifference of his stepmother, had been buttressed by the tightfistedness of his father. It had no basis in logic or in principles, but the day when there would be a change in his way of thinking was far, far away. He decided to give up the work of correspondence clerk. He also did not object as strongly to sitting in the shop as he had before. However, he could not bring himself to accept any money from his father for his own studies. He would have to find some other means to pay for them. Thus for some time there was a kind of truce between Sukhada and him.

During this period, something occurred to further weaken his thoughts of independence.

Sukhada had not been to her mother's house for nearly a year. Her widowed mother had repeatedly been asking her to come. Lala Samarkant also wanted her to visit her mother for a month or two, but Sukhada was not ready. She was not easy leaving Amarkant. It was as if she were riding a horse that had to be trained everyday. If he were left unsaddled for five or ten days, he would not let a hand be placed on his shoulder. For this reason, she could not leave him.

In the end, her mother decided to come to Kashi and live there herself. For a whole month, Amarkant was busy with preparations for her visit. With great difficulty a suitable house—neither too big nor too small— was found on the bank of the Ganges. It took several days to clean and whitewash it. Hundreds of household items had to be accumulated. His mother-in-law had sent Amar a money order for a thousand rupees. By economizing, he was able to manage in half the amount. Every penny was accounted for. When his mother-in-law arrived in Benaras in March, after stopping in Prayag for a bath in the Ganges, she was very pleased with the arrangements.

Amarkant tried to return to her the five hundred rupees that he had saved.

Surprised, Renuka Devi said, 'What, the whole thing cost only five hundred rupees? I can't believe it.'

'Yes, only five hundred rupees.'

'You deserve a reward for this. The remaining money is yours.'

Amar felt embarrassed and said, 'When I need money, I will ask for it. Right now there is no need.'

Renuka Devi was not old in body or health, but in beliefs and manners. She did not believe in charity or piety but she could not disregard public mores. A widow's life is one of austerity and penance. Public opinion would not tolerate any infractions of that. Therefore, Renuka had to go through the sham of religion. Nonetheless, life needs some sort of an anchor. Just as eating chutney and pickles does not satisfy hunger, similarly indulgence and lotus eating, travel and entertainment do not satisfy the human spirit. The anchor has to be something real, something tangible. In Renuka's life this anchor was her love for animals. She had brought a whole menagerie of birds and animals with her. Her pets included parrots, mynah birds, peacocks, monkeys, cats, dogs, deer, and cows; and she felt fulfilled as she participated in their joy and pain. Each pet had a name, separate living quarters, and utensils for food and drinking water. Unlike other rich people, her love for pets was not a fashionable affectation or amusement; rather, it was her whole life. She played with their offspring with the tender maternal love of a grandparent. Surprisingly, the animals also seemed to understand her.

The day after Renuka's arrival, mother and daughter were conversing.

Renuka said, 'You must be very much in love with everybody at your in-laws ?'

Sukhada said bashfully, 'What can I do, *Amma*? I am in such a predicament that I don't know what to do. The father and son are completely at odds with each other. Dadaji wants his son to look after the house business. He says he hates that business. I don't know what would have happened if I had left. I am in constant fear that he may leave the house and wander around the country or go abroad. What can I say, you have pushed me into a well.'

Renuka said anxiously, 'I thought I had fully considered both the house and the groom before the marriage, but fate deals strange hands. Do you now get along with the boy or is it still the same as before?'

Sukhada's cheeks turned red with embarrassment. Bowing her head, she said, 'He doesn't find time away from his books and meetings.'

'A beautiful girl like you cannot control a simple, plain lad? What is his character like, is he chasing after other women?'

Sukhada was aware that Amarkant had no such fault, but at this time she could not bring herself to say it openly. To say that could have been interpreted as a slur to her femininity. She said, 'How can I know, Amma, what goes on in the mind of anyone? So much time has gone by, he has not given me a single present. It's as if he doesn't care whether I live or die.'

Renuka enquired, 'Do you ever ask him for anything, make anything for him to eat, or groom his hair?'

Sukhada said haughtily, 'If he doesn't ask about me, then why should I care. If he talks to me, I talk also. I won't be a slave to anyone.'

Renuka rebuked her, 'Daughter, do not take this amiss but it seems to me that the fault is mostly yours. You are very proud of your looks. You think that he is so enamoured of your beauty he will grovel at your feet. I know that there are men like that, but that kind of love never lasts. I can't understand why you are so terse with him. To me he seems a very humble and thoughtful boy. Honestly, I pity him. The poor fellow lost his mother in childhood. The stepmother was a virago, and the father turned into an enemy. He could never consider his house a home. Feelings that are so suppressed by anxiety need to be nurtured with affection and care before the seed of love can be sown.'

Sukhada, getting annoyed, said, 'He wants to live away from home and work as a labourer, and he wants me to live with him like a hermit, eat coarse food and wear rough clothes. I can't do that even if it means permanent separation from him. If he follows his own inclinations and doesn't care at all about my well-being, then I won't be sitting here waiting for his approval.'

Renuka glanced at her reproachfully and said, 'What will happen if Lala Samarkant goes bankrupt tomorrow?'

Sukhada had never even considered this possibility. Bewildered, she said, 'Why should he go bankrupt?'

'It is possible.'

Self-respect prevented Sukhada from saying—whatever you have is mine also. Instead, irritated at her mother's harsh question, she said, 'If death comes, one dies, but one doesn't jump into fire knowingly.'

During this conversation, it had become apparent to her mother that a child, an heir to her fortune, was on its way. She had been very anxious about her daughter's future but this knowledge assuaged her worries.

Overjoyed, she embraced Sukhada.

CHAPTER 5

Amarkant had not experienced the joy of a mother's love in his life. He was only a child when his mother had passed away and the memories of that distant past were dim and therefore pleasant and joyful. Renuka Devi seemed to be his mother who had descended from heaven and, hearing his agonized wails, had picked him up in her arms. The child forgot his crying and experienced heavenly bliss in those loving arms. Amarkant would decline, but the mother, lovingly catching hold of him, would offer him sweets and dry fruits. He could never refuse her. She was always cooking something special for him and was so happy feeding him that he felt a wave of affection and respect for her. After college, he would head directly for Renuka's house, where she would be waiting with some refreshments for him. He even started to breakfast at her house. He couldn't get enough of her motherly love. On holidays he would often spend the entire day at Renuka's house. Sometimes Naina would accompany him because she liked playing with Renuka's pets.

Blossoming in this affection, Amarkant began to lose his churlishness. Sukhada became closer to him as he was no longer afraid of her love of luxury, and he started taking her and Renuka for outings and to shows. Every few days Renuka would lovingly insist on giving him ten or twenty rupees, which he couldn't refuse. New suits were tailored, new shoes bought, a motorcycle purchased, and many other fancy articles obtained for him. In five or six months this devotee of simple living, the rebel against luxury, was transformed into a rich man's son. He began to have the selfish outlook of the sons of the wealthy. He always had ten or twenty rupees in his pocket. He would dine out and host his friends and spend money like water. His zeal for studies was replaced by a passion for cards and the game of *chausar*. But he was more enthusiastic than ever about public meetings because there he had a chance to achieve recognition. He was not a bad speaker, and with practice he had become a polished one. He liked to read the daily news and current literature, especially as Renuka liked the news read out to her.

Amarkant developed a proficiency in political affairs through reading the newspapers. His blood would boil at the injustices of the ruling class against his fellow countrymen. He started to sympathize with organizations that were working toward national betterment. He became a member of the local Congress committee and started to participate in its affairs.

He, along with Salim, was part of a group of college students on a fact-finding mission regarding the economic state of villages. Professor Shantikumar was its leader. When the group was returning in the evening after surveying several villages, Amar said, 'I had never imagined that the condition of our farmers was so desperate.'

Salim said, 'The four or five houses of boatmen along the pond had nothing except one or two iron pots and pans. I had thought that the villagers would have *silos* full of grain, but none of the houses had even a bin of grain.'

Shantikumar responded, 'All farmers are not so poor. The big farmers have granaries in their houses. But there are no more than three or four such farmers in a village.'

Amarkant disagreed, 'I didn't find even a single big farmer in these villages. Moneylenders and officials prey on these poor people. Don't they even pity them?'

Shantikumar said with a smile, 'Moneylenders and officials have been tested for compassion and dharma for a long time and have been found to be wanting in those attributes. Now the time has come for testing their sense of justice.'

Shantikumar was about thirty-five years old, very fair and handsome. His clothes and manners were at first glance English and with his blue eyes and brown hair, he appeared English. He had a doctorate from Oxford University. He was a man of cheerful disposition, sympathetic and helpful, and always ready with a joke. He greatly valued independence and was strongly opposed to marriage. He was friendly with the students and participated fully, but privately—not coming out openly—in political organizations. However, on social issues, he expressed himself quite freely.

Amar said sadly, 'I can't forget the face of the man who has been sick for six months and can't afford any medicine. Yet the landlord obtained a court order to collect the rent and had everything in the house auctioned. Even the oxen were sold. I have begun to doubt that any rational force governs this unjust world. Did you see, Salim, the poor fellow didn't even have rags to cover his body? His old mother was crying so bitterly.'

Salim had tears in his eyes. He said, 'The old woman was so overwhelmed when you gave them money that I couldn't bear to look at her.'

The group was moving along talking thus. They were on a paved road, lined on both sides by tall trees that darkened the path . On each side of the road, but lower down, there were fields of sugarcane and a legume, *Citisus cajan*, as well as other crops. Occasionally, the group came across a labourer or two or some other passer by.

Suddenly, they noticed a party of ten or twelve men and women standing apprehensively under a tree. They were all staring at the legume field in front of them and whispering to each other. Two white soldiers, each with a cane in his hand, were standing on guard on the earthen fence bordering the field. Curiously, Salim asked one of the men, 'What is going on, why are you people assembled here?'

All of a sudden they heard a woman screaming from the legume field. Taking hold of their sticks, the student, rushed toward the field. They now understood what was happening.

One white soldier, flaunting his cane, said threateningly, 'Go away, or else I will beat the hell out of you.'

No sooner had he uttered these words than Dr Shantikumar charged in and boxed him on the face. The soldier tottered, but he was an expert boxer and when he retaliated, Doctor sahab went down. Salim hit the soldier on the head with his hockey stick. The soldier fainted and fell. Amar and another student were tackling the other soldier, but he was heavier than both youths. Salim was free and rushed to their aid—now they were three against one. Salim's hockey stick felled this soldier as well. Meanwhile, a third white man emerged from the field. Taking hold of himself, Dr Shantikumar rushed to tackle him, but the white man took out a revolver and fired. Doctor sahab fell to the ground. Now the situation was very tense. The three students tended to the doctor, afraid at the same time of a second bullet. Their lives were hanging by a thread.

So far, the labourers had watched the drama from the sidelines, but when Doctor sahab fell down, they became very agitated. Like fear, courage is also infectious. Catching hold of their sticks, they all rushed towards the white man. He fired his revolver, but missed. Before he could fire a third shot, he fell under a hail of sticks. It was lucky that the bullet had hit Doctor sahab's thigh. All the students knew first aid and they stopped the flow of blood and bandaged the wound.

At that moment a young woman stumbled out of the field. Hiding her face and rearranging her clothes, she crept away. She didn't say anything; the poor, embarrassed woman just wanted to get away from everyone's sight. Who could give her back the priceless virtue that she had lost? One's sense of justice may be appeased by slaughtering the wicked culprits, but what she had lost was lost forever. If she wept for her loss, lodged an appeal, or even if the whole world sympathized with her, what good would that do?

Salim stared at the young woman a moment. Then, in a frenzy, he started hitting the three men on the ground with his hockey stick.

Doctor sahab shouted, 'What are you doing, Salim, what good does that do? It is inhuman to hit someone who is down.'

Salim, taking a quick breath, said, 'I won't leave any of these devils alive, and I won't be sorry if I am hanged. They should be made an example of so that no wicked man would ever dare do such a thing again.'

Then, turning towards the labourers, he said, 'There are so many of you and you just stood there gaping. Don't you have any sense of shame? You don't even protect the honour of your daughters and daughters-in-law. You may think that it was not your daughter or daughter-in-law, but indeed all the daughters of this country are your daughters; all daughters-in-law are your daughters-in-law; all mothers are your mothers. You all witnessed this evil act and still stood there gawking like cowards. Why don't you all go and drown yourselves.'

Suddenly it struck him that, although he was angry, he had no right to chastize these poor souls. He calmed down feeling somewhat abashed.

They requisitioned a bullock cart from a nearby village. People lifted Shantikumar and laid him down in the cart; the cart had begun to move when Doctor sahab asked, startled, 'Are you leaving those other three men here?'

Salim said with a frown, 'We are not responsible for their transport. I would rather dig graves and bury them.'

After considerable persuasion by the doctor, Salim agreed to load the three white soldiers also on the cart, and the cart moved on. The labourers, with their heads bowed like culprits, walked behind the cart some distance. Doctor Shantikumar thanked them profusely and bid them farewell. They reached the nearest railway station at about 9.00 p.m. The white men were left in the charge of the local police and Doctor sahab and his students boarded the train for home.

After a while, Salim and Amar started talking and laughing, discussing the fight. They told it to the stationmaster, other passengers in the train, and whomsoever else they could find, about it. Salim bragged about his courage and bravery as if he had conquered a fort and the public ought to crown him and take him out in a procession. But Amarkant soon fell silent and sat quietly next to Doctor sahab. He would never be himself again after today's experience. He kept going over the incident in his mind. How could those miserable two-bit soldiers dare to act so? Those white soldiers represented men of the lowest class in England. How could they be so bold? Because India is a subject nation! They knew that the people were terrified of them and no one would dare squeak no matter what evil they perpetrated. He realized that this feeling of terror would have to be thrown off and the chains of subjugation broken. He started planning various schemes to break these chains, schemes that had elements of youthful rebellion, childish intensity, and, yes, the folly of an immature mind.

CHAPTER 6

Doctor Shantikumar was fully recovered after a month in hospital. He didn't know what had happened to the three soldiers, but the first thing that he did on recovery was to take a *tonga* to the military cantonment and inquire about those soldiers. He learned that the three had stayed in military hospital for some days and then had been transferred to another unit. The Captain of the regiment apologized to Doctor sahab for the crime committed by his men and assured him that in the future the soldiers would be kept under strict control. During Doctor sahab's hospitalization, Amarkant was in attendance day and night. He went home only for meals and to visit Renuka, who also visited Doctor sahab two or three times.

Once Amarkant finished tending Dr Shantikumar, he participated in the work of Congress much more vigorously and soon no one could match him in contributions to that organization.

Once at a public meeting he had spoken with such passion that the police superintendent had called in Lala Samarkant and warned him to control the boy. Lalaji did not speak directly to Amarkant; instead, he spoke to Sukhada and Renuka. He knew perfectly well who had the most influence over Amarkant.

Recently he had become more affectionate toward his son. In the past, when he had to pay Amar's tuition fees, he had resented his attending school. He had wanted Amar to work and would lose his temper when he wouldn't. Now there were no tuition fees, to be paid, so there was no cause for complaint. Instead, now if he couldn't find the key to his safe or felt too lazy to get up and open it, he would borrow money from his son. Amarkant would never call in the loan, and his father would never repay.

Sukhada's delivery time was approaching. Her face had become pale, her appetite had diminished, and she talked and laughed very little. She had bad dreams that made her anxious. Renuka brought her several books related to childbirth, but she would worry even more after reading them.

When she thought of the child she would be overjoyed but she was also anxious about what might happen.

One evening she was in a bad mood when Amarkant came to her. She said severely, 'Why don't you give me some arsenic, you will be rid of me, and I will be free of this mess.'

Amar was an ideal husband these days. Sukhada's beauty excited him, while at the same time, the pale, sickly woman, burdened with child, filled his heart with compassion. He would sit next to her and play with her uncombed hair and rough hands. He was responsible for her condition; so to make her burden bearable he attended to her every wish. He would have been ready to pluck even the stars out of the firmament for her. All the time he tried to make her happy by reading good books to her. Thoughts of the child made him happy, but he worried about Sukhada. So he replied nervously, 'Why do you say such things, Sukhada? If I have made a mistake, please tell me.'

Sukhada was lying down. Raising herself on a pillow, she said, 'You keep on speaking harshly against the government at public meetings. It will serve no purpose other than your arrest and, then this house will also fall. Some senior police officer has said so to Dada. You don't help him at all; instead, you are bent on reducing all he has done to ashes. I am dying as it is, and these antics of yours are making me worse. You were involved with Doctor sahab for a month; now that that is finished you have taken up this mess. Why can't you sit peacefully? You are no longer your own master that you can do whatever you wish; you are shackled now. Why don't you see this?'

Amarkant tried to defend himself, 'I don't think I have given any speech that could be considered vehement.'

'Was Dada lying then?'

'What this means is that I should button my lips.'

'Yes, you may have to button your lips.'

Both kept staring at nothing. Then Amarkant, defeated, said, 'Alright. From now on I will seal my lips. You may call me on it if in the future you hear any more complaints.'

Sukhada softened and said, 'I hope you are not making this promise in anger because I really dread it when you are angry. I also realize that we are a subject people and detest this subjugation as much as you do. Our feet are tied with two separate sets of shackles, one social, and the other governmental. But one has to be cautious. The duty we owe our country we owe in greater measure to our parents and, to an even greater extent, to our children. If what you do for your country is at the expense of your father's happiness and your child's welfare it is like setting your own house on fire for personal glory. I want the child that I am nurturing to mean everything to you as he does to me. I want him to be the sole recipient of all your love and allegiance.'

Amarkant listened to this admonishment with bowed head. He was contrite and felt that he had been unfair to both Sukhada and the child. An imaginary picture of the child arose before his eyes, and his whole conscious being was absorbed in contemplation of that child, buttery-soft, playing in his arms. A beautiful print of the child Krishna was hanging on the wall. Today that print gave him profound joy such as he had never experienced before. He had tears in his eyes.

Sukhada, giving him a *bira* of paan, said, 'Amma says that she wants to take the child to Lucknow. I said, "Amma, you may not like it, but I am not parting with my child".'

Amarkant asked curiously, 'Did she resent it?'

'No, no, there was nothing to resent; but she must have felt a little badly. I can't part with my child even in jest.'

'Dada must have told Amma what the police officer had said.'

'Yes, I know he has told her. When you go there today you will get quite an earful.'

'I won't go today.'

'Oh, I'll come with you and intercede on your behalf.'

'Pardon me! You will embarrass me even more.'

'No, honestly. Achcha, tell me, who will the baby look like, you or me? I say, he will look like you.'

'I wish he would be like you.'

'Why? I want him to be like you.'

'If he takes after you I will love him even more.'

'Alright. Is there any news of the woman who was abused by the white soldiers?'

'No, I haven't heard anything.'

'Why don't you people go and find out some day, or do you think that giving speeches frees you of any obligation?'

Embarrassed, Amarkant said, 'I will go tomorrow.'

'You must be careful that no one gets even a whisper of it. If her family members have disowned her you should bring her home with you. Amma will have no objection to keeping her. But if she does, I will keep her with me.'

Amarkant looked at Sukhada with renewed respect. For the first time he understood how kind-hearted, charitable, and courageous she was.

He asked, 'You won't feel any aversion towards her?'

Sukhada hesitated, then said, 'If I say, no, it will be a lie. There will undoubtedly be some, but we have to change our ideology. She has done nothing wrong, why should she be punished?'

Amarkant saw Sukhada in a new light—she was bathed in the glow of serene womanhood, which, becoming personified, was embracing him.

CHAPTER 7

Amarkant gave up speaking at or even participating in public meetings. But he chafed at these restrictions and, at times, would derive some comfort from expressing his feelings in articles that he published in daily newspapers and magazines. Once in a while, especially on holidays, he would mind the shop. He discovered that tending the shop gave him an insight into human nature. The affection and love of both Sukhada and Renuka had tied him down. His anguish, which he had thought justified, and which had been directed at first against his wife and then as rebellion against society, had now been calmed. It was as if a crying child had been given a candy and had forgotten his reason for crying.

One day Amarkant was minding the shop when a client came in and asked, 'Bhaiya, where is *Babuji*? I have some important business with him.'

Amar saw a dark, sturdy, ugly man. His name was Kaale Khan. Amar said gruffly, 'He has gone somewhere. What is your business with him?'

'It is important business. Do you know when he is likely to be back?'

Amar could smell the unpleasant odour of cheap liquor on his breath. Turning his face away he asked, 'Do you drink?'

Kaale Khan laughed and said, 'Who can afford drink, Lala, I can't even afford to buy dry bread. There was a family affair today where some liquor was served.'

He came closer and whispered in Amar's ear, 'I have an ornament to show you. It must weigh at least a hundred and twenty grams. In the market it would cost no less than two hundred and fifty rupees. But I am an old client of yours, and will accept whatever you give.'

He pulled out a pair of gold bracelets from his waistband and put them in front of Amar.

Without touching them, Amar asked, 'Where did you get these bracelets?'

Kaale Khan smiled shamelessly, 'Don't ask me that, son. They are a gift from God.'

Amar looked repulsed. He said, 'You must have stolen them from somewhere.'

Kaale Khan laughed again, 'What is theft, son? It's all labels in our head. It is God's device to give labels to everything. Some get money from service, others from labour, and still others from business; the same God provides for everyone. All right, take out the money. I am getting late. All those policemen need to be paid also, Bhaiya, otherwise nothing works—not even for a day.'

Amarkant felt like booting Kaale Khan out of the shop. He was astonished to learn that Lala Samarkant had business dealings with such criminals. He found these dealings so repugnant that he began to hate the shop, that house, that environment, even himself. He said, 'Take this thing away, I don't want it; otherwise, I will notify the police. I am warning you, never bring this kind of thing here again.'

Kaale Khan was unperturbed. He said, 'Bhaiya, you are saying something totally new. Lala Samarkant would not be a rich merchant today if he had followed that policy. I alone have passed on to him articles worth thousands of rupees. Lala deals with everybody—rich merchants, beggars, and deprived people. Whatever article they lay their hands on, they bring it here without hesitation, take whatever it's worth, and go home. Children are nurtured on this shop. Now take the scales out and weigh these bracelets. I bet they will be more than a hundred and twenty grams. But I am an old client; so, come on, give me one hundred and fifty rupees. There is no point in my running around from place to place.'

Amar said firmly, 'I have told you, I don't want them.'

'Lala, you will be sorry. You will be able to sell them for two hundred and fifty rupees in no time at all.'

'Why are you pestering me? I don't want them.'

'Achcha, come on, give me only one hundred rupees. Allah knows I am squeezed for money, so I will take a loss this time.'

'You are needlessly annoying me. I will not accept a stolen article no matter how cheaply I can buy it. You aren't even ashamed of stealing. You have four limbs, and you are healthy. Why don't you work as a labourer? You are ruining your life both in this world and hereafter by stealing other people's goods.'

Kaale Khan made a bored face indicating that he had heard this sermon before. He said, 'Then you are not taking them.'

'No.'

'Will you take them for fifty rupees?'

'Not even for a *kauri*.'

Kaale Khan retrieved the bracelets, put them in his waistband, and stepped down from the shop. But, turning back a moment later, he said, 'Alright, give me thirty rupees. Allah knows, the policemen will take half the money.'

Amarkant pushing him away said, 'You swine, get out of here. Why do you keep badgering me?'

When Kaale Khan had left, Amar had the shop swept and perfumed with incense. The place was still reeking of liquor. He had never been so disgusted with his father as he was now. He felt that even the air of the house was contaminated. Where he had had vague suspicions before, today he had inescapable proof of his father's unsavoury dealings. He made up his mind that he would have it out with his father. He stood up and scanned the road impatiently, but there was no sign of Lalaji. He decided to close the shop and leave, and when he saw his father, openly tell him that he couldn't carry on with the business. He was just about to close the shop when an old woman leaning on a stick came and said, '*Beta*, isn't Lala here?'

The old woman's hair was white and she was so emaciated that a slight breeze could have blown her away.

Amarkant thought at first to say that Lala was not there and she should come back when he was, but her shrivelled face showed such pitiful anguish and hopelessness that he took pity on her. He said, 'What is your business with Lalaji? He is not here right now.'

The old woman said, disappointed, 'It does not matter, beta. I will come back.'

Amarkant said politely, 'He should be coming soon, Ma. You may come up.'

The shop was three steps above street level. The old woman's legs were not strong; she put one foot on the first step, but could not raise the other foot. Amar came down and supported her up. The old woman blessed him, 'May you have a long life, beta. I am afraid that Lala may be delayed; if it gets dark how will I get home? I can't see anything at night, beta.'

'Where is your home, Ma?'

The old woman looked at him with sightless eyes and said, 'Beta, I live at Govardhansarai.'

'You have no relatives?'

'Everyone was there, Bhaiya. There were sons, daughters-in-law, grandsons, wives of grandsons, but they are not for me. Yes, they were mine, but they can't take care of me. Perhaps, they will look after me when I die.'

'Then those people don't give you any money?'

The old woman said proudly, 'I am not dependent on anyone, beta. Long live my Lala Samarkant. He takes care of me. You were quite young, bhaiya, when my husband was Lala's steward. Through God's grace, his wages were enough to build a house, to marry off the children and still to have some savings. He had a lowly job that earned him only five rupees per month, but he was not indebted to anyone. He was ready to do anything for Lala. Whenever he was called, even if it was midnight, he always went. Even though he was a lowly servant, Lala never addressed him by the familiar *tum*. He always called him, Khan sahab. Many rich merchants would ask him to work for them at twice the salary. But he would always reply, "Once you are with someone, you stay with him; unless he rejects you, you don't leave him." Lala offered us benefits that others would not be able to match. My husband died twenty years ago, but he still continues to pay me his wages. May Allah keep my Lala safe and sound, I have not had to beg at all.'

Amarkant had seen his father's, selfish, covetous, and unfeeling side. Today he learned that he was also kind and affectionate. His heart beat with pride. He said, 'So, you get five rupees?'

'Yes, beta. He gives me five rupees every month.'

'Then I will give you the money and you can go. Lala may be late.'

The old woman, looking shocked, said, 'No, no, beta. I will wait for him. Afterwards I will go home, feeling my way with this cane, which is now my sight.'

'It won't be a problem. I will tell him that you have collected your money. If you delay, you may fall down and hurt yourself in the dark.'

'No, beta. I don't want to do anything that might have repercussions later. I will come back.'

'No. I won't let you go without the money.'

The old woman, though dreading the consequences, responded, 'Alright, give it to me, beta. Don't forget my name—Pathanin.'

Amarkant gave her the money. The old woman took it and tied it with trembling hands in a knot in her sari; after blessing Amarkant, she slowly descended the steps. But she hadn't gone fifty paces when Amarkant caught up with her in an *ikka*, a small horse-drawn carriage, and said, 'Venerable mother, come and sit in the ikka. I will take you home.'

The old woman looked at him with astonishment, 'Oh, no, beta. Why should you take me? I will go home using my cane. May Allah keep you safe and healthy.'

Amarkant had hired the ikka. He picked the old woman up in his arms and seating her in the ikka, asked, 'Where to?'

The old woman clinging to the support in the ikka said, 'Beta, go to Govardhansarai. May you have a long life. My child, you are taking so much trouble on my account, you have come running from so far! You are studying, beta, aren't you? May Allah give you a high office.'

The ikka reached Govardhansarai in fifteen to twenty minutes. A lane led off from the right side of the road. The old woman requested the ikka to stop and she got off. The ikka couldn't have gone any further. The entrance to the lane was so dark that it seemed painted with coal tar.

When Amarkant asked the coachman to take him back, the old woman said, 'No, my son, now that you have come so far, you must come into my house for a moment. You have been of great help to me.'

The lane smelt foul. On both sides ran open sewers. Most houses were built of mud. It was a poor ward. The shopping districts of a city are so different from these lanes. One is like a flower—beautiful, fresh and fragrant; the other like a root, crooked and reeking of mud and mire. But does the flower know that it exists because of the root!

The old woman stopped in front of a house and called out gently, 'Sakina!'

A voice answered from within, 'I am coming, Amma; why were you delayed?'

The front door opened and a young girl holding a leather flask of kerosene oil stood in the doorway. She did not see Amarkant as he was standing behind the old woman, but when the old woman moved forward, Sakina noticed him. At once she hid her face with her scarf, and stepping back asked softly, 'Amma, who is this?'

The old woman put her cane in a corner and said, 'He is Lala's son. He came to see me home. I have never met such a gentle and civil boy.'

Blessing Amarkant repeatedly, she narrated the entire episode to Sakina, then said, 'Daughter, put a *charpai* in the courtyard, so he may sit awhile. He must be tired.'

Sakina put a broken-down cot in the courtyard and spreading a thread-bare sheet on it said, 'What, will you seat him on this! I am ashamed.'

The old woman looked at her sternly, 'What about? Don't they know our state?'

Going out, she beckoned Amarkant. A tattered old gunnysack acted as a curtain on the door, which led to a small courtyard, barely big enough to hold two little beds. On the opposite side was a low verandah with a tiled roof and beyond the verandah was a small room, which was dark. At one end of the verandah stood a stove and a few earthen and tin utensils; there was also a pitcher and a large earthen pot. A fire burned in the stove and an iron skillet for cooking *chapattis* was on it.

Sitting on the cot, Amar commented, 'This is a very small house. How do you manage here?'

The old woman sat on the ground next to the cot and said, 'Beta, now there are only two of us. At one time, a whole family lived in this house. My two sons, two daughters-in-law, their children; everyone lived in this very house. They were all married here, and here they all died. I can't tell you how full life was then. Now it is only my granddaughter and I, Allah has called everyone else to Him. We cook, eat, and sleep here. When Pathan died, it was as if total ruination was visited on this house. Now my only request to Allah is that Sakina get married to some good man while I am still alive. Then I will ask Allah that He take me. You must have many friends, beta. If you don't consider it shameful, mention it to some. Who knows, something may be arranged through your efforts.'

Sakina, dressed in kurta and pajama, her forehead covered with a scarf, was standing in the verandah. As soon as the old woman started discussing her marriage, she sat down by the stove and started kneading the flour. She was annoyed that Amma was telling this man her story. She thought Amma wasn't in the least discerning about what she said to anyone. She would start harping on her marriage to whosoever happened by, as if there was nothing else to talk about. How could Sakina know that the greatest desire of old people is to see their children married. Amarkant, reviewing his Muslim friends in his mind, said, 'I don't have too many Muslim friends, but I will mention it to the one or two that I do have.'

The old woman said pensively, 'They must be rich people.'

'Yes, they are well-to-do.'

'Ah, why would the rich be concerned with the affairs of poor people. Although our Prophet ordains that in marriage no thought be given to wealth, no one really follows that stricture! All of them, Muslims or Hindus, are so only in name. One doesn't see either a true Muslim or a true Hindu anywhere. Beta, what can I serve you; you probably won't even drink water in our house!'

She said to Sakina, 'Daughter, get the handkerchief that you crocheted and show it to Bhaiya. He may like it. What else can we do!'

Sakina came out of the kitchen and brought a big cigarette box from an alcove. She took out a handkerchief from the box. Hesitantly, with bowed head, she quickly put the handkerchief next to the old woman and went away.

Amarkant was gazing down, but seeing Sakina in front of him, he looked up. When an attractive woman stands in front of you, it is discourteous to look away. Sakina was dark and, at first glance, would not be considered beautiful. Nor was her figure something the poets wrote about. But her complexion and grace, her walk and bearing, her disposition and modesty combined to make her a very attractive girl. Hiding her eyes behind long eyelashes and appearing to withdraw within herself, she seemed to radiate a fragrance and glow as she went away, as a vision vanishes after a glimpse.

Amarkant picked up the handkerchief and looked at it carefully in the light of the lamp. The pattern of vines and flowers was neatly crocheted, and in the centre was a peacock. Such good taste in this hut!

Surprised, he said, '*Mataji*, this is a very beautiful handkerchief. Sakina seems very proficient at crocheting.'

The old woman said proudly, 'Bhaiya, I don't know how she learned to do it, but she can do all types of crochet work. Some girls in the ward go to school. Sakina learned to crochet from observing them. Had there been a man in the house, we could have obtained some work. But who is there to appreciate such work in a poor ward. Beta, take this handkerchief as a present from a helpless widow.'

Amar was close to tears as he put the handkerchief in his pocket. If it had been in his power, he would have put in an order, then and there, for a hundred or two hundred handkerchiefs. Even so, the feeling took firm root in his heart.

Getting up he said, 'I will always regard this handkerchief as your blessing. I don't promise, but I am confident that I will be able to get you some work through my friends.'

Amarkant had used the familiar 'tum', with Pathanin. By the time he was leaving, 'tum' had changed to the formal *aap*. Perhaps it was Sakina who was responsible for the origin of the discrimination between 'tum' and 'aap'. He had found courtesy, good judgement, and everything in good taste. Yet there was a shadow of impending doom.

Amar stood up to leave. The old woman, spreading her shawl in a gesture of benediction, blessed him.

CHAPTER 8

When Amarkant arrived home around 9 p.m., Lala Samarkant said to him, 'You closed the shop. Where did you go? Is this any way to run a business?'

Amar explained, 'The old Pathanin came to get her allowance. It was quite dark and I was afraid she might fall down and hurt herself; so I took her home. She didn't want to take any money in your absence. But it was getting late, and I thought I shouldn't make her wait any longer.'

'How much money did you give her?'

'Five rupees.'

Lalaji was relieved.

'Did any other client come? Did you get any money from anyone?'

'No, sir.'

'I am surprised.'

'No one came except that rogue Kaale Khan who wanted to sell a piece of gold jewellery. I told him to go away.'

Samarkant lifted his eyebrows, 'What was the jewellery?'

'Gold bracelets weighing, he said, about 120 grams.'

'You didn't weigh them?'

'I didn't even touch them.'

'Yes, why would you touch them—they were tainted with sin! How much did he want for them?'

'Two hundred rupees.'

'Surely not!.'

'He started with two hundred, but came down to thirty rupees.'

Lalaji exclaimed, 'Even at that price you didn't take them!'

'I wouldn't take them even for a penny. How could I, when I consider such transactions sinful.'

Samarkant said angrily 'Be quiet! Instead of being ashamed, you make excuses. We could have had one hundred and fifty rupees without lifting a finger. You lost them because of your pride in your dharma and now you boast. Do you even know what dharma means? Do you take a dip in the Ganges even once a year? Have you offered homage to the gods even once? Have you ever chanted the name of Rama in your life? Have you ever observed Ekadashi or any other fast? Do you ever read or listen to the ancient myths or texts? What do you know about dharma? Dharma is one thing, business another. Shame on you, you threw away one hundred and fifty rupees.'

Amarkant, quietly amused at this definition of dharma, said, 'You consider bathing in the Ganges and worship and scripture reading as the essentials of dharma; I consider truth, service, and charity as the essentials of the spirit. Bathing, meditation, worship, and fasting are merely the means to dharma, they are not dharma itself.'

Samarkant said sarcastically, 'Yes, you are right, very right. Now the world will recognize you as the learned master of dharma. If I had followed your path of dharma, I would have been dirt poor; you would not be sitting here enjoying the fruits of wealth. You have learned a little English and this is the result. But I know people who have mastered English, but still follow their dharma. You threw a hundred and fifty rupees down the drain!'

Amarkant said impatiently, 'Why do you keep repeating the same thing? I will not deal in stolen articles whether you are pleased or angry. I abhor such dealings.'

'That kind of a conscience is not needed in my business. I want a man motivated by profit or loss.'

'I can't weigh dharma on a scale of profit or loss.'

The only cure for such stupidity was a good slap on the face. Had Amar been hale and hearty, he would have been taught a lesson for abusing dharma; instead, Lalaji swallowed his anger. He said, 'You are the only one left in the world who is an upholder of morality. Everyone else is immoral. Someone else bought the piece of jewellery that you so proudly refused for a few rupees more or less. He earned the money, you are left with nothing. Nothing! You earn one hundred and fifty rupees only when you sell a hundred and fifty yards of cloth or a hundred and fifty bags of sugar. It is easy to be pious while enjoying someone else's earnings. When you have to earn for yourself, then your eyes will be opened.'

Amar was adamant. He said, 'I will never engage in such business.'

Lalaji's anger became tempered with pity. 'Then what business would you engage in? What business is there that will not kill your soul? All business, whether it is receiving or lending, interest or brokerage, dealing in grain or cloth, oil or ghee, involves the ability to take risks and to strike at the right moment. One who understands this earns profits; one who doesn't goes bankrupt. Tell me one business that doesn't involve lying and dishonesty. Show me a high-placed official who doesn't take bribes. Even having a single document copied costs one rupee! Unless bribed, a police officer will not write a report. And which lawyer does not use false witnesses? Which leader doesn't benefit himself from subscriptions to the party? The world revolves around maya—shadow and illusion. How can anyone escape it?'

Shaking his head despondently, Amar said, 'If business is like that, I won't go into business.'

'Then how will you run a household? If there is no flow of water into a well, how long will it continue to give water?'

Wanting to put an end to the discussion, Amarkant replied wearily, 'I may die hungry, but I won't sacrifice my soul.'

'Then will you become a labourer?'

'There is no shame in being a labourer.'

Samarkant, trying a different tack, said, 'It may not be shameful, but I can guarantee that you won't be able to handle it. It is easily said, but one has to sweat from every pore to earn even a *pai*. Labour indeed! You have never even drawn a pail of water from the well. You have servants to carry the smallest item that you buy. You a labourer! Thank your lucky stars that I have earned and saved money. I know that you will not accomplish anything in this life, but I get so annoyed with this talk of yours that I feel like giving away my entire fortune to charity, then we will see what happens to your soul.'

This threat had no effect on Amarkant, 'You may happily do so. Don't worry at all on my account. The day you do this pious deed will be the dawn of my good fortune. Freed of the delusion of money, I will be independent. For as long as I am tied to it my soul won't be nurtured.'

Samarkant had no more weapons. Enraged, he lost his business sense momentarily and said, 'Then why do you stay tied to it? Why don't you develop your soul? Become an ascetic and show what you can do. I don't want you to be tied to anything that you can't respect.'

With these words, he left for the temple where the bell for *aarati* was being sounded.

Amar could not reply to this challenge and his unspoken thoughts began to trouble him like a wound in his heart—he wants to impress me with his wealth. He is so proud of the money that he has accumulated from selling stolen articles, lending money to gamblers at exorbitant interest, and cheating poor farmers and labourers! God forbid that I should be a slave to that wealth.'

He was still lost in these disturbing thoughts when Naina came and said, 'Bhaiyaji, was Dada irritated?'

In Amarkant's rather lonely life, Naina was the only one who had given him affection and comfort. She was his confidante in happiness and sorrow, in victory and defeat, and shared in his plans and resolutions. Even though he was no longer distant from Sukhada; indeed, he had even begun to love her; Naina was still closer to him. Sukhada and Naina were the two banks of the river of his innermost self: Sukhada so high, majestic, and difficult to reach that the waves could touch only her feet; Naina so familiar, level, and easily approached that even gentle waves could touch her innermost being.

Amar hid his anguish behind a mild smile, 'It was the same old thing, Naina, nothing new. Your Bhabhi wasn't downstairs, was she?'

'She was here just a while back. She just went upstairs.'

'Then today I will get a scolding from her as well. Dada very plainly told me today that I should find myself an occupation. I agree that I have to do something. This daily rebuke is getting intolerable. If I have done something wrong, then he can kick me as he pleases, I won't say a word. But I can't do things against my conscience.'

Naina had just made *pakoris* of different kinds—sweet, salty and sour, and many other things; she wanted to serve everyone these delicacies and to eat them herself. She thought disputes about what is dharma and what is not unimportant. She said, 'Come on, let's eat pakoris first; then we will talk about it.'

Amar said listlessly, 'I don't want to eat anything. I can't stomach food that comes with so much abuse. Dada has finally settled that.'

'I don't like you talking like this. I bet you've never eaten such delicious pakoris. If you don't eat, then I won't either.'

Naina's argument weakened his resolve, 'You badger me a lot, Naina. Honestly, I have no wish to eat.'

'Come, sit at the dining table. I'm sure you'll attack the pakoris the minute you see them.'

'Why don't you go and eat? I am not going to die if I don't eat for one day.'

'Does that mean that I will die if I don't eat one day? You don't observe any fasts, but I fast on Shivratri and don't even drink water.'

It was impossible for Amarkant to withstand Naina's cajoling. Lala Samarkant was not in the habit of having an evening meal. Accordingly, the brother, his sister, and his wife used to eat together. When they reached the courtyard, Naina called out to her bhabhi. Sukhada called back from upstairs, 'I'm not hungry.'

Amarkant had to face the task of persuading her. He quietly climbed upstairs; afraid at heart that today the issue was very serious. But he was determined not to back down. On a matter of such fundamental principles there couldn't be any compromise.

Sukhada sat up as soon as she heard Amarkant's footsteps. Her pale face showed such helpless grief that for a moment Amarkant wavered.

Taking her hand, he said, 'Come, let us eat. It is very late.'

'I'll eat later. First we have to discuss one thing. Did you have a fight with Dadaji again today?'

'What does it matter whether I fought with him or if he rebuked me for no reason at all?'

Sukhada said in a tone of philosophical objectivity, 'Then why do you give him an opportunity to rebuke you? I know you don't like his principles. I don't support them either. But at his age you can't expect him to adopt new ways. After all, he is following the ways of the world. You should help him in any way you can. When he is no longer around you can live by your own ideals. No one will hold you back then. For now, you shouldn't feel badly if you have to do something against your principles. At least you will give him the satisfaction of knowing that you won't squander his earnings behind his back. I was listening to both of you today and it seemed to me that you were more at fault.'

Amarkant did not wish to add the burden of anxiety to her burden of pregnancy but, in the present context, he felt it necessary to defend himself. He said, 'He told me clearly today that I have to look after myself. He loves his money more than he loves me.'

That was what had been weighing on Amarkant's heart.

Sukhada was ready with a response, 'You also love your principles more than you do your father. I don't say anything to him. He can't be lectured to at the age of sixty. At least you have no right to lecture him. You may not care for money but great thinkers and warriors have always worshipped goddess Laxmi. Only the brave appreciate the world and they will always enjoy it. Renunciation is for ascetics, not for householders. If you wanted renunciation, why did you marry me? You could have shaved your head and become a disciple of some sadhu or saint. Then I wouldn't have been around to quarrel with you. You can't escape the consequences of your deeds. After all, the responsibilities of family life have made many great men waver from their principles. Even Lord Krishna and Arjuna had to resort to a new argument.'[1]

Amarkant thought it unnecessary to reply to this sermon. He considered such arguments unworthy of serious consideration. He said, 'So, you advise me to become an ascetic.'

Sukhada was annoyed. She couldn't tolerate such a flippant response. She said, 'That is a coward's way. It is not easy to earn money. If an ascetic had to face the difficulties that a businessman faces he would forget asceticism. It does not require much strength, intelligence, knowledge, or courage to seek hospitality at the house of some gentle soul. But to earn money one has to put in one's blood and sweat. It is not an easy thing to do. Money doesn't grow on a tree that can just be harvested.'

Amarkant said flippantly again, 'I don't see Dada doing anything other than sitting on his cushion. And I see all other important seths and moneylenders getting fatter everyday. Only the labourers put in their blood and sweat—they are mere skeletons.'

Sukhada did not reply. It was useless to argue with such a thickheaded person.

Naina called, 'What are you doing, Bhaiya? Why don't you come? The pakoris are getting cold.'

Sukhada said, 'Why don't you go and eat? The poor girl has spent all day making them.'

'I won't go unless you come too.'

---

[1] Sukhada is alluding to Lord Krishna's ability to find practical solutions by bending the rules a little in order to achieve a noble end, that is the victory of the Pandavas over the Kauravas in the epic battle in the Mahabharata. For instance, when Dronacharya—the guru who had taught martial arts to both the Pandavas and Kauravas and is now fighting on the side of the Kauravas—proves invincible against Arjuna, a rumour is spread that Ashwatthama has been killed in battle. Ashwatthama was the name of both Dronacharya's son and an elephant. On hearing the rumour, Dronacharya thinks his son is dead and loses interest in the battle. He asks Yudhisthir, the eldest Pandava who is known to always speak the truth, whether Ashwatthama is dead. Yudhisthir, who has been persuaded by Lord Kirshna from before, replies in the affirmative but adds in an undertone that it is the elephant. Hearing a 'yes', Dronacharya lays down his arms and becomes an easy victim of Arjuna. There are other similar instances of bending the rules a little by Lord Krishna in support of a noble cause, a course of action that many practical people tend to follow.

'Promise me that you will not fight with Dadaji.'

Amarkant said seriously 'Sukhada, I tell you honestly that I have made every effort to avoid these quarrels. Sometimes I am surprised myself at the change in me over the last two years. I now accept things that I used to hate. But now I have reached a limit that if crossed will propel me into a bottomless pit. Please don't push me towards destruction.'

Sukhada took this as a reflection on herself. She could not accept it, 'What that means is that you think I want to destroy you. If this is what you think of me, then you should have poisoned me long ago. If you think that I am a slave to pampered living and argue with you only for selfish reasons, then you are doing me the greatest injustice. I want to tell you this—even if I have been spoiled, I am able to bear pain and suffering such as you can't imagine. I hope to God the day never comes when I am the reason for your downfall. However, I don't believe in digging my own grave. I know that with a little effort, you can safeguard your principles and dharma while preventing the destruction of this house. Dadaji is a well-read man and he is well versed in worldly affairs. If there is any truth in your life, then he will certainly be affected by it. With these daily quarrels, you are only hardening his stance. Even children are driven to obstinacy by punishment. Old people are somewhat like children. Like children, you can get around them with tenderness and love.'

Amar asked, 'Then should I buy stolen articles?'

'Never.'

'But that was the reason for the quarrel.'

'You could have told the man to bring it back when Dada was there.'

'And if he had not accepted that? He wanted the money immediately.'

'Sometimes we have to do things that normally we would never do.'

'That is hypocrisy as practised by hypocrites.'

'In that case, I consider your sterile idealism the hypocrisy of hypocrites.'

Like tired warriors, the two stopped a minute to catch their breath. Then Amarkant said, 'Naina is calling us.'

'I will come only if you will promise.'

Amarkant was unshaken and said, 'I will promise for your sake, but I won't be able to keep it. The alternative is that I disassociate myself from everything that goes on in the house.'

Sukhada said in a determined manner, 'That is far better than fighting everyday. As long as you are in this house, you will have to consider the welfare of this house.'

Amar said arrogantly, 'I can leave the house today.'

Sukhada dropped a bombshell, 'And what about me?'

Amar, stared at Sukhada astonished.

Sukhada continued, 'My relationship with this house is dependent on you. If you don't live here, then what is there for me in this house! Wherever you live, that is where I will live too.'

Amar said anxiously, 'You can stay with your mother.'

'Why should I stay with my mother? I can't be dependent on anyone. My happiness and sorrow rest with you. However you keep me, I will live. I will also see how firmly you adhere to your principles. I promise that I won't ask you for anything. You won't have to bear any hardship because of me. I can also earn something. If it is a modest income, we will live modestly; if it's a lot, then so much the better. If we have to build our hut some day anyhow, then we might as well begin now. You draw water from the well, and I will look after the pots and kitchen. A man that lives in a palace can also live in a hovel. Then at least no one will be able to lord it over us.'

Amarkant was defeated. He wasn't concerned about himself, but how could he subject Sukhada to such hardships.

Abashed, he said, 'That time has not yet come, Sukhada.'

Sukhada said agitatedly, 'Why? Are you afraid that I will cry about my bad fortune?'

Amarkant said shamefacedly, 'It is not that Sukhada.'

'Why do you lie? That is what you are thinking and you can't do me a greater injustice. When it comes to bearing hardship or defending a principle, women have never been less than men. You are forcing me, if for no other reason than to avoid public stigma, to ask Dadaji's permission to live separately from him. Answer me.'

Ashamed, Amar said, 'Forgive me, Sukhada! I promise that I will do whatever Dadaji wants me to do.'

'Because you still doubt about me?'

'No, only because I still lack the strength.'

At that moment Naina came and dragged the two of them away to feed them. Sukhada was happy because she felt that today she had won a great victory. Amarkant, however, was ashamed because his idealism and dharma had been tested and he had been found lacking in the fortitude needed to uphold them against all odds. A camel faced with a mountain had become aware of his own height.

CHAPTER 9

Sukhada's pregnancy gave Amarkant some purpose in life. Now he didn't want to cause her pain or go against her wishes in any way at all. Because she was pregnant, Amar read to her many good books and he developed a special liking for the epics—Ramayana, Mahabharata, and Bhagvad Gita. The upbringing of their child was always in his mind as he constantly strove to please Sukhada. Now he didn't hesitate to take her to a theatre or cinema. Sometimes he brought her garlands of flowers; at other times other trinkets that would amuse her. He also looked after the shop in the morning and evening. He was no longer interested in meetings. Just imagine, he was going to be the father of a son! At times, when alone, he became so overwhelmed that he bowed his head before Lord Krishna's image. While Sukhada was undergoing her trial, Amar was preparing himself to face new responsibilities. Until now, he hadn't had to proceed carefully as he had been on a level field, but now that he was on a hillside, he had to step very carefully.

Lala Samarkant also was much happier during this time. Again and again he would go inside the house to inquire after Sukhada's comfort. He had become especially kind towards Amar and didn't regard his idealism as all that bad. Indeed, one day he summarily ejected Kaale Khan from the shop. He didn't lose his temper with his tenants anymore, nor did he file as many lawsuits as before. He saw a bright future now, and one day while talking to Renuka, he openly praised Amarkant's work ethic.

Renuka wasn't quite so cheerful. She was terrified whenever she thought of the difficulties of childbirth. She said, 'Lalaji, I pray to God that He doesn't give us anguish in the middle of happiness. The first delivery is very difficult. A woman is born again after childbirth.'

Samarkant had no such fears and said, 'I have even thought of a name for the child. He will be named Renukant.'

Renuka said apprehensively, 'Lalaji, please don't pick names yet. A name can be chosen once we are out of danger. I have been thinking that there could be a reading of invocations to the goddess Durga to ward off any

possible misfortune. It would also be useful to hire a midwife now. I
know one who lives in this locality. My child, Sukhada, still doesn't know
many things. The midwife would be able to instruct her.'

Lalaji accepted both proposals happily. When he returned home, he
found Amarkant talking to two white men and a woman sitting in the
shop. Occasionally, white men of the lower class would come to the shop
wanting to sell a watch or some other article. Lalaji cheated them at will.
He knew that they wouldn't go to any other shop for fear of gossip. He
hurriedly took over from Amarkant because Amarkant believed in frank
talk and this was no occasion for frankness.

He greeted the woman, 'What can I do for you, Memsahab?'

All three were very drunk. Memsahab brought out a gold chain and
said, 'Sethji, I want to sell this. Baba is very ill and I have had to spend a
lot of money on his medication.'

Samarkant examined the chain and weighing it in his hand, said,
'The gold is not good quality, Memsahab. Where did you have the chain
made?'

The woman laughed and said, 'Oh! You always say that. The gold is
very good quality. It was made in an English shop. You should take it.'

Samarkant, with an expression suggesting unwillingness to trade, said,
'The big shops are the ones that shave the customer with the dull side of
the razor. Cloth that is sold for six annas per yard in the market here will
be sold for no less than twelve annas per yard in an English shop.
The maximum that I could give you for this chain would be ten rupees
per tola.'

'You won't give any more?'

'No, I couldn't. This too as a special favour for you.'

These whites were the sort of people who sell their souls for liquor
and gambling, travel first class in trains ticketless, deceive hotel staff and
abscond without paying the bill; and, when all else fails, beg, posing as
gentlemen and ladies who have fallen on hard times. The three consulted
among themselves and sold the chain. Taking the money, they went down
to the street and were just getting into a tonga when a beggar woman
came up. The three were lost in the joy of having money when suddenly
the beggar woman took out a dagger and lunged at one of the white
men. The dagger was aimed at his face, but in nervous fright, he tilted his
head backwards and the dagger pricked his chest. He started groaning.
The two remaining whites jumped off the tonga. They were trying to

run into the shop to save their lives when the beggar woman attacked the second white man. The dagger pierced his ribs. He had not been able to climb the steps to the shop and he fell down. The beggar woman dashed up to the shop and charged at the woman when Amarkant rushed to seize the dagger, yelling, 'Stop! Stop!' Seeing him, the beggar woman threw down the dagger, jumped down from the shop and stood there. There was pandemonium in the entire market. Rumours started flying. 'A white man has killed several people.' 'Lala Samarkant has been killed, and Amarkant has been injured.' In such a situation, no one wanted to endanger his life by going to the spot and checking for himself. People closed their shops and started running away.

The two white men were writhing on the ground. Up in the shop, the white woman was standing as if stunned, while Lala Samarkant, holding Amarkant's hand, was trying to drag him indoors. The beggar woman, with head bowed, was standing rooted to the ground, as if she had done nothing. She could have run away; nobody would have dared chase her, but she did not run. She could have committed suicide. Her dagger was still lying on the ground, but she didn't kill herself either. She just stood as if amazement rooted her to the spot.

Several shopkeepers from across the street had gathered. Two burly policemen had also arrived. Everyone started saying, 'That's the woman, that's the woman!' The policemen caught her.

In ten minutes all the officials and almost the entire city had congregated there. The red *pugrees* of police constables were visible everywhere. The civil surgeon arrived and had the injured removed to hospital. Investigation into the crime started. The beggar woman readily confessed to her crime.

The police superintendent asked her, 'Did you have any grievance against these men?'

The beggar woman didn't reply.

Hundreds of voices shouted, 'Why don't you speak, murderess?'

The beggar woman said firmly, 'I am not a murderess.'

'Didn't you assault those sahabs?'

'Yes, I did.'

'Then why aren't you a murderess?'

'I am not a murderess. About six months ago, a group of three white men violated my honour. I didn't go home afterwards, and didn't show my face to anyone. I don't know where I have wandered, how I have lived, or what I have done up to now. I came to myself after I had wounded the two white men. Only then did I realize what I had done. I am very poor. I don't know who gave me the dagger, or where I found it, or how I got so much courage. I am not saying this because I am afraid of being hanged. I pray to God He would take me from this world as soon as possible. What will I live for when my honour is lost?'

Her statement changed the attitude of the public. Everyone who gave a statement to the police testified that she was a madwoman. She was always wandering here and there. If she was given food, she fed it to the dogs. If money was given to her, she threw it away.

One *tongawalah* said, 'She was sitting in the middle of the street once. No matter how much I shouted at her, she didn't move from the path. I couldn't do anything except to go onto the shoulder of the road.'

One *paanwalah* said, 'One day she came and stood in front of my shop. I gave her a bira of paan. She threw it down and started trampling on it with her feet. Then she went away singing.'

Amarkant also gave a statement. Lalaji tried to dissuade him from involving himself in the affair, but Amarkant was so agitated that Lalaji dared not stop him. Amar told the whole story, embellished with a few details of his own making.

The police officer asked, 'Would you testify that this woman is deranged?'

Amarkant said, 'Oh, yes, absolutely. I have seen her dozens of times laughing or weeping alone. If anyone asked her anything, she would just run away.'

That was a lie. This was the first time Amar had seen the woman since that day in the fields. He might have come across her here and there, but he had not recognized her.

When the police took away the madwoman, about two thousand men went with her to the police station. In the eyes of the public, she was no longer an ordinary woman. She had achieved the status of a saint. How could she have had so much courage without some divine power! Throughout the night people from other areas of the city kept coming to the site of attack to have a look. Some men discussed the chain of events endlessly—how she came and stood close to the tonga, how she pulled out the dagger, how she rushed, how the two tried to climb up to the shop, how she attacked the second white man. Had Bhaiya Amarkant not intervened, she would have finished off the Mem as well. At that time her eyes were like burning coals and her face was brilliantly alive.

When Amarkant went inside the house, he saw Naina standing in a state of shock holding her sister-in-law's hand. Sukhada was sitting on a cot. Her eyes were moist with sympathy. She stood up as soon as she saw Amar and said, 'She was the same woman, wasn't she?'

'Yes, she seems to be the same one.'

'So, now she will be hanged.'

'She may escape it, but there is little hope.'

'If she is hanged, there is no justice in this world. She hasn't committed any crime. The scoundrels that raped her deserved this punishment. If I were a judge, I would acquit her completely. One should make an image of such a *devi* and worship it. She has brought credit to all her sisters.'

Amarkant said, 'But it is not justice if one person commits the crime and someone else gets punished.'

Sukhada said angrily, 'They are all the same. A society that harbours such evil people is doomed. If a member of a community commits an evil deed the entire community gets a bad name, and its punishment should be meted out to the entire community. When some man in a border state kidnapped a white woman, in retaliation the government launched an attack against the entire region. It didn't even inquire who the culprit was, in its eyes the entire state was guilty. No one protected this beggar woman. She had only herself to avenge her honour. You should go and consult some lawyers—she must not be hanged, no matter how much it costs. I would even say that the lawyers should plead this case free of charge. Any lawyer who demands payment in this case would be inhuman. You should call a meeting of your organization today and start a campaign for contributions. Even in my condition, I could raise thousands of rupees in this city. There is no woman who will say no in her cause.'

Trying to calm her, Amarkant said, 'What you wish, will be done. We will do whatever we can no matter what the results are. I am going to see Professor Shantikumar for a while. You should go and lie down comfortably.'

'I will also go visit Amma. You can drop me there on your way.'

Amar insisted, 'You should go and lie down peacefully. I'll go and see Amma on my way.'

Sukhada was getting agitated, 'In this situation one who lies peacefully is dead. Even if I have to give my life for this devi, I will give it gladly. You can't tell Amma what I have to say to her. It is impossible for men to feel the agony that a woman feels in her heart for another woman. I will insist that Amma give me at least five thousand rupees for this case. I don't need her money for myself. If contributions come in, that would be fine, otherwise she will have to bear the entire burden. Please have a tonga fetched.'

Amarkant now understood that this apparently frivolous woman had the capacity to feel deeply, a love of her sisterhood, and the ability to sacrifice.

The tonga arrived and they went to see Renuka Devi.

CHAPTER 10

❧

For three months the entire city was in turmoil. Everyday thousands of men abandoned their work and went to the court in the hope of catching a glimpse of the beggar woman. Many women also went. The moment the beggar woman stepped off the lorry, there would be a thundering cry of 'Victory! Victory!' and flowers would be showered. Renuka and Sukhada stayed in court everyday until it ended.

The district magistrate had forwarded the case to a judicial court and depositions were being made daily. A jury of five men was selected. An army of lawyers was made ready for her defence. No proof of guilt was needed in the case as the woman charged with the crime had acknowledged her guilt. The only thing to be ascertained was whether she was sane or insane at the time of the attempted assassination. The witnesses said that she was not sane. The doctor, a Bengali, said that he did not find any signs of mental imbalance in her. When he came out of the court after testifying he met with such taunts and disapproval that the poor fellow had difficulty reaching his house. On such occasions anyone who said a word against the wishes of the public was condemned. The public does not allow any dissent based on personal judgment. There is no room for leniency of any kind in its realm.

Renuka had become the queen of the city. She was shouldering the entire burden of the defence of the case. Shantikumar and Amarkant were her right and left hands. People would come of their own volition and offer further contributions! Even Lala Samarkant was helping secretly.

One day Amarkant saw Pathanin in the courtroom. Sakina, covered in a shawl, was with her.

Amarkant asked, 'Shall I get you something to sit on, Mataji? Today even you couldn't stay away.'

Pathanin said, 'Beta, you may not have seen us, but we come everyday. This girl just insists on coming.'

Amarkant was reminded of the handkerchief; he also remembered the old woman's request to him. But in the turmoil he hadn't even gone to college, let alone keep track of these matters.

The old woman asked, 'What will happen in the case, beta? Will the woman be acquitted or sentenced?'

Sakina stepped closer to her.

Amar said, 'I can't hazard a guess, Mataji. There seems little hope of acquittal, but we will go all the way to the Privy Council.'

Pathanin said, 'It will be an outrage if she is sentenced.'

Amarkant said agitatedly, 'Irrespective of whether she is sentenced or acquitted, she has shown how even the downtrodden women of Bharat can defend their honour.'

Sakina spoke to Amar indirectly by asking her grandmother, 'Amma, will we be able to have a *darshan* of her.'

Amar said eagerly, 'Yes, of course, you can see her. Pathanin come, I'll seat you with the women of my house. You can talk to them as well.'

Pathanin said, 'Yes, beta, this girl has been pestering me from the very first day. We couldn't get through to you to inquire. She made some handkerchiefs, which sold for two rupees. She has saved those two rupees as her contribution. If you will, beta, you take them; we would be ashamed offering two rupees to the women.'

Amarkant felt humbled by the sacrifice of these poor people. He had begun to give himself airs because, wherever he went, people respected him. But seeing their selfless enthusiasm his eyes were opened.

He said, 'It is no longer necessary to contribute, Amma! There is no shortage of money. You should spend it on yourselves. But, come, I will introduce you to the women.'

Sakina's enthusiasm was dampened. Bowing her head she said, 'In a place where the contributions of the poor are not valued, who will acknowledge the poor! There is no point in our going there, Amma. If she comes, we can see her from here just as well.'

Amarkant was mortified and said, 'No, no, it is not that way at all, Amma. Even the contribution of a single paisa is welcomed with open arms. There is no question of rich or poor. I am myself poor. I said that only because I thought it might be inconvenient for you.'

As the two started walking with Amarkant, Pathanin said in a soft voice, 'Beta, I had asked you for something the other day! Perhaps you forgot.'

Amarkant was embarrassed, 'No, no, I remember it. It is just that in the last few months I have been totally occupied with this matter. As soon as there is some free time, I will mention it to my friends.'

As Amarkant came out of the courthouse after introducing the two women to Renuka, he encountered Professor Shantikumar.

The professor asked, 'Where have you been, my friend? The case is coming up and there is no lawyer to be seen. Today the testimony of the accused will be heard. God alone understands these lawyers. They stand up in the court for a few minutes and expect that the entire world should worship them. It would have been far better if one or two lawyers had been retained on fees. Work provided without payment doesn't receive proper attention. My blood begins to boil when I think of the lackadaisical manner in which the case is being argued. They all want to be famous, but no one wants to do any work. If the case had been defended better all the witnesses for the prosecution would have been neutralized. But no one was here to do it. They know that the accused will be called today, but no one cares.'

Amarkant said, 'I have notified each and every one of them. If someone doesn't show up, what can I do?'

Shantikumar said, 'I will take care of them all after the case is over.'

Just then a lorry came into view. Amarkant ran to inform the lawyers. The bystanders rushed from all sides and entered the courtroom. The beggar woman stepped down from the lorry. As she walked and stood in the dock, thousands of eyes followed her and every one of those eyes was filled with respect. Her pale, downcast face was so radiant with dignity that before any scornful stare could be raised, it was overpowered and transmuted into reverence.

The judge sahab was a dark-complexioned large man, short and broad. He had a long nose and his small eyes seemed to be naturally smiling. Formerly, this gentleman had been an ardent servant of the nation, and had chaired some provincial function of the Indian National Congress, but for the last three years he had been a judge. Accordingly, he had divorced himself from the national movement, but those in the know understood that he was still propagating his nationalistic views in newspapers under a pseudonym. Even an enemy would not have dared to say that he would deviate an inch from the path of justice because of pressure or threat. On this occasion, however, his very adherence to justice was perceived as an obstacle to the release of the beggar woman.

Judge sahab asked, 'Your name?'

The beggar woman said, 'Beggar woman.'

'Your father's name?'

'I cannot disgrace my father by giving you his name.'

'Your home town?'

The beggar woman said sadly , 'Why do you ask? What will you do with the information?'

'You stand accused that on the third day of the month you wounded two Englishmen with a dagger so severely that both died the same day. Do you acknowledge the charge?'

The beggar woman said unperturbed, 'You call it a crime; I don't consider it so.'

'You accept that you killed them.'

'The witnesses would not have given false testimony.'

'Do you have anything to say in your defence?'

The beggar woman said in a clear voice, 'I don't have anything to say. I have no wish to offer any explanation to save my life. I am happy to think that my life will soon end. I am a poor, weak woman. I only remember that some months ago everything that I had was taken from me, and after losing it there was no purpose to my life. I died that very day. I am standing here speaking before you, but this body doesn't have a soul. I don't call a person alive who can't show her face to others. So many of my brothers and sisters are needlessly running here and there, incurring expenses on my account, but, after being so disgraced, it is much better for me to die. I do not ask for justice, I do not ask for mercy. I only ask for the death sentence. But I do request my brothers and sisters not to treat my body with disrespect after I die. Please do not be apprehensive or uneasy about touching it; forget that it is the corpse of some unfortunate, sinful woman and give me after my death the respect that is now denied me while I live. I say clearly that I am not grieved by what I did, I have no regrets. God forbid that any of my sisters are in my situation but, if they are, there is no other recourse. You may wonder, "If she is so eager to die, why did she continue to live up to now?" How can I explain that to you? When I regained my senses and saw the two men writhing in front of me, I was frightened. I couldn't think of what to do. Afterwards the gentleness of my brothers and sisters ensnared me in ties of affection; even now I am under the delusion that perhaps the blot on my face has been washed off and that I will get the confidence and respect that my sisters receive. But this may be a figment of my imagination. Even if the government releases me today and my brothers and sisters put a garland of flowers around my neck, and even if gold coins are showered upon me, would I be able to go home?

'I am a married woman, I have a small child. Can I ever call that child mine? Can I ever call my husband mine? Never. The child, on seeing me, will raise his arms to be picked up, but I will have to lower his arms and turn away my face tearfully. My husband may even forgive me, I have not betrayed him and still wish to lie at his feet; but I can't even face him. He may drag me to the house, but I can't step inside. I can't console myself with the thought that I had not sinned at heart. Such rationalization is possible only for someone who desires to live. Whatever one may say or hear, I can't forget that I am impure, that I am untouchable.

'Why does a man want to live? Not because he is happy, for even those who are always in pain and hunger for bread don't love life any less because of their suffering. We love life because we get affection from those who are ours and because we have others' respect. When there is no hope of getting either, life is pointless. Even if those who are mine offer me love, it would be pity, not love. Others offer me respect, that will also be pity, not respect. Now I can get that love and respect only after death. There is nothing in this life for me except scorn and exile. I beg all my brothers and sisters here to pray to God for the redemption of that society which produces such human animals.'

At the conclusion of the beggar woman's statement, the large courtroom was as silent as a tomb. Only the sobbing of a few women could be heard. Women's faces were lit with dignity, while the faces of men were suffused with shame. Amarkant was thinking that the white men had dared to commit such a heinous crime only because they thought themselves the rulers of this country. Shantikumar, meanwhile, had composed in his mind a lecture on the topic, 'Men's oppression of women'. Sukhada was thinking—If she is released, I will keep her in our house and serve her. Renuka was contemplating a women's hospital in her name.

The wife of the judge was sitting near Sukhada. She had been eagerly waiting for a long time for a chance to speak to someone about the case, but had not dared to open her mouth because she didn't trust the ladies sitting close to her—a suspicion that was mutual.

Finally, unable to contain herself, she said to Sukhada, 'This woman is entirely blameless.'

Sukhada said bitterly, 'Only if the Judge sahab also thinks so.'

'I will tell him plainly today that if he convicts this woman I'll think that he is taking direction from his superiors.'

Suddenly, Judge sahab stood up and in a few words instructed the jury to give their verdict in the case, and then busied himself with some paperwork. The jury retired to a back room and after some discussion returned to give their verdict. In their opinion the accused was not guilty. There was a faint smile on the judge's face as he promised to deliver his judgment the next day and got up to go.

CHAPTER 11

Two kinds of preparations gripped the city the day before the judgment. One was for a tragic, the other for a festive outcome. Black flags were made and baskets of fruit were also assembled, but the pessimists outnumbered the optimists. White people had been murdered. How could the judge in this case pass a just verdict, what could he do? Shantikumar and Salim were openly saying that the judge would sentence her to death by hanging! Some spread the news that an entire army regiment had been called up to the court for tomorrow. Some stopped short of saying the army and said armed police instead. Amarkant was confident that the army would be called up.

At ten at night, Amarkant went to Salim's house. He had been there only an hour earlier. Salim asked anxiously, 'Why have you come back, bhai; has something new happened?'

Amar said, 'I have thought of something and want to know what you think. It would be a sign of weakness if we took a sentence of hanging quietly. It may be necessary to teach Judge Kichloo sahab that young India will not tolerate the massacre of justice. We should boycott him socially: I will hire his cook, you hire his coachman; he will be an outcaste everywhere, and wherever he goes he will be ridiculed.'

Salim said with a smile, 'After so much serious thought you have come up with this idea? It sounds like what a *baniya* would say.'

'What else can we do?'

'What will such a boycott accomplish? He will simply write to the police station, and dozens of cooks and coachmen will be offered.'

'At least the fellow will be in trouble for a few days.'

'It is a useless idea, Amar. If you want to teach him a lesson, then teach one that he will remember for some time. We will hire a fellow who will throw a shoe at his face at precisely the moment he sits down after passing his verdict of guilty.'

Amarkant laughed and said, '*Yaar*, you are a great comedian!'

'What is so funny about that?'

'Do you really mean to have him hit with a shoe?'

'Oh, yes. I'm not joking. I want to teach him a lesson so that he wouldn't be able to show his face here.'

Amarkant thought it a shabby idea, but where was the harm! People who are used to being kicked don't listen to persuasion. He said, 'Alright. We'll see. But where will you find the man to do it?'

Salim smiled at his naiveté and said, 'You can find men who will cut someone's throat for payment. This is nothing. All you have to do is to give some ruffian two hundred rupees. I was thinking of Kaale Khan.'

'Oh, that one! I once gave him a dressing down at our shop.'

'That was very foolish. You should keep a few such people on your side; at times, they are very useful. You manage the money, I will take care of everything else. I have already overspent my budget.'

'The month has just begun, bhai!'

'Oh, yes. It is all gone at the beginning of the month. Then I scrape some from here, some from there. Sometimes, I wangle ten rupees from Amma; sometimes, I squeeze out five to ten rupees from *abba-jaan* on the pretext of buying books. But to get a sum of two hundred rupees would be a problem. If you definitely say no, then I will have to squeeze it from Amma.'

Amar said, 'Money is not a problem. I'll go and get it.'

Salim didn't think it wise to bring the money at that time of night. So it was deferred to the next day.

When Amar reached home, it was close to ten thirty. Lights were on at the front door. In the sitting room, Lalaji was consulting with two or three pundits. Amar wondered anxiously why people were awake at that hour of night. What new event had occurred now?

When Lalaji saw him, he scolded him, 'For goodness sake, where have you been? You left at ten o'clock; it is nearly midnight now. Please go and get the lady doctor, the one in the main hospital. Bring her with you.'

Amarkant, asked apprehensively, 'Is someone ill ...'

Samarkant interrupted him sternly, 'What are you going on about, do as I tell you. You people are good for nothing. This court case has taken over everything in this house. Go quickly.'

Amar dared not ask any further questions. He didn't even go inside the house. Slowly he came out on the road, and was mounting his bicycle when Sillo came out of the house.

Seeing Amar, she said, 'Oh, Bhaiya, listen, where are you going? Bahuji is very restless. She has been asking for you for a long time. Her entire body is drenched in sweat. Look, Bhaiya, I will accept nothing but a gold necklace; there will be no quibbling afterwards.'

Amarkant understood. Getting off the bicycle, he rushed like the wind into the house. Renuka, a midwife, a brahman woman from the neighbourhood, and Naina were sitting in the courtyard. Inside the room, Sukhada was wailing in labour pain.

Naina caught hold of Amar's hand and said crying, 'Where have you been Bhaiya? Bhabhi has been restless for a long time.'

Amar's heart was inundated with emotion and he started crying. He went and stood at the door to Sukhada's room, but he could step inside. His heart was bursting.

Sukhada looked at him in great pain and said, 'I won't live now. Oh! It feels like my stomach is being gored with a dagger. Do forgive me for whatever I have said or done.'

Renuka ran up and said to Amarkant, 'You should not be here, Bhaiya. Seeing you she will become even more restless. Send someone to get the lady doctor. Be strong, you are far too wise to cry.'

Sukhada said, 'No, Amma. Tell him to just stay here for a while. I will not live through this. Oh, God!'

Renuka admonished Amar and said, 'I tell you to go, and you are standing here weeping! Go and get the lady doctor!'

Amarkant left in tears and started toward the women's hospital, his heart aching as he remembered Sukhada's agonized face.

The lady doctor, Miss Hooper, was often called out at odd hours. Her fees at night were double those she charged in the day. Amarkant was afraid that she might be annoyed that he had come so late at night, but Miss Hooper welcomed him kindly and after ordering the car to be brought out started to talk to him.

'Is this the first child?'

'Yes, madam.'

'Don't cry. There is no reason to be nervous. It is quite painful the first time. Your wife is not very weak, is she?'

'She has become quite thin lately.'

'You should have come sooner to fetch me.'

Amar lost all hope. How could have he known that this calamity was so imminent. If he had known he would have come home directly from the court.

Mem sahab said again, 'You people don't have your ladies do any exercise. As a result, the inner muscles remain tight. It is more painful for that reason.'

Amarkant said sobbing, 'Madam, now we depend on your kindness.'

'I am coming, but we may have to call the civil surgeon as well.'

Frightened, Amar said, 'If you say, I will bring him with me.'

Memsahab looked at him kindly and said, 'No, not right now. Let me examine her first.'

Amarkant was not comforted. He said in a frightened voice, 'Madam, if anything happens to Sukhada, I won't be able to live.'

When Amar said that, the Mem asked worriedly, 'Is she not alright?'

'She is in terrible pain.'

'I mean is her condition alright?'

'Her face is very pale, sweating ...'

'But how is her condition? Her heart is not failing? Her hands and feet are not cold? Are they?'

The car was ready.

Mem sahab said, 'Come and sit here. My man will return the bicycle tomorrow.'

Amar beseeched her, 'Please go. I will just go to the civil surgeon's residence. The house of Lala Samarkant on Bulanaale ...'

'We know.'

Mem sahab was on her way, Amarkant went to get the civil surgeon. It was already eleven o'clock. The roads were all quiet, and he had to go a full three miles. The civil surgeon lived in the military cantonment. When he arrived there it was midnight. It took more than an hour to get the main gates opened and to have the sahab informed. The sahab was in a bad temper at being woken up. He thundered 'I can't go now!'

Amar said unperturbed, 'You want your fees, don't you?'

'My fees at night are one hundred rupees.'

'It doesn't matter.'

'Have you brought the money?'

Amar upbraided him, 'You don't require advance payment from everyone! Lala Samarkant is not one of those men who can't be trusted for a mere one hundred rupees. He is the biggest moneylender in this city, and I am his son.'

The sahab calmed down somewhat. When Amar told him what the case was, he prepared to go. Amar left the bicycle there and sat in the car with the sahab. In half an hour the car reached the Bulanaale. Amarkant could hear the festive sound of a clarinet in the distance. Guns were being fired as well. His heart blossomed with happiness.

When the car stopped at the front door, Lala Samarkant stepped out of the house, greeted the doctor, and said, 'Everything is alright because of your kindness, illustrious Sir. A grandson has been born to me.'

The doctor and Miss Hooper talked for a while; then the doctor collected his fee and departed.

After he had left, Lalaji scolded Amarkant, 'That was a hundred rupees wasted.'

Amarkant, said exasperated, 'I will give you the money back. Anyone could make such a mistake. I wasn't thinking about money then.'

At any other time, Amarkant would have pondered over this rebuke for hours on end, but now his heart was filled with joy and excitement. Just as an inflated soccer ball is not affected by kicking, he started planning what charitable donations he would make to mark the occasion. Now he was the father of a son! Who could now lord it over him! It was as if the newborn had brought with him the blessing of hope and immortality from heaven. He was very anxious to see and adore this child!

Seeing his eager looks, Miss Hooper said, 'Babuji, you won't be able to see the baby boy just like that. You will have to give me a big reward first.'

Amar said courteously, 'The baby boy is yours. I am only your servant. How is the newly delivered mother doing?'

'Very well. She has just gone to sleep.'

'Is the baby healthy?'

'Yes, he is. He is very handsome also, like a little doll with a face like rose petals.' Then she turned and went into the delivery room.

Dozens of women from the neighbourhood had congregated and were singing and making music. Their united voices, like a heavy rope, were binding Amar to domesticity. At that very moment, Miss Hooper, with the baby boy in her arms, gestured to Amar to come toward the delivery room. Joyfully, Amar moved forward, but suddenly he was filled with a strange uncertainty. His steps faltered—how could he accept such a divine gift when his heart was impure and he was in no way worthy to receive it? When had he done any penance for it? It was through God's extreme grace that he had been bestowed such a treasure. God, how kind you are!

Just as the light of dawn emerges from a bluish-black horizon, so did Amarkant feel a light emerging from the meanness and pettiness of his inner being and enveloping his life with a silvery radiance. The light of lamps, the sound of music, and the stars in the firmament were like the beauty, grace, and creativity of the child.

Sillo came to him and started crying. Amar asked, 'What happened? Why are you crying?'

Sillo said, 'Memsahab won't allow me to see the baby. She shooed me away. Would I have put an evil eye on the child? I have had children, I have brought them up. What could happen if I saw him for a moment?'

Amar said laughing, 'Sillo, you are such a silly girl. She must have stopped you for fear that the child might be exposed to air. These English lady doctors have peculiar ways. They neither understand, nor explain, they just keep making up excuses as they go along. But, after all, today is her day to reign, after that only the midwife will remain. You will be the one who will take care of the baby, who else is there to look after him?'

Sillo smiled through her tears and said, 'I have seen him from a distance. He looks just like you, though, in complexion, he takes after Bahuji. Let me tell you, for my gift I will accept only a necklace.'

It was around two o'clock in the morning when Lala Samarkant called Amar and said, 'Sleep is impossible now. Why not sit down and prepare a list of things to do for the festivities tomorrow? When you were born, my business was not as large, and Naina was a girl. God has given us this son today after a twenty-five-year wait. Some people are opposed to dancing and music, but I don't see any harm in it. These are happy occasions. Relatives and friends come; they listen to songs and music and participate in a festive dinner. These joys are what life is all about, what else is there in this world?'

Amar objected, 'But dancing by prostitutes does not become this auspicious occasion.'

Lalaji said, 'Keep your high opinions to yourself. I am not asking for your advice. We have our customs and we need to support them. Angels danced on the happy occasion of the birth of Shri Ramchandra. In our society it is considered auspicious.'

Amar said, 'In English society such festivities do not take place.'

Lalaji, seizing the opportunity as a cat seizes a mouse, said, 'In English homes instead of prostitutes, daughters and daughters-in-law dance—as in the untouchable community here. Instead of the daughters and daughters-in-law dancing, it is much better that prostitutes dance. At least, I and older people like myself wouldn't like to see our daughters and daughters-in-law dancing.'

Amarkant couldn't think of any answer. He knew Lalaji wouldn't be persuaded to change his mind. Even if he stayed away the dancing would still go on. Besides, Salim and some of his other friends would come and there would be lots of fun. He sat down and started making a list.

CHAPTER 12

The next morning Salim got up earlier than usual. He summoned Kaale Khan, and put the previous night's proposal before him. Two hundred rupees was not a small sum. Kaale Khan, slapping his chest said, 'Bhaiya, throwing one or two shoes is nothing; if you want, I will throw fifty shoes in the court. I wouldn't be sentenced for more than six months; whereas two hundred rupees will go a long way toward feeding and clothing my little ones.'

Salim was thinking that Amarkant would bring the money, but eight o'clock came, then nine o'clock, but still there was no sign of Amar. 'Why didn't he come; was he ill? Well, he must be arranging to get the money from some source. His father wouldn't give him a penny; so, he would have to get it from his mother-in-law.' Finally, it struck ten o'clock. Salim was about to set off for Amarkant's house when Professor Shantikumar arrived. Salim stepped up to the front door and welcomed him.

Professor Shantikumar, reclining on a settee, gestured for the fan to be turned on. 'Did you hear?' he said, 'Amar's wife has had a baby boy. He won't be able to go to court today. His mother-in-law is also at his house. I don't know how we will manage affairs at the court today. We won't be able to put up a demonstration without him. If Renuka Devi had been able to come, we would have managed somehow, but she is also busy.'

Salim said looking at Kaale Khan, 'It is unfortunate that his child was born on this particular day. What shall we do now, Kaale Khan?'

Kaale Khan was unperturbed. He said, 'It doesn't matter, bhaiya. I will do your work and collect the money later. I'll go now, buy a few rupees worth of goods for the household, and then go on to the court. As soon as you give me the signal...'

When he had left, Shatikumar asked, suspecting a plot, 'What was he saying, I couldn't understand him?'

Salim, making light of the matter, said, 'It's nothing. Just a test to see what kind of a man Kaale Khan is. Amarkant feels that Judge sahab should be taught a small lesson today after he has given his verdict.'

Doctor sahab sighed deeply, 'What you are saying is that you people have lowered yourselves to the level of hoodlums. It is also sad to know that it was Amarkant's idea. He is not here, but since this plot has been hatched with your participation, you are equally responsible. I consider it petty and loathsome. You have no right to assume that judge sahab will sacrifice justice in order to please his superior officers. A man much more knowledgeable, intelligent and experienced than you people, and with such a good reputation will not swerve from the path of justice. I am even more grieved because I had thought you both civilized and honourable.'

Salim's face fell. He had never been so rebuked in all his life. He had no argument, no words to offer, in his defence. To put the blame on Amarkant's shoulders, he said, 'I tried to stop Amarkant, but I had to go along when he wouldn't be persuaded.'

Doctor sahab retorted angrily, 'You lie. I can't accept that. This is your mischief.'

'There is nothing I can do if you don't believe me.'

'Such a thought wouldn't even enter Amarkant's head.'

Salim kept quiet. Doctor sahab said, 'Even assuming that Amarkant made this proposal, why did you accept it?' He didn't have a response to that question either.

After a moment, doctor sahab looked at his watch and said, 'I am so angry with this rascal, Amar, that I feel like whipping him fifty times. He has been involved in this case for so many days, and today when the judgment is to be passed, he is sitting at home celebrating his son's birth. I don't know when, if ever, we Indians will develop a sense of responsibility. What is there to celebrate in childbirth? A man's duty is to be steadfast in battle; celebrating happy occasions is for pleasure lovers. Would you believe it, he started laughing when I rebuked him? A man formulates his life's goal, and then follows it throughout his life and doesn't waver from it; he is not a stringless kite that turns in whichever direction the wind is blowing. Are you ready to go to court? I have nothing more to say. If the verdict is favourable, then the beggar woman will be carried in a procession to the bank of the Ganges. There everyone will take dips and then they will go to their respective homes. If she is sentenced, we will congratulate her and bid her adieu. In the evening, I will give a speech on Educational Reform. I have to think about that too. Will you speak also?'

Salim said hesitantly, 'What would I say on that subject?'

'You are conversant with my thinking. Why not say something along similar lines. This borrowed English education system is destroying our character. We have made education a business. The more capital you invest in business, the more profit you make. It is the same with education; the more schooling you receive, the higher the office you obtain. I want the highest of the high education to be free to everyone, so that the poorest of poor can attain a high level of competence and rise to the high office. The doors to a university should be open to everyone, and the government should bear the full cost. The country needs education far more than it does an army.'

Salim asked doubtfully, 'If there is no army then who will defend the country?'

Doctor sahab said seriously, 'The country will be defended by you, me, and the hundred million youth in the country who are second to none in this world in bravery and courage. Just as you and I when confronted by thieves at night come out of our houses wielding sticks instead of calling the police.'

In order to put an end to the argument, Salim said, 'I won't speak, but I will come for sure.'

Salim called for the car and both men went to the court. The crowd today was much bigger than ever and as unwieldy as a wedding party without a bridegroom. Groups of fifty to a hundred were standing or sitting, staring at nothing. If somebody started speaking, people would gather around him. As soon as they saw the doctor sahab, hundreds of people rushed toward him. Doctor sahab, after instructing the main workers, was going towards the court chamber when he saw Lala Samarkant distributing invitation cards. The festivities at his house were currently the talk of the court. Eagerly, people were enquiring which courtesans had been called. Were eunuchs coming? Was there special arrangement for non-vegetarians? A group of ten or twelve gentlemen was discussing the subject of dancing. Seeing doctor sahab, one man asked, 'Tell me, are you going to the festivities, or is it against your principles?'

Dr Shantikumar replied disdainfully, 'I have more important things to do.'

One gentleman asked, 'What do you have against dancing anyway?'

Doctor sahab responded reluctantly, 'Because you and I consider dancing for pleasure a vice. Dancing is not for indulgence, it is a means of worship and spiritual joy. But we have made it into a thing of embarrassment and shame. To treat women as objects of pleasure and lust is to insult our mothers and sisters. We have moved so far from the truth that we can't even see its real face. Dance is as pure …'

Suddenly, a young man approached Doctor sahab and greeted him with folded hands. He was a tall slim man with a pinched and sad face; his hair was dusty, and he was wearing dirty and worn-out clothes. In his arms was a one-year-old boy, hale and hearty and full of life, but somewhat frightened.

Doctor sahab asked, 'Who are you? What can I do for you?'

The young man looked around him carefully, as if he didn't want to say anything about himself in front of all those people, and said, 'I am a Thakur. I come from village Muhli, about twelve-thirteen miles from here.'

Doctor sahab looked at him sharply. He understood, and said, 'Oh yes, the village on the western side of the road. Come with me.'

Doctor sahab took him into a nearby garden and, seating himself on a bench, looked at him expectantly.

The young man said hesitantly, 'The woman in this case is the mother of this child. The two of us with our child were the only people living in the house, there was no one else. I used to look after the farming, while she would go to the market once in a while to purchase things. On that day she had gone, in the company of other villagers, to purchase a sari for herself. It happened when they were returning. All the men from the village ran away, abandoning her. After that day, she never came home. I didn't search for her either, and I have no idea where she wandered. Looking back, it was just as well that she didn't come home, otherwise either one or both of us would have lost our lives. I was particularly worried about this child. He kept wanting his mother, but I kept diverting him. I lived for him. At first it seemed that he would not survive, but gradually he forgot his mother. In the beginning, I was his father, now I am both father and mother; rather less of a father, more of a mother. I thought that she had probably drowned herself somewhere. The village people would sometimes say that a woman answering her description had been seen in the military cantonment, but I didn't believe them.

'The day I heard that a woman had killed two white men at the shop of Lala Samarkant and that she was being tried, I realized that it must be her. From that day onwards, I have come to every hearing. I stand in the very last row and I have not dared to say anything to anyone. Today I thought that she might be gone forever; so I brought the child so that she may at least see him and satisfy her longing. You and your friends have contributed a lot of money and effort to save her, but what is ordained by fate can't be averted. I have only this one request of you; that after judge sahab has given his verdict, I be allowed to see her for a moment. Babuji, I say to you honestly, if she is released, then I will drink the wash water off her feet and take her home and worship her. My relatives will frown, but when respectable people such as yourself are on my side, then I am not afraid of being socially ostracized.'

Shantikumar asked, 'Were you here the day she gave her testimony?'

The young man said with tears in his eyes, 'Yes, Babuji. I was standing at the door behind everyone and crying. I felt like throwing myself at her feet and saying—"Munni, I am your servant. Until now you were my woman, from now on you are my goddess." Munni has redeemed my ancestors from perdition, Babuji, what else can I say.'

Shantikumar asked again, 'Supposing she is freed today. Will you take her home?'

The youth answered ecstatically, 'Without question, Babuji. I will carry her home on a chariot, and as long as I live, will justify my life by serving her.'

After a moment he asked eagerly, 'Is there any hope of her acquittal?'

'Others don't think so, but I am hopeful.'

The youth fell crying at Doctor sahab's feet. They were the first encouraging words he had heard, and it seemed that his inner self was singing out of sheer joy. Can a man control his tears in the face of extreme happiness?

Both looked towards the court at the sound of a car horn. Judge sahab had arrived. That vast sea of people surged from all sides towards the court chamber. Then the beggar woman was brought in. Seeing her, the public shouted a victory salute. Some people threw flowers. Lawyers, barristers, policemen, and officials all moved to sit at their appointed places.

The judge glanced fleetingly towards the public. All around there was utter silence. Countless eyes were raised toward him, as if saying—you are the judge—the decision maker—on you depends our fate.

Judge sahab took out a typed decision from an attaché case and, after clearing his throat, started reading it. The people moved in closer. Most people didn't understand a word of the decision, but everyone was listening carefully. They were hopeful that rupees might be scattered for the poor, along with rice and *batasha*s, in celebration of the judgment.

For about fifteen minutes, judge sahab read the decision and the public listened, anxiously waiting.

In the end, the judge sahab said, 'It is evident that Munni has committed homicide...'

Many hearts sank. Some looked at each other with defeat in their eyes. The judge completed the sentence, 'But it is also evident that she committed it while in a state of mental imbalance brought on by the atrocity committed against her. Therefore, she is acquitted.'

The last word of the sentence was drowned in a tidal wave of joy. After months of anxious waiting, joyful relief, like a freed calf, vaulted in leaps and bounds. People rapturously embraced each other. Intimate friends slapped each other on the back. Some threw their hats in the air. Comedians thought of tossing up their shoes. Suddenly, Munni, accompanied by Doctor Shantikumar, wearing a solemn smile and looking like a queen with her chief minister, came out. Her appearance calmed the crowd's boisterousness. Who could be impertinent before a queen?

The programme had already been drawn out. After a showering of flowers, a victory garland was to be placed around Munni's neck. This honour had been reserved for the wife of judge sahab, who had become an object of reverence for the public. Then the band started. Two hundred youths of the Seva Sabha wearing saffron-colored robes were ready to march with the procession. Workers of the National Assembly, wearing khaki uniforms and holding flags, were also assembled. Almost a thousand women were there as well. It had been decided that the procession would march to a bank of the Ganges, where a large meeting would be held and Munni would be presented with a purse, after which the meeting would be dispersed.

Munni looked calmly at this celebration for a while, then turning to Shantikumar said, 'Babuji, I am not worthy of all this honour which you people are bestowing on me. My only request to you now is that you let me go to Haridwar, or some other place of pilgrimage. There I will spend my days begging for alms and serving the pilgrims. All this procession and ceremony doesn't become an unfortunate woman like myself. Please tell all these brothers and sisters to go home. I was lying in dust, and you people have raised me to heaven. I am not capable of rising any higher now. I beg of you, please take me to a railway station from here.'

Shantikumar was astonished at this self-effacement, 'Sister, how can you say such a thing! So many men and women are assembled here. At

least consider their love and devotion. They will all be so disappointed if
you don't go in the procession. I don't think that these people will ever
leave unless you come.'

'You people are making a mockery of me.'

'Don't say that, sister. By offering you homage we are honouring
ourselves. And why do you have to go to Haridwar? Your husband is here
to take you home with him.'

Munni looked at the doctor in astonishment, 'My husband! He is here
to take me with him? How do you know?'

'I met him a short while ago.'

'What did he say?'

'Only that he will take you with him and will regard you as the
goddess of the house.'

'Was there a child also with him?'

'Yes, your little boy was in his arms.'

'The child must have become very thin?'

'No, he seemed quite healthy to me.'

'Did he look happy as well?'

'Yes, he was laughing lustily.'

'He was not crying for his mother?'

'He didn't cry in my presence.'

'He is probably walking by now?'

'He was in his father's arms. But it is possible that he is walking.'

'Achcha, how was his father? He must have lost a lot of weight?'

'I had never seen him before! But yes, he looked sad. He must be here
somewhere. If you allow me, I will search for him. He might even be on
his way here.'

After a moment, Munni said tearfully, 'Babuji, I beg of you, don't let
those two come near me. Please tell these people to go home, and take
me to the railway station. I will not totally destroy my husband and son
by my *moh* for them. I must leave here today. Seeing me esteemed in this
manner my honoured husband is ready to take me in; but I know his
feelings. He won't be happy living with me. Now I am only fit for a
place where no one knows me! There I will sustain myself by labour or
by begging.'

She was quiet for a moment, wondering what the response of doctor
sahab would be. When Doctor sahab didn't reply, she spoke to the people
in a loud, but faltering, voice, 'Sisters and brothers! How can I praise you

enough for the honour you have given me. You have redeemed an unfortunate woman. Now please let me go. Do not insist on taking out a procession for me. I am only fit to hide my blackened face in a corner. I am not so worthy that my misfortune should be treated as anything noble.'

There was a loud outcry from the people; leaders tried to reason with her and women attempted to persuade her, but Munni did not agree to a procession and continued to request that she be taken to the railway station. In the end, Doctor sahab was forced to bid the crowd farewell and seat Munni in the car.

Munni said, 'Let's go now, and please take me to some distant railway station where none of these people is likely to be present.'

Shantikumar looked around expectantly, and said, 'Sister, don't be in such a rush. Your husband is here. He will certainly come when these people have gone away.'

Munni said agitatedly, 'Babuji, I don't want to see him, I never want to see him. If he comes near me I will die of shame. I will die for sure. Take me away quickly. If I were to see my child such a storm of affection would rage in my heart that all my discretion and reason would be blown away like a blade of grass. In that moh I will forget that my taint will ruin his life completely. I feel most uneasy. You must take me away from this place at once. I don't want to see my child because if I see him it would lead to his destruction.'

Shantikumar started the car, but they had gone no more than ten or twenty yards, when Munni's husband, with the child in his arms, came running and shouting, 'Stop the car! Stop the car!' Seeing him, Munni put her head out of the car window and, signalling 'no' with her hand, shouted, 'No, no! Go back. You must not follow me! For God's sake, don't follow me.' Then she spread out her arms as if she were embracing the child and fell down in the car in a faint.

The car sped away. The young Thakur with the child was left standing and crying, while thousands of men and women stood gaping at the car.

CHAPTER 13

News of Munni's acquittal spread through the city like wildfire. Very few people had expected this decision. Someone said that judge sahab's wife had forced him to pass that verdict by threatening to leave him and go to her father's house otherwise. If a woman is adamant about getting something, how can a man say no? Another opinion was that the government had ordered judge sahab to acquit her because there was fear of a riot in the city should the beggar woman be sentenced. Amarkant was busy with preparations for the feast at his home; but when he received the news he forgot his arrangements for a while and began to take the entire credit for the decision. Going inside the house, he said to Renuka Devi, 'Did you see, Ammaji, wasn't I saying that I wouldn't rest until she was acquitted; and that's what happened. I alone know what mental gymnastics I had to go through with lawyers and witnesses.' Outside the house, he boasted in the same way to friends and shopkeepers across the street.

One friend remarked, 'She is a very determined woman. Her poor husband kept throwing himself at her feet, but she wouldn't go with him.'

Amar offered a philosophical analysis, 'If you don't look after a job yourself, it is never done properly. I was occupied here and no one there could make that woman understand. Had I been there, she wouldn't have been able to go away just like that. Had I known that this would happen I would have left everything here and gone to plead with her. I thought that doctor sahab and dozens of other men were there to manage things in my absence, but no one there seems to have been concerned! They are all heroes now, it doesn't matter whether the job gets done properly or falls apart.'

Lala Samarkant freely spent money on the festivities. The same Amarkant who had always been severely critical of such frivolous pursuits now stayed mum; in fact, he defended them, 'If those who have money don't spend it on such festive occasions, when will they do so? Such is the beauty of wealth; but, of course, it is foolish to burn down the house in order to enjoy the show.'

Amarkant had become especially attached to his home. He had gone back to University, but no longer felt like attending meetings and societies. Now he was not as averse to the business of lending and borrowing as he had been and he would sit in the shop morning and evening and work industriously. He was also getting to be a little careful with money. He was still kindly disposed towards hard-pressed souls but not to the extent of compromising the shop's income. His infant child, like the ring in a camel's nose, had taken complete control of his life. It was as if a tiny object by coming in front of a lamp had dimmed its light.

Three months had gone by. It was evening. The child was sleeping in the crib. Sukhada was sitting on a *morha* (reed chair) holding a fan in her hand. After her delivery, she had become slender and was now blooming with the radiance and strength of motherhood. Her beauty didn't have the nimbleness of a maiden, nor did it have the languid restlessness of a pregnant woman; instead, it had the serene contentment and bliss of a mother.

Amarkant came home directly from the college, looked worriedly at the child for a moment, and then said, 'His fever is gone?'

Sukhada gently felt the baby's forehead. 'No, he doesn't seem to have one. He fell asleep in my arms just now, so I laid him down.'

Amar, unbuttoning his kurta, said, 'I couldn't concentrate at the shop at all today. I only pray to God that this child remains well. I don't want anything else in the world. Look how he is smiling.'

Sukhada said gently chiding, 'Your constant doting has cast an evil eye.'

'I wish I could kiss him.'

'No, no. Sleeping children should not be kissed.'

Suddenly, someone approached the entrance and called. Amar came out and saw the old woman, Pathanin, standing there holding a cane. He said, 'Come, Pathanin, you must have heard that a baby was born in this house.'

Pathanin came inside and said, 'May Allah keep him healthy and add my age to his life. Beta, why was the entire city invited but we weren't asked! Are we the only strangers? Allah knows, the day we heard the good news we asked for His blessings for the little one's safety and well-being.'

Amar said shamefacedly, 'Yes, it was my fault, Pathanin, please forgive me. Come, see the baby. I don't know why he was feverish today.'

The old woman stepped softly across the courtyard and went to the verandah, blessed the bahu, and looking at the child said, 'It is nothing beta. It is the mischief of an evil eye. I will give you an amulet, Allah willing, he will be laughing and playing in no time at all.'

Sukhada had become polite after becoming a mother. She touched the old woman's feet with the border of her sari, and said, 'He has not been well for four days, Mataji. There is no old and wise woman in this house. What do I know about what needs to be done? I have a mother, but she cannot come here every day, nor can I go to her every day.'

The old woman blessed her again and said, 'Do call me, beta, whenever something needs to be done. I have no other reason to live. Just come with me Bhaiya, I will give you the amulet.'

The old woman took out a silk kurta and cap from the pocket of her garment and, putting them near the baby's head, said, 'This is a present for my little treasure, beta; do accept it. I am not able to do anything else. Sakina stitched these a few days ago. I can't walk well anymore, beta, it took a lot of doing for me to come here today.'

Sukhada had been given many fine and beautiful clothes for the child by relatives, but she had not received them with such joy as she did this simple gift. This gift was not given to reflect the donor's wealth nor was it given to fulfil arid custom. In it was the soul of a well-wisher showering love and blessing.

When the old woman was leaving, Sukhada gave her a packet of sweets, offered her paan, and walked with her to the door to bid adieu. Amarkant went outside, hired an ikka, and sitting in it with the old woman, went to get the amulet. He did not believe in charms and amulets but he did believe in the blessings of old people.

On the way the old woman said, 'I had spoken to you about something, beta; have you forgotten?'

Amar had indeed forgotten. Ashamed, he said, 'Yes, Pathanin, I have forgotten. Please forgive me.'

'It was regarding Sakina.'

Amar, striking his forehead in chagrin, said, 'Yes, it had indeed slipped my mind.'

'Then do think of it now, beta. Who else is there for me to ask. Meanwhile, Sakina has made several handkerchiefs, and has crocheted several panels for caps. But when the things are not sold, one gets discouraged.'

'Give them to me. I will have them sold.'

'Won't it be a bother for you?'

'No bother at all. What trouble could there be in that?'

The old woman did not invite Amarkant inside. Lately her material condition had deteriorated even further. Even bread had become scarce. Every bit of the house was evidence of her poverty. How could she have brought Amar into her house? Old people, despite being free of most proprieties, want to keep some things private. Leaving him in the ikka, she went inside, and in a little while came out with the amulet and an attaché case of handkerchiefs.

'Tie the amulet around his neck. Then tell me his condition tomorrow.'

'Tomorrow is a holiday. I'll talk to a few friends. If possible I will come in the evening; otherwise I will come some other day.'

Returning home, Amar tied the amulet around the baby's neck and then went to tend the shop. Lalaji asked, 'Where have you been? You should not be missing during business time.'

Amar said apologetically, 'Pathanin came today and said that she would give me an amulet for the baby. I went to get it.'

'I just saw him. He seems well now. The little rascal caught hold of my moustache and pulled it, so I gave him a sound cuff. Oh, I remember something now. You mind the shop, I will go to Shastriji to get the baby's horoscope. He promised to give it to me today.'

When Lalaji had gone, Amar went back inside the house and, taking the child in his arms, said, 'Why, you! You have been pulling my father's moustache ! Be careful, if you touch his moustache again, I will knock out your teeth.'

The baby caught hold of his nose and tried to swallow it as if the monkey king, Hanuman, was swallowing the Sun god.

Sukhada said laughingly, 'First save your nose before thinking of your father's moustache.'

A loud shout from Salim nearly shook the house.

Amarkant went outside and said, 'Hey, you devil! You shouted so loudly you made me nervous. Where have you been? Come on, let's go into the sitting room.'

The two men went into the adjoining room. Salim had composed a ghazal during the night, and had come to recite it. After he composed a ghazal, he could not rest in peace until he had recited it to Amar.

Amar said, 'But, you may be sure, I won't praise it.'

'I'm certain that you will even if you don't want to ...'

If these are the ways of the world, let them be;
Congratulations on your laughter, if someone cries, let him cry.

Amar swayed with pleasure, 'It is a priceless couplet, bhai! No kidding, honestly, how compelling! Great!'
Salim recited the second couplet:

I swear—no on will reproach you for your faithlessness,
I weep at my own doing, to my heart's content let me cry.

Amar said, 'The couplet is so full of pain that I get goose bumps. It is as if someone is reciting what he has experienced first hand.'
Salim recited the entire ghazal, and Amar listened to it swaying in ecstasy!
Then the two began to talk. Amar showed him Pathanin's handkerchiefs. 'An old woman left them here. She is a poor woman. Would you like to buy a few?'
Salim looked at the handkerchiefs, 'It is good workmanship, my friend. All right, I will take a dozen. Who made them?'
'The old woman has a granddaughter.'
'Oh, is she the girl who came to the court once during the mad woman's trial? You certainly chose a good lady-love, my friend.'
Amarkant tried to justify himself. 'Honestly, I have never even looked at her.'
'You needn't protest! You are welcome to her. I have no wish to take your paramour. How much are a dozen handkerchiefs?'
'Pay whatever you think is right.'
'The price will depend on who has crafted them. If that beauty has made them then it is five rupees per handkerchief. If the old woman or somebody else has made them then it is four annas per handkerchief.'
'You are joking. You don't want to buy them.'
'Tell me first who made them.'
'They were made by Sakina.'
'So, her name is Sakina! Then I will pay five rupees per handkerchief. The only condition is that you show me where she lives.'
'With great pleasure; but if you make any mischief then I will become your mortal enemy. If you come with empathy, come. I want her to get married to some good man. Do you know of anyone? Understand that he would be a very lucky man. I haven't met a girl who has her modesty

and civility. And, believe me, she has everything a woman needs to entice a man.'

Salim smiled and said, 'It seems you have fallen for her charms. Yet her beauty is not equal even to the soles of your wife's feet.'

Amar, replied critically, 'Beauty is not the most lovable attribute in a woman. I tell you honestly that if I were not married and there were no religious obstacles, I would marry her and consider myself fortunate.'

'What causes you to be so smitten?'

'That is something I don't understand myself. Perhaps it is her simplicity. Why don't you marry her? I can say this—that with her you would be in bliss.'

Salim was not convinced. 'The woman I dream about is cast in an entirely different mould. Perhaps she does not exist outside of my imagination. If I can think of some man who may marry Sakina, I will let you know. For now I will buy this handkerchief, I can't give less than five rupees! Can Sakina sew garments as well? I am sure there would be plenty of work for her at our house. I will give you some friendly advice as well. I have no suspicions about you, but you should not go there very frequently otherwise you will get a bad name. Your reputation will suffer less, but that poor girl's life will be ruined. There is no lack of do-gooders who will hound you, giving the whole thing a religious twist. No one will help them, but there will be many to point their finger at you.'

Amarkant was not foolhardy, but replied exasperatedly, 'Such contemptible people are not worthy of notice. If your heart is pure, then nothing will affect you.'

Salim did not take affront at Amar's remark and said, 'My friend, you are more innocent than is necessary. I am afraid some calamity may befall you.'

The next day Amarkant closed shop, pocketed the five rupees, and, arriving at Pathanin's house, called out. He thought how happy Sakina would be to receive the money!

A voice answered from within, 'Who is it?'

Amarkant gave his name.

The doors were opened immediately and Amarkant stepped inside, but he saw darkness all around. He asked, 'You didn't light an oil lamp today, Amma?'

Sakina said, 'Amma has gone somewhere to get a stitching job.'

'Why is it dark? Isn't there any oil in the lamp?'

Sakina said softly, 'There is oil.'

'Then why don't you light the lamp? Are there no matches?'

'There are matches as well.'

'Then light the lamp. One of the handkerchiefs that I took yesterday sold for five rupees. Come on, light the lamp right away.'

Sakina didn't answer. Instead, he heard her sobbing. Surprised, Amar asked, 'What is the matter Sakina? Why are you crying?'

Sakina said, sobbing, 'It's nothing. Please go, I will give the money to Amma.'

Bewildered, Amar said, 'I won't go unless you tell me what's wrong. If there is no oil, I will go get some. If there are no matches, I will get them. Tomorrow I will bring a regular lamp. You will ruin your eyes if you continue to work in the light of a small leather lamp. What do you need to hide from me, one who is almost family? If I considered you a stranger, why would I come here so often.'

Sakina, stepping up to the front shed, said, 'My clothes are wet. I extinguished the lamp when I heard your voice.'

'Then why are you wearing wet clothes?'

'My clothes were dirty. I washed them. Please don't ask me any more questions. I wouldn't have opened the door for anyone else.'

Amarkant's heart was wrenched. Oh! Such abject poverty! She doesn't even have a second set of clothes to wear. Now he realized the extent of Pathanin's sacrifice yesterday when she gave the gift of a silken kurta and cap for his baby. It must have cost at least two rupees. Two rupees would have bought two pajamas. How generous are these poor souls. They are willing to bear such hardship for what they consider their duty.

In a trembling voice he said to Sakina, 'Go and light the lamp, Sakina. I will soon be back.'

He flew like the wind from Govardhansarai to the main market, but the market had closed. What should he do now? Sakina must still be sitting in wet clothes. Why had all the shops closed so early today? He left there and, running swiftly, arrived at his house. Sukhada had many saris. Some were quite ordinary. Surely she could spare some of those? But she would ask—what do you need them for? What answer would he give? If he were frank, she might become suspicious. No, this was not the time to explain things. Sakina, in those wet clothes, must be awaiting his return. Sukhada was downstairs. He went upstairs softly, opened her cupboard, took out four saris and stepped out quietly.

Sukhada asked, 'Where are you going now? Why don't you have dinner?'

Amar replied from the outer vestibule, 'I am coming back soon.'

After he had gone some distance, he realized that there would be real trouble if tomorrow Sukhada opened her cupboard and didn't find the saris. The servants would be blamed. Would he dare at that time to admit that he had given those saris to a poor woman? No, he wouldn't be able to say that. Then should he take the saris back? But Sakina would be sitting there in wet clothes! Then he thought how happy Sakina would be to get the saris. That thought intoxicated him. Walking as rapidly as he could he reached Sakina's house.

Sakina opened the door as soon as she heard his voice. A lamp was burning. In the interim, Sakina had lit a fire and dried her clothes; she was standing in a kurta and pajama, her head covered with a veil.

Amar put down the saris on a cot and said, 'I couldn't find any in the market, so I had to go home. There is no need for concealment from friends.'

Sakina looked at the saris and said hesitatingly, 'Babuji, you shouldn't have brought the saris. When Amma sees them, she will be very annoyed and it may become difficult for you to come here. Amma has been praising your civility and sympathy, which I have received in even greater measure. Also, you shouldn't come here very often; people will needlessly start suspecting something. I don't want anyone to cast aspersions on you because of me.'

She had a sweet voice, and had expressed herself with great politeness and frankness, but there was none of the joy Amar had imagined she would feel. If the old woman viewed this simple affection with suspicion, then certainly his visits would come to an end. He searched his heart to ascertain whether there was any cause for this suspicion. His heart was clean, there were no impure thoughts of any kind about Sakina. Even so, the possibility of not being able to meet Sakina was unbearable to him. His male ego, which had been dictated to at home, could appear in its natural state with her. It was as if Sukhada's brilliance, resoluteness, and independence had been constantly overwhelming him. His soul, that hankered after some sort of self-importance, was left unfulfilled. He was unable to assert himself and felt vanquished in front of Sukhada. Sakina, by contrast, made him feel nine feet tall. Sukhada was his business office; Sakina was his home. There he was slave, here he was master.

He picked up the saris and, with a heavy heart, said, 'If that is so, then I will take back these saris, Sakina, but I can't tell you how much that will hurt me. As to my visits here, if you don't want me to come, I won't come even by mistake, but I really don't care what the neighbours say.'

Sakina said tenderly, 'Babuji, I entreat you, please don't say these things. Since you started coming here, the world has changed for me. I find such strength and enthusiasm in my heart that I feel intoxicated, but one has to be careful of false accusations.'

Amar said wildly, 'I am not afraid of false accusations, Sakina, not one bit.'

Immediately afterwards, however, he was conscious that he had gone too far, and said, 'But what you say is correct. The world may not do anything else, but it can certainly ruin reputations.'

The two sat quietly for a minute, then Amar said, 'Do make more handkerchiefs, Sakina. I am making arrangements for you to stitch clothes as well. I will go now, and take these saris with me.'

Sakina looked at Amar's face. It seemed to her that he was close to tears. She felt like picking up the saris and embracing them, but her self-discipline wouldn't allow her to even lift her hand. Amar took the saris and with unsteady steps staggered out of the doorway.

Chapter 14

Amarkant was again disenchanted at home and Sakina was constantly on his mind. Her words—'The world has changed for me. I find such strength and enthusiasm in my heart . . .' were forever ringing in his ears. In those words, his masculinity found such a delightful thrill that he forgot himself. His liking for the shop began to diminish again. After a taste of Sakina's politeness and unassuming charm, Sukhada's brilliance and passion left him drained. Sakina offered him simple fare amid verdant leaves, whereas Sukhada offered him delicacies arranged in platters of gold and silver. There it was a case of simple affection, here it was a display of pride. He was being drawn towards the gift of unadorned affection, while being repelled by opulent grandeur. He had been deprived of a mother's love since childhood and had spent fifteen years of his life under an arid rule, at times being berated by his stepmother, sometimes facing his father's bad temper, with only Naina's tenderness soothing his injured heart. When Sukhada came, she had the same authority and hauteur. He did not receive affection even there. Like a thirsty bird that had returned disappointed from the dried up shores of a lake, he yearned for love, seeking rest and fulfilment. He sought refuge under the cool shade of Sakina's affection. And here was not only cool shade, but water as well. It was not surprising if the bird stayed there!

Amar had been deeply affected by Sakina's poverty. His rebellious spirit that had been calmed a while rose up again twice as strong. He started pursuing his dharma—what he thought was right—with even greater zeal. He had been conscious of the bonds of wealth since his childhood. The bonds of religion were, in comparison, much more strict, far more unbearable, and far more difficult to comprehend. The pursuit of religion should result in creation of peace and unity in the world. Instead, it has led to the creation of differences and animosity. What had religion to do with eating habits and customs and usage? I may commit theft or murder or deceive someone, but my religion won't disown me; but if I drink water from the hands of an untouchable, I lose my religion. What kind of religion is this? We cannot relate at the level of the soul to anyone outside our religion. Religion has tied down souls, has restrictions even on love. This is not religion, this is a disgrace to religion.

Amarkant was lost in this mental turmoil. Once every month, sometimes two or three times a month, the old woman would bring a package of handkerchiefs and Amar would buy them at whatever price she asked. The money that Renuka gave him as pocket money was all spent on handkerchiefs. Salim was also a participant in these transactions and, among his friends, there was no one who had not purchased a dozen or so hankies. Some stitching jobs were also made available at Salim's house. The old woman had become acquainted with Sukhada and Renuka as well. So there was work—embroidering of saris and mantles of fine muslin. But since his last visit, Amar had refrained from going to the old woman's house. He started to go several times with firm intent, but turned back when he was halfway there.

Once during this period a debate on the subject of 'dharma' was held in the college. Amar's speech on that occasion was being discussed throughout the city. Now he thought that the revival of the country would occur only through revolution—a revolution that would be all pervasive, that would put an end to life's false ideals, its greed, and dishonest principles and conventions. This revolution would usher in a new era and create a new world order, which would demolish the countless gods with clay feet, thus delivering mankind from the hold of a government that depended on money and religion for its continuance. Every atom of his being was crying, 'Revolution! Revolution'. But the generous Hindu society does not say anything to anyone until there is an open attack on its social order. Revolution or anarchism, as long as it's all at the level of preaching, it does not care. But the moment someone steps beyond the bounds of lecturing into the field of action, society goes for his throat. Amar's revolution so far had been limited to speeches and writing. He wanted to act only after he was finished with the degree examinations. The examinations were still a month away when an incident occurred that compelled him to take immediate action. The incident was Sakina's upcoming marriage.

One evening Amarkant was in the shop when the old woman came with a muslin sari of Sukhada's and said to Amar, 'Beta, Sakina's marriage has been arranged through the grace of Allah. The wedding is on the eighth day of the month. I have arranged for everything, but you could help with money.'

Amar's face paled, as if his vessels had been drained of blood. Stammering, he said, 'Sakina's marriage! What's the big rush?'

'What choice do I have, beta? We can barely subsist, and she is a young girl! It is possible for her to get a bad name.'

'Is Sakina willing?'

The old woman said in a simple manner, 'Beta, do girls say anything directly? She keeps on saying no.'

Amar said loudly, 'Even so, you are marrying her off?' Then regaining his composure, he said, 'You will have to speak to Dada for money.'

'I will speak to him myself, beta, but you might appeal on my behalf.'

'Who am I to recommend you? Dada knows you far better than I do.'

Leaving the old woman standing there, a bewildered Amar rushed to Salim. Seeing his distraught look, Salim inquired, 'Is everything alright? Why are you so upset?'

Amar took hold of himself, 'I am not upset. But you might be.'

'Alright then, I will recite to you a freshly composed ghazal. The couplets will thrill you, I guarantee.'

It was as if a noose had tightened around Amarkant's neck, but how could he say—I don't want to hear it. Salim read the first couplet:

(You) divert my heart through to dawn with things concerning him,
my heart agonizes like his on wet monsoon nights.

Amar said in a superficial tone, 'It is a good couplet.'

Salim was not fazed. He recited the second couplet:

Something was said by the lifting of my eyes, something was said by the
    lowering of his,
The quarrel that wouldn't have been settled in years, was settled in a trice.

Amar was swayed in spite of himself, 'How wonderfully you recite, bhai! Great! Splendid!! Let me kiss your pen.'

Salim went on:

It was not the silence of remembering when I listened with hope,
Even though I knew that in those sweet words there was only deception.

Amar was thunderstruck, 'It expresses extraordinary agony, my friend! It is heart-wrenching.'

After a moment, Salim teased, 'Sakina hasn't sent any handkerchiefs in the last month. Why is that?'

Amar said, getting serious, 'My friend, you must be joking! She is getting married in a week.'

'You'll go in the marriage procession on the bride's side, I on the groom's.'

Amar said resolutely, 'This marriage will take place over my dead body. I tell you, Salim, I would give up my life for Sakina. I will pound my head at her door and die.'

Salim asked nervously, '*Bhai-jaan*, what kind of talk is this? Are you in love with Sakina? Had I guessed correctly?'

Amar, with tears in his eyes, said, 'I can't tell you, Salim, why I am in this state; but ever since I have heard this news, it seems as if my heart is being torn asunder.'

'What do you want after all? You can't possibly marry her.'

'Why not?'

'Don't be a child! Just use your intelligence.'

'Of course you mean that she is a Muslim and I a Hindu. I don't hold religion as important as love, not at all.'

Salim said with a feeling of disbelief, 'I have heard your thoughts during debates, and have read them in newspapers. Those thoughts are very lofty and pure and revolutionary. Many have achieved fame by expressing such ideas. But a learned discussion is one thing, to put it into practice another. People will gladly listen to a learned discussion on revolution. But if you lift a sword in its cause, the entire society will turn against you. A learned debate does not injure anyone. Revolution results in throats being cut. Have you even asked Sakina whether she is ready to marry you?'

Amar hesitated, for he had not considered this possibility. He had perhaps thought in his heart that he had only to say it for her to agree. After the words he had heard, he didn't think it necessary even to ask.

'I believe that she would be agreeable.'

'What is the basis of your belief?'

'She has said certain things that can't have any other meaning.'

'Did you say to her, "I wish to marry you"?'

'I don't think it is necessary to ask her.'

'Then a statement that was made to you in your role as a sympathetic listener, you have taken to mean as a promise for marriage. Really! What intelligence! Have you eaten opium, or has your brain become soft from reading too much? You are ready to sacrifice everything—a wife more beautiful than a fairy, a lovely child, and all the gifts that the world has to offer, for a comely and possibly well-mannered weaver's daughter! Do you think that this is a discourse or an article? *Janab*, the whole city will be in turmoil, it will be like an earthquake. Not only in the city but in the whole province; no, even all of India. What is the matter with you? It wouldn't be surprising if you lost your life.'

Amarkant had thought these objections through. They didn't move him one bit. If society punished him for this, he couldn't care less. He thought it much better to die for his belief than, forsaking it, live like a coward. Society had no right to ruin his life. He said, 'I know all that, Salim, but I do not wish my soul to be a slave to society. I am prepared to face the consequences. This matter is between Sakina and I, society has no right to come between us.'

Salim, shaking his head in doubt, said, 'Sakina will never agree if she loves you. But, yes, if she wants to see your love being ridiculed, then she might agree. But I ask you what is so special about her that you are determined to make such a big sacrifice yourself and ruin so many other lives?'

Amar didn't like what he was hearing. Grimacing, he said, 'I am not making any sacrifice, nor am I ruining anyone's life. I am only following the path that my soul tells me to take. I can't allow relationships or wealth to act as a chain around my neck. I consider fulfilling life's desires as living. For me to be alive, I need a heart that has the ability to feel desire and pain, to sacrifice and to negotiate; one that can cry with me, burn with me. I feel my soul getting rustier day by day. In these last few years, I alone know how wretched I feel deep down. I keep getting more and more tied up in chains. Only Sakina can liberate me. With her alone can my soul soar to heights, with her alone can I discover myself. You say I should first ask her. You think that she will never agree. I am confident that no one can reject something as priceless as the gift of love.'

Salim asked, 'What if she says that you must become a Muslim?'

'She can't say that.'

'Assuming she does?'

'Then I will call a *Maulvi* and confess to being a Mohammedan. I do not see anything in Islam that my soul could not accept. Ethical principles are the same in all religions. I have no objection to accepting the most eminent Mohammed as the emissary of Allah. Hindu religion rests on the foundation of service to others, self-sacrifice, kindness, and purification of the soul; the Islam rests on the same foundation. Islam doesn't forbid me from revering Buddha, Krishna, or Rama. I am not a Hindu by choice, but only by birth. Even then, I wouldn't want to become a Mohammedan, unless Sakina so wishes. My personal belief is that religion is a chain around one's soul. My religion is what my intellect accepts. The rest is rubbish.'

Salim was left speechless. He had never imagined such a mental state. He equated love with mere lust. He thought it madness to build such a grand facade for the trifling sentiment of love to make such sacrifices for it, to get a bad name, and to cause such turmoil.

He shook his head and said, 'Sakina will never agree to it.'

Amar said calmly, 'Why do you think so?'

'Because if she has the least bit of intelligence, she will not destroy a family.'

'That means she loves my family more than she does me. Also, why should my family be destroyed. Dada and Sukhada both love money more than they love me. I can still love the child as before. All that would happen is that I may not be able to go to the house and not touch its pots and pans.'

Salim asked, 'Have you mentioned this to Doctor Shantikumar?'

Amar said, as if despairing of his friend's intelligence, 'No, I have not considered it necessary to mention it to him. I have not come to you seeking advice either, only to lighten my heart's burden. My intention is firm. If Sakina refuses me, I will end my life. If she accepts me then the two of us will slip quietly away somewhere; no one will be informed. After three or four months, I will inform them at home. There will be no turmoil, no storm raised; that is my plan. I am going to her now. If she accepts me, I will return; if she rejects me, then you will not see me again.'

So saying, he stood up and walked rapidly toward Govardhansarai. Despite wanting to stop him, Salim could not do so. Perhaps he realized that at this time Amar was being driven by the devil and would listen to no one.

It was a winter night in the month of Magh and bitterly cold. A smoky haze covered the sky. Amarkant pushed on in manic intoxication. He was becoming angry with Sakina. She could have written to him to inform him of what was happening! Then a strange fear gripped his heart. Could it be that Sakina would get annoyed? Her words had not meant that she was ready to go with him anywhere? It was possible that the old woman had arranged her marriage with her consent. Possibly, her intended husband had had free access to her house. He might be sitting there right now. Should that be the case, Amar would leave quietly. Sakina would be even more embarrassed if the old woman had returned; he wanted an opportunity to talk to Sakina in private.

His heart was palpitating as he arrived at Sakina's door. He listened carefully for a moment. There was no sound, and the courtyard was lit. Perhaps Sakina was alone. His dearest wish had been granted. Gently he rattled the chain. After inquiring who it was, Sakina immediately opened the door and said, 'Amma has gone to your place already!'

Amar replied standing, 'Yes, I met her, and the news that she gave me has driven me insane. Sakina, I had hidden my heart's secret from you, and had thought to keep it hidden for some more time, but this news has forced me to reveal it to you now. My life will depend on what you decide after hearing it. I kneel at your feet; you may kick me away or raise me up and embrace me. I cannot tell you why this fire was ignited in my heart, but the first time I saw you that day, an ember was lit in my heart, which has now become a conflagration. And if it is not quenched soon, it will burn me to ashes. I have tried to contain myself, Sakina, I have been choking inside, but you had told me not to come and I didn't have the courage to come. I sacrifice everything that was mine at your feet. My house is worse than a prison for me. My beautiful wife seems like a marble statue that has no heart, no sympathy. I will have everything if I have you.'

Sakina became very nervous. Where she had asked for a pinch of flour, the patron saint had presented her with a full banquet platter. Where would there be room in her small basket for such a treasure? She couldn't think how to accept it. Even if her shawl and skirt were both overflowing, she wouldn't be able to contain it. Her eyes became wet and her heart began to leap. Bowing her head shyly, she said, 'Babuji, God knows how much I love and respect you in my heart. Even a glance from you would be enough for me to sacrifice everything on. You have, as if, given this beggar woman the riches of all the three worlds,[2] but what will the beggar woman do with the riches? She wanted just a small crumb. It is more than sufficient for me to think that you have considered me worthy of this honour. But I don't consider myself so worthy. Just think what I am—a poor Muslim woman who lives by hard labour. I have neither

[2] The three worlds in Hindu philosophy are *swarg* (heaven), *narak* (hell), and *prithvilok* (earth).

culture, nor etiquette, nor learning. I cannot even rise above the foot-steps of Sukhada Devi. A female frog can't fly up to sit on a tall tree. If you suffer disgrace because of me, I will kill myself. I will not taint your life.'

People become somewhat poetic on such occasions. The intensity of love is the subject of poems, it can't be expressed in ordinary language. Catching a breath, Sakina continued, 'You lifted an orphaned, poor girl from the ashes and raised her to heaven—gave her a place in your heart—so I will keep this lamp of love lit with blood from my heart as long as I live.'

Amar said, breathing deeply, 'This thought does not comfort me, Sakina. This lamp will be blown out by a gust of wind, and in its place another lamp will be lit. Will you remember me then? I can't accept that. You should stop thinking that I am some great man and that you are of no account. I have laid all that I have at your feet and now I am nothing but your worshipper. Undoubtedly, Sukhada is more beautiful than you, but you have something that has distanced me from her and fall in love with you. I can't bear the thought that you may belong to someone else. The day that happens you will hear that Amar is dead. If you need any proof of my devotion, I offer you these drops of blood.'

So saying he took out a dagger from his pocket. Sakina rushed forward and quickly seizing the dagger from his hand, said in a sweetly chiding tone, 'Proof is needed by those who do not accept your word or who want something in return. I want only to worship you. Because a god is silent, it does not mean any less devotion on the part of the devotee. Love is its own reward. I don't know what life holds for me, but whatever happens, whomsoever takes possession of me, my heart will always be yours. I want to keep this love free of desire. I am content with the belief that I am yours. My darling, I say this to you honestly—this faith has so strengthened my heart that it can happily bear the greatest hardship. I stopped you from coming here because I was afraid not only that you would get a bad name but that I would as well. But now I am not afraid at all. I not only have no worries for myself, I also have none for you. No one will be able to harm you in any way as long as I live.'

Amar burned to embrace Sakina, but her high ideals of love cooled him. He said, 'But you are soon to be married.'

'I will refuse now.'

'Will the old woman agree?'

'I'll tell her that if she even mentions my marriage, I will take poison.'

'Why don't you and I go away somewhere right now?'

'No, that is only superficial love. Real love is one where separation and union are the same thing, where separation does not exist, where the lover sees herself embracing her beloved even if he is a thousand leagues away.'

Suddenly Pathanin opened the door. Amar turned to her and pretended, 'I thought you must have come home a long time ago. Did you get detained somewhere?'

The old woman said sourly, 'Bhaiya, you made me cry today when you replied so gruffly. I depended on you and you were so unhelpful. But through the grace of Allah, Bahuji has promised to give me whatever money is needed. That is why the delay. Beta, are you annoyed with me for some reason?'

Amar consoled her, 'No, Amma, why would I be annoyed with you. I had just had an argument with Dada, and I was still upset. Afterwards I felt very ashamed and ran to beg your pardon. Will you pardon my misbehaviour?'

The old woman said crying, 'Beta, we have lived on scraps from your table all our lives. How could I go before God were I to be angry with you? If my skin is used to make shoes for your feet, I would have no complaint.'

'Enough said, Amma. I came only to satisfy myself on that score.'

Sakina, closing the door after Amar, said, 'Do come tomorrow.'

Amar was drunk with joy, 'I will certainly come.'

'I will be anxiously waiting.'

'You won't be angry if I bring you a present?'

'There can be no present bigger than the gift of your heart.'

'A present has to be accompanied by something sweet.'

'Whatever you give I will accept most willingly.'

Amar departed strutting as if he were the king of the world.

Sakina closed the door and said to her grandmother, 'Amma, you are needlessly running around tiring yourself. I am not going to marry.'

'Then you will stay as you are?'

'Yes. I will marry when I want.'

'I won't be here forever.'

'You will still be around when I get married.'

'This is no laughing matter. I have made all the arrangements.'

'No, Amma, I will not get married; and if you pester me, I will poison myself. The mere thought of marriage makes me panic.'

'What has come over you, Sakina?'

'Nothing, except I don't want to marry. I don't want to take on this headache until I am satisfied that there is a man with whom I can spend my life in comfort. You are bent on marrying me in a household where my life would be ruined. Marriage shouldn't entail spending one's life in misery.'

Pathanin sat down in front of the *angithi* and held her head in her hands thinking—how shameless this girl is.

Sakina had her meagre supper of millet bread and lentil *daal*, lay down on the broken cot and covered herself with a tattered blanket, curling her feet under her because of the cold, but her heart was filled with happiness. All the wealth of the world was worthless in comparison with the treasure that she had received today.

CHAPTER 15

There was a new purpose to Amarkant's life these days. Until now people at home had been scornful of everything he did, trying all the while to steer him. He had been like a horse that had neither wind nor enthusiasm, but now there was a human being who was encouraging him and stroking his neck. In place of disdain, or at least arid indifference, there was now a woman's encouragement—the gift that can move mountains and bring the dead to life! His desire to accomplish things, which had been constrained by his bondage, was strengthened and intensified! He had never known himself to be so self-reliant. Sakina nourished his inspiration through her reservoir of love. While that reservoir could not protect her, like the gift of a saint who begs for alms himself, her love showered riches on others. Amar no longer went to Sakina's house without definite purpose and he was not as overbearing as before. Now his actions were governed by considerations of time and opportunity. Trees that are deep-rooted do not require frequent watering—they draw moisture from the earth and grow and flower and fruit. The love of Sakina and Amar was that kind of a tree. They didn't have to meet frequently to keep it alive.

Examinations for degrees were held, but Amarkant did not take them. The teachers were confident that he would get a scholarship, even Dr Shantikumar did his best to persuade him, but he stood fast in his resolution. To succeed in life education is necessary, not a degree. The real degree is our desire to serve others, politeness, and a simple life. If we don't get this degree, if our souls are not awakened, then a paper degree is worthless. He had begun to hate this type of education. When he saw his teachers slavishly imitating fashion, running sycophantically around their superiors, and wanting maximum payment for minimum work, he felt disgusted. And to think that the reins of the nation were in the hands of these great souls! They are the makers of society, yet they do not care that the poor in India subsist on two *annas* a day. The common man does not make more than fifty rupees a year, while teachers need fifty rupees a day. At such moments, Amar was reminded of the gurus of olden times who lived in huts, having renounced selfishness and temptation and, leading virtuous lives, serving others without any hope of personal gain. They took very little from society and gave it their all. They were indeed great souls. The teachers of today are not at all different from common businessmen or government functionaries. They have the same arrogance, the same greed for money, and the same thirst for power. Educational institutions today are no different than a government department, and the teachers are an organ of the same government. They themselves are in darkness, how can they spread enlightenment? They are prisoners of their own mentality, slaves of their own cravings, and they make their students prisoners and slaves too. Amar's youthful imagination would start dreaming of an imaginary nation, where workers automatically served others and teachers lived as ascetics in huts, subsisting on simple fare and above the pettiness of envy and temptation, daily disagreements and quarrels that were common these days. What was the need for so many courthouses? What were all these big departments for? They seemed to be a coterie of vultures ready to pounce on the dead bodies of the poor. The higher the degree one held, the more selfish one was. As if temptation and selfishness were the badges of education. The poor may not be able to afford bread, they may hunger for clothes; but our educated brothers must have cars, bungalows, and platoons of servants. If man is the architect of this world, then he has been unjust; if God is the architect, then what could one say!

These feelings kept rising in Amar's breast like waves.

He would get up in the morning and go to Shantikumar's Sevashram and there teach boys until noon. The school was in Doctor sahab's bungalow. Doctor sahab also taught there until nine o'clock. No fees were charged, but even then very few boys came. Government schools were overcrowded and had little space even though they collected fees, fines, and subscriptions on any pretext; while here, with difficulty, two hundred to two hundred and fifty boys could be mustered. The main goal of the school was to let the young children, in all their honesty and simplicity, develop naturally so that they would pass out as confident courageous citizens with a natural inclination to service. The two friends constantly debated how ethics, the core of human nature, could be developed by separating students from a polluting environment and how sympathy for others, instead of conflict, could be nurtured. Their educational system was an evolving one, with methods devised to accomplish the main goal by keeping it constantly in sight. The inspirational lives of great men, their firmness of character, their sacrifices, their service to others and to causes were often discussed to fire the young minds with similar purpose. They had two other associates. One was Atmanand, an ascetic, who having renounced the world, was trying to find a justification for his life in charitable work. The other was a music teacher of the name, Brajnath. With the arrival of these two associate teachers, the school was able to widen its activities.

One day Amar said to Shantikumar, 'How long do you intend to continue with your professorship? It does not seem right that you should stay within a system that we want to uproot.'

Shantikumar smiled and said, 'Bhai, I am thinking the same myself, but then I wonder where the money would come from. Even though there are no great expenses, we still need at least five hundred rupees per month.'

'You needn't worry on that score. Money will come from somewhere. Anyway, why do we need money?'

'There is the house rent, books for the boys, and many other expenses; too many to count on our finger tips.'

'We could teach the students under trees, two under each tree.'

'You take leave of common sense in your pursuit of idealism. Pure idealism is only an imaginary feast.'

Amar was astonished and said, 'I thought that you were also an idealist.'

Shantikumar said, parrying this thrust, 'There is a place for common sense in my idealism.'

'That means that you eat *gur*, but avoid sweets.'

'Until I can raise money from some other source, how can I resign from service? I have started the school and I am responsible for its operation; if it closes down, I will get a bad name. I would resign today if you could make stable arrangements for its operation. But I can't do anything without support. I am not such a staunch idealist.'

Amarkant had not yet learned how to compromise with his principles. He had not yet faced the harsh realities of the world, and realized that to pursue one's ideals there had to be some give and take unless one wanted to forsake them altogether. He still had that absolute devotion to principles that characterizes neo initiates and so his respect for Doctor sahab suffered a severe setback. He felt that Dr Shantikumar was brave in words only; he said one thing, and did another. Which meant in plain words that he deceived the world. How could he be associated with such a man? He said threateningly, 'Then you won't resign?'

'Not until there is some other arrangement for money.'

'Under the circumstances, I can't work here.'

Doctor sahab said politely, 'Look, Amarkant, I have much more experience of the world than you do and I have been tested many times in my life. The lesson that I have learned from all that is that our life is based on compromise. Now you may think whatever you like of me, but there will come a time when the realization will hit you that in life realism is just as important as idealism.'

Amar said loftily, 'To die in the field of action is much better than abandoning the field.' And he left instantly.

First he encountered Salim. Salim called the school a juggler's pageant where a touch of the magic wand would convert dirt into gold. He was preparing for a Master of Arts degree. He was hoping to get a good government post and live his life in contentment. He had no special love for reform, organization, and national movements. When he heard the news, he said happily, 'You did very well by getting out. I know Doctor sahab very well. He is one of those people that warm their hands after setting another's house on fire. He would die for community but only in words.'

Sukhada was also happy. She had never liked Amar's enthusiasm for the school. She was annoyed with Doctor sahab for making Amar dance to his tune. Also, she felt that Amar's disenchantment with home was due to his influence.

But in the evening when Amar mentioned it to Sakina, she sided with Doctor sahab, 'I think Doctor sahab's reasoning is correct. One can't remember even God on an empty stomach. If one is worried about day-to-day existence, how can one serve the community? And if he does, he will do so by sacrificing his integrity. A man cannot remain hungry. There are the expenses associated with the school. Even assuming that the school can be held under trees, where is the park for that? It is essential to have some place where the boys can sit and study. The students need books, paper, a floor to sit on, and rope and pail for drinking water. These things have to come either from contributions or from someone's earnings. Just think how great a sacrifice a man makes when he lays the foundation for a project while working in a job against his principles. You are sacrificing your time, but he is sacrificing his conscience. I consider such a man worthy of much greater respect.'

Pathanin said, 'Beta, you shouldn't be taken in by the words of this young lass. Go and look after the affairs of your household. Such idle ramblings are for those that have nothing to do at home. Allah has given you prestige, rank, and a family; you shouldn't be getting embroiled in such nonsense.'

Amar had now been relieved of selling handkerchiefs. The old woman was getting so much muslin work through Renuka Devi that there was no time for crocheting hats. Enough work also kept coming from Salim's house and, through him, from other houses as well. Sakina's house had begun to look a little prosperous. The house had been painted, the door had a new curtain, two new cots had arrived, the cots had new bed mats, and some new pots and pans had been purchased. There was no lack of clothing either. An Urdu newspaper was on a cot. Even in her better days Pathanin had never been as well off. Her only grief now was that Sakina would not agree to getting married.

Amar left Sakina's home feeling ashamed that he had doubted Dr Shantikumar. One sentence from Sakina had quietened all his misgivings. His belief in Doctor sahab had again become as deep as ever. Sakina's wisdom, reasoning, perception, and fearlessness had astonished him and captivated him. The more he knew Sakina, the deeper her influence became. Sukhada dominated him with her brilliance and passion, a domination that he chafed against. Sakina dominated him with her softness and grace, a domination that he liked. Sukhada had the pride of possession. Sakina had the humility of surrender. Sukhada thought herself wiser and abler than her husband. Sakina thought herself nothing in comparison to Amar.

Doctor sahab smiled and asked, 'So, you are determined that I should resign. In fact, I have already written out my resignation; I will hand it in tomorrow. I can't lose your cooperation; I won't be able to do everything myself. After you had left I thought calmly and discovered that I was attaching needless importance to money. After all, what did Swami Dayanand have when he laid the foundation of the Arya Samaj?'

Amarkant also smiled, 'No, when I thought calmly, I discovered that I was in error. Don't resign till there is some alternative arrangement for money.'

Doctor sahab said, astonished, 'You are being sarcastic?'

'No, I have been impertinent to you. Please forgive me.'

Chapter 16

For some time now, Amarkant had been a member of the Municipal Board. Lala Samarkant was influential in the city and the public liked Amarkant so much that he was elected without spending a *dhela*. His opponent was a well-known lawyer, but he didn't receive even a quarter of the votes that Amar did. Both Sukhada and Lala Samarkant had tried to dissuade Amar from serving on the Board because they wanted him to be involved in household affairs. Now that Amar had given up studies, Lalaji wanted to retire and have him assume the entire load of running the house. If he kept frittering away his time and energy on this and that work, how would he be able to attend to the needs of the family! A little storm was brewing and one day it broke. Lalaji and Sukhada were on one side, Amar on the other, and Naina was in the middle.

Lalaji said, caressing his big belly, 'A *dhobhi's* dog belongs neither at home nor at the ghat. You go to school at dawn, attend to affairs of the Congress in the evening, and now you are getting involved in a new affliction. Why don't you burn down the house?'

Sukhada voiced her support, 'Yes, you should now think of your home and not get entangled in these useless jobs. Up to now you were studying, but now that you have finished, you should look after your family. Those that have other men in their household can better undertake this type of work. A single man is fully occupied with the responsibilities of running a household, how can he do outside work also?'

Amar said, 'What you people consider an affliction, extra work, and useless entanglement, I consider no less important than running the house. Also, as long as you are around, why should I worry? And the fact is that I have no turn for Dadaji's kind of work. A man is successful only at the work that his heart is in. My heart is not at all in the business of trade and borrowing and lending money, and I am always afraid that I may ruin some well-laid scheme.'

Lalaji was not impressed with this logic. It was impossible that his son should be an amateur at the business of trade. He said, toothlessly chewing paan, 'All this is rhetoric, nothing else. If I were not here wouldn't you take care of your family? You just want to wear me out. There are sons who support their families and thus relieve their fathers, but you don't want to leave even my bones in peace.'

Then matters took a turn for the worse. Sukhada, seeing that things were getting uncomfortable, fell silent. Naina, plugging her ears with her fingers, went and sat inside the house. Meanwhile, the two adversaries kept wrestling. The young man was fit, agile, and able to twist and turn. The old man had craft, stamina, and authority. The old warrior tried repeatedly to crush him down, but the young stalwart always managed to wriggle out from underneath. No stratagems seemed to work.

In the end, Lalaji lost his cool and said, 'Then, baba, you should leave with your family. I cannot shoulder your burden. If you live in this house, then you will have to quietly pay the rent plus half the household expenses. I have not undertaken to support you throughout your life. If you consider this house as yours, then whatever is here is yours. If you don't think so, then nothing here is yours. When I am dead, you may come and take whatever is left.'

Amarkant was thunderstruck. Before the baby was born and he had been at odds with Lalaji, he had once or twice feared that such a blow might fall; but, since the birth of the baby, Lalaji had shown some of the tenderness and love of a parent for his progeny. Amar no longer had any such apprehension. Having given him the toy of a grandson that Lalaji had hoped for, Amar had become carefree; but he discovered today that the toy was unable to overcome the attraction of worldly goods for his father.

He could have understood a father's anger at his son's recalcitrance or his admonishment or sulking, but that a father should ask his son for rent or living expenses, that was the height of crass material greed. The only solution was to have no further dealings with his father and move somewhere else with Sukhada and their child. If Sukhada objected then he would abandon her as well.

He said in a steady voice, 'If that is your wish, it is alright by me.'

Lalaji said, feeling somewhat abashed, 'You are relying on the support of your mother-in-law.'

Amar said reproachfully, 'Dada, please don't add insult to injury. If there is no place for me in my father's house where I was born, then do you think that I would depend for my livelihood on my in-laws? I have not fallen so low, thank you. I can do hard work and feed myself from the sweat of my labour. I will lose all self-respect if I have to beg for kindness from anyone. God willing, I will show you that I can serve the public even as a labourer.'

Samarkant thought that Amar was still indulging his pipedreams; he would come to his senses after a month or two of facing the problems of running a household. Quietly, he went out; at the same time, Amar left to search for a house.

After Amar had left, Lalaji went in again. He had hoped that Sukhada would comfort him, but she ignored him although she saw him at her door. She couldn't imagine that a father could be so heartless. After all, what was the use of his several lakhs? Until now, she had felt badly that Amar kept aloof from household affairs. That Lalaji should rebuke the son on that score was only fair; but to ask for expenses for bread and board was tantamount to breaking the relationship. If he could break the relationship, she would not bow to him for support. She wouldn't care if the house burned down. She took off all of her jewellery—after all, Lalaji had given it to her. She put aside even the gifts her mother had given her, for whatever her mother had given was part of her dowry. Those gifts must also have been entered in Lalaji's account books! She would leave this house in only the sari that she was wearing. May God keep her child safe and sound; she didn't care about anything else. That priceless jewel was hers.

At this moment she felt a real sympathy for Amar. After all, what was so bad about serving on the Municipal Board? Who does not like respect and honour? People spend lakhs of rupees to become members. Why? Are all Board members considered no-goods at home? A person aspires to make a name for himself, to do something worthwhile. If Amar didn't pursue the selfish goal of personal ambition, he had also not done anything for which he deserved to be punished. Some other man would have considered himself lucky and praised his good fortune at having a son with such a zeal for public affairs.

Suddenly Amar came and said, 'You heard what Dada had to say today. What do you advise?'

'What is there to advise? We should leave immediately. After such a rebuke, I would rather die than drink water in this house. You should arrange for some other house.'

'I have already found one. It is a small house, clean and tidy, in Nichibagh. The rent is ten rupees.'

'I am ready.'

'Then should I get a tonga?'

'It is not necessary. We will walk there.'

'We will have to carry a trunk, bedding, etc.'

'There is nothing in this house that is ours. I have taken off all my jewellery. The women of labourers do not sit around wearing ornaments.'

Amar was amazed to see how proud this woman was. He said, 'But the jewellery belongs to you. No one else has any claim over it. Also, you brought more than half of it with you.'

'Whatever mother gave me was as part of my dowry. Whatever Lalaji gave me, he gave with the understanding that it was going to remain in the house. Every single item is entered in his account book. I consider jewellery also charity given out of kindness. Now we can claim only those things that we have bought from our own earnings.'

Amar fell into a deep reverie. She was breaking the relationship so completely that not even a shred of connection would remain. He knew how dearly a woman loves her jewellery. After husband and child, it is their jewellery that is precious to them. At times, for jewellery, they may be at odds even with their husband and children. Right now the wound is fresh, there is still no pain. In a few days, this contentment would be replaced by resentment and unhappiness. Then for every little thing there would be sarcasm, and every little thing would set off tears. It would become difficult to live at home.

He said, 'Sukhada, I wouldn't advise that. It isn't wrong to take with us what belongs to us.'

Sukhada looked at her husband proudly and said, 'You must be thinking that I will sit in a corner crying for the jewellery and bemoaning my fate. You have no idea of the degree of sacrifice that a woman can make if there is occasion for it. After this rebuke, I consider it a sin even to glance at, let alone wear, this jewellery. If you are afraid that I will soon be pestering you for it, I can assure you that you may cut off my tongue if I ever mention the jewellery. I also tell you that I am not going to be dependent on you. I will earn my own keep. Food does not cost much. Real expense comes only from trying to keep up with the Joneses. Once you have abandoned the trappings of the wealthy, you can live very cheaply.'

Naina had seen her bhabhi taking off her jewellery. She couldn't imagine how she would live alone in this house. She couldn't survive without the child even for a moment. She was angry with everyone; her father, brother, and sister-in-law. What had come over Dada? There was so much money in the house—what was it for? If Bhaiya had tended the shop for a few hours everyday what harm would there have been in that? Bhabhi, too, was acting on a whim. If she didn't go with him, Bhaiya would return after a few days. If she went with Bhabhi, then who would cook for Dada? He would not eat food cooked by anyone else. She wanted to pacify bhabhi, but how could she do that! These two would not even look at her. Bhaiya has already turned away. Naina's distress was boundless.

She went to her father and said, 'Dada, Bhabhi has taken off all her jewellery.'

Lalaji was worried, he didn't say anything. Perhaps he hadn't heard.

Naina said a bit more loudly, 'Bhabhi has taken off all her jewellery.'

Lalaji raised his head listlessly and said, 'What is she doing with the jewellery?'

'She is taking it all off.'

'So, what am I to do?'

Naina replied, 'Why don't you go and speak to her?'

'What can I do if she doesn't want to wear it?'

'You must have told her that she couldn't take the jewellery if she left. Will you take back even the jewellery given to her at her wedding?'

'Yes, I will take back everything. There is nothing in this house that belongs to her.'

'You are being very unjust.'

Lalaji rebuked her, 'Go sit inside and stop this useless twaddle.'

'Why don't you go and talk to her?'

'If you feel so badly, why don't you talk to her yourself?'

'Who am I to explain things? If you are taking back your jewellery, why would she listen to me?'

Both were silent for a while. Then Naina spoke again, 'I can't see this injustice being done. The jewellery is hers. You cannot take her wedding ornaments.'

'Since when have you learned this fine point of law?'

'One doesn't have to learn what is just and what is unjust. Even a child would protest if he were punished without cause.'

'You seem to have acquired these ideas from your brother.'

'It is no bad thing if I learn about justice and injustice from my brother.'

'Achcha bhai, don't bite my head off. I said, go inside. I am not going to persuade anyone or make anyone understand anything. It is my house, and I own everything in it. I have sweated my life blood for it, why should I let anyone take it away?'

Naina bowed her head in resignation and said, 'Then I, too, will go with bhabhi.'

Lalaji's manner hardened, 'Go, I won't stop you. It would have been better to remain childless than to have a child like you. Leave my house, and leave today. I will really enjoy being alone. There will be nothing to worry about. I won't have to listen to your constant moaning, "We don't have this and we don't have that". What happiness have you given me by living here?'

In tears, Naina went to Sukhada and said, 'Bhabhi, I want to come with you, too.'

Sukhada said in disbelief, 'With us! We don't even have a house yet. We have no money, no pots and pans, no servants. How can you come with us? And who will live in this palace?'

Mad Sillo came guffawing, guffawed and said, 'You should all go away and I will be the queen of the house. I will sleep happily in this bed in this room. If a beggar comes to the door, I will chase him away with a broom.'

Amar understood the turmoil in the heart of the madwoman, but how could he possibly take them all with him? There was only one livable room in the house. Where would Naina stay? If the madwoman came also, life would be intolerable.

He said to Naina, 'Naina, if you come with us, who will cook for Dada? We are not going far away. I promise to come to see you everyday. You and Sillo should both stay here, but let us go.'

Naina started crying, 'Just think, how can I live in this house without you. What will I do but lie around all day? I won't be able to stay here for even a moment. I will cry all the time missing Munna. Bhabhi, see, he won't even look at me now that he is leaving.'

Amar said, 'Then we will leave the boy here. He will stay with you.'

Sukhada voiced her protest, 'What! What are you saying? He will cry himself to death. And what about me? I will not accept that.'

In the evening they left the house, followed by a laughing Sillo. The shopkeepers opposite the house thought they had been invited out, but were puzzled because they were not wearing any jewellery, shawls, or expensive clothes, normally worn on special occasions.

Lala Samarkant was sitting in his room smoking his *hukkah*. He didn't look up at them.

He got up after an hour, locked the house, and lay down in his room.

One of the shopkeepers came and asked him, 'Lalaji, where have Bhaiya and his wife gone?'

Lalaji replied, turning his face away, 'I don't know. I have thrown everyone out of the house. I have not earned money so that others may enjoy life at my expense. One who understands the value of money may enjoy it, but one who considers it dirt will have to learn the value of money. Even these days I work eighteen hours a day, but I won't do it for children who think money is dirt. Children who were raised in my arms lose their temper with me, I keep giving out money only to hear abuse! No, I am supposed to hold my tongue if the household work doesn't get done or even if someone sets fire to the house. If one is happy wasting time on associations and meetings, then go, let the meetings support you. My house is not for such children. A child should listen to what he is told; if he goes his own way, what kind of a child is he!'

As soon as Sillo gave Renuka the news, she came running as if a great calamity had befallen her daughter and son-in-law—why hadn't they come to her, was she a stranger, weren't they related to her? They had taken a separate house and not even informed her. What! Was this child's play? The two ragamuffins! Her daughter was not like that, but the boy seems to have turned her head.

It was eight o'clock in the evening. It was still warm outside. The dust hanging in the air dimmed the stars in the sky. When Renuka arrived, the three outcasts were sitting with heavy hearts on a *charpai* on the roof. The entire house was in darkness. The poor souls had the unfamiliar burden of managing a household. They didn't have a penny and didn't have the least idea what to do.

As soon as Amar saw her, he said, 'How did you hear, Ammaji? Achcha, that witch Sillo must have gone and informed you. I will take care of her, where is she?'

Renuka was winded after climbing the stairs in darkness. Taking off her shawl she said, 'What was the harm if she told me, am I an enemy? Don't I have a home, and don't I have bread in my house? I won't allow you to stay here for even a moment. There is plenty of room in my house, why are you all crammed into this cubbyhole. Come, let us go. The baby must be wilting in this heat. There are no cots here, how will you sleep in this little space? You were not like this, Sukhada, what has come over you? If old people reprimand you, you should patiently hear them out, not just march out of the house. Have you two lost your wits?'

Sukhada narrated the entire story and did so in a manner that Renuka also came to believe that Lala Samarkant had exceeded the bounds of reason. If he was so conceited about his wealth, then he could keep it. He could take it with him to his grave.

Amar said, 'Dada probably never thought that Sukhada and Naina would also leave the house.'

Sukhada was not to be so readily appeased. She said, 'Come, come! He said plainly there was nothing of yours there. Couldn't he have come and asked even once, "Where are you people going?" We left the house, he continued to sit in his room and stare after us. He didn't even take pity on the child. He is so conceited, aren't we humans, too? He can live in his palace, we will live by our own sweat and toil. Amma, you have never seen such a greedy person! When Naina went to talk to him, she was also scolded. The poor soul came away in tears.'

Renuka, taking Naina's hand, said, 'Achcha, whatever has happened, has happened for the good. Come on, it is getting late. I have asked the cook to make dinner. Cots have also been laid out. If Lala's house hadn't been deserted, how could mine have been inhabited.'

Downstairs, Sillo lit an earthen lamp using mustard oil. After escorting Renuka to the house, she had run to the market to buy the lamp, oil, and a broom. After lighting the lamp, she swept the house.

Sukhada, handing the child to Renuka, said, 'Amma, please excuse us today, we will come some other time. Why should we give Lalaji any excuse to say that Amar finally ran to his in-laws? He has made it awkward for us to come to your house. Let us stay here a few days. We want to see that we can live on our own; then we will come to you.'

Amar was feeling mortified. He wasn't concerned about himself. He could go to Salim or the Doctor's house; but how would Sukhada and Naina sleep without cots. Also, where would he get money tomorrow? But how could he contradict Sukhada?

Cuddling the baby, Renuka said, 'You can do that when I am gone. Right now, I am very much alive. My house is your house. Come on, let's go.'

Sukhada said firmly, 'Amma, until we can live on our own earnings we will only come as guests to visit you.'

Renuka appealed to Amar, 'Beta, listen to her, she acts as though I am a stranger, not her mother.'

Remorsefully, Sukhada said, 'Amma, please don't take it amiss. I have learned from Dadaji's behaviour today how much wealthy people value their money. Who knows, you may develop similar ideas some day? I'd rather not let that happen. When we come as guests ...'

Amar, thinking how much Renuka must be hurt by what Sukhada said, interrupted, 'Sukhada, there is no harm in your going. It will be very difficult for you here.'

Sukhada said sharply, 'Does it mean that you are the only one who can bear hardship? I can't do so? If you are afraid of hardship, then you go. I'm not going anywhere yet.'

The upshot was that Renuka dispatched Sillo to her house to get her bedding. Since the food was ready, it was also brought. The roof was swept clean, and, like travellers in an inn, they ate their meal and passed the night. Now and then they would tease and joke with each other. It was not as if it was pitch dark. It was dark, but it was the darkness before dawn. They were miserable, yes, but they were not intimidated by their misery, rather they gloried in it.

Renuka went back home the next morning. Once again she tried to persuade everyone go with her, but Sukhada remained adamant. She would not accept anything—clothes, pots and pans, or cots and beds—to the point that Renuka got angry. Amarkant also felt annoyed—he felt that she was dictating to him even in their poverty.

After Renuka had left, Amarkant began thinking about where the money was to come from. It was time for him to go to the free school. It was essential that he go there. Sukhada was still enjoying her morning sleep, and Naina was sitting anxiously wondering how the household would be managed. Amar went to school, but his heart wasn't in it. Sometimes he felt angry with his father, sometimes Sukhada, and sometimes himself. He didn't say anything to Doctor sahab about his banishment. He didn't want anyone's sympathy. Today, he didn't go to any of his friends because he was afraid that after hearing his story, people might think that he wanted some help from them.

When he returned home at ten o'clock, he saw that Sillo was kneading dough and Naina was in the kitchen cooking vegetables. He dared not ask where the money had come from. Naina said on her own, 'Hear this, Bhaiya, today Sillo is giving us a feast. She brought everything from the market—wood, ghee, flour, and daal. She has also borrowed pots and pans from someone she knows.'

Sillo spoke up, 'I am not giving any feast. All expenses will be added up and I will collect them.'

Laughingly, Naina said, 'She has been fighting with me for a long time. She says that she will collect her money. I say, "you are giving us a feast". Tell us, Bhaiya, isn't she giving us a feast?'

'Yes, it's a feast alright, what else!'

Amarkant had guessed what was in silly Sillo's mind. She knew that unless she said that it was only a temporary loan, these people would refuse to accept things bought with her money.

Sillo's shrivelled face lit up, as if she had risen in her own esteem, and her life had been justified. Her plain emaciated face was suffused with grace. She was flying in air when she put water out for Amarkant to take his bath.

Amar had hoped that even now Dada would perhaps send someone or come himself to fetch Sukhada and Naina, but when no one came, he felt badly.

Quickly he bathed, but then remembered that he didn't have a clean dhoti to wear. So, instead, he wrapped his neck shawl about his waist. He ate his meal and was going out to search for a job when Sukhada said peevishly, 'You have been sitting so content as if you have arranged everything here. The only thing you seemed to know was how to get us here. You disappeared in the morning, only to return at noon. Have you asked anyone for a job or some work, or do you expect a miracle from God? This won't do, you understand?'

Amar was saddened at this change in Sukhada's feelings in less than twenty-four hours. Yesterday she had spoken so loftily, today she was perhaps already sorry for having left the house.

He said dryly, 'I haven't spoken to anyone yet. I am going now to search for a job.'

'I will also visit the judge sahab's wife and speak to her about some work. I don't know about now, but in former days she thought highly of me.'

Amar didn't say anything. He realized that there were testing times ahead.

Amarkant was well known to everyone in the market. From a *khaddar* shop, he took several bolts of khaddar cloth, saris, jumpers, kurtas, and *chadars* to sell on commission. Loading them on his back, he prepared to move.

The shopkeeper said, 'Babuji, what are you doing? Get a labourer. What will people say? It is not right.'

A rebellious storm was brewing inside Amar's breast. If he could, he would have done away with all the wealthy people who made this world such hell. By carrying the load on his back he wanted to show that he considered it much better to live off his own labour than to be a freeloader. 'All you pot-bellied people, you are all freeloaders! You think lowly of me because I am carrying a load on my back! Is this load any more shameful than the load of impropriety and immorality that you carry? You carry it around on your head and are not even ashamed about it, instead you are proud of it!

If a rich man had teased Amarkant at this time he would have fared very badly indeed. He was like a keg of gunpowder, a live electric wire.

Chapter 17

Amarkant had been selling *khadi*. It was about three in the afternoon, and it was very hot, with dust rising up in swirls. The shopkeepers were taking siesta in their shops, rich people resting in palaces, and labourers under trees; while Amar, with a load of khadi on his back, perspiring, and with red face and eyes, was wandering from lane to lane.

A lawyer acquaintance of Amarkant, raising the curtain of khas, saw him carrying the load and shouted, '*Arre* yaar, what is this shameful thing you are doing! At least think of your reputation as Municipal Member. You are embarrassing us all. Wasn't there a labourer available?'

Amar, still weighed down by the load, said, 'Labouring doesn't detract from the prestige of a Municipal member. What does detract is earning your living through deceit and trickery.'

'Come bhai, which of us earns money through chicanery? Do lawyers, doctors, professors, wealthy merchants, and moneylenders live off deceit and trickery?'

'You should put this question to their hearts. Why should I speak ill of anyone?'

'But you must know something to be speaking so.'

'If you insist on asking me, I can say, yes, some do live in such a way. If one person can live on ten rupees, why should another person need ten thousand? Such an imbalance will last only as long as the eyes of the public are not opened. Pardon me, but it is neither just nor righteous that one man should sit under a fan cooled by khas-khas, while another toils under the midday sun; it is wicked.'

'Bhai sahab, rich and poor there have always been and will always be. You cannot make everyone equal.'

'I can't change the world; but if justice is a good thing, it will prevail, even if people don't always follow it.'

'What it means is that you don't accept individualism, but are a follower of socialism.'

'I am not a follower of any –ism. I worship only just-ism.'

'I see. So, have you broken off completely with your father?'

'My father is not responsible for my life.'

'Alright, let's see what you have!'

The lawyer then sorted through the load and purchased fabrics worth ten rupees.

Amar had become very ill-tempered and rude these days. He was ready to pick a fight and argue any time. Even so, his sales were going well, and he earned one to one and a quarter rupees each day.

People who are ascetics fall into two categories. One type finds joy in abandon, and experiences both contentment and fulfilment in relinquishing worldly goods. His sacrifice encompasses magnanimity and compassion. The other type is the angry ascetic whose sacrifice is a sign of revolt against his situation; whose fetish for justice is his revenge against the world and his compensation; one who burns himself and thus burns others as well. Amar was of this second type. If a healthy man takes a bitter pill he happily swallows it, but a sick man takes it after a fuss, and bemoaning his fate.

On the recommendation of Judge sahab's wife, Sukhada had found a job in a girls' school at fifty rupees per month. Amar couldn't say anything openly, but he was furious at heart. All the household jobs—looking after the child, cooking, and shopping for essentials—were his responsibility. Sukhada didn't even go near household chores. If Amar said mango, Sukhada said tamarind. They were always at odds with each other. Sukhada was dominating him even in their poverty. Amar said a pint of milk was enough. Sukhada said a quart was needed and so ordered it. He didn't drink milk himself, so even that became a cause for daily strife. He said, 'We are poor, we are labourers, and should live like labourers.' She said, 'We are not labourers and will not live like labourers.' Amar considered her an obstacle to his self-development, and fumed at himself for not being able to remove that obstacle.

One day the child developed a cough. Amar prepared to take him to a homeopath, but Sukhada said, 'Don't take the child, he might catch a cold. Get a doctor to visit, at worst he will charge his fees.'

As a result, Amar had to call a doctor. After two days the child recovered.

One day they received the news that Lala Samarkant had a fever. In the last month, Amarkant had not gone to his father's house at all. He didn't go even after hearing the news. He thought it none of his business whether his father lived or died—he loves his money, he can keep it close to his heart; he doesn't need anybody.

But Sukhada couldn't remain apathetic. She at once marched off taking Naina with her, while Amar fumed.

Samarkant wouldn't eat food cooked by anyone except his family members. For the first few days after his family left, he didn't eat anything and drank only milk. Then for many days he subsisted on fruit; but he kept pining for roti and daal. Many delicious things were available in the market, but not rotis. One day he couldn't contain himself. He cooked rotis and, in his enthusiasm, ate too much. He had indigestion, then the next day he had loose bowels, after that he developed a fever. He was already weak from the fruit diet; so he nearly died after being sick for two days.

Seeing Sukhada, he said sarcastically, 'Bahu, why did you rush here, you could have waited a few more days, and this worshipper of money would have been dead. That boy thinks I love money more than my children. For whom did I accumulate it—for myself? Why did I have children? That same child I carried in my arms when he was ill, calling in occultists and physicians who practice Ayurvedic and Arabic medicine has now become my enemy. I didn't spend my money on fancy food and clothes for myself—for whom then did I accumulate it? I became a miser; cheated, flattered others, and killed my soul— why? The very same boy I did all these things for now calls me a thief.'

Sukhada, with head bowed, cried.

Lalaji said again, 'I am not a fool, I know that if God has given anyone hands he will be able to take care of himself. But parents always wish that their children suffer no grief; that their children don't have to bear the same hardships as they did. They wish their children to be spared the good and bad deeds they had to do and the blows they had to face. The world calls them selfish and greedy. They don't care about that, but when their own children insult them, then imagine what goes through the heart of an unfortunate father. He feels that his entire life has been useless. That magnificent edifice which he had assembled brick by brick, for which he had suffered the heat of summer and pelting rain of August, has fallen down and its bricks and stones lie scattered. The house has not been demolished, his life has been demolished; all that he had wished for in his entire life has been demolished.'

Sukhada took the child from Naina's arms, laid him down on her father-in-law's bed, and started fanning him. The child, with his eyes big and wide, noticed his old grandfather's moustache and, seeing no purpose for it, tried to pull it out with both hands. Lalaji yelped with apparent pain, but didn't remove the child's hands. Hanuman, the monkey God, had probably not destroyed the gardens of Sri Lanka with such vehemence, but even then Lalaji didn't take the child's hands away from his moustache. His paternal instincts, which had been suppressed so long, had come alive with the child's touch. The child had suffused every fibre of his being and had released latent emotions in his grandfather like churned up butter.

For two days Sukhada, Naina, and Sillo stayed in their old home with Lalaji. But Amarkant didn't go to see his father. He would come home in the evening, cook his meals, eat, and be off to the Congress office or the office of the Youth Association. Sometimes he would speak at public meetings, sometimes he would solicit subscriptions.

On the third day Lalaji felt better. Sukhada stayed with him all day, but requested permission to go to her house in the evening. Lalaji looked at her affectionately and said, 'Bahu, if I had known that you had come only to nurse me, then I would have stayed sick for five or ten more days. I haven't done any wrong knowingly, but pardon me if I have done something inappropriate.'

Sukhada wanted to forgive her father-in-law, but it didn't seem right to stay with him when after such hardship they had begun to establish their own home. Also, in her new home she was mistress, she controlled the household. Every article was her own and indicative of her self-respect. Everything reflected her good taste, every article bore her stamp on it. In this house there was nothing she could take personal pride in and, despite everything, her dreams of being mistress would never be fulfilled. But to make Lalaji understand this required some tact. She said, 'Dada, what are you saying? We are your children. Whatever you say to us, good or bad, I know you say for our benefit. I really don't want to go, but what will be accomplished if I came back here alone. I am embarrassed also at what people might be saying about us. As soon as possible, I will bring everyone back here. Until a man gets kicked around for a while, his eyes are not opened. We will come and cook for you everyday. Some days Naina will come and other days I will.'

From then on, this was Sukhada's schedule. In the morning she would go to Lalaji's house and return home after feeding him. Then, after eating herself, she would go to the girls' school. In the afternoon, after Amarkant left to sell homespun cloth, she would again go with Naina to her father-in-law's for two or three hours. At times, when she would visit Renuka, she would send Naina to her father-in-law's. Her idea of self-respect was tempered with tenderness. Whatever irritation there had been with her father-in-law was long forgotten, she couldn't bear to see the old man suffering.

What bothered her most these days was that Amarkant would go around with the load of khadi on his head. Many times she had harangued him on the subject, but the more she said the more stubborn he would become. Therefore she had stopped discussing it. But one day when returning home with a woman of the neighbourhood, she saw Amarkant with a load of homespun. Sukhada was very embarrassed.

As soon as Amar came home, she tackled him on the subject, 'I realize how true to your word you are, but why don't you consider my feelings? The world knows the importance of hard work, but I feel so badly about you carrying the load on your head like a common labourer. You may not feel ashamed, but my honour is tied to yours. You have no right to keep insulting me in this fashion.'

Amar was ready for the fight. He said, 'I know that I have no rights anywhere, but may I ask whether there is any limit to your rights or are they unlimited?'

'I don't do anything that brings dishonour to you.'

'If I said that I feel insulted by your working just as you feel insulted by my working as a common labourer, you probably wouldn't believe it.'

'I can't help it if your ideas of respect and disrespect are unique in the world.'

Amar rejoined, 'I am not a slave to the ideas of the world. If you want to be a slave that is your business, but you can't force me.'

'If I don't work, how do you expect the household to run on your wages of twenty annas per day?'

'Most people in this country live on a lot less than that.'

'I'm not "most" people. I say this for the last time—I can't tolerate your carrying a load like a common labourer. If you don't listen to me, I will throw the load down myself. I don't want to say or hear any more about it.'

For the last month and a half Amarkant had not gone to Sakina's house. He thought of her everyday, but he didn't get the chance to go see her. After the first two weeks, he began to feel uncomfortable as to what he would say when she asked—why didn't you come for so many days?

He avoided dealing with the situation for another month. Finally, he received a card from Sakina asking how he was and whether he could go see her for a few minutes. Her *Amma-jaan* was going to visit her relatives and friends in the community and it was a good opportunity for a brief visit. Amarkant was fed up with life. He had come to realize that he was never going to be happy with Sukhada. He wouldn't change, and neither would she. So where was the hope of a happy life? They had different sentiments, different ideals, and different goals for their lives. He couldn't give up his values and his struggle for inner fulfilment for the sake of saving his marriage. The purpose of human life was much loftier than just eating, working, and dying.

That day, after dinner he didn't go to the Congress office. He had to solve the most important problem of his life. He couldn't put it off any longer. He didn't care about his reputation. The world was blind and ignorant and wanted to keep others the same way. It wouldn't be surprising if narrow-minded people scoffed at him when he carved out a new path for himself. He took two khaddar saris as a present for Sakina and rushed to her house.

Sakina was waiting for him. The minute she heard his knock, she opened the door and taking his hand said, 'You forgot me. Is this what you call love?'

Ashamed, Amar said, 'It is not that, Sakina. I didn't forget you for even a moment. It is just that I have had so many problems to deal with lately.'

'I heard, and Amma also said that you had moved away from your father's house; I couldn't believe it. We also heard that you are selling khaddar, carrying the load around on your head. I would never have let that happen, I would have put the load on my head and walked behind you. Here I have been comfortably lying around while you were labouring in the hot sun. But my heart was breaking.'

How loving and tender were these words! Had Sukhada ever been so sweet? She always wanted her own way. Sakina's words gave him power and strength. He didn't want to hurt Sakina, so he decided he would no longer carry the bundle.

He said, 'Sakina, I was disgusted with my father's selfishness. He must have thought I wanted only his money. I wanted to show him and others like him that I could do physical labour. I don't care about money. Initially, Sukhada moved away with me, but one day Dada pretended he had a fever. That was a good excuse for her to go there. Since then, she cooks his meals both in the morning and in the evening.'

Sakina asked simply, 'Why do you resent that? The old man lies in the house all alone. If she goes to help him, what's so bad about that? I respect her for it .'

Amar was embarrassed, 'She doesn't go because she feels it is the proper thing to do, she does it because he is wealthy. She was never concerned or even pretended to be concerned about how I was feeling. But the minute she heard of his "illness" she had to go help him. I can't understand this. His wealth draws her, nothing else. Sakina, I am sick of this pretentious life. Honestly, I will go mad. Sometimes I think of abandoning everything and running away to some place where people are humane. You will have to decide today, Sakina. Let's go and build a small hut somewhere, get away from this selfish world and spend our lives in honest labour. If I lived with you, I wouldn't need anything else. I desperately need your love, not the kind of love where separation is union, but where even union is separation. I want to fully experience love with all its passion and desire. I want to drink the real wine, not the imaginary wine of poets.'

He reached for Sakina to embrace her. Pathanin entered at that moment, and Sakina and Amar slipped apart. Quickly he said, 'Where were you, Amma? I came here to give you these saris. You know, don't you, that I am selling khaddar.'

Pathanin didn't reach out for the saris. She ignored his gift. Her dry, shrivelled face was red with anger. Her nearly sightless eyes were inflamed. She said furiously, 'Come to your senses, you scoundrel. Take these saris and give them to your wife and sister. We don't want your saris. I thought you were a gentleman's son, and decent, so I told you of our situation. I didn't expect you, the son of a gentleman to be capable of such licentious behaviour. Now, go, don't say a word, otherwise I will have your eyes ripped out. What arrogance! If I shout just once, my whole neighbourhood will be here. We are poor and deprived, we need bread. Do you know why that is so? Because we value our reputation. Don't you ever dare come here again. Go and hang your head in shame.'

Amar felt paralysed, a mountain had come crashing down, he was thunderstruck. One could only imagine his thoughts after these harsh words. He seemed to be like a stone statue, devoid of all senses. He stood like that for a minute, then he took both saris and with his head down, like a wounded animal he stumbled towards the door.

Suddenly Sakina, catching hold of his hand and crying said, 'Babuji, I am coming with you. Those that love their reputation may lick it. I will live without it.'

Amarkant gently removed her hand and said softly, 'If I live, we will meet again, Sakina. For now, let me go. I am not thinking straight.' So saying and after some reflection, he handed over both saris to Sakina and left.

Sakina asked sobbing, 'When will you come?'

Amar turned back and replied, 'When people here stop thinking of me as low and licentious.'

Amar went away and Sakina with the saris in her hand, stood at the door gazing into darkness.

Suddenly, the old woman called out 'Will you come and sit down now or are you going to stand there all night? You are already defamed, what else are you bent on doing?'

Sakina gave her a furious look and said, 'Amma, I fear for your soul. Why do you make false accusations against an innocent man? You are not even ashamed to say such things. How could you return his generosity in this manner? If you searched the whole world, you wouldn't find such a good person.'

Pathanin rebuked her, 'Keep quiet, you shameless hussy. Instead of being ashamed, you talk back. Had there been a man in the house, he would have cut his throat. I will go and tell Lala Samarkant. I won't relax until this scoundrel has been thrown out of the city. I will ruin his life.'

Sakina said decisively, 'You must understand; if his life is ruined, mine will also be ruined.'

Pathanin grabbed Sakina's hand and pulled her inside so roughly that she nearly fell down. The old woman stepped out of the house, shut the door and locked her in. Sakina called repeatedly, but the old woman didn't even look back. That weak old woman, for whom it was difficult to take even one step, was now running in her agitation to Lala Samarkant.

Chapter 18

Amarkant came out of the lane onto the road wondering where to go. Pathanin would go at once to Dada, that was certain. He thought—what an awful situation it was! What upheaval it would cause! Some would say he had lost his dharma; some that he had lost his sense of decorum and propriety. Deception, fraud, fabrication, betrayal, and earning by dishonest means all can be forgiven; even praised. People who practise such things are often the pillars of society. A man who frequents prostitutes and is amoral is often kowtowed to, but it is an unpardonable sin to love anyone with a pure and honest heart. No, Amar could not go home. That door was closed for him. Besides, when did he ever feel comfortable at home? It was only a place to eat and sleep. Who wants that?

He paused for a moment. Sakina had been ready to go with him, why shouldn't he take her with him? People may wail and curse him to their heart's content. This was, after all, what he had wanted; but the mountain, which had seemed like a small hill from afar, now when viewed from near, was an insurmountable barrier. There would be uproar throughout the country. Everybody would say that a Municipal member had run away with a Muslim girl! Dada may even poison himself. His adversaries would be clapping their hands with glee. He remembered a story by Tolstoy in which a man runs away with his mistress; but the story ended so tragically! Had Amar heard a similar report about someone other than himself, he would have hated him. A skeleton covered with flesh and blood appears so beautiful, but the same skeleton looks so frightful when flesh and blood have been stripped away. These rumours erase what is beautiful and sweet and, instead, highlight what is hideous and loathsome. No, Amar could not go home now.

Suddenly he remembered his son. He was the one light in the darkness of his life. His heart rushed towards that light. The child's lovable image stood in front of him.

Someone called, 'Why are you standing there, Amarkant?'

When Amar turned around to look, Salim said, 'What have you been up to?'

'I just went to the main market.'

'Why are you standing here? Perhaps you are going to meet your lover?'

'Yes, I just came from there. It has been a disastrous day. That Satan's aunt, the old woman, came home suddenly and blasted me with such vile accusations that I can't repeat them.'

The two started walking together. Amar told him the entire story.

Salim asked, 'So, now you won't go home. That's very foolish. Let the old woman babble. We will all testify to your good morals. But yaar, you are stupid, what else can I say? One who doesn't know how to charm a scorpion shouldn't be putting his finger in a snake's mouth. That sums you up. I told you many times not to go to her place. Ultimately what I feared has happened. The saving grace was that the old woman didn't summon the neighbourhood, otherwise there would have been bloodshed.'

Amar said philosophically, 'At any rate, whatever happened was for the best. Now I only wish to live in a quiet corner of the world as a farmer. I've seen this world and had enough of it.'

'Where will you go?'

'I don't know. Wherever fate takes me.'

'I could go and explain things to the old woman.'

'It won't be of any use. Perhaps it is my destiny. I've never had happiness, nor probably ever will. If I have to die crying, I could die anywhere.'

'Let's go to my house. We'll get Doctor sahab to come as well, and we'll talk about it together. What is this? An old woman scolds you and you run away from home! I have been reprimanded many times like this, but never taken it to heart.'

'I keep thinking that the old woman will curse Sakina to death.'

'What do you see in her? Why are you so captivated by her?'

Amar, putting his hand on his heart, said, 'Bhai-jaan, what can I say? Sakina is the epitome of grace and loyalty. God alone knows how that jewel came from such miserable surroundings. But the few memorable moments that I have had in my unfortunate life have been spent in her company. All I ask of you is to take care of her. I can't describe to you the turmoil I feel in my heart. I don't know whether I will live or die. I am sitting in a boat, but I don't know where it will take me. I have no idea when or where it may come ashore; very probably it will sink midstream. If I have learned anything from life, it is that there is no just God in this world. One doesn't get what one deserves. In fact, the very opposite happens. We are tied up in chains and can't move even a hand or foot by ourselves. We are given something and then we are told we have to abide by it all our lives! Our dharma tells us that we should honour it as we do our dead ancestors, even though we may hate it. If we want to try a different path in our lives, we are caught by the scruff of our necks and trodden on. This is what the world calls justice. I can't live in this world.'

Salim said, 'You are not going to live forever, so why unnecessarily endanger your life for a trifle. You come from a wealthy family, your father would give his life for you, you have a beautiful wife, and you are running away from it all for the sake of a weaver's daughter. I consider that sheer madness. At the most what will happen is that you may accomplish something, whereas I will not. But the final outcome in both cases will be the same. You will die a Hindu to the chant of *Ram-nam satya*, whereas I will die a Muslim to the call of *Innallah razeoon*.'

Amar said remorsefully, 'If my life had been like yours, perhaps I would also think the same way. I am a tree that was never watered. A human being needs love early on. If a plant is watered when it is a sapling its roots are strong for the rest of its life; but if it does not get its share of moisture, then it withers. My mother died when I was a child, and from then on, I did not receive any love. I have been hungry for that love my entire life. Wherever I find even the least bit of affection, Nature's immutable law irresistibly draws me towards it. If someone calls me guilty for that, he may do so; I consider only God responsible for it.'

So conversing they reached Salim's house.

Salim said, 'Let's eat something. So how long do you intend to remain in exile?'

They went in and sat down. Amar replied, 'Who understands my suffering here? My father doesn't care, he may even be happy that I am no longer around. Sukhada can't even look at me without feeling sorry for herself. Among my friends, you are the only one who matters. We will meet each other once in a while. If my mother were alive, her affection would probably have kept me here. But then my life would not have taken such a turn. One who has lost his mother is the most unfortunate person in the world.'

Remembering his mother, Amar started crying. The image that came to him was one of her picking him up when he cried and how happy he was resting his head in her arms.

Salim went to the inner quarters and quietly sent his servant to Lala Samarkant with the message that Amarkant was running away from home and to come quickly. He commanded him to bring Lala Samarkant back with him immediately and threatened him that if he were even a minute late, he would be shot.

Then, going outside, he kept talking to Amarkant, 'But have you thought what will happen to Sukhada Devi. Don't misunderstand me, but supposing she also meets someone who she feels attracted to?'

Amar, thinking it unlikely, said, 'A Hindu woman would never be that shameless.'

Salim laughed and said, 'So, now we are on to religion. Bhai-jaan, in matters like this, no one is held back because they are Hindu or Muslim. It depends on individual temperament. There are virtuous women as well as prostitutes among both Hindus and Muslims. Also your wife is a modern woman—educated, freethinking, and pleasure loving. She goes to the cinema, and reads newspapers and novels. God save us from such women! They are influenced by European culture. There is hardly anything that these modern women won't do. In former times the man used to take the first step, flirtation used to be initiated by men; now flirtation is started by women.'

Amarkant replied unmoved, 'That may concern those who have some joy in life. It means nothing to one who is sorry to be alive! She can do as she pleases. I am not anyone's slave, nor do I wish to enslave anyone.'

Defeated, Salim said, 'That's the limit! If you think like that, then why shouldn't women think that they can do anything they want! My blood boils at the mere thought of it.'

'Women feel the same anger at the faithlessness of men.'

'Men and women differ in temperament, physical structure, and mental processes. A woman has been made to belong to one man. A man, by contrast, has been made to roam freely.'

'That is man's self-serving rhetoric.'

'No, no, it's a fact of life.'

The discussion kept branching away. The issue of marriage came up, then the problem of unemployment. Finally, food was served and they started eating.

They had just taken a few bites when the gatekeeper announced the arrival of Lala Samarkant. Quickly Amarkant got up, rinsed his mouth, and hid his plate under the table.

'How could he know so quickly? It hasn't been that long yet. The old woman must really have stirred him up.'

Salim was smiling.

Amar said angrily, 'It seems like your doing. You brought me here with this purpose. What good will it do to bring my father here? Will you get anything out of my humiliation? I consider this an act of an enemy, not a friend.'

The tonga stopped at the door and Lala Samarkant entered.

Salim was looking at Lalaji as if to ask whether he should stay in the room or leave. Lalaji, reading his thoughts correctly, said, 'Why are you standing, son, do sit down. Hafizji and I are friends of long standing, you and Amar are like brothers. There are no secrets from you. My son, I have heard everything. The old woman came to me crying. I gave her a thorough scolding. I told her that I didn't believe a word of what she said. Why would a man whose wife looks like the Goddess Laxmi sacrifice his life for a seductress? Don't worry, even if something untoward has happened. Everybody makes mistakes. The old woman will be given three or four hundred rupees; and the girl will be married off in a good family. That will be the end of the matter. You don't need to run away from home and thereby broadcast this news all over town. I am not thinking of myself, but God has blessed you with a wife and child. Just think about how many people would be bereft if you left. Your wife would suffer, your sister would cry herself to death; and then there is Renuka Devi, who moved to this city for the love of you all. If you were not here, she would move away taking Sukhada with her. My house would be ruined and I would be alone like a ghost in that house. Salim beta, tell me, am I saying anything that I shouldn't be? Whatever has happened, has happened; only be careful in the future. You know yourself what is what, what can I tell you? One's natural instincts must be curbed by a sense of duty, otherwise who knows where the fickleness of one's nature might lead. God has given you everything. You can do things at home as well as serve your community. Life is short, you should enjoy it. It is senseless to wander around getting knocked about to no purpose.'

Amar sat through this as if it was a mad man's ramblings. To himself he thought, you have ruined my life and, today, you are trying to ensnare me by flattery. I am in this situation because of you. You have never let me think of your house as mine. You want me to be like an ox who goes around and around in a mill and follows the beaten path. Amar didn't respect his father, rather he knuckled down under him. He felt like interrupting him many times.

No sooner had Lalaji stopped than he said impertinently, 'Dada, my life has been ruined in your house, and I don't want it to be ruined any further. A man's life is not simply about eating and dying, nor is it for accumulating wealth. My situation has become unbearable to me. I am going to start a new life where manual labour is not a shameful thing and where a wife doesn't drag her husband down, but instead brings joy and enlightenment to his life. I don't want to remain a slave to custom and propriety. In your house I would have to fight against these obstacles everyday and that struggle would finish me. Can you say with a truthful heart that there is a place for Sakina in your house?'

Lalaji asked with fear in his eyes, 'What do you mean, in what form?'

'As my wife.'

'No, not once, but a hundred times, no.'

'Then there is no room for me either.'

'You have nothing else to say?'

'No, nothing.'

Lalaji got up from the chair and moved toward the door, then turned around and said, 'Could you tell me where you are going?'

'I have not yet decided.'

'Go, may God bless you. Don't hesitate to write to me should you need anything.'

'I hope that I won't have to cause you pain.'

Lalaji, his eyes brimming with tears, responded, 'My son, don't add insult to injury. A father's heart is inconsolable. At least do this much, write letters once in a while. You may not want to see my face, but please don't stop me from visiting you occasionally. Be happy, wherever you are, I bless you.'

PART 2

CHAPTER 19

❧

Nestling among the northern mountain ranges is a small pleasant village. In the foreground, the river Ganges burbles along like a young maid; laughing, skipping, dancing, and singing. In the background, a high mountain stands like an aged yogi with long hair; calm, serious, and thoughtful. Like the yogi's childhood memory or some golden pleasant dream of his youth, the village is tinged with joy and happiness. He lets those memories slumber in his heart and holds that dream close to his bosom.

The village has no more than twenty to twenty-five huts, constructed of small stones placed one above the other, covered by thatched roofs. The doorways are made of wood and thatch. From time immemorial, people in the village have been living in such pigeonholes with their cows and bullocks, sheep and goats.

One evening, a thin young man of darkish complexion arrived in this village. He was wearing a kurta of coarse fabric, a dhoti to the knees, and cheap shoes. He carried on his shoulder a small metal pail and rope for hauling water from a well, and held a small bundle under his arm. He asked an old woman, 'Mother, would it be possible for a stranger to find accommodation for the night here?'

The old woman had a bundle of firewood on her head and was returning from the pasture urging on an old cow. She took in the young man from head to toe—he was sweaty, his head and face were coated with dust, and he had sunken eyes, as if searching for a refuge in his life. Taking pity, she said, 'Bhaiya, only low caste Chamaars live here!'

Amarkant had been wandering through similar villages for months. He had passed through about fifty small and large villages and become acquainted with numerous people, many of whom had helped him, many others had become his devotees. This delicate young man from the city had lost weight, but he had become hardened to bear hot sun and wind, storm and rain, hunger and thirst. This was the preparation, the penance for his future life. He had been fascinated by the simplicity, generosity, affection, and contentment of the villagers. To see these simple guileless souls being subjected to daily persecution made his blood boil. The peace that he had hoped to find for himself in village life was not found anywhere. Instead he had found injustice everywhere, and Amar was looking for ways to raise the flag of rebellion against that injustice.

Amar said, politely, 'I don't believe in the caste system, Mataji. A Chamaar is worthy of respect if he is honest; whereas a Brahman, if he is deceitful, false, and licentious, is not worthy of respect. Please give me the bundle of wood, let me carry it.'

He took the bundle from the old woman's head and put it on his own. The old woman blessed him and inquired, 'Where are you going, beta?'

'Mata, I am not going anywhere in particular, I just beg and eat. Would it be possible to find a place somewhere to sleep?'

'There is no shortage of places, bhaiya. You may sleep in the temple courtyard. I hope you have not become entangled with some sadhu or saint. One of my boys got caught in their web and has been lost to the world. He would have been the father of several boys by now.'

The two reached the village. The old woman, opening the door to her hut, said, 'Do come in, beta, put the wood down here. You must be tired. Here is some milk to drink. Only this one cow is left, all the others have died. She gives only about a *paav* (eight ounces) of milk every day. She doesn't get enough to eat, how can she produce any more milk?'

Amar couldn't refuse this gift of simple affection. The abject poverty visible in the hut wrenched his heart. He contrasted it with the luxurious living of high society with its bungalow and cars. Why didn't the system that perpetuated such stark contrast come crashing down?

The old woman poured the milk into a brass cup, and picking up a pail started on her way to fetch water. Amar said, 'I will draw water, Mata; the rope must be at the well.'

'No, beta, I can't allow that. You are here for one night, and I should ask you to fetch water!'

The old woman kept saying 'no, no', but Amarkant picked up the pail and started toward the well. She couldn't stay back and followed him.

Several women were at the well waiting to draw water. Seeing Amarkant, one young woman asked, 'Is he your guest, aunt Saloni?'

The old woman laughed, 'If he wasn't a guest, why would he be coming to draw water! Don't you have guests like that come to visit you?'

The young woman, glancing sideways at Amar, said, 'Our guests don't do anything, not even get themselves a glass of water, auntie. I would like to have such a humble guest in our house.'

Amarkant's heart stopped. This young woman was the same Munni who had been acquitted of the murder charge. She was no longer emaciated and anxious. Instead, she was graceful and well proportioned, with a pretty happy face. The essence of life is joy, it doesn't dwell on the past. Munni hadn't recognized Amarkant, however. His appearance had changed so much—the delicate city youth now looked like a village labourer.

Shyly, Amar said, 'I am not a guest, devi, I am a stranger to this village. I happened to come here today, so you may consider me a guest of the entire village.'

The young woman replied smilingly, 'Then you won't be able to get away with filling just one or two pails. You will have to fill two hundred pails, or else give me the pail. Am I not right, auntie?'

She took the pail from Amarkant's hand, quickly put the rope around it, threw it in the well, and in no time at all drew it up.

After Amarkant left with the pail, Munni said to Saloni, 'Auntie, he seems to come from a good family. You saw how shy he was. Do take some pickles from my house. Do you have any flour?'

Saloni said, 'I have some millet flour. Where would I get wheat flour?'

'Then I'll bring you some flour. No, you come with me and get it. I may get involved in other chores and forget to do it.'

Three years ago the son of the village Chaudhary had brought Munni from Haridwar. She was in a bad state and for a week had been lying at the entrance to a *dharmshala*, a house for pilgrims. Well-to-do people used to stay at the dharmshala and would give away hundreds and thousands of rupees in alms, but no one took notice of this poor woman. That young man of Chamaar caste used to go there to sell shoes. He took pity on her, put her on a cart, took her home, and gave her some medication. The Chaudhary was irritated and wondered why he had brought home someone who was nearly dead. The young man looked after her assiduously. There was no doctor of western or ayurvedic medicine nearby, and the villagers relied on blessings or ashes of cow dung smeared over the body for treatment. One day they heard of an occultist who was reputed to bring even dead people to life. The son wanted to get him that very night, but his father said, 'Wait until morning, then go.' The young man didn't listen, and went anyway. The Ganges was in spate and flooding but he thought he could swim across—it was not very wide; he had done it hundreds of times before. So, he confidently entered the water. The current was strong and he lost his foothold. He tried to balance himself, but he was swept away by the current. The next day, his body was found four miles down, caught on a rock. His death coincided with the recovery of Munni and since that time she had remained in the Chaudhary's house. This house was now her house. Here she was respected and regarded. She was a high caste Thakur, but she had forgotten her caste and the customs and conduct that go with it. She was living happily among untouchables as an untouchable. She was the mistress of the house. She attended to all the outside work, while the wives of the two younger brothers attended to the kitchen and other household work. She was not a stranger; instead, she had acquired the role of eldest bahu, the eldest daughter-in-law of the Chaudhary.

Taking Saloni home with her, Munni arranged some flour, pickles, and curd on a platter and offered it to her. Saloni was uncomfortable taking the platter home till after dark because she felt that her guest would be waiting at the door and he would think there wasn't even any flour in her house.

Munni asked, 'What are you thinking, auntie?'

'I am thinking of going only after it has become a bit darker. If he sees me returning with the platter, what would he think?'

'Then I'll take it there. What do you think he will say? Does he think that rich merchants live here! You'll see that he will eat rotis made of millet flour. He won't even touch bread made of wheat.'

The two arrived to see Amarkant sweeping the entrance. It had not been swept for months. It seemed like someone had passed a comb through entangled and stray hair.

Saloni, taking the platter, quickly went inside. Munni remarked, 'If you are going to be this kind of guest, you may never be able to leave.'

She stepped up to Amar and seized the broom from his hand. Amar gathered the rubbish together with his feet and said, 'The entrance looks so much better after it has been swept.'

'When you go away tomorrow, we'll remember you for these things. Who can trust a stranger, but will you ever come this way again?'

Munni's face was downcast.

'If I come this way again, I will certainly visit you. I have never seen a more picturesque village, with a river, a mountain, and a forest. I wish I could just stay here and not think of going anywhere else.'

Munni said eagerly, 'Then why don't you?'

But then after some thought, said, 'There must be other people in your family, why would they let you stay here?'

'There is no one in my family who cares whether I live or die. I am alone in this world.'

Munni said insisting, 'Then do stay here. Who are you, bhai?'

'I have completely forgotten Bhabhi, I don't know anymore. Now anyone who talks to me and feeds me a roti with affection is my brother.'

'Let me visit you tomorrow then. You won't just slip quietly away?'

When Amarkant went inside the hut he saw that the old woman was trying to light the fire in the stove. The wood was wet and the fire wouldn't catch. The shrivelled mouth hadn't strength enough even to blow.

Seeing Amar, she said, 'Why have you come into this smoky room, beta; go sit outside. Take this mat with you.'

Amar came close to the stove and said, 'You move aside, I will light the fire.'

Saloni said in a severe, but affectionate tone, 'Why don't you go outside? It is not proper that men should be in the kitchen.'

The old woman was afraid that Amar might see the two kinds of flour. Perhaps she wanted to impress on him that she also ate wheat flour. Unaware of this, Amar said, 'Alright, give me the flour, I will knead it.'

Saloni said exasperated, 'Bhai, what kind of a boy are you! Why don't you go and sit outside?'

This exchange made her remember the days when her own children would surround her calling 'Amma, Amma' and she would admonish them. In her deserted house, today a lamp was lit; tomorrow there would be the same darkness, the same emptiness. Why was she feeling such affection for this young man? Who knew where he had come from, or where he was headed. But despite this, her parched motherly instincts seemed to be nourished by Amar's guileless, simple childlike behaviour, his repeated forays into the house, and readiness to undertake any work. It seemed as if the echo of her own departed children's voices were coming to her ears from far away.

A child carrying a lantern and a *durrie* on his shoulder came and, putting both things down, sat down near Amar. Amar asked, 'Where is the carpet from?'

'Auntie has sent it for you. The same auntie who was here a short while ago.'

Amar, stroking the child's head affectionately, said, 'Oh, so you are her nephew! Does your aunt ever spank you?'

The child shook his head and said, 'Never. She plays with us. Not with Durjan, though. He is very bad.'

Amar smiled and asked, 'Where do you study?'

Pouting, the child said, 'We are not allowed inside the school. Where can we go, who will teach us? One day, Dada took us both to the school. Panditji wrote down our names, but we were seated away from all the others. The boys teased us, calling us, "Chamaar-Chamaar". So, Dada took us out of the school.'

Amar wanted to meet the Chaudhary. He seemed like a self-respecting man. He asked, 'What is your Dada doing?'

The child, playing with the lantern, said, 'He is sitting with a bottle of liquor and roasted chick-peas. Now he will soon begin to jabber, yell and scream, hit someone, and abuse somebody else. He is usually quiet all day. But the minute he starts drinking, the shouting starts.'

Amar realized it wouldn't be wise to meet him at that time.

Saloni called, 'Bhaiya, rotis are ready. Come and eat while they are hot.'

Amar washed his hands and face and went inside. On a brass plate rotis were arranged, curd in a stone bowl, pickles on a leaf, and water in a metal pitcher. Sitting down in front of the plate, he asked, 'Why don't you also eat?'

'Beta, you eat. I will eat later.'

'No, that I can't allow. You must eat with me.'

'The cooked food would be defiled, wouldn't it?'

'It doesn't matter. I am the only one eating with you.'

'God resides in cooked food. It shouldn't be defiled.'

'Then I will not eat either.'

'Bhai, you are a very troublesome boy.'

There were no other plates in the kitchen, so Saloni took the millet rotis in her hand and left the cooking area. Amar saw the millet rotis and said, 'I won't have this, auntie. You have given me thin, puffed up rotis of wheat, while you have taken the delicious rotis yourself.'

'Beta, you can't eat millet rotis! You're here for one day and I should feed you millet rotis!'

'Don't think of me as a guest. Just imagine that your lost son has come back.'

'Even that boy would be treated as a guest the first day. What kind of hospitality would that be, offering you plain rotis? There is neither liquor, nor game.'

'I don't even touch liquor or game, auntie.'

Amarkant didn't want the old woman to feel badly, so he didn't insist on having millet rotis. They started eating. Presently, the old woman spoke, 'Youth is the time for eating and drinking, beta, not for being a saint! Being pious and abstaining from meat and intoxicating drinks is for the elderly.'

'Auntie, I am not pious. I just don't like meat or drink.'

'Your mother and father must have been holy people.'

'Yes, both were holy.'

'Both are still living, aren't they?'

'My mother is dead. Dada is still alive. I don't get along with him.'

'So, annoyed, you have run away from home.'

'We had a disagreement about something, so I left.'

'You have a wife at home, don't you?'

'Yes, I do.'

'The poor woman must be crying her eyes out. Do you ever write her a letter or send her a note?'

'She doesn't much care for me, auntie. She is a girl from a wealthy family, and her comforts and luxury mean more to her. I said, "We should go to some village and become farmers, but she likes city life more".'

After Amarkant had finished eating, he took the plate and going outside, started washing it. Saloni followed him and said, 'Would it have been demeaning for me to have washed your plate?'

Amar laughed and said, 'Well, would I be demeaned if I washed my own plate?'

'It doesn't seem right that one should be a guest for a day and wash one's own plate. You must be wondering—why did I stay at this beggar woman's?'

But she smiled as she said it, lest it hurt Amarkant.

Amar was enchanted and said, 'Auntie, your simple, pure affection has given me such happiness as can't be obtained anywhere other than in a mother's arms.'

He washed the plate and put it away and, after spreading the cotton carpet on the ground, was about to lie down when a group of fifteen to twenty boys came up. Except for two or three boys, all were scantily clad. Curious about them, Amarkant sat up wondering if some show was about to be performed. The boy who had brought the carpet stepped forward and said, 'Almost all the boys in our village are here, only two or three didn't come because they were afraid you might cut off their ears.'

Amarkant got up, stood them in a row and asked everyone's name. Then said, 'Which of you wash your hands and face everyday? Raise your hands.'

None of the boys raised his hand. They didn't understand the question.

Surprised, Amar said, 'What, none of you washes his hands and face every day?'

They all looked at each other. The boy who had brought the carpet raised his hand. Seeing him, others raised their hands also.

Amar asked again, 'Which of you bathe everyday? Raise your hands.'

At first, no one raised his hand. Then, one after the other, they all raised their hands. Not because they all bathed everyday, but because they didn't want to be left behind.

Saloni was standing there. She said, 'Oh, Jangalia, you don't bathe even once a month; why are you raising your hand?'

Jangalia felt insulted and said, 'So Goodar doesn't bathe everyday either. Bhulai, Punnoo, Ghasite, none of them bathe.'

All of them started telling tales on each other.

Amar rebuked them, 'Alright, don't fight amongst yourselves. I will ask one thing, you reply. Is it a good thing to wash your hands and face everyday, or is it not?'

All said, 'It is a good thing.'

'And bathing?'

All said, 'It is good too.'

'Do you say it from the heart or are you just mouthing it?'

'From the heart.'

'Alright, go now. I will be back in a few days and then I'll see who has spoken the truth and who hasn't.'

When the boys had gone, Amar lay down. He was tired of his continuous wandering for the last three months. He wanted to rest a while. He thought—why shouldn't I stay in this village? Who knows me here? He imagined constructing a small house where he lived with Sakina and they had cows and bullocks. Finally he fell asleep.

CHAPTER 20

Amarkant got up in the morning, bathed in the Ganges, and went to meet the Chaudhary whose name was Goodar. There was no landlord living in this village. So, Goodar's frontyard served as the *chaupal* of the village. Amar noticed a wooden platform under the neem tree. There were also two or three bamboo cots covered with straw cushions. Goodar was about sixty years old, but was still quite robust. His older son, Payag, was sitting in front of him sewing a shoe. The second son, Kashi, was looking after the feed and water for the bullocks. Munni was shovelling out the cow dung. Teja and Durjan, the grandchildren, were running to get water from the well. Off to the side, Goodar's two daughter's-in-law were scrubbing pots and pans.

Amar greeted the Chaudhary and sat down on a straw cushion. The Chaudhary welcomed him in a fatherly way, 'Sit comfortably on the cot, Bhaiya. Munni told me about you last night. You are not leaving today, are you? Stay for three or four days, then you can go. Munni was saying that you might stay if you could find some work.'

Amar said hesitantly, 'Yes, something like that had crossed my mind.'

Goodar was smoking a hand-held water pipe made of coconut shell. Exhaling smoke, he said, 'There is no lack of work here. Even if you cut grass you can earn a rupee a day; otherwise, there is leatherwork. You can make soles for shoes, or leather buckets for drawing water. One who is willing to work hard doesn't die of hunger, it is only lazy people who don't get anywhere.'

Seeing that Amar didn't take to either of the two propositions, he suggested a third one, 'You can do farming if you wish. Saloni bhabhi has fields, you can till them.'

Payag said, using the awl, 'Farming is a tricky business, bhaiya, avoid it. It doesn't matter whether your field produces anything or not, as a tenant farmer you still have to pay the rent. You are faced with one or other calamity all the time, hail or frost, drought or flood. On top of that, if your bullock dies or the crop catches fire, you lose everything. The best alternative is to cut grass. You are no one's servant or lackey, you don't borrow from or lend to anyone. You take your sickle to cut the grass in the morning, and by early afternoon you are back at home.'

Kashi piped up, 'Labour and farming can't be compared. A labourer may be rich, but he will still be called a labourer. He is at the beck and call of everyone. He may be walking down the road carrying a load of grass on his head when someone may call from this side or that—"O, Grass cutter!" Also, you get cursed and abused if you happen to cut grass on the boundary of someone's field. Farming is much more respectable.'

Payag's awl ceased, 'Respect be damned. Farming is a bottomless pit in which whatever you earn from any source gets swallowed up.'

Chaudhary rendered judgment, 'There is loss and gain in every business, bhaiya. Even the big and wealthy merchants go bankrupt. There is no occupation like farming provided your earnings and luck hold out. Do you have the custom of giving gifts and presents to your landlord where you come from, bhaiya?'

Amar said, 'Yes, Dada, it is the same everywhere, more or less. They all suck the blood of the poor.'

Chaudhary said, 'I can't understand why God differentiated between poor and rich. After all, they are all His children. Why doesn't He treat them the same?'

Payag, opined dogmatically, 'It is the result of previous incarnation. As one has acted in his former life, so shall he reap in the present one.'

Chaudhary objected, 'All this wisdom is just to make the poor reconcile to their lot, beta, so that the pleasures of the rich are not curtailed in any way. But is it just that even our children have to work, and still don't have enough to eat; whereas every government official gets a salary of ten thousand rupees? So much miney that even a mule can't carry.'

Amar said smilingly, 'Dada, you are just an atheist!'

Chaudhary said humbly, 'Beta, you may call me an atheist or a fool, but when you are hurt to the core, you have to express your pain. You must be an educated man?'

'Yes, I have studied a bit.'

'You have not read English, have you?'

'Yes, I have studied some English too.'

Chaudhary was pleased and said, 'Then, bhaiya, we won't let you go. Call your family and stay here and teach our children. Then they will be able to go to the city where no one cares about your caste and community. They will simply declare there that they are Kshatriyas.'

Amar smiled, 'And if it comes out in the end?'

Chaudhary was ready with an answer, 'Then we will say our ancestors were Kshatriyas although we are a bit ashamed to call ourselves so. We have heard that the Kshatriyas gave away their daughters in marriage to Muslim kings. You mustn't have had any breakfast, bhaiya. Teja, where are you? Go get some breakfast from bahu. Bhaiya, ask for His blessing and do stay here. Saloni has three or four *bighas*. You can share about two bighas with us. That will be enough for farming. God willing, you won't lack anything to eat.'

But when Saloni was called and the Chaudhary put this proposition before her, she balked, and said severely, 'Your intention is that I should register my land in his name and that I should just starve. Isn't that right?'

Chaudhary laughed and said, 'No, no. The land will stay in your name, you nincompoop! He will only till the land. Just imagine that you are sharing it with him.'

Saloni, not listening, replied, 'Bhaiya, I won't register my land in anyone else's name. This way he is our guest. He may stay here for a while. I will serve and welcome him to the best of my ability. If you want to do crop sharing with him, do so. But how can I give someone, whom I have never seen nor have heard of before and whom I don't know, a half-share of my land?'

Payag looked at the Chaudhary disdainfully and said, 'Are you satisfied now? You say women are foolish. Aunt Saloni is so sharp she could sell off both you and me in the blinking of an eye. She only talks sweetly.'

Saloni bristled, 'Oh, yes, just because you say so, I should abandon the land of my ancestors. I thought you wished me well, but here you are trying to cut my throat.'

Kashi sided with Saloni, 'She is right. How can she hand over her land to someone she does not know and has never heard of?'

Amarkant was amused. He smiled and said, 'Yes, auntie, you are perfectly right. How can one trust a stranger?'

Munni was standing in the doorway and listening to everything. She said, 'Auntie, have you gone mad? Will anyone carry away your fields on his head? We are here. Don't you think we would intervene if someone tries to defraud you?'

A cornered animal goaded by a crowd becomes even more agitated. Saloni was sure that they were all colluding to rob her. Having once said no, she couldn't say yes. She left in a hurry. Payag said, 'She is a witch, a witch.'

Amar said, abashed, 'Dada, you spoke to her needlessly. It is immaterial to me whether I stay in this village or some other village.'

Munni's face paled.

Goodar said, 'No, bhaiya, what a thing to say! You stay here and be a shareholder with me. I will speak to Mahantji and arrange for you to have another two to four bighas of land. You will have your own hut and no worries about food or drink. At least there will be an educated man in the village. As it is, everybody gets nervous and frightened whenever a *chaprasi* comes to the village.

In half an hour Saloni returned and said to Chaudhary, 'Why don't you take my fields for sharecropping?'

Chaudhary snorted and said, 'I don't want them. You keep your fields.'

Saloni appealed to Amar, 'Bhaiya, tell me, did I say anything untoward? Does anyone give his possessions to one he has never known or heard of?'

Amar consoled her, 'Auntie, you did perfectly right. Trusting in this manner leads to betrayal.'

Saloni was a little comforted, 'I have known you only since last night, beta. Isn't that so? The person who has my fields these days is a relative of mine. If I take the land away from him and give it to you, what would he say? If you think I am saying anything wrong, you may slap my face. I know he cheats me but, after all, he is my flesh and blood. Tell me, would you think well of me if I were to seize bread from his mouth and give it to you?'

Whether Saloni had thought of this argument on her own, or whether someone else had suggested it was immaterial, but it left Goodar without argument.

CHAPTER 21

Two months went by.

The cold night in the month of Poos was covered in a dark blanket. The tall mountain, standing like some grand and important design, was wearing a crown of stars. The huts scattered below were like small yearnings that he had rejected.

A lantern was burning in Amarkant's hut. The school was in session. Fifteen to twenty boys were standing listening to the story of Abhimanyu. Amar was standing, narrating the story. All the boys were happy. Their pale faces and eyes were shining. Perhaps they, too, were dreaming of being as brave and dutiful as Abhimanyu. How could they know that one day they would have to bow before Duryodhans and Jarasandhs, the evil kings of this world. How many times would they try to escape the enemy soldiers arranged in circles, only to find they couldn't.

Chaudhary Goodar was sitting in the chaupal with his keys and alcohol, lost in thought. Then he threw away the keys, put the bottle back in the alcove, and calling Munni, said, 'Tell Amar bhaiya to come and eat his dinner. This good man never seems to get hungry; even at this late hour he is oblivious to food.'

Munni, looking at the bottle, said, 'I didn't call him so you could finish your drinking.'

Goodar said, indicating a distate for the liquor, 'Tonight I don't feel like drinking, beti. It is not a good thing.'

Munni stared at the Chaudhary in astonishment. It had been more than three years since she had come, she had never seen Chaudhary miss his drink or heard any talk of aversion to it. Getting worried, she said, 'Are you not feeling well today, Dada?'

Chaudhary laughed and said, 'Why wouldn't I be well? I bought it for my pleasure, but now I don't feel like drinking it. What Amar bhaiya said registered with me today—in a country where eighty per cent of people die of starvation, drinking liquor is like drinking the blood of the poor. If somebody else had said it, I wouldn't have paid any attention, but what he says somehow hits you in the gut.'

Munni got worried, 'Dada, you shouldn't listen to him. Giving it up now may harm you. You may develop aches in your body.'

Chaudhary dismissed these misgivings and said, 'I may have pains, or may develop rheumatism, but I am not going to drink anymore. In this life I have drunk away thousands of rupees worth of liquor. All my earnings have been frittered away in drinks. Had I used that money for some charitable work the village would have benefited and I would have had some acclaim. I have been a fool and a bad person. English officers, I have heard, drink a lot; but they are a class of their own, they are the rulers here, their money comes from robbing us; if they didn't drink, then who would? Have you noticed that Kashi and Payag are beginning to like reading and writing?'

School was over. Amar, holding Teja and Durjan's hands, came and said, 'I am late today, Dada; haven't you had your drink and dinner?'

Chaudhary was overwhelmed with affection, 'Yes, of course, I have been hard at work since early evening; I took some shoes to Rishikesh! If you are going to kill yourself doing all this work, then I will have to close down your school.'

Girls were also attending Amar's school now. His happiness knew no bounds.

After dinner, Chaudhary went to sleep. Amar was getting up to go when Munni said, 'Lala, you won a great victory today! Dada, didn't take even one drop of liquor.'

Amar jumped up ecstatically, 'Did he say anything?'

'He was singing your praises, of course. I thought he would quit drinking only when he died, but what you said to him seems to have worked!'

For several days Amar had been wanting to ask Munni how she had reached here, but had had no occasion. Today, taking the opportunity, he said to her, 'You haven't recognized me, but I know who you are.'

Munni's face lost all its colour. Looking at Amar searchingly, she said, 'Now that you mention it, I also seem to remember that I have seen you somewhere.'

'Think back to the court case in Kashi.'

'Oh yes, now I remember. You used to go around collecting money with Doctor sahab. Why are you here?'

'I had a quarrel with my father. How about you, how did you come to be here with these people?'

Munni, entering the house, said, 'I will tell you some other time, but I beg of you not to say anything to anyone here.'

Going to his hut, Amar got out a pair of dhotis from under the bedding, and went to Saloni's house. Saloni was lying inside singing herself to sleep. When she heard Amar's voice, she got up and opened the door and said, 'What is it, beta? It is very dark tonight. Have you had your dinner? I was spinning yarn on the wheel. My back began to ache, so I lay down.'

Taking out the dhotis Amar said, 'I have brought these for you, please take them.' Then added, 'I will accept your yarn as payment when you have finished spinning it.'

Saloni was feeling embarrassed for having doubted Amar some time back. How could she have doubted such a good man? Ashamed, she said, 'Why are you giving them to me now, bhaiya? You could have given them to me when I had finished spinning the yarn.'

Amar held the lantern. The old woman took the pair and opening the folds, looked at them covetously. Suddenly she said, 'There are two of them, beta! What will I do with two? You should take one back.'

Amarkant said, 'You keep both of them, auntie! How can you make do with just one?'

Saloni had never had two saris in her life before. Even while her husband and son were alive and she was well to do, she had never had more than one dhoti. And today she was getting, no, being forced to accept, these two beautiful saris! She was swept with a wave of affection for Amar, and blessed him maternally with every fibre of her being.

Amarkant left, while Saloni wept tears of joy.

Going back to his own hut, Amar was undecided what to do, then sat down to write in his diary. At the same time, the door to Chaudhary's house opened and Munni came out with a metal pail to fetch water. Seeing a light in Amar's house she headed towards it and arriving at the door said, 'You're not sleeping yet, Lala. It is quite late.'

Amar coming outside, said, 'Yes, sleep has eluded me so far. Isn't there any water in the house?'

'No, all the water is finished. If anyone gets thirsty, there isn't a drop to drink in the house.'

'I will go and fetch it. You shouldn't be out alone in this dark night.'

'People in the city are afraid of the dark. We are villagers.'

'No, Munni, I won't let you go.'

'Is my life more precious than yours?'

'It is worth a hundred thousand times mine.'

Munni looked at him lovingly and said, 'Why didn't God make you a woman, Lala? I have never seen a man with such a tender heart. Sometimes I think, Lala, it would have been better if you hadn't come here.'

Amar smiled 'Have I done something wrong, Munni?'

Munni said in a trembling voice, 'No, you have done no wrong wilfully. But is it not wrong to give an orphan child sweets and toys when he has no one to love him? How is he to go back to leading a deprived existence after those treats?'

Amar said compassionately, 'It is me who is the orphan, Munni. You have given me love and affection while I have been nothing but a burden to you.'

Munni put the pail down and said, 'I can't win an argument with you, but I will tell you this that I was very content before you came. I did the household chores, ate whatever coarse, tasteless food there was, and slept. You have robbed me of that contentment. You must be thinking what a shameless woman I am. But when a man acts like a woman, then a woman will have to act like a man. I know that you avoid me. I also know that I can't have you, I'm not that fortunate. But I won't let you go. I don't want anything from you except that you consider me one of your family. Then I will know that there is someone to take care of me and that my life as a woman has been worthwhile.'

Amar had so far looked at Munni in the fashion that every young man looks at a beautiful woman—not with love, but with the thought of making love but he was shaken by this self-surrender. Men are thrilled to see the full udders of a milch cow, anticipating the amount of milk. They are not prepared to catch the cow and milk it, but it is a different story if the milk is given to them in a cup.

Amar extended his hand towards the cup of milk, 'Let's you and I go some place, Munni. I will tell them there that this is my . . .'

Munni put her hand over his mouth and said, 'Stop, don't say anything else. All men are the same. You completely misunderstood me. I don't want to marry you, I won't be your kept-woman either. It is enough for me that you consider me your servant.'

Munni picked up the pail and walked off toward the well. Amar was astonished at this revelation of the feminine heart.

Munni called out, 'Lala, I have some fresh water. Shall I bring a pitcherful?'

Even though he wanted a drink, Amar said, 'I am not thirsty just yet, Munni.'

CHAPTER 22

❦

Amar had not written a letter to anyone for three months as he had had no free time. He was pining for some news of Sakina, and he also thought about Naina—the poor girl must be crying herself to death. The laughing, flower-like face of his son kept coming to him all the time. But how could he have written to them when he hadn't stayed in any one place for long and when he hadn't known where he was going to be the next day. Some time after coming to this village he wrote three letters; one each to Sakina, Salim, and Naina. He had enclosed Sakina's letter in the envelope for Salim. Today the postman had delivered the replies. Amar went to a lonely spot on the bank of the Ganges to read the letters. He didn't want to be interrupted by village boys who might ask who the letters were from.

Naina wrote, 'At long last you have remembered me. I never thought that you would be so unrelenting. You and I are different; so you can't imagine how hard it has been for me living here without you. Four and a half months have gone by and there has been no letter from you, no news of you. I can't tell you how many tears I have shed. Except for crying, what have you left me here to do! I didn't realize that my life would be so empty without you.

'I understand why you have been silent for so long; it is because you have a misconception about our relationship. You are my brother, my hero. If you are a king, you are my brother; if you are destitute, you are still my brother. The world may laugh at you, you may be reviled in the whole country, but you are my brother. If today you convert to Islam or Christianity, wouldn't you still be my brother? Can you break the relationship that God has ordained? I don't think you are that strong. I don't believe that there is any other relationship in the world that is so dear. A mother has love for her child. I don't know what a sister has, but it is certainly more tender than the love for a child. A mother punishes a transgression, but a sister is forgiveness personified. The brother may be just or unjust to her, rebuke or love her, hold her in esteem or insult her, but the sister has nothing for him except forgiveness. She only hungers for his affection.

'Ever since you left, I haven't wanted to glance at books even. I just keep crying. I don't feel like doing anything. The spinning wheel has also been abandoned. The only joy I have is Munnu. He is the garland around my neck! He doesn't leave me even for a moment. Now he is asleep, so I am able to write this letter; otherwise, he would have been writing in his baby hieroglyphics which even the most learned scholars wouldn't have been able to decipher. Bhabhi is not as affectionate to him now as she used to be. She doesn't mention you even by mistake. She has become especially fond of religious discourse and devotion. She talks less to me as well. Renuka Devi wanted to take her to Lucknow, but she didn't go there. One day Renuka Devi hosted a feast for thousands of religious people from the city to celebrate the mating of her cow. We also attended the feast. She has bequeathed ten thousand rupees to the local home for cows.

'Now let me tell you about our father. These days Dada is busy having a *thakurdwara* constructed. He had purchased the land earlier; now the building stones are being collected. Raja sahab will be invited to lay the foundation stone of the temple. I don't know why, Dada is never angry with anyone anymore. He doesn't even raise his voice. He, who used to throw his plate if the daal was even a bit salty, now doesn't even say a word, no matter how much salt has been put in. I hear he is not as strict with his tenants either. He intends to pardon the outstanding debts of many tenants the day the foundation stone is laid. Instead of five rupees, Pathanin now gets twenty-five rupees per month. There are many other things to tell you, but I won't write more now. If you come here, come disguised, because people here are mad at you. No one comes to our house any more.'

The second letter was from Salim. 'I thought that you had drowned in the Ganges. So, with the aid of onions, I shed a few tears in your name and, for the salvation of your soul, even donated a *kauri* shell to a brahman; but I was saddened to learn that you are alive and my mourning was to no purpose. I am not sorry about the tears—after all the eyes benefited somewhat, but I am certainly sorry about losing that kauri. My good man, how could you be silent for five whole months! The only thing that saves you is that you are not here. You pride yourself on being a great servant of the community. How can a man who is so faithless to his friends serve his community?

'I swear by God, I remember you everyday. I go to college, but my heart is not in it. With your departure, the enchantment of college has also gone. On the other hand, my *abba-jaan* keeps pestering me about the Civil Service. Do you ever intend to come back or are you determined to stay banished for life?

'College is as usual—the same card games, the same cutting lectures, the same cricket matches. But, yes, the convocation address was good. The Vice Chancellor emphasized simple living. You would have enjoyed the address, had you been here. I thought it was kind of dull. Everyone lectures about plain living, but nobody leads by example. Are these countless lecturers and professors examples of simple living? Of course not, they all live life well. Then why wouldn't the students also want a high standard of life? I can't understand why the Vice Chancellor doesn't lecture his staff on simple living. Professor Bhatia has thirty pairs of shoes, some worth as much as fifty rupees. But leave him aside. Professor Chakravarty is known for his parsimony. He has no family, but do you know how many servants he has? A total of twelve! So, bhai, we who are young, desire new products and new styles. We will ask our parents for them, if they don't give them we will quarrel with them, get loans from our friends, or flatter the shopkeepers, but we will certainly get them and live in style. The teachers are going to hell, we will go there too, but after them.

'You want some news of Sakina, don't you? We sent them clothing and money so many times through the ayah, but they didn't accept anything. The ayah understood that Sakina eats just half or one chapatti throughout the day, otherwise, she just lies around listlessly. She doesn't speak to her grandmother. I sent your letter to her the minute I received it yesterday. Her reply is reproduced below verbatim. You will get to see the original only when you come here.

'Babuji, I am very sorry that I have caused you so much suffering. What else can I say! I live only to I remember you. My only wish is that I see you once before I die, but even that will bring disgrace to you. I, of course, have already been disgraced. I received your letter yesterday, Since then I have considered so many times whether or not I should come to you. Would you be angry if I did? I don't think so. But when I think about it, I know that I will probably never come. For some time, I was so angry that I didn't open your letter, but how long could that go on? I opened the letter, read it, and cried; read it again and again cried. Crying is so pleasant that one never gets sated with it. I can hardly bear the anguish of waiting for you. May God keep you well.'

Salim continued, 'See, how painful this letter is! I don't cry very often, but when I was reading her letter I couldn't control myself. You are very fortunate.'

When Amar raised his head, he was intoxicated—an intoxication that didn't dull, but invigorated the senses; that didn't result in blurred, but clear vision; that didn't lead to stupor or oblivion, but to awareness. He had never had such a shattering revelation. His soul had never felt such compassion, such grandeur, or such joy. He imagined Sukhada and Sakina as two statues in front of him. Sukhada immersed in luxury, bedecked with jewels and full of pride, and Sakina adorned with simple grace, her head bowed in well-bred humility. His thirsty heart was drawn toward the cool water offered by Sakina and away from the fragrant *sharbat* presented by Sukhada. He reread Sakina's letter. Agitated, he started pacing along the bank of the Ganges. How could he meet Sakina? Would she like this village life? She was so delicate and tender—how would she be able to lead such a harsh life? How could he persuade her to come to him? He remembered her face when she said—'Babuji, I am also coming.' Oh! What tender affection! He was sorry that he hadn't insisted that she do so. He had been like a foolish labourer who finds a jewel while digging, and in his ignorance mistakes it for a piece of glass.

'My only wish is that I see you once before I die.' This stuck to his heart. He imagined he was swimming on the waves of the Ganges searching for Sakina. He was so immersed in gazing at the waves, he felt as if he were being carried by them. Startled out of his dream, he started walking towards his house; his eyes were moist and his cheeks were wet.

Chapter 23

One of the village men had become engaged. There was dancing, singing, and feasting to celebrate the occasion. At his doorstep, small drums were being played. All the village was assembled there, and dancing had begun. Amar's school was closed, and he had been dragged to the festivities.

Payag said, 'Come, Bhaiya, give us a performance. We hear that people in your part of the world dance a lot.'

Amar, begging to be excused, said, 'Bhai, I don't know how to dance.' He wished that he knew, so he could dazzle everyone present.

Young men and women were dancing in pairs. Each pair danced along for ten to fifteen minutes. Amar had never understood the excitement and pleasure of dancing.

A young woman, pulling further the veil that covered her face, stepped on the stage. Payag joined her and the two began dancing. People were enchanted with the young woman's graceful movements that so accurately mirrored her emotions.

A second couple followed this pair. The man was a sturdy youth with a gold coin hanging on his broad chest. He wore a loincloth wrapped round his hips and thighs and tucked in at the waist. Amar was startled when he recognized the young woman as Munni. She was wearing a *lehanga*, with a rose-coloured veil covering her face, and she had tied tiny bells around her ankles. Her cheeks glowed like two rose petals. The two were caught in the frenzy of dancing. They would touch each other's hands, then move their hands to their waists, and follow the beat with a coquettish sway of their hips. Entranced, everyone watched the elegant craft of these two artists. What agility, what flexibility! Every swing and movement of their bodies expressed deep understanding of each other and complete obliviousness to their surroundings. Touching each other's hands and quickly moving their feet, the two danced their way to the end of the stage never missing a beat.

Payag said, 'Look, Bhaiya, Bhabhi is dancing so well. She has no competition.'

Amar said in a detached tone, 'Yes, I am watching.'

'If you want to dance, get ready; I will call that boy away.'

'No, I am not going to dance.'

Munni was still dancing when Amar got up and went home. He couldn't bear such shameful behaviour.

Within moments Munni followed him and said, 'Why did you leave, Lala? Didn't you like my dancing?'

Amar said turning his face away, 'Do you think I am a man who sees evil in good things?'

Munni said coming closer, 'Then why did you leave?'

Pretending to be sorry, Amar said, 'I have to go to a Panchayat meeting. People are probably waiting for me there. Why did you stop dancing?'

Munni said simply, 'Whom would I dance for if you aren't there?'

Amar said, gazing into her eyes, 'Munni, are you being honest with me?'

Munni, looking straight into his eyes, said, 'I have never lied to you.'

'Then do one thing for me. Please don't dance any more.'

Munni, replied sadly, 'So you were displeased with a little thing like that. Just ask anyone how long it has been since I danced. I have not been near the drums for two years. People tried to persuade me but to no avail. I went there only for you and now you are angry with me!'

Munni went home. A little while later, Kashi came to call her, 'Bhabhi, what are you doing here? Everybody is asking for you at the dance.'

Munni pretended to have a headache.

Kashi went to Amar and said, 'Why did you leave, Bhaiya? Perhaps you didn't like the singing and dancing of the villagers?'

Amar said, 'No, no, nothing of the kind. I have to go to a Panchayat meeting, and I am going to be late.'

Kashi said, 'Bhabhi is not going back either. After seeing her dance, the other dancers seem very dull. If you ask her, she might change her mind. Such community celebrations are rare. If we don't go people will say that when there is a celebration we avoid going.'

Amar was caught in a moral dilemma, 'You didn't explain this to her?'

Then, going to her courtyard, he called to her, 'You are angry with me, Munni.'

Munni came out into the yard and said, 'Who is angry, you or I?'

'Alright, I am asking you to come.'

'You are playing with me, Lala, the way cats play with mice. You make me cry or laugh whenever you wish.'

'Please forgive me. I made a mistake in leaving the dance, Munni.'

'Lala, now I will only dance when you hold my hand and say—"Come, let us dance." I am not going to dance with anyone else.'

'Then I will have to learn to dance.'

Munni sensing victory said, 'If you wish to dance with me, then you will learn.'

'Will you teach me?'

'You are teaching me to cry, so I will teach you to dance.'

'Alright, let's go.'

At college functions, Amar had taken part in several plays. He had even danced and sung on stage; but there was a world of difference between that dancing and this. The college dances had been amorous dalliances of sensuous people, whereas this was the spontaneous frolic of working people. He felt himself incapable of such uninhibited dancing.

He said, 'Munni, I have to ask you for a gift.'

Munni paused and said, 'You don't want to dance?'

'Yes, that's the favour I ask.'

Munni turned back towards her house while Amar kept calling out, 'Wait! Wait!'

Amar then returned to his hut and, after changing, went to the Panchayat. He was gaining the respect of people. Whenever there was a Panchayat meeting in the neighbouring villages, he was invariably invited.

CHAPTER 24

❦

There had been an influx of boys into the school and the one small room in Amar's hut was proving insufficient to hold them all. No one had asked Saloni for a place, nor had any pressure been put on her. One day Amar and Chaudhary were sitting together and discussing where to build a new school—in the village itself there wasn't enough room even to tie up the bullocks—when Saloni, who had been listening to the conversation, piped up, 'Why don't you take my house? About twenty paces behind my house, there is some vacant land. Won't that much land do for you?'

Both men gaped at Saloni in astonishment.

Amar asked, 'And where would you live, auntie?'

Saloni said, 'Oh! What do I need a house and grounds for, beta! A corner in your hut would do for me.'

Goodar did a mental calculation and said, 'There would be plenty of space alright.'

Amar shook his head, 'I don't want to take auntie's house. I'll meet Mahantji and we will plan to have a school built outside the village.'

Auntie was hurt 'What is the matter, Bhaiya? Is my place contaminated by my touch?'

Goodar decided the issue. Auntie's house would be taken over for the school. A room would be added to it for Amar to live in. Auntie would move into Amar's hut. In one corner of the hut, the cow and bullock would be tied; in another corner, she would sleep.

Saloni was happier with this decision than she had ever been before. The old woman who would pick a quarrel with anyone who tied their livestock in front of her house, and who wouldn't let children play marbles in front of her door, today, after donating her ancestral home to the school, considered her life justified. It may seem contradictory, but only the miserly can be charitable. But, of course, the recepient of the charity must be worthy of the wealth that has been accumulated through sweat and tears.

Construction started immediately. Lumber was gathered from homes, and rope, money and labour were all donated without anyone having to be asked. This was their school where their boys and girls were to be educated. And in the past six or seven months the children had shown some positive effects of their education. By and large they were cleaner, told fewer lies, made fewer false excuses, swore less often, and did not steal things from home. And they were not as obstinate as before. Whatever needed to be done at home, they did with pleasure. Who would not be supportive of such a school?

The cool dawn of the month of Phagun, wearing golden clothes, was playing on the mountaintop. Amar and several boys had just returned from a bath in the Ganges. But today no one seemed to be working. What was the matter? On other days when he returned from his bath craftsmen were already at work. It was so late today, and yet nobody was about.

Just then, Munni arrived with a pitcher of water on her head. The same cool, golden light of dawn was playing on her fair face.

Amar smiled and said, 'See, the Sun god is staring at you.'

Munni taking down the water pitcher and holding it in her hands, said, 'And there you stand happily, doing nothing!'

After a moment she said, 'It seems as if you don't live in the village any more. We hardly ever see you now that the school is being constructed. I am afraid that you might drive yourself crazy working so hard.'

'I am here all day but what about you? I don't know where you are! Where has everyone gone today? No one has come.'

'There is no one in the village?'

'Where has everybody gone?'

'What! You haven't heard? Early last night a cow belonging to the Thakur of Siromanpur died. Everyone has gone to the Thakur's house. Tonight meat will be cooked in all the houses in this village.'

Amar said in a disgusted tone, 'A dead cow?'

'It's eaten in our house too.'

'I didn't know. I never noticed. You ...'

Munni, making a disgusted face, said, 'I don't even glance at it.'

'You don't explain to them why they shouldn't be eating such meat?'

'Oh, they won't listen to reason, especially coming from me!'

Because of his traditional upbringing as a devotee of Vishnu, Amarkant felt revolted. He was truly nauseated. He had rid himself of former prejudices about untouchability and other caste differences, but he still felt the old loathing about forbidden foods. And to think that he had been eating food cooked in the homes of these carrion eaters for the last ten or eleven months!

'I won't eat today, Munni.'

'I will cook your food separately.'

'No, Munni. I cannot eat in a house where that thing will be cooked.'

Suddenly, hearing loud noises, Amar raised his eyes to see fifteen or twenty men coming his way carrying the dead cow on bamboo staves. In front were several boys jumping up and down and clapping in glee.

It was such a dreadful sight! Amar couldn't bear to watch, and he started to run toward the banks of the Ganges.

Munni said, 'What will be accomplished by running away? If you feel badly, then go and make them understand.'

'Who will listen to me, Munni?'

'If they don't listen to you, then who would they listen to, Lala?'

'And if no one accepts what I say?'

'And if they do! Come on, let's make a bet.'

'Alright, what do you bet?'

'If they accept, then you will bring me a good sari.'

'And if they don't, then what will you give me?'

'One kauri shell.'

In the interim, the people had come much closer. Chaudhary was charging ahead of the group like a commander-in-chief.

Munni stepped up and said, 'I see you are bringing the dead cow, but Lala is leaving.'

Goodar asked curiously, 'Why! What has happened?'

'It is the same old thing about eating dead cows. He says he won't even drink water from your hands.'

Payag said defiantly, 'Let him go on. If he doesn't drink water from our hands, it won't lower us any.'

Kashi said, 'We have meat today, after such a long time. And now, there is this obstacle.'

Goodar said in an attempt to settle things, 'Well, what does he say?'

Munni replied exasperatedly, 'Why don't you go ask him? Why do we continue to eat what the upper castes won't touch? That is why people consider us low caste.'

Payag, responded agitatedly, 'So what? We don't look for matches for our daughters in the homes of Brahmans and Thakurs. We also don't go begging for alms at any door like Brahmans do. Different people have different customs.'

Munni rebuked him, 'Is it a good thing that we are considered low caste by everyone because of what we eat?'

The cow was put down. Two or three people ran to get a meat cleaver. Amar noticed that Munni was trying to stop them but nobody was listening. He turned away afraid that he might vomit. Even though he was no longer looking, the sight kept floating before his eyes. How could he ignore the fact that fifty steps away from him a dead cow was being hacked to pieces? He fled towards the Ganges.

Goodar, seeing him headed toward the Ganges, said worriedly, 'He is indeed running away. He is a very resolute man. I'm afraid he might drown himself.'

Payag said, 'You do your job. Nobody is going to drown himself. No one's life is that onerous.'

Munni threw him an angry look and said, 'Life is dear to those who are born low and want to stay low. One who is honourable and who doesn't bend to anyone could easily sacrifice his life on such a matter.'

Payag shot a barb, 'You are being very partial toward him, Bhabhi. Have you become betrothed to him?'

Munni said in a distressed voice, 'Dada, you hear what he says and yet you don't say anything. If I became engaged to him, wouldn't people make fun of you? And if I was so inclined nobody would be able to stop me either. To get back, I won't let the cow come into the house. They'll have to chop off my neck, first.'

Munni moved into the crowd, sat next to the cow and challenged, 'Now, whoever wishes to wield the cleaver, let him wield it; here I sit.'

Nervously, Payag said, 'You are taking advantage of the fact that no one will dare to kill you.'

Munni said, 'It is the likes of you who have brought infamy to our community. Besides, when someone tries to explain things, you pick a quarrel with that person.'

Goodar Chaudhary was lost in thought. He had some inkling of the way the wind was blowing in the rest of the world. Several times in the past he had had conversations with Amarkant on this topic. He said solemnly, 'Brothers, everybody from the village is assembled here. Speak up, what do you think?'

A broad-chested youth said, 'Everyone will follow whatever you advise. You are Chaudhary after all.'

Payag, seeing his father vacillate, said, challenging others, 'Why are you all standing there gaping? There are many of you. Why don't you forcibly remove Munni? I am ready with the cleaver.'

Munni said angrily, 'So go ahead, kill me and eat my flesh? After all, it is also meat.'

Seeing no one else move, Payag stepped forward and catching Munni's arm was about to pull her away when Kashi pushed him aside forcefully and said with eyes blazing, 'Bhaiya, there will be bloodshed if you touch her—I am telling you. There isn't going to be any smell of this cow meat in our house. Who do you think you are?'

The broad-chested young man said in a conciliatory tone, 'What is so delicious about a dead cow's meat that everyone is ready to die for it? Let's dig a hole and bury it after skinning the pelt. But only if Amar bhaiya so advises. We have to follow his advice. We will be redeemed if we follow his example. The entire world considers us untouchables. Why? Because we drink hard liquor, eat meat of dead animals, and do leatherwork. We do nothing else that can be called bad. We have already given up hard liquor—we didn't give it up, rather the changing times made us—so why can't we give up dead meat? What is left is leatherwork. Nobody can call it bad, and if they do, we don't care. There is nothing bad about making leather products and selling them.'

Goodar looked at the young man with respect, 'You have all heard what Bhure has said. Is that what everyone feels?'

Bhure said, 'If anyone wishes to object, they should do so.'

One old man said, 'What will be accomplished if you or I give it up? The whole community will still eat dead meat.'

Bhure replied, 'If the community eats it, they will continue to be low caste. We should do what our individual dharma dictates.'

Goodar said, 'You are right Bhure. Just take the case of the boys' education. Did anyone send their boys to school at first? But when our boys started going to school, boys from other villages also came.'

Kashi said, 'The community will not punish us for not eating the meat of dead animals. I will take responsibility for that. You will see that by this evening this news will have spread, and other people will start following our example. Amar bhaiya is well respected. Who would dare to contradict what he says.'

Payag realized that he wasn't getting anywhere. So, berating everyone, he said, 'Now it's the women who rule. They are in charge of everything.'

So saying, he left for home taking the cleaver with him.

Goodar rushed swiftly towards the Ganges and shouted loudly, 'What are you standing here for, bhaiya. Come home, the squabble has been settled.'

Amar was lost in thought. He didn't hear him.

Chaudhary said, coming closer, 'How long will you continue to stand here, bhaiya?'

'No Dada let me be. You people will be cutting up and butchering meat there, which I won't be able to stand. I'll return when you have finished with that.'

'Bahu was saying that you are not going to eat at our house any more?'

'Yes Dada, I won't eat today. I would be sick if I did.'

'But in our house, it is a common occurrence.'

'I will get used to it in a few days.'

'You must be thinking that we are demons.'

Amar, putting his hand on his breast as if he were swearing an oath, said, 'No Dada. I have come here to learn something from you, to serve you and to improve myself. People have different customs. In China, which is a very big country, many people worship the Buddha as god. In their religion, it is a sin to kill any animal. For that reason, those people eat animals that have died. Dogs, cats, foxes, none are spared. Then are they even lowlier than us? No, never. Even in our country there are many Brahmans and Kshatriyas who eat meat. They slaughter animals for their gourmet taste. You are much better, at least you eat only dead animals.'

Goodar laughed and said, 'Bhaiya, you are a very wise man, nobody can win against you in a discussion. Let's go, no one will eat dead animals any more. We have decided; well, no, we haven't, Bahu has decided. But we won't have to throw away the skin, will we?'

Joyously Amar responded, 'No Dada, why should you throw away the skin? Making shoes is a great occupation. Was Bhabhi really displeased?'

Goodar said, 'She was not only displeased, she was prepared to lay down her life. She sat down next to the cow and said, "Now wield your cleaver, the first blow will be on my neck!" No one dared to do it.'

Amar's heart was filled with respect for Munni.

CHAPTER 25

꧁꧂

Several months went by. The meat of a dead animal didn't appear again in the village. The strange thing was that Chamaars of other villages also gave up eating carrion. Good endeavours are contagious!

Amar now ran his school in a new building. People had developed such keenness for education that not only did young people attend school but older people also came. Amar's style of imparting education consisted of critical reviews of different topics—the main subjects being the progression of social and political thought in other countries, new inventions, discoveries, and new ideas. Everybody listened with great fascination to tales of customs and traditions, and thinking and behaviour in different countries. He was sometimes astonished to see how easily these illiterate people understood complex social issues. It seemed as if new life was flowing through the entire village. The issue of 'untouchability' had more or less disappeared. Upper caste people of other villages would often attend the school as well.

After a hard day's work, Amar was lying down reading when Munni came and stood near him. Amar was so engrossed in reading that he didn't notice her. He was reading about the self-immolation of the brave women of Rajasthan, that pure self-sacrifice which has no parallel in the history of the world, and which, even today, makes one proud. Who else would have considered life so insignificant! Where would one find such an example of defending the family honour? No matter how much those brave women were belittled by the so-called learned people of today, we will always bow our heads in homage to them. Munni, standing quietly, stared at Amar's face. The little bit of cloud that had come flying like a bird in her heart's sky about a year ago, had gradually spread over the entire sky. In its cool shade the desires that had been singed by flames of the past were becoming green again. Her arid life, like a fragrant, cultivated garden, had begun to sway with new blossoms. Her sisters-in-law cooked for everyone else, but she would cook for Amar. The poor soul ate only two rotis, and those uncouth women would make thick cakes of bread! If Amar asked her to do anything, her face would glow with rapture. She would start imagining a new heaven—dreaming of a new happiness.

She remembered one day when Saloni had said smilingly, 'It is your good fate, Munni, that has brought Amar bhaiya here. Your life will take a turn for the better now.'

Munni had said with suppressed excitement, 'What are you saying, Auntie, there is no comparison between us. He must be several years younger than I. Also, he is so learned, so wise! I am not worth even the sandals on his feet.'

Auntie had replied, 'That may be true Munni; but I see that you have charmed him. He seems to be a shy man; so he doesn't say anything to you; but believe me you have captured his heart. Don't you understand that! You will have to help him overcome his shyness.'

Overjoyed, Munni, had said, 'With your blessings, Auntie, my hopes will be fulfilled.'

Munni watched Amar for a moment, then, going inside the hut, she brought out his cot. Amar's concentration was broken. He said, 'Let it be. I will lie down shortly. If you pamper me so much Munni, I'll become lazy. Come here, I will read you tales of Hindu devis.'

'Is it fiction?'

'No, it is a true account.'

Amar, recounting the attacks by Muslims, the self-immolation of the Kshatriya women, and the bravery of the Rajput warriors, said, 'Those devis preferred death by fire rather than being looked at by some man other than their husband. They died for their honour. Such were the ideals of our devis! What are the values in Europe now? During the First World War when German soldiers marched into France, there were no men left in the villages, so the French women made love to German soldiers.'

Munni said in a disgusted tone, 'They were very fickle. But how could the Kshatriya women stand being burned alive?'

Amar, closing the book, said, 'It must be a very difficult thing to do, Munni! We are in so much pain if a little burning ember falls on us. That is why the entire world respects them. When I read their story, my hair stands on end. I just feel like taking the ashes from the holy ground where they were cremated, smearing them on my head and face, and dying there.'

Munni, lost in thought, was gazing at the ground.

Amar said again, 'Sometimes the women would commit self-immolation even before the battle so that men would be freed from their love and affection for their family. Man holds life so dear that even old people don't want to die. Even severe ailments don't lessen our love for life. Renowned ascetics and great souls are also not able to renounce life, but for those devis, life was less dear than honour.'

Munni was still standing silent. Her face was drained of all colour as if she was suffering unbearable pain.

Amar, with concern, asked, 'What's the matter Munni? Why are you so pale?'

Munni smiled faintly and said, 'Are you asking me? Do you want to know what happened to me?'

'There is something wrong. You are keeping something from me.'

'No, no. Nothing is the matter.'

After a moment she said, 'Will you listen to my story today?'

'Willingly! I have asked you many times to tell me, but you didn't want to.'

'I was afraid how you might react. After hearing what I have to say, you may think me contemptible or even worse.'

Amar said, as if disappointed, 'Alright, don't tell me. I am who I am. I can't change into what you would like me to be.'

Munni said tiredly, 'You get annoyed very easily, Lala. That's why you don't get along with women. Alright, listen; you may think whatever you like.

'For some time after I left Kashi, I wasn't at all conscious of where or why I was going, or even where I was going from. Then I started crying. The love of my dear ones swept over me like a sea in which I kept sinking and surfacing. Then I realized what I was losing by going away. It seemed as if my child was straining to come into my arms. I had not felt such affection for him before. I started thinking of him, remembering every little thing—his laughter and crying, his childish prattle, and his unsteady footsteps. I remembered showing him Uncle Moon to divert him and singing lullabies to him. That little world of mine had been so joyful! Holding my jewel in my arms I was as happy as if I held the wealth of the world. I would not have exchanged that joy for the bliss of heaven. It was as if all my hopes and desires had found a focus in that child, and all the sharp thorns of living—our ramshackle hut, ragged clothes, worries about debt and prices, poverty and ill fate—turned to flowers. Leaving all that behind, I didn't know where I was going that day. I was distraught. As the train sped along, like the trees that were flying by, my memories kept running and, with them, my child also seemed to be running with me. Finally, I couldn't go any further. I thought, the world may laugh at me, let it; I may be excommunicated by my community, let it be so; I won't leave my son behind. I can still find work as a labourer; at least I will be able to have my son with me. No one could take him away from me! I have nursed him and lived for him. He is mine. No one else has any right to him.

'I got off at Lucknow. I had decided that I would return to Kashi by the next train. And let whatever has to happen, happen.'

'I don't know how long I stood on the platform. The station was lit with electric lights. I kept asking porters when the train for Kashi was due. I understood that a train was arriving at ten o'clock. I rearranged my luggage. My heart started beating loudly as the train arrived. Passengers started getting off and on. The porter came and asked, "Should I put your luggage in the women's compartment or in the men's"?'

'I couldn't speak.'

'The porter looked at me and again asked, "Should I put the luggage in the women's compartment"?'

'Distressed and unsure, I said, "I'm not taking this train."

"The next train won't come until ten tomorrow morning."

"I will take that train."

"Then should I carry the luggage outside the station or to the passenger waiting room?"

"To the waiting room."

Amar asked, 'Why didn't you take that train?'

Munni said in a trembling voice, 'I don't know what I thought—it was all a jumble. It was as if somebody had tied my hands and feet because I was going to slaughter a cow. How could I hold my baby with these leprous hands? I was also angry with my husband. Why hadn't he come with me? If he had cared for me, would he have let me come alone? He could have come on the same train. If he didn't wish to have me, then I would also not go back. And I don't know what other thoughts came to me to stop me from going.

'I was sitting in the waiting room sulking, when a man and his wife arrived and, spreading a durrie next to me, sat down. The woman had a child about a year old in her arms. He was a beautiful chubby child, with a rosy complexion and saucer-like eyes. I became so absorbed watching him that it seemed as if he were my own child. He climbed out of his mother's arms and slowly crawled toward me. I moved backwards. The child again moved towards me. I moved to the other side. The child thought I was avoiding him and started crying. I still didn't go near him. His mother looked at me angrily and ran and picked the child up, but the boy kept struggling and stretched his hand towards me. But I stayed away. It seemed as if my hands had been severed; I felt as if that beautiful child would become contaminated by my touch.

'Putting him down, the woman said, "Just hold the boy for a minute, devi; you act as if you are running away from him. The miserable child doesn't go to those who love him; instead he runs towards those who turn away from him."

'Babuji, I can't tell you how hurt I felt at these words. How could I explain to them that I was tainted and sinful, that my touch would bring some harm, some evil? And knowing that would they ever ask me to hold the boy again?

'Coming closer and looking at the boy affectionately, I nervously extended my arms to lift him. Suddenly the boy shrieked and ran towards his mother as if he had seen some terrifying apparition. Now, on reflection, I understand that children often behave that way, but at that time I thought there was something hideous in my very appearance. I was very embarrassed.

'The mother said to the boy, "She wants to hold you, why don't you go to her now?" Then turning to me, she asked, "Where are you going, Sister?" I replied, "Haridwar." They were also going to Haridwar. They had missed their train and since they lived far from the station, were staying in the waiting room. I was very happy that at least until Haridwar we would travel together. But the little boy didn't come to me again.

'In a little while the couple fell asleep, but I stayed awake. The child also was asleep, clinging to his mother. I had a strong desire to lift the boy and cuddle him, but I was afraid that he might start crying or that his mother might wake up and think it very strange. I looked at the beautiful face of the boy. He was smiling, probably dreaming of something. I couldn't control myself and picking him up, embraced him. But the next moment I came to my senses and laid him back. That momentary cuddle had been blissful! It had seemed as if I held my own child.

'Deviji was very hard-hearted. She would admonish the boy for every little thing. I got so angry with her that I felt like scolding her. I had never known that a mother could be so angry with her own child.

'By the next day when we sat in the train to Haridwar, the child had already adopted me. How can I explain to you, Babuji? I felt milk seeping from my breasts, and soon I relieved his mother of this responsibility as well.

'In Haridwar, we stayed in a dharmshala. Ensnared by affection for the child, I followed that couple. I was the child's servant. It became my job to wash him, feed him, and nurse him. His mother was freed of all these chores, but I enjoyed looking after him. Lalaji was just as courteous and kind as Deviji was indolent and vain. His personality was somewhat like yours. He would never raise his eyes to look at me. If I were alone in a room, he would never come in. His life with that shrew was like that of a mouse in the claws of a cat. She would berate him for everything, and the poor man would just look sheepish and downcast. I used to pity him.

'Two weeks went by. Deviji wanted to return home, whereas her husband wanted to stay on for a few more days. An argument ensued. I was standing in the verandah holding the child. Getting angry, she said, "If you want to stay, then stay. I will go today; I don't have to follow you."

'The husband said, apprehensively, "What is the harm in staying here for another five or ten days? I haven't noticed any improvement in your health as yet."

"Please don't worry about my health. I am not going to die just yet. Can you honestly say that you want to stay here because of my health?"

"Why else did we come here?"

"Whatever the reason may be, you are not staying here for my health. Tell these stories to women who don't know you. I know all your tricks. You want to stay to play around . . ."

'Babuji, folding his hands in supplication, said, "Binni, please, let it be; don't vilify me. I will also leave today."

'Deviji wasn't pleased with such an easy victory. She hadn't yet given expression to her pent up feelings. She said, "Yes, why wouldn't you leave, you wanted to do that in the first place. To stay here costs money, doesn't it? So, take me home and leave me in that dungeon. You couldn't care less whether I live or die. If I die, another would take my place—a new and novel one to boot. No matter what happens, you benefit. I thought that I would stay here for a few more days, but because of you I can't! May God deliver me from this misery."'

Amar asked, 'Had Babuji really behaved ill, or was it a false accusation?'

Munni said, turning her face away and smiling, 'Lala, you are very obtuse. That witch was accusing me obliquely. Babuji was being compliant lest she accuse me openly. He was supplicating her with folded hands; entreating her, but she was not to be placated.'

Munni continued her story. 'Rolling her eyes, the wife said, "I am not blind, God has given me eyes too. While I lie in the room groaning, you make merry outside! You have to have someone to dally with for your amusement."

'Slowly the knot began to unravel for me. I felt so angry that I could have clawed her face. I am not hiding anything from you, Lala. I had never even raised my eyes to look at Babuji, and the shrew was slandering me! If I had not respected Babuji, I would have taken care of her. Where even a needle wouldn't prick, I would have plunged a ploughshare."

Finally, Babuji lost his temper. He said, "You are telling lies, all lies!"

"I am telling lies?"

"Yes, absolute lies."

"Swear on the life of your son."

'I should have left quietly, but what can I do about my heart that can't bear injustice. My face was red with anger. I went to her and said, "Bahuji, now, just hold your tongue, otherwise it won't be good for you. I keep ignoring you and you keep making things worse. I stayed on with you because I thought you were a civil person. Had I known that you were so petty and mean, I would have avoided even your shadow. I am not a prostitute, nor am I a destitute woman. By God's grace, I too have a husband and child. It is a twist of fate that I am staying alone here. I don't consider your husband even remotely comparable to my husband. Just stay here for a couple of days, I will call him, then you can see for yourself."

'I had said only half what I intended, when my husband, with my son in his arms, came and stood in the courtyard, and seeing me hastened toward me. I became very nervous seeing him. I felt as if I was facing a lion. At once I ran into my room and bolted the door from within. My heart was pounding, but I was watching through a crack in the door. My husband's face was darker and his hair was matted with dust. He carried a long bamboo stick and had a blanket and small metal mug and rope on his back. He stood there, bewildered.

'Babuji came outside and said to my husband, "So, you are her husband. You came just in time. She was just talking about you. Come in and change your clothes. But why did sister run inside? Why should she go into purdah in this distant land?"

'Lala, you have seen my husband. Next to him, Babuji looked like a small bull in front of a prize steer.'

'Without returning an answer, my husband came to my door and said, "Munni, what is this outrage you are perpetrating? I have been searching for you for three days, and, when I find you today, you go and lock yourself behind a door! For God's sake, open the door and listen to my sad tale. After that you may do as you please."

'Tears were flowing from my eyes. I wanted to open the door and take my child in my arms. But I don't know, someone sitting in a corner of my heart was saying—"Beware, don't take the child in your arms!" It was as if a man dying of thirst and seeing a pail of water jumps for it, only to hear someone say that the water is impure. On the one hand, my heart was saying—don't dishonour your husband, the relationship of wife and mother created by God can't be broken by anyone; on the other hand, it was saying—you can't call your husband, husband anymore, or your son, son. Are you going to corrupt both of them under the impulse of a momentary affection?

'I moved away from the door!

'The child, trying to force the door open with his small hands, lisped to me to open the door.

'His words were so sweet. When in utter solitude we are frightened by some misgiving, we begin to sing—hearing our own voice, we imagine that we are not alone.

'I, too, trying to restrain the surge of affection, spoke up, "Why are you pursuing me? Can't you understand that I am dead? You are a Thakur, but have such a soft heart. You are sacrificing your family honour for a worthless woman. Go, get married and take care of the boy. In this life I am no longer related to you. But, yes, I beg of God that you may be mine in the next life. Why are you intent on making me break my vow, why are you snaring me again in ties of affection? You will not be happy living with a sinful woman. Have pity on me, please go away right now; otherwise, I swear I will poison myself."

'My husband said with gentle insistence, "I will give up everything for you, family honour, brothers, and kin. I don't care for anyone else. I don't care if the house burns down. I will either take you back with me, or I will drown myself in the Ganges here. God may punish me with a hundred hells if I have even an iota of disrespect for you. If you are not going to come then I will entrust your child to you and go. You may save him or kill him; I will not come to you again. If you ever care to, just give me a handful of water in offering."

'Lala, just think, What a terrible dilemma I was in. I knew that my husband would do what he said. I was also aware of how little he cared for his life. Even so, I steeled my heart. The smallest little weakening on my part would lead to a total disaster. So, I said, "If you leave the child with me, then his death will be on your conscience, because I won't live to see his misery. You are responsible for his upbringing, whether you like it or not. If I had any happiness in life, it was to know that my son and husband are well. You want to snatch that too away from me, so take it, but remember that it is the foundation of my life."

'I saw my husband lift the child, whom a moment earlier he had put down, and retrace his steps. Tears were streaming down his eyes, and his lips were trembling.

'Deviji courteously tried to persuade him to sit down. She began to ask him what the matter, was, why I was displeased, but my husband didn't answer. Babu sahab saw him to the gate. I can't say what they talked about, but my guess is that Babuji must have praised me. I was still afraid that my husband may indeed commit suicide, and so invoked all the gods and goddesses to protect my loved ones.

'The minute Babuji returned, I gently opened the door and asked him, "Which way did he go? Did he say anything else?"

'Babuji looked at me disdainfully and said, "What could he say, he was choking with emotion and sobbing bitterly. It is not too late for you to go and stop him. He has gone towards the Ganges. You are so kind and yet so hard-hearted, I discovered today. The poor man was weeping bitterly like a child."

'When confronted with disaster one reaches a stage when one treats strangers as if they are one's own. Rebuking him, I said, "Even so you came rushing back here! It wouldn't have hurt you to stay with him a little bit longer, you wouldn't have been belittled nor would anybody have abducted your deviji here. He is not himself right now, and yet you left him."

'Deviji spoke up, "Had he not run back here, who knows where I might have gone. Come and sit in the house. I will go. I am not my father's daughter if I don't catch him and drag him back here!"

'Dozens of travellers were staying in the dharmshala. They were all standing at their doors looking on. Four or five men joined Deviji as she left. They all returned in half an hour saying that my husband had gone toward the railway station.

'But I couldn't relax until I had seen him get on the train. The train would be leaving next morning. He would stay at the railway station all night. I arrived at the station. as soon as it was dark. He had spread out the blanket under a tree and was sitting on it. My child, pretending that the metal mug was a carriage, was pulling it with the rope. He kept falling down, getting up, and pulling at it again. I sat behind a tree, hidden from view, watching. A jumble of thoughts came to my mind—it is, after all, fear of community that is keeping me away from my loved ones. What can the community do if I live with my husband some place else? But after what had happened, can I ever be what I had been before? These thoughts were turning themselves over and over in my mind. My husband has spoken clearly, and his heart is pure. He is always candid, so why would he say things just to please me. He is also big enough to let bygones be bygones. He used to be so much in love with me. And he still is. I am unnecessarily vacillating and ruining both his life and mine! But can I ever be what I was before? No, I can't.

'I know that my husband will now hold me in even greater regard than before. He would not utter a word of reproach even if I spilled the most precious nectar. He would continue to love me as before. But it will not be the same as before. Now I am a tainted woman.

'Then why should I live? Life is worthless if there is no joy and no hope. If you are alive only to cry for a few more days, what is the point? Who knows what other disgrace I may have to bear or what other misfortune may befall me. It is much better to put an end to it all.

'Having come to a decision, I got up. I could see that my husband was asleep, and so was the child. Oh! How strong are the ties of affection. They are like the hoard of a miser. He doesn't use his money, nor gives it away; he has no satisfaction other than that he has wealth, but that thought gives him so much strength. I was going to break that illusionary affection.'

'Apprehensively, as if taking my life in my hands, I approached my husband, but I couldn't stay even a moment. I was being drawn towards his lips like a magnetic pull on a piece of iron. Exercising all my will-power, I broke that temptation and, in the same distraught state, ran to the bank of the Ganges. I was still very much under the temptation, when I jumped into the Ganges.'

Amar said, feeling very distressed, 'I can't bear to hear any more, Munni. Tell me the rest some other time.'

Munni smiled and said, 'Oh! We are nearly finished. I can't tell you how long I was in the water, but when I regained consciousness I was lying in this house. Apparently, I kept floating and was carried by the current. In the morning, Sumer, the oldest son of Chaudhary, went to bathe in the Ganges and he found me and brought me here. Since then, I have been here. I can't describe to you the happiness and peace that I have found in this hut of untouchables. Kashi and Payag call me Bhabhi, but Sumer used to address me as sister. I had not totally recovered when he passed away.'

There was a niggling doubt in Amar's mind. It had been partially resolved, but not altogether.

He asked Munni, 'Sumer must have been in love with you?'

Munni's hackles rose, 'Yes, he was. Not a little, but a lot. But what could I do about it? When I recovered, one day he expressed his love to me. Laughing off my anger, I said, "Are you asking for a return for your kindness to me? If so, then take me and drown me in the Ganges again. If you saved my life with that intent, you did me a grave injustice. Do you know who I am? I am a Rajput woman. Don't you ever say such a thing to me again, even by mistake; otherwise, the Ganges is not far from here." Sumer was so ashamed that he didn't talk to me again. But it broke his heart. One day I was having a pain in my ribs. He thought I was possessed by a demon, and when he went to get an occultist, he drowned in the swollen river. I was as saddened by his death as I was at the death of my real brother. I discovered only after coming here that there are such good people even among low castes. Had he lived longer, this house would have prospered. He used to attend to the needs of the entire village. He would never answer back, even if someone swore at him or abused him.'

Amar asked, 'Since then you've no news of your husband and child?'

Tears fell from Munni's eyes as she began to cry bitterly. Sobbing, she said, 'The next morning, my husband went again to the dharmshala. When he learned that I hadn't been there that night, he began to search for me. He kept wandering from place to place for a whole month, looking wherever anybody said they had spotted me. In his hopelessness and anxiety, he turned somewhat unstable. He returned to Haridwar again, but this time the child wasn't with him. If someone asked, "What happened to your child," he would begin to laugh. When I became well and started walking again, one day I thought of going to Haridwar to see what had become of my possessions. It had been more than three months. I didn't expect to recover anything, but I wanted to use that excuse to get some news of my husband. I thought of writing him a letter. When I got to the dharmshala, I saw a crowd gathered at the gate. I joined the crowd. A man's corpse lay there. People were saying that it was the mad man who used to wander around searching for his wife. I recognized my husband. From talking to people in that neighbourhood, I put together the pieces of the story. All I could do was wail in agony. The disaster that I had feared had come to pass. Had I known that this was going to happen, I would have gone with my husband! God has punished me twice over, once when I lost my honour, then when I lost my husband. But man is very shameless. Now I couldn't even die. For whom would I die? So I eat and drink, laugh and talk, as if nothing has happened. That's it. That is my story.'

PART 3

CHAPTER 26

❦

Although Lala Samarkant was not the kind of person to rest till his dying day, he had hoped that in the twilight of his life, after giving away all of his belongings to his son and getting his daughter married, he would finally stay in solitude and sing devotional songs. These hopes of Lala Samarkant had been dashed to pieces. For a while, he had felt encouraged to hope that Amar was getting attuned to the routine of middle class life. Amar may have had any number of faults, but there had never been any doubt about his character. However, when he fell into bad company, he lost his common sense—he lost not only his moral principles, but also his character and his family honour. Lalaji did not consider extramarital affairs to be especially wrong. After all, the rich had always had dalliances since olden times; but to be willing to abandon one's religion and to openly flout social values, was sheer lunacy. No, it was stupidity.

Samarkant's business life was completely separate from his religious life. In business and trade he considered deception, fraud, and trickery as excusable practices. It was acceptable to mix rubbish in jute and cotton, and to mix potatoes or *ghujian* in ghee. But, when it came to religion, he would not even drink water without taking his bath first. In forty years, perhaps there hadn't been a single evening when he had not performed aarati or put *tulsi-dal* on his forehead. On Ekadashi he would fast without even water. In short, his religion, which was all for appearance, served no real purpose in his life.

On returning from Salim's house, the first thing that Lalaji did was to berate Sukhada. Then it was Naina's turn. After making them both cry, he went into his room and started crying himself.

During the night, news of Amar's departure spread throughout the city, and different interpretations were put on his leaving. Samarkant didn't go out of the house the next day, not even for his bath in the Ganges. Many tenants came by to pay their rent. When Lalaji's clerk came to get the keys to the safe, he was admonished so angrily that he went away quietly. The tenants also left without paying their rent. The servant brought the silver hukkah, put it in front of him, and lit the tobacco, but Lalaji didn't even put the stem of the hukkah to his mouth.

At ten o'clock, Sukhada came and asked, 'Won't you have something to eat?'

Lalaji looked at her angrily and said, 'I am not hungry.'

Sukhada went away. No one ate anything all day.

At nine that evening, Naina came and inquired, 'Dada, aren't you going to the temple for aarati?'

Startled out of his reverie, Lalaji said, 'Yes, yes, why wouldn't I go? Did you people eat anything, or not?'

Naina said, 'Nobody wanted to eat.'

'So, is the entire household going to die because of him?'

Just then Sukhada came and said, 'If you are giving up your life, you have no right to be angry with others for wanting to do the same thing.'

Lalaji, wrapping a shawl around himself, said, 'There is no reason for me to give up my life. What happiness did Amar ever give me while he was here? I haven't known the joy of having a son. He used to infuriate me then, and he is still infuriating me. Go and cook food, I will eat when I come back. Whoever has gone, let him go, those who are still here will have to make up for his absence. Why should I give up my life? I raised a son, arranged his wedding, and built up this household. The running of this house has been my responsibility; now, it will continue to be so for much longer. What I can't understand is what came over the boy. Pathanin's granddaughter can't be that beautiful, why is he so captivated with her? It wasn't in his character to be like this. This is what is called God's *lila*.'

There was a crowd of people in the temple. No sooner did they see Lala Samarkant than several gentlemen inquired, 'What happened, Sethji? Has Amar gone away somewhere?'

Lalaji said, as if warding off a blow, 'Nothing really. He has had this wanderlust for a long time; he was probably an ascetic in his former life. If he could, he would squander away my entire fortune in one day. I wouldn't let that happen, that's what the dispute was about. I have known poverty as well as wealth, but he has not tasted poverty as yet. In six months or a year, when he has tasted it, he will come to his senses. Then he will realize that only people with money can do public service. He wouldn't even have become a Board member if he didn't have the security of assured meals at home.'

Nobody dared ask anything else. But the foolish priest couldn't resist asking, 'We heard that he was mixed up with the daughter of some weaver?'

Other people bit their tongues and turned away at this blunt question. Lalaji looked with bloodshot eyes at the priest and said loudly, 'Yes, he was. So? Didn't God Krishna enjoy the company of a thousand queens? Didn't King Shantanu enjoy the company of a fisherman's daughter? What king doesn't have two hundred queens in his palace? If he did it, it's nothing new. That is the answer for people like you. For those who are wise, the answer is—if one's wife is as beautiful as a nymph, why go after a plain girl. Those who dine on delicacies do not munch dry chickpeas.'

So saying, Lalaji turned towards the idol, but tonight he couldn't summon the same faith as before. The poor believe in God out of hope, the rich out of fear; the belief of the poor increases with their suffering, whereas the rich, if they suffer, begin to rebel—they want even God to bend before their wealth. Tonight, Lalaji's troubled heart did not get the message of peace and contentment from that idol resplendent in gold and silk. Until yesterday, the idol had bestowed on him strength and encouragement. Tonight, his grief-stricken heart rebelled against the same idol. It questioned, 'Is this the reward for my belief? Is this the result of my bathing in the Ganges and my fasting and devotion?'

When he was leaving, the brahmachari said, 'Lalaji, we are thinking of having the Shri Valmiki *Katha* in the temple.'

Lalaji said, turning around, 'Yes, yes, go ahead.'

One babu sahab said, 'There are no funds to bear the cost. Only if you contribute, can it be done.'

Samarkant said enthusiastically, 'Yes, yes, I am ready to shoulder the entire burden. What better use of money can there be than arranging for readings of God's kathas?'

People were astonished to see such enthusiasm on his part. He was known for his frugality and did not take a leading role in any religious function. People had been expecting no more than ten or twenty rupees from him. Seeing him cornering all the glory, other people also warmed up. Seth Dhaniram said, 'You are not being asked to shoulder the entire burden, Lalaji. Admittedly, you are wealthy, but others are also faithful. Let it be by voluntary contribution.'

Samarkant said, 'In that case, let others pool their contributions. Whatever deficit remains, I will fill it.'

Dhaniram, fearing that this arrangement might let off Lala Samarkant very lightly, said, 'No, you write down whatever you feel like donating.'

Becoming competitive, Samarkant said, 'You write first.'

Paper, pen, and ink were brought in. Dhaniram wrote down one hundred rupees.

Samarkant asked the brahmachariji, 'How much do you think will be the total cost?'

Brahmachariji estimated one thousand rupees.

Samarkant wrote down eight hundred and ninety nine rupees, and walked away. Lacking true faith, he wanted to fill the void with money. For every void in one's dharma, there is a corresponding increase in vanity.

CHAPTER 27

❧❧❧

When Naina went inside with the letter from Amarkant, Sukhada asked, 'Who is it from?'

Naina had read the letter the minute she received it. She said, 'It is from Bhaiya.'

Sukhada asked, 'Achcha, it is from him? Where is he?'

'He is in some village near Haridwar.'

In the last five months, the two had never discussed Amarkant. It was like an open sore that sent shivers through their hearts by merely touching it. Sukhada didn't delve any further, and continued sewing a playsuit for her son.

Naina wanted to respond to the letter right away. She began, 'You finally remembered me after such a long time.' She wanted to write many other things. She finished writing the letter several hours later. She took the letter to Sukhada but she didn't want to read it.

Dejected, Naina asked, 'Shall I write something on your behalf?'

'No, nothing.'

'Will you write something yourself?'

'No, I have nothing to write.'

Naina left almost crying. The letter was mailed.

Lately, Sukhada was annoyed even at the mention of Amar's name. There used to be a framed photograph of Amar in her room but she smashed it and threw it away. Now there was nothing in her room to remind her of him. Her anger even disaffected her from the child, who now stayed mostly with Naina. Instead of affection for Amar, she now felt pity. However, her humiliation at his hands had not caused her to despair; instead, her feeling of self-worth had increased manifold. She had also become much more self-reliant. She did not try to belittle anyone anymore and she rebelled against any kind of pressure, except the pressure of love. Her desire for comfort and luxury seemed to have been supplanted by her desire for respectability.

The surprising thing was that she didn't feel at all resentful of Sakina. She felt her to be as grieved as herself, if not more so. Sakina had been slandered so much and still the poor woman was crying for that heartless man. All that frenzied passion had gone. How could one trust such a sordid man? He must have ensnared some other prey by now. She wanted very much to meet Sakina, but it remained only a wish.

One day she learned from Pathanin that Sakina was very ill. Sukhada decided to visit her that day and took Naina with her. On the way, Pathanin said, 'She won't say anything in front of me; indeed, she hasn't spoken to me since that day. I will point out the house to you and go somewhere else. I had arranged such a good marriage for her, but she wouldn't accept it. I keep quiet. I will see how long she waits for him. As long as I am alive, Lalaji won't be allowed to step inside our house. After that, I can't say.'

Sukhada asked, 'What would you do if someday a letter comes from him and Sakina goes away?'

The old woman said angrily, 'She wouldn't dare go away like that! I would kill her if she did.'

Sukhada inquired again, 'If he agrees to become a Muslim, what objection could you have?'

Pathanin protested, 'Arre beta! Shall I benefit at the expense of someone to whom we are indebted for life? That is not what civilized people do. I cannot understand why Bhaiya fell for the girl, anyway.'

After pointing out the house, Pathanin went to a neighbour's, while the young women knocked at Sakina's door. Sakina opened the door. Seeing the two, she felt so nervous that she wanted to run away—how could she welcome them, where would she seat them?

Sukhada said, 'Don't worry, sister, we will sit on this cot. You seem to be wasting away. You fell for the tricks of a faithless man, but why are you sacrificing your life because of that one mistake?'

Sakina's pale face became red with shame. It seemed to her that Sukhada was asking her to explain why she had ruined her home. Sakina had no answer. She had herself been caught unawares. At first, there was just a small bit of cloud in one corner of the sky. In no time at all, the entire sky was filled with cloud and there was a storm of such force that she herself was lifted off the ground. How could she explain to Sukhada what had happened? Seeing that little bit of a cloud how could anyone have predicted that a storm was brewing.

Bowing her head, she replied, 'What else is a woman's life, sister! She is helpless in matters of the heart. One whom she expects to be faithful deceives her. What can she do? But if one didn't love the faithless, then what would be the joy of loving. Accusations and complaints, crying and wailing, perplexity and uneasiness—these are the joys of love. And I never expected fidelity. I knew even then that this storm would last only a few hours, but it was enough that a man, whom I respected more than anyone else, thought me worthy of the honour of marriage. I am consoled and will be able to cross the sea sitting in that fragile paper boat.'

Sukhada realized that the young woman's heart was totally free of guile! Somewhat disappointed, she said, 'These are the wiles of men. First they pose as *devatas*, as if they are paragons of civility, afterwards they turn their eyes like parrots.'

Sakina said stubbornly, 'Sister, one doesn't become a devata by posing. You may be a year or two older than me, but in these matters I am more experienced than you. What I am going to say is said out of shame, not pride. Among the poor, beauty is a curse. May God never make a poor man's daughter beautiful. Not only the rich and important but everybody thinks she is easy of access. Amma is very protective and always nearby. She must think that I am a virtuous woman; she doesn't let any young man come near the door. But now that the subject has come up, I must say that I have had plenty of opportunity to see and judge men. They all looked upon me as an object of dalliance and wanted me for their enjoyment, taking advantage of my poverty. If anyone treated me with respect, it was Babuji. As God is my witness, he never even once looked at me or said anything that could smack of sordidness. He offered me marriage, which I accepted. As long as he doesn't revoke that offer, I am bound to him, even though I may have to live my entire life like this. In four or five brief meetings, I have come to trust him so much that I can wait for him for the rest of my life. I'm sorry now that I didn't go away with him. My presence might have been of some comfort to him, and I might have been of some service to him. You may be sure that it is not complexion and beauty that attracted him. He wouldn't even raise his eyes to look at a celestial beauty, but he is easily attracted to service and affection. That is my fear. I say it to you honestly, sister, that I would be very pleased if you two would get together again and the misunderstandings between you are resolved. I would be even happier then. That was the reason I didn't go with him. But if you don't mind, I would like to say one thing more.'

She waited for Sukhada to answer. Sukhada assured her, 'You have been so frank with me that I will not feel badly about anything you say. Please feel free to speak.'

Thanking her, Sakina said, 'Now that you know his address, you should go to him at once. He craves attention and you can win him back through service.'

Sukhada asked, 'Is that all, or is there anything else?'

'That is all. What else can I tell you? You are far wiser than I.'

'He has betrayed me. I cannot humble myself before a man who has betrayed me. If today I ran away with some other man, do you think that he would come to plead with me? He would probably cut my throat. I am a woman, and a woman's heart is not that hard, but I wouldn't sweet-talk him even while breathing my last.'

So saying, Sukhada got up. Sakina regretted that by being more familiar than necessary she had angered Sukhada. She begged forgiveness until they reached the door.

When the two sat on the tonga, Naina said, 'You get angry very easily, Bhabhi.'

Sukhada said sharply, 'Of course you would say that. You are, after all, his sister. What woman in this world would go to placate such a husband? Yes, perhaps Sakina might go, but then she would be getting what she had hoped for.'

After a moment, she spoke again, 'I came to offer her sympathy, but am going back defeated. Her faith has vanquished me. This girl has all the virtues that attract men; it is such women that rule the hearts of men. I never had such faith. I had thought that my duty toward him ended with gay conversation, laughter and joking, and displaying my beauty and youth. I never loved, nor did I receive love. What she got in a few hours, I couldn't get in years of marriage. Today I have learned a little about where I have erred. This girl has opened my eyes.'

CHAPTER 28

The reading of the katha had been going on in the thakurdwara for a month. Pundit Madhusudanji was an expert in the art of reading. When he read, both the aural and visual aspects of the story were evoked. He could get his audience to laugh just as easily as he could make it cry. He had volumes of examples at his disposal, and he was such a proficient actor that when he played a character, the character came to life. The entire city would rush to hear him. Renuka Devi went to the thakurdwara early in the evening. Vyasji and his entire company of hymn singers were her guests. Naina, with Munna in her arms, also attended. Only Sukhada was not interested in the katha. Despite Naina's repeated efforts to persuade her, she still refused to go. She was so angry and humiliated by Amar's behaviour that she wanted to take revenge on the whole world. At times she felt so anguished that she wanted to break away from the shackles of society and religion. She thought that the only punishment for such men was that their wives treat them exactly the same way. Then only their eyes would open and they would understand what it means to burn with jealousy. Why should she alone mourn in the name of family honour! But then she thought that such atrocities would not continue much longer. No one should be under the delusion that a husband could do whatever he liked and his wife would still worship him, consider him her devata, massage his feet, and believe that she was fortunate if he talked to her pleasantly. Those days were long gone. She had written many articles on this subject for the newspapers.

One day, Naina began to argue, 'You say that one should examine a man's behaviour and thought processes before marriage. But can't one be deceived even after an assessment? Aren't people in the West getting divorced every day?'

Sukhada replied, 'So, what's the harm in that? At least the man doesn't go on amusing himself while the wife keeps on mourning her loss.

Naina repeated the hackneyed phrase, 'If there is no love, there can be no happiness. Premarital assessments accomplish nothing.'

Sukhada teased, 'It sounds like you have been studying this subject these days. If there are occasional deceptions in marriages where the parties are known to each other, then in those where they do not know each other, there are deceptions all the time. Divorce should be legalized, then our lives would be much happier.'

Naina couldn't come up with an answer. Yesterday, Vyasji had compared the Western practice of marriage to the Indian custom. She remembered only bits and pieces of his comparison. Changing the subject, she said, 'Tell me, are you coming to the katha or not?'

'You go, I am not going.'

When Naina reached the thakurdwara, the katha had already started. There was a bigger crowd than usual that day. The students and teachers of the Youth Congress and Sevashram were there as well. Madhusudanji was saying, 'The story of Rama and Ravana is the story of this life, the story of our world. You will hear it whether you want to or not. We can't escape it, because Rama is within us, so is Ravana, and so is Sita, and...' Suddenly, there was a commotion in the last few rows. Brahmachariji, shouting loudly, was pulling some people up and forcing them to stand. A riot was in the making. People elsewhere were getting up and congregating near him. The reading had stopped. Samarkant asked, 'What is the matter, Brahmachariji?'

Brahmchari, his eyes red with sanctimonious wrath, said, 'What's the matter you ask! Do these people come to listen to Bhagwan's katha or to soil our religion! Sweeper, Chamaar, whosoever, comes barging in—is it a temple for *Thakurji* or is it an inn?'

Samarkant said harshly. 'Throw them all out, by force if necessary.'

One old man, folding his hands in respect, said, 'We were sitting here at the door, Sethji, where shoes are kept. We are not so ignorant as to come and sit amongst you.'

Beating him with a shoe, Brahmchari said, 'You scoundrel, why did you come here? See this carpet, which indicates seating for the upper caste? Now everything is ruined for everyone! There is *prashad, charanamrita*, and *Gangajal*. Isn't all that contaminated now? Won't all these people have to bathe and wash themselves in this cold frosty weather? I tell you, Mithua, you have grown old, your days are numbered, but you have not learned anything. And here you come posing as a great devotee!'

Samarkant asked irately, 'Have you been coming here on other days as well, or just today?'

Mithua said, 'We come here everyday, Maharaj. We just sit here at the door and listen to Bhagwan's katha.'

Disgusted, the brahmachari struck his forehead with his palm. These rogues have been coming here everyday, touching everyone! Everyday people have been eating the prashad soiled by their touch! What a calamity!! What greater offence could there be against religion? The anger of the religious souls knew no bounds. Several men, taking shoes in their hands, started beating the poor people. In God's temple, by the hands of God's devotees, God's devotees were being beaten with shoes!

Doctor Shantikumar and his teachers had been standing watching the spectacle. When the untouchables began to be beaten with shoes, Swami Atmanand sprang toward Brahmachari, with his thick bamboo stick poised for attack.

Doctor sahab, seeing that a catastrophe was about to take place, leapt up and seized the bamboo stick from Atmanand's hands.

Atmanand looked at him with blazing eyes, and said, 'You may be able to witness this scene calmly, but I can't.'

Shantikumar calmed him down and in a loud voice said sarcastically, 'Hooray for you, devotees of God! Hooray for you! What can one say about your devotion! The more you hit with shoes, the more will God be pleased. You will get all four objects.[3] You will be whisked straight to heaven! But now, you may hit as much as you like, your dharma has been ruined.'

Brahmachari, Lala Samarkant, Seth Dhaniram, and the other custodians of dharma looked at Shantikumar in astonishment.

Shantikumar, dressed in kurta and dhoti, with sandalwood tilak on his forehead and a shawl around his neck, looked like the younger brother of Vyasji. Dressed so, he could not be accused of being an atheist. Doctor sahab challenged again, 'Why did you people stop? Keep on hitting as hard as you can! And why shoes? Get your guns and put an end to these offenders against dharma. The government would not intervene. And you offenders against dharma, all of you, sit down and take as much beating as

---

[3] Ancient Hindu mythological texts, the Puranas, mention *dharma*, *artha*, *karma*, and *moksha* as the four aims that human beings are supposed to achieve. So if one achieves these, he/she has achieved all that there is to achieve.

you can. Haven't you heard that this is the house of the God of seths and *mahajans*! How dare you step into their God's temple! Your God is probably in some hut or under a tree. This God wears jewel ornaments and eats rich sweets and cream. He doesn't want to see the faces of those who wear rags or chew dry chickpeas.'

Like the mythological Parasuram, Brahmachariji adopted a fearsome look and said, 'You are causing a lot of trouble, Babuji. Where is it written in the Shastras that people of low caste should be allowed inside a temple?'

Shantikumar said, excitedly, 'No! No! The Shastras tell you to sell ghee mixed with tallow, take bribes, hoodwink others, and fawn on those stronger than yourself, even if they flout the Shastras. If that is what is written in your scriptures, follow it. In my scriptures, it is written that in God's sight no one is big or small, pure or impure. His arms are open to all.'

Samarkant realized that several people were ready to side with the untouchables. In an effort to calm them, he said, 'Doctor sahab, you are needlessly getting angry. Only scholars know what is or what is not written in the scriptures. We simply do what is customary. These scoundrels know the situation here, they are not strangers, they should have thought about it before coming here.'

Shantikumar was still enraged, 'Why did you people hit them with shoes?'

Brahmachari said rashly, 'What else should we have done? Should we have welcomed them with paan and flowers?'

Getting agitated, Shantikumar replied, 'Maharaj, all this time, you have been throwing dust in the eyes of blind devotees and profiting from them. Those times are passing; you won't be able to get away with that very much longer. Soon even God will be bathing in water, not milk.'

Everybody kept on saying, 'Don't go, don't go!' But Shantikumar, Atmanand, and the students from Sevashram got up and left. The leader of the hymn-singing troupe, Brajnath of Sevashram, also went with them.

CHAPTER 29

There was no more katha that day. Some people began to blame Brahmachari. After all, the poor fellows had been sitting in a corner, where was the need to eject them? And even if they had to be thrown out, it could have been done politely. What had been gained by beating and hitting them?

The next day the katha started at the regular time, but the audience was much depleted. Madhusudan tried his best to enthrall them but people kept yawning, and in the back rows some even shamelessly dozed. It seemed that the courtyard of the temple had become smaller and the doors a bit lower than they had been yesterday; the absence of the choir group made it seem all the more quiet. Elsewhere, in front of the office of the Youth Congress, Shantikumar was holding his own katha in the open field. Brajnath, Salim, Atmanand, and others were welcoming the audience. Carpets had been laid on the ground to seat the people; but the audience outgrew the seating capacity and soon even the field was too small to accomodate everyone. Most people in the audience were poorly clad; some wore rags. They reeked of sweat and tobacco. Women wore dirty, wrinkled dhotis or lehangas and were bare of ornaments. Silk, perfume, and dazzling ornaments were nowhere to be seen. But these people had kind hearts and a sense of duty, community service and self-sacrifice. When newcomers arrived they did not take up more space by spreading out their legs or stare at them as if they were enemies; rather they gathered themselves in closer and obligingly made room for them.

The katha started at nine o'clock. This was not a katha of gods and goddesses and their various incarnations, nor was it a recital of the penance and subsequent enlightenment of great ascetics, nor was it a saga of the valour and magnanimity of Kshatriya princes. Rather it was an account of the edifying character of the man for whom purity of mind and action are the essence of dharma. One whose mind is pure is a higher being, one whose mind is impure is a lesser being. It was the story of the man who did not make one segment of the society drunk and blind with power and the other untouchable by fabricating the sham of skin colour; who did not slam the door on improvement and betterment for anyone. It was the story of the man who did not anoint the forehead of one person with the mark of greatness and of another with the black mark of lowliness. In this character, there was a vital message of self-improvement. It seemed to the audience who heard it that the bonds that had tied them down were at last broken and that the world was a holy and beautiful place.

Naina was also irritated by the hypocrisy that was practiced in the name of dharma. Amarkant often used to talk to her on these matters. The previous day at the temple, her blood had boiled at the injustice being done to the untouchables. Had she not been afraid of Samarkant, she would have rebuked Brahmachariji. Accordingly, she was overjoyed when Shantikumar joined issue with the fake custodians of religion. She had heard accounts of him many times from Amarkant. This time she felt such a rush of respect for him that she wanted to step up to him and say 'You are the true devata of dharma, I salute you.' Seeing the men around her getting angry, she was afraid that they might attack him. She wanted to go and stand next to Doctor sahab and protect him. She was thankful when he left with several people; then, she went home.

Sukhada had heard the news and remarked to Naina, 'I don't know where those scoundrels came from, and then Doctor sahab was ready to pick a fight on their behalf!'

Naina said, 'God did not make anyone higher or lower.'

'If God didn't, then who did?'

'Injustice did.'

'High and low rank have always been in the world, and will always be.'

Naina didn't think it very fruitful to continue this discussion.

The next day when she heard that the Youth Congress was holding a separate katha for the untouchables that evening, she was very tempted to go. She went to the temple with Sukhada, but her heart was not there. Back at home, when Sukhada started dozing in the evening earlier than usual, she quietly slipped out and, catching a tonga, went to the office of the Youth Congress. Seeing gaslights and a crowd of people from a distance and afraid that she may not be able to get in, she thought of turning back so that Sukhada might not know of her departure. As she drew closer she could hear the sound of Brajnath's singing. When the tonga reached the site, Shantikumar was already on the dais. There was a sea of people and

Doctor sahab's image was overshadowing that sea like an immense, all-pervading soul. For a little while, Naina sat in the tonga listening as if mesmerized, and then getting out she stood in the last row behind everyone.

An old woman said, 'How long will you keep standing, little one? Get inside and sit down.'

Naina said, 'I am very comfortable. I can hear everything.'

The old woman was standing in front of her. Taking Naina by the hand, she pulled her up to where she was and moved back herself. Naina could now see Shantikumar clearly. His face had a divine radiance at that moment, and he seemed to be in some celestial world where the very air was ambrosia. These wretched people, whom she had witnessed being showered by abuse, were so proud today; as if they were the masters of some new treasure. She had never before seen them so gracious, so polite.

Shantikumar was saying, 'God has not brought you into this world so that you should bear the burden of slavery. You serve others with all your heart, but you are slaves and society has no respect for you. You are the foundation of society, it depends on you, but you are untouchables. You can't enter temples. Such injustice would not prevail anywhere else except in this unfortunate country. Do you wish to remain downtrodden and outcaste all your life?'

A voice rose, 'What can we do about it? We don't have any control.'

Shantikumar said agitatedly, 'You have no control as long as you think that you have none. A temple does not belong to any one man or a group of people, it is symbolic of the Hindu religion itself. If someone stops you from entering, he is being high-handed; stay firmly at the door of the temple, don't move even if you are shot at. You can lose everything, even your life, over a little thing. This is a matter of dharma, and dharma is dearer to us than our lives. Dharma has always been defended by the sacrifice of lives, and so it will continue to be.'

The people were agitated by yesterday's beating and had discussed it all day. A powder keg was ready, and it lacked only a spark. Shantikumar's words provided that spark. People adjusted their headgear, changed positions, and looked at each other as if asking 'Are you coming or is there still more to think about?' Being part of a group added to their courage. Then the moment passed and they quietened. Courage, like a mouse, poked its head out of the hole and then withdrew it. The old woman next to Naina said, 'They can keep their temple, we don't need it.'

Naina, supporting Shantikumar's ideas, said, 'The temple doesn't belong to any one man.'

Shantikumar said resoundingly, 'Who will come with me to have a darshan of their Thakurji?'

The old woman said, doubting, 'Will they allow us to enter?'

Clenching his fist Shantikumar, said, 'We will see who stops us! Our God is not the property of any single individual or a group that He can be kept under lock and key. This matter must be decided today, once and for all.'

Many men and women marched with Shantikumar towards the temple. Naina's heart was palpitating; but, ignoring it, she walked behind the crowd. Thinking how happy Bhaiya would have been had he been there motivated her though she also had many misgivings about this march.

More and more people joined the crowd as it advanced towards the temple, but their courage waned, as they got nearer. They were not that hungry for a right that they had never known; they only remembered the pain from the beatings. The faith that arises out of knowing what is just, what is right, was not there. Even so, the number of people increased as they marched. There were few who were prepared to give their lives, but the hope that they might win by the force of their numbers kept impelling them forward.

When the crowd reached the temple it was already ten o'clock. Brahmachariji and several priests and acolytes were standing at the door holding lathis. Lala Samarkant was also pacing back and forth.

Naina was feeling so cross at Brahmachari that she wanted to scold him, 'You pose as a great soul, yet you gamble in this temple half the night, sell your honour for a kauri, bear false witness, and beg at every door; even so, you claim to be a custodian of dharma! Fie on you, even your touch defiles the gods!'

She couldn't control this impulse and, tearing through the crowd, she was approaching the temple door when Shantikumar spotted her. Startled he said, 'Why are you here, Naina? I thought you would be inside the temple listening to the Katha.'

Naina said jokingly, pretending anger, 'You are blocking my passage. How can I enter?'

Shantikumar, directing the throng away from the front of the temple, said, 'I didn't see you standing there.'

Naina said hesitantly, 'You want to defile our Thakurji, don't you?'

Shantikumar didn't understand that she was joking and said sadly, 'Naina, do you also think that?'

Naina said still teasing, 'Won't the God be defiled if you fill the temple with untouchables?'

Shantikumar said gravely, 'I thought that God purifies the defiled, He is not Himself defiled.'

Suddenly, the brahmachari roared out, 'Have you people come here to the door of Thakurji's temple to incite a riot?'

One man came forward and said, 'We haven't come here to incite a riot, rather we have come to have a darshan of Thakurji.'

Samarkant pushed the man backward and said, 'Had your father or grandfather ever come to have a darshan or are you the first brave one?'

Shantikumar supported the man, 'Lalaji, are grandsons and great grandsons prohibited from doing what their fathers and grandfathers couldn't do? Our fathers and grandfathers didn't even know of electricity and telegraph, so why do we use these things today? Ideas keep on evolving, you can't stop them.'

Samarkant said sarcastically, 'So now your thinking has evolved to the point that you have given up faith in Thakurji and, instead, have chosen to offend Him?'

Shantikumar countered, 'I am not offending Thakurji. Those who won't allow His devotees to worship Him are his offenders. Don't these people follow the sacraments of Hindu religion? Why have you shut the doors of the temple to them?'

Brahmachari said angrily, 'People who eat meat and drink liquor and do menial work can't be allowed inside the temple.'

Shantikumar replied calmly, 'Many Brahmans, Kshatriyas, and Vaishyas eat meat and drink liquor. Why don't you stop them? Probably everyone here partakes of *bhang*, yet they all pose as teachers and priests!'

Samarkant took hold of a stick and said, 'These people won't be persuaded so easily. They will have to be turned out of here by force. Someone should go to the police station and report that these people have come here to incite a riot.'

By this time many priests and acolytes had gathered. They started to disperse the crowd using the heavy end of their lathis. People began to run in all directions. Shantikumar was hit on his head, but he stood where he was exhorting people—'Don't run, don't run, all of you just sit down where you are; sacrifice yourselves in the name of Thakur, for dharma ...'

But he was hit on his head a second time with such force that he couldn't finish what he was saying and fell down. He wanted to take hold of himself and get up again, but he was hit repeatedly until he lost consciousness.

CHAPTER 30

Naina went to the door repeatedly, but withdrew when she saw Samarkant sitting there. It was eight o'clock in the morning, but he hadn't yet gone for his bath in the Ganges. Naina had been awake all night thinking of the terrible incident she had witnessed.

She had seen Shantikumar being hit and fall, but she had stood there frozen. Amar had taught her the rudiments of first aid, but on this occasion, she felt paralysed. She saw a crowd of men surrounding him; she saw a doctor come and put Shantikumar on a stretcher, and take him away; but still she stayed rooted to the spot. Just as a tethered animal tries repeatedly to run away but is held back by its rope, she had tried to go to him several times, but was held back by her diffidence.

Finally, she steadied her heart and went out into the verandah.

Samarkant asked, 'Where are you going?'

'Just to the temple.'

'The passage to the temple has been blocked off. I don't know where these jackals of Chamaars came from, but they are sitting at the door and won't let anyone go in. The police are trying to remove them but they just won't listen. This is all owing to that Shantikumar's wickedness. Today he has become their leader. He had already lost his dharma when he went to England. Now he is trying to destroy the Hindu religion by digging it up by its roots. He is neither cultured nor civilized and he eats and drinks with that rogue Salim. What else will these rebels against religion think of next? Keeping company with such people has ruined Amar. I don't know who made Shantikumar a teacher.'

Naina pretended that she would watch the scene at the temple from a distance and then come back. But, after going some distance towards it, she turned into a lane and went towards the hospital. Looking warily right and left, she walked rapidly, as if she were a thief out to steal.

When she reached the hospital, she saw crowds of people milling around, and university students running back and forth. She also spied Salim. She didn't want to be recognized, and was about to turn back when Brajnath, surprised at seeing her, shouted, 'Oh, Naina Devi! What brings you here? Salim and I sat with Doctor sahab all through the night but he was unconscious all the time. He has just opened his eyes.'

With so many acquaintances present, Naina felt uncomfortable staying there. She turned back. But her visit had not been entirely fruitless. She had at least learned that Doctor sahab had regained consciousness. She was on her way back home when she saw hundreds of people running towards her. She hid in a lane and wondered if there had been an armed conflict. How would she reach her house now? By some chance, Atmanandji met her. He recognized Naina and said, 'Bullets are flying at the temple now. A police Captain came and ordered firing.'

The blood drained from Naina's face and she turned pale. She said, 'Have you just come from there?'

'Yes, I was almost killed. I hid from lane to lane. We were just standing there when the Captain ordered firing. Where were you?'

'I was returning after my bath in the Ganges. When I saw people running, I came this way. How will I get home now?'

'Right now it is dangerous to go that way.'

After a moment, perhaps feeling ashamed of his cowardice, he said, 'But going through the lanes is not dangerous. Come, I will take you home. If someone asks, just say that you are the daughter of Lala Samarkant.'

Naina thought to herself—this gentleman poses as an ascetic, but he is such a coward. He initially incited those poor people and when things got rough, he was the first to run away. The time was not right; otherwise she would have berated him thoroughly. They reached her home at about ten o'clock by a circuitous route via several lanes. Atmanand returned the way he came. Naina didn't even thank him; she had lost all respect for him.

When she entered the house, she saw Sukhada standing at the main door and people running in the street in front.

Sukhada inquired, 'Where have you been, Naina? The police have been firing and the poor people are running to save their lives.'

'I found that out on my way, so I came home cautiously, hiding in the lanes.'

'People are such cowards! They have even shut their doors.'

'Why doesn't Dadaji go and have the firing stopped?'

'He is the one who asked the police to fire. How can he ask them to stop now?'

'Achcha! Dada is behind the firing?'

'Yes, he approached the Captain and asked him, and now he is hiding in the house. I don't condone the untouchables entering the temple, but it makes my blood boil to see bullets being fired. A religion that needs to be protected by bullets has lost its claim to truth. Look! A bullet has hit that poor man, his chest is bleeding!'

So saying, she went to Lala Samarkant and asked, 'Lalaji, rivers of blood may flow, but the door to the temple will never be opened, will it?'

Calmly, Samarkant said, 'What nonsense, Bahu! You want me to let these Dom-Chamaars into the temple! You go even further than Amar. If we can't drink water from the hands of these people, how can we let them inside our temple?'

Sukhada didn't discuss the matter any further. She was a smart woman. Her keen intelligence had made her proud; it was at the root of her love for comfort and luxury. It had stopped her from mixing with the common people and wouldn't let anyone dominate her. That intelligence was now transformed into the ability to sacrifice. She left the house extremely agitated and, standing in front of the policemen, challenged those who were running away.

'Brothers, why are you running away? This is not the time to run, it is the time to bare your chests and stand firm! Show them how you can sacrifice your lives in the name of dharma. Only those that have faith attain God. Those who run away don't ever win.'

People stopped running momentarily. Seeing a woman standing up to bullets, even cowards were ashamed. An old woman came near her and said, 'Beta, I hope you don't get hit by a bullet.'

Sukhada said firmly, 'When so many people have already died, my death won't be any particular loss. Brothers and sisters don't run! Thakurji will be pleased with you only when He receives the sacrifice of your lives!'

Like cowardice, courage is also contagious. Instantly, those running away, like leaves dispersed in a storm, formed a solid wall of men. Now, they were not afraid of either lathis or bullets.

Many guns were fired. One bullet whined past Sukhada. Several men fell down, but the wall stayed unbroken.

Guns were again fired. More men fell, but the wall did not break.

Sukhada was holding up the wall. Just as one bulb illuminates the whole house, one brave soul gave the entire crowd fortitude.

It was a terrible sight. Their loved ones were writhing in front of them, but the people shed no tears. Where did they get such courage! Do armies always remain steadfast in the battlefield? The same army that on one day fights fearlessly, on another day flees at the first sound of gunfire. But that is true for mercenaries who do not have the conviction of truth and justice, who fight only for their living or for the spoils of war. This throng had the strength of truth and justice. Every man and woman, no matter how ignorant, understood that he or she was fighting for his or her rights and dharma. To sacrifice one's life for dharma was as much a matter of pride in the code of the untouchables, as it was in the code of the higher castes.

But what has happened? Why have the policemen taken the bayonets off their guns? Why have they put guns on their shoulders? Oh, look! They have wheeled around and are forming a column four abreast. They are being ordered to march back towards the temple. No constable is left behind. Only Lala Samarkant is talking to the police superintendent, and the people are standing, as before, immovable, behind Sukhada. After a moment, the Superintendent also left. Lala Samarkant stepped closer to Sukhada and said loudly—'The temple is open to all. Whoever wishes can go and have a darshan of Thakurji. No one will be stopped.'

There was an uproar. Intoxicated with victory, people touched Sukhada's feet and then raced towards the temple.

After a few minutes, the crowd returned to the scene of the carnage, embraced the corpses of their dear ones, and wept. The students from the Sevashram brought stretchers and took away the injured people, while arrangements were made for the cremation of those who had fallen fighting for the cause. Cloth merchants donated yards of cloth for shrouds, others provided bamboo staves and ropes for biers, and ghee and firewood for cremation. The untouchables had won a victory not only over dharna, but also over hearts. Everyone in the city was eager to pay his respects.

In the evening the biers of the dead heroes were taken out in a procession. The entire city poured out of their homes to pay their respects. The procession first went to the temple. Both doors to the temple were wide open, and there was no sign of the priest or Brahmachari. Sukhada fetched sacred tulsi leaves from the temple and put it on the biers, and some drops of holy water in the mouths of the dead ones. This terrible carnage had occurred only to have the temple doors opened. Now those doors were wide open to welcome them but they couldn't enjoy the welcome. How strange was this victory! What detachment towards the temple for which they had given their lives.

After a little while, the biers were taken towards the river. The same Hindu society that had shunned these untouchables an hour ago was now showering flowers on their biers. There is so much power in self-sacrifice!

And Sukhada? She was the goddess of victory. At every step, the crowd cheered her name; sometimes they showered flowers; at other times, dry fruits; at still others, rupees. A little while ago she was unknown in the city, now she was its queen. Few get such acclaim! Walking in the procession, she felt humbled—it seemed to her that the tall houses on both sides were a bit higher and the people standing along the road a bit taller. Her head was bowed under the weight of this acclaim and glory; she had never before known such modesty and humility.

On the bank of the Ganges, funeral pyres were burning. Elsewhere, the temple was incandescent with lights in joyful celebration, as if the souls of the brave had been left there to shine.

CHAPTER 31

❧❦❧

It isn't necessary to recount the celebrations that took place at the temple or the commotion or festivities in the city the next day. All day the devout kept pouring into the temple. Brahmachari was again in his seat and he had probably never in his entire lifetime received the donations he received that day. Accordingly, his opposition to the entry of untouchables was diluted a good deal. But the higher castes who entered the temple continued to avoid bodily contact with the untouchables and sidled away with their noses pinched. Sukhada stood at the temple door and welcomed the people. She hugged the women and children, and greeted the men.

A dramatic change had occurred in Sukhada between yesterday and today. The woman who had been devoted to a life of comfort and luxury was now the epitome of service and compassion. She was touched to see the devotion, faith, and enthusiasm of the poor untouchables. They were in rags, they were half blind, and they couldn't walk straight because they were so weak. But, drunk on devotion, they kept coming as if they were the rulers of the world, as if misery and sorrow had disappeared from the world. Sukhada was carried away by such simple, guileless devotion. Intelligent, energetic, and ambitious people often have a nature like hers. Only the brave truly enjoy life.

Irrespective of whether they were rich or poor, everybody considered Sukhada worthy of respect. This respect had fuelled a very worthy feeling of community service in Sukhada. What she had accomplished yesterday had been done in a fit of passion. She had not cared in the least what the result would be. At such moments considerations of what is advantageous or disadvantageous weaken the will. But today she was indeed interested in what she was doing, and she felt good about it. She now knew her strengths and abilities. Drunk on that feeling she forgot to think about her own welfare and became absorbed in service to others. It was as if she had found her soul.

Sukhada was now the leader of the city. She inaugurated every work of social welfare in the city. She was the chief participant in all ceremonies, all charitable works, and national movements. Her devotees pressed her to attend these functions whether she wanted to go or not, and her presence was the key to the success of any function. The surprising thing was that she began to make public speeches as well. Her speeches may have lacked wit and polish, but they came from the heart and, therefore, were much appreciated. The city had a number of public societies; some were social, some political, and some religious. They had all been lying dormant. Sukhada's arrival infused new life into them. The Temperance Society had been inactive for years. There had been no advertising or organization. One day its secretary convinced Sukhada to attend. The very next day, the Society had a choir group, several instructors, and many lady volunteers who agreed to go from door to door spreading the gospel of temperance. Panchayats were formed in each locality. The society was reborn.

Now Sukhada had many occasions to see the wretched condition of the poor. Until now her knowledge of the subject had been based on hearsay and she discovered that there was a big difference between seeing and hearing. She saw the dark narrow lanes in the city where fresh air and light never penetrated. Not only the ground but also the walls of houses were perpetually damp; one couldn't breathe because of the stench. There the working children of India, downtrodden and miserable, were struggling to seize a short existence from the jaws of death. Now she understood the reason for Amarkant's opposition to wealth and luxury. She felt mortified at living in her palatial house, wearing fine clothes, and eating good food. She stopped using servants for her work, and washed her own clothes and swept the house. The woman who used to wake up at eight o'clock in the morning now arose while it was still dark and got busy with the household work. Naina almost worshipped her now. Lalaji, seeing the condition his house was in, would fret and fume, but couldn't do anything. It seemed to him that Sukhada held court daily where important leaders and scholars came and went. Therefore, he felt a little subdued in front of Sukhada; but he was becoming dissatisfied with all the work that was required to maintain a home. When no one in the house listened to him or had any sympathy for him, how could he feel any attachment to the house? Your house is where your wishes are the law; those who follow your wishes are your real relatives. This house had become like an inn to him; but he was afraid of saying anything to either Sukhada or Naina.

One day Sukhada said to Naina, 'I don't want to live in this house any more. People will say, "You live in a mansion and then lecture us about temperance." I have been running around for months in efforts to reform alcoholics, but I have had no effect on them. They don't listen to what I have to say. Most alcoholics drink to forget their misery, why should they listen to me. We will be effective only when we live like them.'

For some days it had been quite wintry. It had rained a little and the cold air of the month of Poos, now moist, covered the sky with fog. In some places it had even become frosty. Munna, now a toddler, wanted to go outside and play but Naina restrained him, afraid he might catch cold. Putting a woollen hood over his head and ears, she said, 'What you say, Bhabhi, is correct, but we have to see whether we can live like them. It would probably kill me within a month.'

Sukhada said, as if she had made up her mind, 'I have been thinking of taking a small house in some lane and living there.' Turning to Naina, she said, 'Why don't you take off his hood and let him be? Children should not be treated like potted plants that will dry out with a gust of hot wind. They should be toughened like forest trees, which are able to withstand sun, rain, hail, and frost.'

Naina smiled and said, 'He has not been brought up like that, and now you want to toughen him up! If he catches cold, then what will you do?'

'Achcha, bhai, dress him as you please. It is you who takes care of him, not I.'

'Why? Won't you keep him with you in the small house?'

'He is your child, do with him as you wish. Who am I to say anything?'

'If you had lived like this when Bhaiya was here, he would have been your slave.'

Sukhada said proudly, 'What I was then, I am still today. When your brother was upset at Dadaji and moved to a separate house, didn't I stay with him? He thought I loved luxurious living, but I was never a slave to it. Yes, I didn't want to alienate Dadaji; that was my error. Now I will ask his permission before I live separately. You'll see, I'll raise the matter with him in such a fashion that he won't object at all.' Then, changing the subject, she said, 'Let's go visit Doctor Shantikumar for a while. I haven't been able to go there for some time.'

Naina had been visiting Shantikumar frequently, usually once a day, but she hadn't told Sukhada. He was now starting to walk around, but he was still so weak that he couldn't walk without a cane. He had been badly hurt and had been bedridden for six months. Yet Sukhada had reaped all the glory! His jealousy added to his misery. He didn't confide his mental anguish even to his most intimate friends, and so the thorn continued to prick him. Had Sukhada not been a woman as well as the wife of his favourite student and friend, he would probably have left the city. The greatest misfortune was that in these six months Sukhada had not visited him more than two or three times. Sukhada, in her turn, had no special regard for him because he was a friend of Amarkant.

Naina had no objection to going with Sukhada. Her mother, Renuka, had had a car for some time, used primarily by Sukhada. The two got into the car; Munna couldn't be left behind, so Naina took him along as well.

After going some distance, Sukhada remarked, 'These are all luxuries of the rich. If I wanted, to I could live on two or three annas per day.'

Naina laughed and said, 'Show me first, then I will believe you. I know I couldn't do it.'

'As long as I live in this house, I can't do it either. That is why I want to live on my own.'

'But you will have to have somebody with you.'

'I don't think it is necessary. In this very city thousands of women live alone. Why should it be so difficult for me? There are many who will protect me. I can also defend myself.' Then she smiled and said, 'But, yes, it would be a different matter if I fell for someone.'

Shantikumar was sitting in a chair wrapped from head to foot in a blanket. There was a lighted angithi nearby and he was reading a book on health care. These days he was obsessed with getting well as soon as possible. When he was told that the two ladies had come to visit him, he put his book down, took off the blanket, and put it away. He wanted to remove the angithi as well, but he didn't get a chance. He greeted the two ladies as they came into the room and, indicating chairs, said, 'I am jealous of you both. You are wandering about in this cold weather and I am lying here with this lighted angithi. What can I do, I can't even stand up. Six months of my life have been lost; no, rather half my life has been lost! Even if I get well, I will still have only half my strength. I am so ashamed that ladies can go out and work, while I lie closeted indoors.'

Consoling him, Sukhada said, 'Considering the awakening that you have brought to the people in this city, you have accomplished as much as someone might in four lifetimes. In contrast, I have done nothing to merit the glory.'

At such praise from Sukhada, Shantikumar's pale face glowed with pride, and he felt that his life was justified. He said, 'You are very kind. Only you could have accomplished what you have done and are still doing. When Amarkant returns, he will discover that there is no work left here for him to do. Even in his dreams, he wouldn't have imagined what has happened here in the last year. The number of boys in Sevashram has increased rapidly. If it continues like this we will have to move to another location. I don't know where we will get the teachers. At times, I get very concerned at the apathy of our civil society. Everyone you see is busily pursuing self-interest. The more important they are, the greater is their selfishness. This is the blessing we have received from worshipping European culture for one hundred and fifty years! But, despite that, I have no doubt that our future is bright. The soul of India is still alive and I am confident that the time is not far when we will return to the old ideals of service and renunciation. Then the accumulation of money won't be our goal in life, and we won't be valued on the basis of our bank balances.'

Meanwhile, Munna had climbed up on a chair and picked up the inkpot from the table. He was happily dabbing black ink all over his face. Naina ran and seized the inkpot from his hands and gave him a gentle smack.

Shantikumar, unsuccessfully trying to get up, said, 'Why did you smack him, Naina? He is a great man! Only great minds freely admit their defects. He is unconcernedly showing those black stains on his face, whereas we would be ashamed and hide our faces behind a veil.'

Naina, depositing the child in his arms, said, 'Then take this great man. It is difficult to sit peacefully with him around.'

Shantikumar hugged the child. That warm and cuddly touch gave his soul a sense of fulfilment and contentment that was new to him. The affection that he had for Amarkant was condensed into this small body, and had become substantial and weighty. Thinking of Amar and this joy that he had deprived himself of, Shantikumar's eyes became moist and he felt humbled. Today, for the first time, he became aware of a lacuna, an emptiness in his own life. The desires he thought he had completely subdued came alive like embers hidden in ashes.

Munna, having painted Shantikumar's face with the ink on his hands as if he had gone to his arms just for that purpose, was trying to get down. Naina laughed and said, 'Just look at your face, Doctor sahab! This great man has played Holi with you! He is naughty.'

Sukhada couldn't contain her laughter either, and Shantikumar chuckled when he saw his face in the mirror. At that moment, the stain of the black ink seemed to him to be even more joyful than the mark of glory.

Suddenly Sukhada asked, 'Why didn't you marry, Doctor sahab?'

Shantikumar had structured his life on the basis of service to others and austerity; that foundation had been shaken in the days that he had been bed-ridden. He was no longer a firm believer in what he understood to be the truth of life. On many occasions during those difficult times he considered his life a burden. There was no lack of people ready to look after him; at all hours two or three people were there at his call. The important leaders of the city were also constantly coming and going. But it seemed to Shantikumar that those services and visits were done out of feelings of obligation or civility toward him. They lacked the sweetness and the tenderness that satisfy and nurture a soul. But a beggar has no right to refuse the kindness of any one; whatever charity he gets, he must accept. During this period, he often remembered his mother. Affection like hers was so difficult to get. Without knowing why, he felt in some way more alive whenever Naina came for a short time to inquire about his condition. As long as she was there, his ailments seemed to disappear. The minute she was gone the same moaning and groaning and restlessness would be back. In his mind it was this simple affection of Naina that had saved him from the jaws of death, but she was unattainable like a goddess from Heaven!

Hearing this question from Sukhada, he said smilingly, 'Because I haven't seen anyone happy after marriage.'

Sukhada thought this was a blow directed at her. She said, 'You probably also thought that it is always the woman's fault. Didn't you?'

Shantikumar, sensing Sukhada's resentment, said, 'I didn't say that. Perhaps, it is just the opposite. Not perhaps; indeed, it is mostly the man's fault.'

'Good, at least you accept that much. Thank you. But all it proves is that if a man wants to be, he can be happy in marriage.'

Shantikumar continued, 'But a man has a little of the animal in him which he may not be able to subdue despite his intention to do so. That same animal trait makes him a man. Developmentally, man is behind woman. When fully developed, he will become like a woman. A parent's love for a child, affection, tenderness, kindness—these are the bases on which the world rests and these are womanly virtues. If a woman understood this, then they would both be happy. Unfortunately, the woman living with an animal, becomes an animal, then both are unhappy.'

Sukhada said facetiously, 'That is certainly a novel thought. We have always been told that a woman is silly, that she deserves to be punished, that she is a noose around a man's neck, and God knows what else. The man wins either way. If a man were lowly, then why would he object to being ruled by a woman? But, you were too afraid to marry and put your hypothesis to the test.'

Shantikumar said abashed, 'Even if I wanted to now who would look at an old man?'

'Achcha! Now you are an old man! Then you should marry an old woman like yourself.'

'When a thoughtful woman such as yourself and a serious man such as Amar could not make it together, I didn't think it necessary to take any kind of an examination. I am not as modest and self-sacrificing as Amar, and someone as kind-hearted as you....'

Sukhada interrupted him, 'I am not kind, nor am I thoughtful. But yes, I do recognize my duty towards the man. You are older and much wiser than me. You are like an elder brother to me. I sense your gentleness and understanding today, and so I feel comfortable in asking you this: What right does a man who does not fulfil his obligations towards his wife have to expect that she maintain her vows toward him? You are a wise and honest man. I ask you, would you have excused my behaviour if I had treated him as he has treated me?'

Shantikumar said, without hesitation, 'No.'

'Did you consider his behaviour excusable?'

'No.'

'And knowing that, you still didn't say anything to him? You didn't even write him a letter? Why were you so apathetic? It must have been that in this case a woman had been wronged. If the situation had been reversed, then would you have been so apathetic? Please tell me.'

Shantikumar burst into tears. The accumulated pain of a woman's heart, expressed today in the form of this terrible revolt, touched him deeply.

Sukhada continued in the same agitated way, 'They say that a man is known by the company he keeps. I can't understand how someone who keeps the company of such eminent men as yourself, Muhammad Salim, and Swami Atmanand could forget his duty to such an extent. I don't say that I am blameless, no woman can make such a claim, nor can any man make it. I have met Sakina. It is possible that she has the virtues that I lack. She is more pleasant, more tender in temperament. It is possible that she may be more loving; but if all men and women start making such comparisons, then what state would the world be in? There would be nothing but rivers of blood and tears.'

Defeated, Shantikumar said, 'I acknowledge my mistake, Sukhada Devi. I didn't know you and I was under the impression that you had overstepped your bounds. I will immediately write to Amar....'

Sukhada interrupted again, 'No, I didn't come here to ask you that, nor do I want you to beg him for kindness on my behalf. If he wants to run away from me, I don't want to hold him back. A man has been given freedom, he is welcome to it; he can sell his body and soul wherever he pleases. I am quite content in my state of bondage. I pray to God that He keeps me within these bounds and that He gives me death before I vacillate from this course because of jealousy or a grudge. I am so gratified to have met you. I have told you things today that I have never told even my mother. Naina praised you highly; but you are even more gentle than she described. I am not going to let you remain single. May God soon bring the day when I see Bhabhi in this house.'

When the two women left, Doctor sahab, walking with the help of a cane, accompanied them to the gate to see them off. Afterwards, when he came back to his room and lay down it seemed to him that he had been rejuvenated. Sukhada's words, so full of pain, kept ringing in his ears, and he saw Naina with the child, Munna, in her arms standing in front of him.

CHAPTER 32

Shantikumar wrote a letter to Amar that night. He was one of those people who have time for everything but writing letters. The closer the friendship, the less was the reason to write. Their friendship was far deeper than could be expressed through letters. Shantikumar received all Amar's news through Salim and felt no need to write to him. He had blamed Sukhada that Amar had fallen in love with Sakina. But after meeting Sukhada today, he no longer blamed her. He wrote a long letter detailing the entire happenings of the past year. Everything that had occurred in the city since Amarkant's departure was described in full; he also asked for advice in connection with his own future. So far, he had not resigned from his position as university professor, but since the start of the movement, it didn't seem fitting for him to stay on in his position. His conscience bothered him about drawing a salary of five hundred rupees per month from the government when he was acting as an advocate for the poor against the same government. If you can't live like poor people, then you should abandon their cause, and eat, drink and live comfortably like everyone else. But in his heart he could never accept such indifference to the lot of the poor. The question was how would he live. Go to some village and take up farming? Even if he didn't work, his board wasn't a problem because Sevashram received enough contributions, but the mere thought of living on charity hurt his pride.

Four days had passed since he wrote the letter, and still there was no reply. He was beginning to worry now. He watched for the postman all day, but still there was no letter. What was the matter? Had Amar moved to some other place? Was it possible that Salim had given him the wrong address? It should take only three days for a reply to come from Haridwar; and now almost eight days had passed. He had urged Amar to reply immediately. Had he fallen ill? His letter was not an ordinary letter. It was a whole year's history of the city, and it would be very difficult to write a second ten-page letter. It had taken a full three hours to write it; and he didn't want to do it again. Also, Salim hadn't visited him for the last eight days. Nowadays he lived in a different world altogether. He was obsessed with entering the Indian Civil Service (ICS). Why would he come here? He probably feels a bit embarrassed with me. How selfish can he be? There was a time when he hated the very name of the Service. He was a member of the Youth Congress and of the Indian National Congress; wherever you looked he was present, and he wasn't an ordinary member, but one who took a leading part. And now he is fixated on the ICS. He would never get into the Service on his own, there is no chance of cheating and deception there; but he will get nominated nonetheless—Hafizji will exert all his influence. He would never have passed a single examination at the university without pilfering the question papers, or copying the answers, or outright bribery; he is a real rogue. And people like him get into the ICS!

Suddenly, a car arrived. Salim got out of the car and shaking hands with Shantikmar, said, 'You are looking much better. Do you still find it difficult to move around?'

Shantikumar said, mildly complaining, 'What does it matter to you whether I find it difficult or not! You haven't shown your face here for a whole month. What do you care whether I live or die? No one wants to be around when trouble comes, and you are no exception!'

'No, Doctor sahab, these days I am preoccupied with the examination. I hate it. God knows, my soul trembles at the thought of the Service; but what can I do, my dear father is determined. You know that I can't even write a sentence correctly, but who cares for ability. There they look only for a label. Whoever can follow the official directives; there is no doubt about his ability. I am learning this art these days.'

Shantikumar smiled and said, 'Congratulations! But it is not easy to get the designation of ICS.'

Salim didn't say anything, but the look on his face said, 'What would you know about these things. Salim is an old hand at these tricks. Getting a Bachelor of Arts degree was mere child's play. ICS will be a test of my skills. I won't show my face if I don't make the list of selected candidates in the Gazette. My name will be at the bottom, but if I wanted to I could even top the list. The salary will still be the same, so why bother?'

Shantikumar asked, 'Then will you also suck the blood of the poor?'

Salim said shamelessly, 'I have been nurtured on the blood of the poor. Why would I change? I have been sponging off other people's money since I first began school. But, to be honest, I don't feel right about it. After serving for a while in the ICS, I will move to the country where I will keep some cows and water buffalo and cultivate crops. I will live by the sweat of my labour and feel whole as a man. For now, however, like a bedbug I will have to subsist on the blood of others. But no matter how low I sink, my sympathy will always be with the poor. I will show that even as an officer one can serve the public. We are a farming family. My father is a self-made man. The idle rich can never have the love that I feel for the poor. Sometimes when I visit our villages, I feel as if I belong there. I respect the people for their simplicity and hard work. I don't know how anyone can abuse them or oppress them. If I could, I would sentence all those wicked officers to penal servitude.'

It seemed to Shantikumar that this young man had not yet been corrupted by the arrogance of officialdom. He still had a healthy attitude. He said, 'Until the public gets some authority in its own hands, the officers will continue to be high-handed. I am indeed pleased to hear these thoughts from you. I don't see a single good man anywhere. Like vultures, they are all aggregated at the corpse of the poor, picking away at their bones. But the whole thing is beyond our control.'

Continuing fatalistically, he said, 'One has to console oneself with the thought that when God wills the poor will acquire that authority. A revolution is needed, a full-fledged revolution. Until that happens, things will continue as they are. The fire will cool itself when there is nothing left to burn. Until then we warm our hands. Do you have any news of Amar? I sent him a letter, but he hasn't replied.'

Salim, startled, pulled out a letter from his pocket, saying, 'Oh, damn, I completely forgot this letter! It came four days ago, and I put it in my pocket. I meant to bring it everyday and everyday I forgot.'

Shantikumar took the letter after a few words of mild rebuke, and started to read. 'Bhai sahab, I am alive and am fulfilling your mission to the best of my ability. Naina's letters have been giving me some of the news, but I was astonished when I read your letter. In such a short time there has been what seems like a revolution in the minds of men. The credit for this awakening goes to you entirely. And Sukhada, she has become sacred to me. I feel distressed when I think how terribly mistaken I was in my understanding of her. How different she has turned out from what I thought her to be! With all my insight, wisdom, and gifts, I couldn't achieve in my lifetime what she has accomplished in a moment. Sometimes

I feel so proud, at other times I am so ashamed. I weep when I realize how ignorant we are about the people who are closest to us. What colossal ignorance! I wouldn't have ever dreamed that luxury-loving Sukhada could renounce her comforts so completely. This ignorance has left me nowhere. I want to beg Sukhada to forgive me, but how can I face her? I am in darkness, impenetrable darkness, and I can't think of any solution. My self-confidence has been shattered. It seems as if some unseen force wants to trample me while seeming to play with me. I am like a fish caught in a hook; a hand pulls the line and I get pulled, then the line is relaxed and I run. I will not complain about this pitiless game because now I know that man is a puppet in the hands of fate. I don't know where I am; I don't know where I am headed. I have no confidence in the future either. Whatever I believed has proved wrong, and whatever I dreamed has turned out to be untrue. I say to you honestly that Sukhada is making me dance; I am like a marionette in the hands of that illusionist. First she frightened me with one aspect of herself, now she is defeating me with another. What she is in reality, I don't know. I don't know whether or not the Sakina I knew was the real Sakina either. I don't even know who I am myself. I don't know what I am today and what I will become tomorrow. The past is painful, the future is unpredictable, and so I can live only in the present.

You asked me for advice regarding yourself. What can I say? You are far wiser than I. I think that those who have made a career of serving others have the right to take subsistence—food, clothing, and shelter—from the community. It would be even better if they could eliminate any selfish desires.'

Dissatisfied with the letter, Shantikumar put it down. Amar had dismissed in two sentences the subject that he had specially sought advice on.

Unexpectedly, he asked Salim, 'Have you also received a letter?'

'Yes, sir, it came with yours.'

'Did he write anything about me?'

'Nothing special, only that the country needed true missionaries and God knows what else. I didn't even read it to the end. That our lives should depend on charity—I consider such things sheer lunacy.'

Doctor sahab said somberly, 'It is much better that life is sustained by charity than supported by oppression. Government is not essential. Educated people have formed a union to suppress the poor, and that is called government. If you remove the differences between the rich and the poor, government will also come to an end.'

'You are talking theoretically, of course. As long as the world is not populated by angels, a government will be needed.'

'A man must always bear in mind his ideals.'

'But the Department of Education is not an instrument for oppression. When you donate a large portion of your income to Sevashram, there is no reason why you should leave that Department's service and become an ascetic.'

This argument appealed to the Doctor. Now he had found a way to assuage his conscience. Undoubtedly, the Department of Education did not rule over the people. The better the government, the more its educational effort would be extended. Then there would be no need for Sevashram. Dissemination of knowledge by a group following the ideal of service can't be objected to under any circumstances. The dilemma that had perplexed Doctor sahab for months was resolved today.

Saying goodbye to Salim, he went to Lala Samarkant's house. He wanted to please Sukhada by showing her the letter from Amar. He was also beginning to have some doubts about the dilemma that he had just resolved. It was necessary to set them to rest. Samarkant didn't greet him with open arms, but Sukhada called him in the minute she heard he was there. Renuka *bai* was also visiting.

As soon as he saw her, Shantikumar pulled out the letter from Amarkant, put it in front of Sukhada and said, 'Salim has had it in his pocket for the last four days, and here I was getting worried that there might be something wrong.'

Sukhada glanced at the letter and said, 'So, what am I supposed to do with it?'

Shantikumar was amazed, 'Just read it. Many of your misgivings may be resolved.'

Sukhada replied dryly, 'I have no misgivings about anyone. I know what is written in that letter. He probably praises me a lot. I don't want praise. During the uprising I became angry as anyone else would have; my actions were motivated by rage, and nobody admires rage.'

'How do you know that this letter praises you?'

'It is possible that he has also expressed regret.'

'Then what more do you want?'

'It is useless for me to say anything if you can't even understand that much.'

So far Renuka bai had been sitting quietly. Noting Sukhada's diffidence, she said, 'Until he returns home, how can one know that he is truly changed. He would have praised Sukhada even if she had not been his wife. So, what is the result? One can tell when a man and woman live happily together that they love each other. But love is very rare; even leaving it aside, one must do one's duty. What is the point of the husband sitting a thousand leagues away applauding his wife, and the wife sitting a thousand leagues away praising her husband?'

Vexed with her mother, Sukhada said, 'You talk without understanding anything, Amma. Life can be happy only when you find the right person. He has found someone better than me. He is happy even though she is not with him. I have not found anyone better than him and I am not going to find anyone in this life; that is my misfortune. It is no one's fault.'

Renuka looked towards Doctor sahab and said, 'Did you hear that, Babuji! She burns me up like this everyday. I have said to her so many times, "Let's go and bring him home; he won't be able to refuse. Everyone does something foolish when they are young." But she won't go with me nor will she let me go by myself. Bhaiya, not a single day passes that she eats a morsel without crying. Why don't you go, Bhaiya! You are his teacher. He respects you. He cannot ignore what you tell him.'

Sukhada smiled and said, 'Yes, now that you have asked him he will go immediately. He must be very pleased that at least one of his pupils has followed his ideals. These people consider marriage a social blemish. According to their rules, no one should marry, and if a man can't control his lust, then he should keep a mistress. Miyan Salim is another of his pupils. I don't know what pressure was put on our Babuji to get him married. Now he is atoning for that transgression.'

Abashed, Shantikumar said, 'Deviji, you are wrongly accusing me. In my case, yes, I decided to spend my life alone because from the outset I had the ideal of community service.'

Sukhada asked, 'Is it impossible to follow the ideals of service in married life? Or is a wife so blind with selfishness that she will always impede your work? A man who lives alone can never accomplish the kind of service that a family man can, because he has no experience of the difficulties of life.'

Trying to find a way to end the argument, Shantikumar said, 'This is a contentious issue, deviji, that can't be resolved. I need your advice on another matter. It is fortunate that your mother is also here. I have been thinking that I should resign from my position at the university and work full-time for Sevashram. What do you think?'

Sukhada answered as if the question were redundant, 'If you think that you can live without having to beg, then resign by all means. People in community service are usually supported by their organization. But to serve without any concern for selfish desires would be even nobler.'

The logic that Shantikumar had used to quell his conscience gave way. Once again he was in the same perplexed state.

Suddenly, Renuka asked, 'Do you have any cash reserves in your Ashram?'

The Ashram didn't have any reserves up to now. The contributions were not enough to build up any savings. Taking this as a slight on himself, Shantikumar said, 'No, we haven't been able to build up any reserves as yet, but if I got leave from the University, then I could make an effort in that direction.'

Renuka asked, 'How much money do you need to run your Ashram?'

Sensing a ray of hope Shantikumar, said, 'If I could get three or four lakh of rupees, I could make the Ashram into a university and achieve more than the University does with twenty lakh rupees.'

Renuka smiled and said, 'If you could form a Trust, then I could help you to some extent. The thing is, there is no one now to enjoy the money that I had been saving so far. You already know Amar's bent. Sukhada is also headed that way. So I have to decide for myself. The Trust could give me a hundred rupees per month for my living expenses apart from bearing the cost of feeding and taking care of my animals.'

Shantikumar said hesitantly, 'I can accept your proposal only if Amar and Sukhada happily grant permission. And what about the child's rights?'

Sukhada responded, 'As far as I am concerned, I don't need her money; as for the child, his grandfather's wealth is not insignificant. I can't speak for others.'

Renuka said wearily, 'Amar cares far less for money than others do. Wealth is not like a light bulb that spreads illumination. Why should one be saddled with it if one doesn't need it? Wealth is not an easy burden to bear. I cannot bear it by myself. It would be so much better if it could be put to some good purpose. Lala Samarkant advises me to donate it to temples dedicated to Shiva but I am not inclined that way. There are so many temples already that there is a dearth of worshippers. The gift of education is the greatest of all gifts, especially for people whom society has always shunned. I have been thinking about this for several days, and I was going to meet you. I would have vacillated for another three or four

months, but since you have come my uncertainties have disappeared. There
is no dearth of people wanting to give money, only of deserving people.
A person wants to give money to charity where it will be spent according
to the wishes of the donor, not to someone who, getting free money,
blows it, or for appearance's sake, spends a little on the cause and keeps
the rest for himself on one pretext or another.'

So saying, she asked Shantikumar with a smile, 'You wouldn't deceive
me, would you?'

Shantikumar took the jest seriously, 'I don't myself know what my
intentions would be. You have no reason to have such confidence in me.'

Sukhada came to the rescue, 'That is not at issue, Doctor sahab; Amma
was only teasing.'

'Poison has its effect even when mixed with honey.'

Sukhada returned, 'It was not said to insult you.'

'I don't feel insulted. I am not yet worthy of such great confidence, let
me be tested for five or ten years first.'

Renuka said resignedly, 'Achcha, sahab. I take back my question. Come
to my house tomorrow, I'll send the car for you. The first thing is to form
the Trust. I have no misgivings. I have complete confidence in you.'

Doctor sahab said, thanking her, 'I will do my best to retain your
confidence.'

Renuka said, 'I want to finish this business soon. Naina's wedding is
coming close, then we won't have free time for months.'

Shantikumar shuddered at what he heard, 'Achcha, Naina Devi is getting
married! That is very good news. I will see you tomorrow and settle
everything. Should I also inform Amar?'

Sukhada said harshly, 'There is no need.'

Renuka said, 'No, you should inform him. Perhaps he will come, I
certainly hope he will.'

As Doctor sahab was leaving, Naina was getting out of the car with
the child.

Shantikumar said sadly, 'You will go away now, Naina?'

Naina bowed her head, but her eyes were moist.

CHAPTER 33

❧❧❧

Six months passed.

Sevashram Trust had been formed. Only Swami Atmanandji, who was the chief officer of the Ashram and an excellent procurer of goods, was dissatisfied with the arrangement and had resigned. He didn't want the rich to gain an entry to the Ashram, so he tried his utmost to prevent the formation of the Trust. In his opinion they were selling the soul of the Ashram for money—a serious blow to the Ashram. It was because money reigned supreme that Hindu society had enslaved the lowly. It was because of money that a distinction existed between high and low castes. Why should the independence of the Ashram be sacrificed for that money? But Swamiji was overridden and the Trust was formed. Sukhada laid its foundation stone. There were festivities, dining, songs, and music. The next day Shantikumar resigned from his position at the University.

Salim's ICS examinations were also over, and his name appeared at the very bottom in the Gazette just as he had foretold. Shantikumar was astonished. According to regulations, he had to go to England for two years, but Salim didn't want to do that. He would gladly have gone for a pleasure trip for three or four months, but he would not countenance a two-year stay. He should not have been accommodated, but he pressed so hard and pulled so many strings that he was exempted from this regulation. When the chief medical officer of the province attests that to expose this young man to the cold English air for two years would be hazardous to his health, then who would be prepared to take such an awesome responsibility! Hafizji Halim was ready to send his son, he was ready and willing to spend the money, but if the boy's health were ruined then who would comfort him. Ultimately, Salim was victorious. He was posted to the district where his friend Amarkant was already residing. He had chosen the district himself.

Salim's life had also undergone a major transformation. He was still as jovial as before, but he had become more fashionable and eclectic in his taste. He had lost some of his passion for composing verse. He was also more inclined towards marriage now. It is hard to say whether this change in Salim occurred suddenly or gradually, but, for a little while now, he had been visiting Sakina at her house and they had been secretly corresponding as well. Despite the fact that Amar's ardour had cooled, Sakina was still harbouring love for him in her heart so much that Salim felt vanquished. He now wanted to spend his life basking in her warm glow. His ayah's talk of Sakina's intense love for Amar would often reduce him to tears. His poetic heart, which had once, like the bumblebee, flitted from flower to flower sucking honey, was now filled with affection for one only. She was the grand passion of his life.

During this time Naina also got married. Lala Dhaniram was the richest man in town. His eldest son, Lala Maniram was a very gifted young man. Samarkant did not have much hope that the connection would materialize, because Dhaniram, since the day of the temple incident, had considered Samarkant's family unfit to associate with. But finally Samarkant's money won. Grand preparations were made for the wedding. Amarkant didn't attend, nor did Samarkant ask him to. Dhaniram had let it be known that if Amarkant participated, there would be no wedding and this news had reached Amarkant. Naina was neither happy nor sad at her marriage. She couldn't say or do anything. What could she say before her father's wishes? She heard all kinds of rumours about Maniram—that he was a drunk, he was licentious, he was a fool, he was egotistical—but she felt obliged to bow her head to her father's wishes. She would not have protested even if Samarkant had offered her as a sacrifice to some deity. She wept only when she was bidding farewell and leaving her home, but even then she was careful not to hurt her father's feelings. In Samarkant's eyes, money was the most valuable commodity. What experience did Naina have of life? In such an important matter as marriage her father's decision must be acceptable to her. She was uneasy but she would do her duty, even at the cost of her life.

Meanwhile, the collaboration between Sukhada and Shantikumar grew closer every day. There was no lack of money. Branches of Sevashram were being opened in every locality, and a vigorous boycott of intoxicating substances was being implemented. Sukhada's life was becoming highly disciplined. She was now exercising morning and evening. The watchword in her diet was nutrition rather than taste. Restraint and reserve were now the two principles of her daily life. Instead of reading novels, she chose to read historical and philosophical books. Her oratory had so developed that her audience was riveted. Real pain and feeling at the sorry condition of her country and society was reflected in her speeches, and that is the secret of the effectiveness of the spoken word. One more thing had been added to the reform platform she was associated with— the question of housing for the poor. It was now felt that until the problem of public housing was solved no reform proposals would be successful. But this was something that could be handled only by the Municipality, not by contributions. The Municipal Board was nervous handling such a large project. Hafiz Halim was Chairman, Lala Dhaniram was Vice Chairman, and it was difficult to make such antediluvian gentlemen see the necessity and importance of this question. A few men had come forward and were prepared to invest three or four lakhs of rupees once land had been granted. Lala Samarkant was one of them; even if he received interest at the rate of one quarter of one per cent he was satisfied. But the question was where to get the land. Sukhada couldn't see why the Municipality which provided land for mills, schools, and colleges, couldn't donate the land for this work.

It was evening. Shantikumar had come to Sukhada with a bundle of plans and he was showing her each plan as he unfolded it. These were building plans for the houses to be built. One plan was for housing at a rent of half a rupee per month, the second at one rupee per month, and the third at two rupees. Those at half a rupee per month rent had one bedroom, a sitting room in front, a kitchen, a verandah, and a small courtyard. Those at one rupee per month had two bedrooms; while those at two rupees had three bedrooms.

In all the houses, the rooms had windows, and the floor and walls up to a height of two feet were of *pucca* material. The roofs were of earthen tiles. The houses at a rent of two rupees also had a lavatory. The others had a communal lavatory between every ten houses.

Sukhada asked, 'Have you estimated the cost?'

Shantikumar responded, 'Why else would I have the plans made! The houses at half a rupee rent would cost about two hundred rupees, the ones at one rupee would cost about three hundred and those at for two rupees, about four hundred. The interest will be one quarter of one per cent.'

'How many houses are to be built in the first stage?'

'I have calculated about a minimum of three thousand. About that many houses will be needed for the southern end. Some people will put up the money only when the land is obtained, but we will need at least ten lakh.'

'That's murder! Ten lakh! For only one end!'

'If we can find partners who would put up five lakh, then the public itself will provide the rest of the money. There will be considerable savings in labour costs. The bricklayers, plasterers, diggers, carpenters, and ironsmiths are all prepared to work for half the wages. Those pushing the carts or carriages, even the ikka and tonga operators, are ready to work for free.'

'We will see, it may work. Dadaji might put up two or three lakh of rupees. Amma must still have some money left. For the rest, we will have to do something. The biggest difficulty is getting the land.'

'It is not difficult. If only ten bungalows of the wealthy were demolished there would be enough land.'

'Do you think it would be easy to demolish the bungalows?'

'No, I don't think it easy, but what is the alternative? No one wants to live outside the city. So the land has to be found within city limits. Some bungalows are so huge that a thousand men could live there with room to spare. Even your house is not small by any means! It could house ten poor families comfortably.'

Sukhada smiled, 'You want to wield your knife even on us!'

'You have to lead by example.'

'I am prepared to do so, but doesn't the Municipality have some empty plots?'

'It certainly does. I know about them, but Hafizji declares that all those plots are spoken for.'

Just then Salim got out of his car, and called out for Shantikumar. The latter beckoned him inside and asked, 'Where have you been?'

Salim said joyously, 'I am leaving tomorrow night for my new posting. I came to say goodbye. Fortunately, on that pretext I have been able to see Deviji as well.'

Shantikumar asked, 'What, you want to go away just like that? No festivities, no dinner, nothing? *Wah!*'

'There are going to be festivities tomorrow evening. A card has been sent to your house. But it isn't enough just to see you at the party.'

'Then, since you are going, help us out a little bit. Have the Municipality donate to us the plots located in the southern part of the city.'

Salim's face became grave. He said, 'Most likely those plots are already spoken for. Several members have indicated they want to buy them in the names of their sons and wives.'

Sukhada was astonished, 'Achcha! These wicked deals are going on in secret within the Municipal Board! Then we need your help all the more. It is your duty to break this vicious web of corruption.'

Salim said embarrassed, 'My father won't listen to me at all on this matter. And the fact is that it is not correct to force reconsideration of something that has already been decided.'

So saying, he shook hands with Sukhada and Shantikumar and, insisting that they both come to the party, left. He didn't feel comfortable staying there any longer.

Shantikumar said, 'Did you hear that? He has not yet taken up his post, but already he reeks of officialdom. What a peculiar spell there is about officialdom that it intoxicates you with a sense of power. He used to be such a staunch supporter of this scheme, but how he wriggled out of it today! If he had applied the least bit of pressure, it would have been impossible for Hafizji to disagree.'

Sukhada's face was alight with pride, 'We are fighting for a good cause. Justice is on our side. We are not dependent on the help of anyone else.'

Lala Samarkant came just then. When he saw Shantikumar sitting there, he hesitated, then asked, 'Tell me, Doctor sahab, what did you find out from Hafizji?'

Shantikumar narrated to him whatever he had done to date till then.

Samarkant said with some dissatisfaction, 'You people, all sahabs educated in England, what can I say to you. If you think that you will get the land by simply chanting justice and truth, you might as well keep quiet. To accomplish this work, ten or twenty thousand rupees will have to be spent. You should meet every Board member separately; see what kind of temperament, thinking, and peculiarities the man has. Then use the right approach to win his support—if he needs to be flattered to change his mind, flatter him; if he needs to be bribed to agree, give him lucre; blessings, amulets, hocus-pocus, whatever is needed to accomplish the aim, use it. Hafizji is an old acquaintance of mine. Send a bag of twenty five thousand rupees to his house via his ayah, and then you will see how quickly the land is given us. Promise to give the building contract for the new housing to Sardar Kalyansingh; then he will be under your control. You can get Dubeji on your side by presenting him with five vials of Chandrodaya, the Ayurvedic medicine. Talk to Khanna about yogic experience and introduce him to some yogi who can teach him three or four yogic positions. Name your new locality after Rai Sahab Dhaniram.

He may even give you some money. These are the ways to get things done. Don't worry about money. The Baniya community may have a bad name, but in matters of charity they are always the first to give. I myself will underwrite up to ten lakh rupees. I have the support of many of my fellow businessmen. I can't sleep at night thinking of how to make this project successful. I won't rest easy until it is completed.'

Shantikumar said in a subdued tone, 'I still have to learn these skills, Sethji. I have no experience in either accepting graft or offering it. Proposing something like this to a good man embarrasses me. I'm afraid he might consider me self-serving and might even rebuke me.'

Samarkant said as if reproving a dog, 'Then you may as well forget about getting the land. Teaching boys in Sevashram is one thing, making deals is another. I, myself, will make the deal.'

Sukhada said, deeply hurt, 'No, we are not prepared to offer bribes. Ours is a just cause and we have justice on our side. We will be victorious on the strength of that.'

Samarkant said, disappointed, 'That will be the end of your project.'

Sukhada said, determinedly, 'The project will be implemented, even if it gets delayed, or slowed down, but it won't be stopped. The days of injustice are over.'

'Alright. We'll see.'

Samarkant went out, very annoyed. He kept a distance from those who wouldn't accept his wisdom.

Shantikumar said, very pleased, 'Sethji is a peculiar being. He sees nothing but money. He won't accept the value of being human.'

Sukhada said with pride, 'Don't go by what he says, Doctor sahab. At heart he is more kind and giving than both of us combined. You don't know how much his nature has changed. A year and a half ago if his son had made this proposal, he would have exploded with anger. It is not usual to be willing to give away everything that one has, and especially for a man who has pinched pennies all his life. This transformation has been wrought by his love for his son. This is what I consider true asceticism. You should meet the Members first and, if you think it necessary, take me with you. I am hopeful we will get the majority vote. No, you shouldn't go alone. Come tomorrow morning and we will go together. We will be back by ten o'clock at night. Now, I have to go meet Sakina for a while. I hear she has been sick for months. I have developed a kind of respect for her. If I have time, I will go see Naina as well.'

Doctor sahab stood up and said, 'She has been gone almost two months. When is she coming back?'

'We have asked for her many times, but Seth Dhaniram doesn't send her.'

'Naina is happy, isn't she?'

'I have seen her many times, but she hasn't said anything about herself. When I asked her, she only said—I am quite well. But she didn't seem happy to me. She is not a girl to complain. She wouldn't leave the house even if those people kicked her out, nor would she say anything to anyone.'

Shantikumar's eyes became moist, 'I can't even imagine anyone being unhappy with her.'

Sukhada smiled and said, 'Her brother has chosen a wrong path in his life, isn't that reason enough for them to be displeased?'

'I have heard that Maniram is a first-rate scoundrel.'

'If you used that term in front of Naina, you would have a fight on your hands.'

'I would like to meet Maniram at least once.'

'Please don't do that. If you say anything to him, he will take it out on Naina.'

'I won't fight with him. Even though I don't know the art of flattery, and I will hate doing it, I will beseech him on Naina's behalf. I can't see her unhappy. My life would be worthless, if I saw her suffer who is the epitome of self-sacrifice, and didn't do everything in my power to help her.'

Shantikumar went out quickly for he could barely hold back his tears.

CHAPTER 34

Sukhada asked the driver to stop the car on the street where she thought Sakina's house was and stepped out to look for it. Even though she went up and down the street two-three times, she couldn't find the house. The adobe wall of the house and the curtain of rotting sackcloth were nowhere to be seen, instead there was what looked like a new room, which had been freshly painted. Finally she asked a man and discovered that what she had been thinking of as a new room was in fact the door to Sakina's house. She called out for Sakina, and in a moment the door was opened. Sukhada found herself in a clean but small room, which had two or three rattan chairs. Sakina brought forward a chair for her and asked, 'Did you have to search for the house? With the addition of this new room, it is difficult to know which one it is.'

Sukhada, looking at her pale, emaciated face, said, 'Yes, I went around two or three times. Now it can be called a house; but why are you in this condition? I didn't recognize you.'

Sakina tried to laugh it off and said, 'I was never very plump.'

'Now you are much thinner than before.'

Pathanin arrived unexpectedly and hearing her, said, 'She has had a fever for months, beti, but she won't take any medicine. What can I say; she won't even talk to me. Allah knows, I kept thinking of you, Bahuji, but how could I come and show my face. It is only a little while ago that Lalaji himself left. May God bless him with a long life. I didn't go to collect my allowance because Sakina had forbidden me. So he came himself to give it to me. Such large-hearted people are rare in this world. Anybody else wouldn't have even looked at me. His prosperous household was destroyed because of ill-fated me. But Lala is still as kind and thoughtful and charitable to me as ever. I don't know what came over me that I accused that innocent boy. May God punish me so that I don't even get a shroud at my death. Lately I have thought about it a lot, beti! Everyone reproached and reviled me; this girl even stopped talking to me. Ask her, she's standing here. She says things that pierce my heart. It is God's will, so I listen. If I hadn't done what I did, then I wouldn't have had to hear those things. I got suspicious when I saw him with her in that darkened house. And when he realized that the poor girl might get a bad name, then for her sake he was even willing to give up his religion. Wretched me, in my anger, I didn't understand that I was painting my own face black.'

Sakina said sharply, 'Alright, it is all over and done with. How long will you cry over your sad tale? Will you let anyone else talk?'

Pathanin appealed to Sukhada, 'Beti, she keeps berating me so and won't let me speak. Ask yourself, if I don't tell you my guilty story, who else can I tell?'

Sukhada asked Sakina, 'Achcha, why did you refuse the allowance? It has been going on for a long time.'

Sakina was going to say something when Pathanin interrupted, 'She keeps quarrelling with me on that score, Bahu. She says we shouldn't accept charity from anyone. She doesn't know that we have been supported all these years on charity. Nowadays, she has this mania for sewing. She is ruining her eyes sewing until midnight. Just look at her face. She has developed a fever for the same reason, but she won't take any medicine. I tell her, first take care of your health, then work. Who do we have to feed—a whole army? There are just the two of us. But she has this obsession—the house and everything in it should be perfect. We have plenty of work these days and the wages are good too, but all of it is blown on doing up the house. A Christian lady lives not too far from here. She comes every morning to teach her English. In my days, beta, it was customary to pray and fast. Messages for marriage came from many places ...'

Sakina said harshly, 'Oh, be quiet now. It is all over and done with. What can I offer you, sister? At least you remembered this unfortunate person after so long.'

Sukhada said in a generous spirit, 'I thought about you often, and wanted to come to see you, but I was afraid what you might think. Today I heard from Miyan Salim that you are not well. When all of us are prepared to help you in every way, why are you sacrificing your life working so hard?'

Sakina replied, mortified, 'Sister, I may die but I am determined not to be poor any more. Had I not been so destitute, Babuji wouldn't have felt sorry for me. He wouldn't have come to my house, wouldn't have acquired a bad name and wouldn't have run away from his home. The root of all trouble is poverty. I am determined to end it.'

After a moment she said to Pathanin, 'Go and get some paan from a tambolin. Sister, that is the least we can offer you.'

Getting the old woman away under that pretext, Sakina said in a low voice, 'I have a letter from Mohammad Salim. When you are so kind to me, how can I hide anything from you? Whatever had to happen has happened. Babuji came here several times. God knows that he didn't even once raise his eyes towards me. I also respected him and yes, I was certainly affected by his civility. When he suddenly heard the news of my upcoming marriage he was shocked into coming and expressing his love for me. As God is my witness, sister, I am not making up a single word. When I heard his endearing words, I also lost my senses. That such a cultured man should love a woman like me swept me off my feet. He was sacrificing his body and soul for me. I was overcome getting that gift; after all, I wasn't a wooden marionette. I don't know what special thing he saw in me. From what he said, I gathered that he wasn't very happy with you. Sister, please excuse me, I am being very candid. He certainly had some grievance against you. Just as a rich man after a long period of hunger forgets the sweet taste of saffron rice and greedily devours gruel, in the same way his heart having become disenchanted with you leaped toward me. His soul was hungering for love and affection. Perhaps he had never been given that gift. He is not a fickle man who goes for novelty. He wants to be committed to someone body and soul and wants the same commitment from her. I am sorry now that I didn't go with him. The poor man fell for the gruel and that, too, was snatched away from him. You can still win his heart. You have only to write him a letter expressing your love. He will come running the very next day. Meanwhile, I have found a diamond, and won't let it go until someone snatches it out of my hands. Just the thought that I have the diamond will keep my heart strong and happy always.'

She rushed into the house and brought out a scented envelope. Giving it to Sukhada, she said, 'This is the letter from Miyan Mohammad Salim that I mentioned. You can read it. There is no secret in it. At first he wanted to marry me off to his personal valet. Now he wants to marry me himself. Earlier he may have been whatever he was, but now there is nothing sordid about his intentions. His ayah keeps telling me about him, and whatever he knows about me he too, must have heard from the ayah. I have caught him staring at our door several times. I hear he has some high office. It seems that my luck has finally turned for the better, but the delicate chain that ties me to love cannot be broken by the mightiest force. Until I know that Babuji has given me up I will be true to him; and even when he has given me up, I will continue to cherish his love. A moment of such pure love is enough to keep a person euphoric for life. I have replied to Salim along these lines. Tomorrow he leaves for his posting. He started crying when he read my letter. Now he is resolved that either he will marry me or remain a bachelor forever. He is going to the district where babuji is. The two friends will , I think, talk about me and decide. That's why he is in such a hurry to leave.'

The old woman returned with the paan wrapped in a *gilauri*. Sukhada, lost in thought, absently took the paan and put it in her mouth. Today, she felt completely vanquished by Sakina. In spite of being wealthy and belonging to an illustrious family, Sukhada felt like a beggar before Sakina, finally acknowledging her failings. So far she had used logic to tell herself that this young woman had ensnared Amar by coquetry and gay wantonness, for men, after all, are fickle and like butterflies flit from flower to flower. She discovered today that Sakina had no coquetry, no wantonness, and no flirtatious glances. Instead she was like tender and soothing music that can only be appreciated by those who have a heart. In her was none of the spice that arouses the senses and is sought by whoremongers and voluptuaries. With a magnanimity that had been forged in the fire of resentment, she hugged Sakina and said, 'Sister, what you have said today has lightened the load on my heart. It is possible that the charge you have levelled against me is just. I hold no rancour against you any more. I will also say that if Babuji had any grievance against me, he should have told me about it. As God is my witness, I have never knowingly done anything to displease him, but yes, I can now see that he may have interpreted certain things as my callousness. But, I still can't forgive him for the insult that he has dealt me. If he was hungry for love, so was I. What he wanted from me was what I wanted from him. When he himself couldn't give me what he wanted me to give him, why did he act so arrogantly? Is it because he is a man, and a man may treat his wife like the slipper on his feet, but the woman's duty is to stick to his feet? Sister, just as you have hidden nothing from me, so I am telling you everything honestly. If you put yourself in my place for a moment, you will understand how I feel. If

I am at fault, then he is equally at fault. Why couldn't he have become reconciled to his fate, as I had? Then perhaps things would have been easier. But until he offers his hand to me, I cannot extend my hand to him, even if I have to spend my entire life in this condition. A woman is weak and is therefore hurt more in matters of respect and prestige than men. Now allow me, sister, I have to go and see Naina for a little while. Please come and visit us sometime, I will send a ride for you.'

For some reason, when Sukhada left, Sakina was crying.

CHAPTER 35

It was nine in the evening when Sukhada arrived at Seth Dhaniram's house. It was a palatial building reaching up to the sky. Two guards flanked the main door, which was illuminated by a powerful electric light. When they saw Sukhada arriving, there was a commotion inside and out. Lala Maniram came out of the house and escorted Sukhada to a sofa in the formal drawing room on the second floor. The ladies in the house peeked at her through the curtains, they didn't dare come into the room.

Sukhada asked, 'Is everything alright?'

Maniram lit a cigar and blowing out smoke said, 'You have perhaps not seen the paper. Papa has had a fever for the last two days. I called in Dr Lancet from Calcutta because I don't trust anyone here and I also notified the press. Papa is getting old. I tell him that he should rest peacefully, and he wants to, but people won't let him. The Governor was on a visit to Allahabad. His private secretary sent a special invitation to Papa, so he was obliged to go there. Nobody else in the city was invited. How could he refuse such an honour! He caught a cold there. Anyone can earn enough to keep body and soul together, but it is being respected that is the main thing in life. There is a constant procession of the city's elite coming to the house from dawn to dusk. This morning the Deputy Commissioner of the District and his memsahab came. The Commissioner of the Division sent a telegram of sympathy. A few days of sickness is nothing if one receives this kind of honour. I spend the whole day hosting officials.'

A servant brought a plate of paan and cardamoms. Maniram, offering the plate to Sukhada, said, 'My house needed a woman familiar with social etiquette, who could have entertained the ladies. That objective has not been attained by this marriage, so I will have to marry again. There is no dearth of women of the old school in our house, but they can't be good hostesses. They can't even be presented to the ladies. It would be embarassing to bring these stupid, uncouth women out before them.'

Smiling, Sukhada said, 'Then why didn't you marry some lady?'

Without any compunction, Maniram replied, 'We were taken in, what else. How could we have known that a girl from such an educated family would be so uncultured? My mother, sisters, and women of the neighbourhood are very taken with the new bahu. She observes fasts, does puja, and puts vermilion tika on her forehead, but I have to accomplish something and make a name for myself in the world. I don't need a woman who worships and reads scriptures; but now that the marriage has taken place, it can't be broken. Therefore, I will have to marry again. When ladies come to visit, which is almost everyday, they have to be entertained. They must think us all so ignorant.'

Sukhada was beginning to despise this twenty-one year old man's world-view, which he stated without any qualms. His self-indulgence seemed to have so crushed his better feelings that he had become a buffoon.

'For such work you can hire women for a small wage, who will not only entertain the ladies, but also their men.'

'You can't be expected to comprehend these business-related problems. Agents from big mills come here. If my wife could converse with them, then we could increase the commission rate somewhat. This task can only be accomplished by a woman.'

'I would never do such a thing, even if the entire business went to the dogs.'

'As far as I understand the meaning of marriage, the wife should be *sahgaamini*, an associate of the husband. Among English people, women are their husbands' helpmeets.'

'You have not understood the meaning of the term "sahgaamini".'

Maniram was curt and rude. His aides called him direct and plainspoken. Even his jokes began with a vulgar expression. He said, 'You, of all people, don't have any right to lecture me on this subject. Had you understood the meaning then you wouldn't now be separated from your husband, and he wouldn't be wandering in lanes and hovels seeking solace.'

Sukhada's face burned with shame and anger. Getting up from her seat, she thundered, 'You have no right to comment on my affairs, Lala Maniram; absolutely none. You claim to be a great devotee of English culture. Do you think that Western clothing and a cigar are its principal features? Its chief ingredient is respect and honour of women; that is something you still have to learn. No woman from a good family would accept losing her self-respect in that fashion.'

The entire house shook at her outburst, and Maniram seemed to be struck dumb. Naina was sitting in her room waiting for her sister-in-law. Hearing her, she knew something had happened. She went running to the door of the drawing room.

'I was waiting for you, Bhabhi, and here you are!'

Sukhada, ignoring her, continued angrily, 'It is a good thing to earn money, but not by selling your self-respect. And the purpose of marriage is not what you think it is. I now know how low a self-seeking man can fall.'

Naina came and took hold of her hand saying, 'Are you coming with me or not?'

Sukhada said with even greater vehemence, 'Why didn't I go with my husband? Because I wasn't prepared to make as much sacrifice as he. You love your business and wealth more than the self-respect of your wife. My husband refused both. You mentioned lanes and hovels; if you mean by that what I think you do, then it is a base charge. You had better stick to making money. For you to cast aspersions on that noble soul is like a dog yapping at an elephant.'

Sukhada was trying, though unsuccessfully, to match his one great blow by several small hits. She could not bring herself to utter a sentence as sharp as the prick of that single sentence of Maniram.

Naina couldn't help saying, 'Bhabhi, why are you needlessly quarrelling with him?'

Maniram clenching his fist in anger said, 'I won't tolerate such insult in my own house.'

Naina, folding her hands in supplication before Sukhada, said, 'Bhabhi, have pity on me. For God's sake come away.'

Sukhada asked, 'Where is Sethji? I want to say a few things to him.'

Maniram said, 'You can't see him now. He is not well and he won't want to hear unpleasant things.'

'Alright, I won't see him. Naina, do you know that there will be an English "second wife" in this house soon?'

'It is just as well. Who cares how many people come into the house. One, two, as many as he wishes, it doesn't affect me.'

Maniram lost his control at this facetions exchange. As Sukhada started walking with Naina, he blocked her way and said, 'You can't go any further into my house.'

Sukhada stopped and said, 'Alright, I will leave but, remember, insulting me like this won't be good for you.'

Naina fell at Sukhada's feet in supplication; but, Sukhada left in a fury. In a moment, all the women and children in the house had assembled and comments about Sukhada started flying. Someone said—'She is shameless'—another said—'If she wasn't, then why would her husband have left her and gone away?' Naina listened with her head bowed. Her soul was berating her—this injustice is going on in front of you, and you sit silent listening to it! But opening her mouth then would have been disastrous. She was the daughter of Lala Samarkant—she could not erase that stigma even with all her open and guileless service. Samarkant had sown the seeds of a grudge when he had bested Lala Dhaniram at the time of Valmiki's Ramayana katha. Before that the two Seths had been friendly with each other. Resentment had begun that day. Dhaniram had accepted the proposal for this marriage only to revenge himself on Samarkant. After the marriage, the flame of his rancour had cooled somewhat.

Maniram, putting his feet up on the table, said disdainfully, 'What could I say to a woman? If it had been a man I would have said something that he would never have forgotten. Lala Samarkant amassed his wealth through gambling. Now he is reaping the harvest of that sin. She came here to berate me. Her mother has been fooled by that rogue Shantikumar and has signed away all her wealth to him. Now she is dependent on him for the smallest bit of money. Samarkant is also going the same path. And this lady has embarked on a route that she thinks will benefit the country! Her husband is wandering destitute from pillar to post and she is engaged in reformation of the country. She had the temple opened up to untouchables and now she thinks she is better than anyone else. Now she is fighting with the Municipality for land; she will suffer a defeat that she will always remember. As for business acumen, I have carried out more business in two years than Lala Samarkant would be able to achieve in seven lives.'

The entire household deferred to Maniram. He earned good money and even though the people in the house might not like his conduct and behaviour, they listened to him. After all, it was he that had opened the agencies for paper and sugar. Lala Dhaniram dealt in ghee and knew that business very well. It was profitable to a limited extent. Maniram was the sole agent for paper and sugar and profits were unlimited. This success had turned his head. He didn't think anybody else worth anything. If he respected anyone, it was Lala Dhaniram. He alone could curb him somewhat.

They were still talking when Lala Dhaniram, coughing and walking with the help of a stick, came and sat down.

Maniram immediately switching off the fan said, 'Why did you trouble yourself, Babuji? You could have called me. Doctor sahab has prohibited you from walking around.'

Lala Dhaniram asked, 'Did Lala Samarkant's bahu come here today?'

Maniram said, a bit frightened, 'Oh, yes. She has just left.'

Dhaniram said angrily, 'And you didn't inform me. Do you think I am already dead?'

'I tried to stop her, but she went away annoyed.'

'You must have upset her, otherwise she would never have left without seeing me.'

'All I said was that you were not well.'

'So you think that if someone is not well, he should be allowed to die alone? A man doesn't want to die alone. His dearest wish is that in times of trouble, his near and dear ones be around him.'

Lala Dhaniram had a coughing spell. After a while, he resumed, 'Have you gone crazy or something? Being successful in business doesn't mean that you have succeeded in life. Do you understand? A successful man is one who has others do his work for him while making them feel obliged to him. Boasting does not prove that you are successful, it only proves that you are shallow. If she had come to me, she would have gone away happy. Her support is very useful. You are perhaps not aware how much respect she commands in the city. If she wants to harm you, she could ruin you in a day. And she will ruin you, believe me. She is an exceptionally purposeful woman. One who doesn't care for her husband, or her life. I don't know when you will grow wiser!'

Lala Dhaniram had another attack of coughing. Maniram rushed to support him and stroked his back. After about a minute, Lalaji was able to breathe again.

Worried, Maniram said, 'You don't seem to be getting any better with this doctor's medication. Shouldn't we call Kaviraj? I can send him a telegram right away.'

Dhaniram took a deep breath and said, 'I will certainly get better, Beta, with a pinch of ash from some saint's hand. But, yes, if you want to make a show of all these doctors and medicine men coming here, do so by all means. Even this doctor was not a bad one. I am not opposed to spending a few rupees for such a spectacle, but for the time being I have had enough. I will tell doctor sahab tomorrow that he can go, I am much better.'

Maniram asked apprehensively, 'Do you want me to go and see Sukhada Devi?'

Dhaniram said proudly, 'No, I don't want you to suffer indignity. I have to see how magnanimous she is. I have suffered reverses many times, but never have I lowered myself before anyone. I know Samarkant. He may seem very bad, but he has a good heart. He is always guided by compassion and dharma. Now I have to test his bahu.'

Having said this, he picked up his stick and slowly walked toward his room. Maniram supported him with both arms.

CHAPTER 36

Naina returned to her father's house in the month of Saavan. Even though her in-laws' home was very close to her father's house, she had had no opportunity for six months to visit. If it had been in Maniram's power, he would still not have allowed her to go, but the entire household was ranged on Naina's side. It was tradition that all daughters-in-law go to their parents' house in Saavan. He could not go against that tradition.

Saavan's rain was pelting down. Occasionally a house would fall or a roof collapse. Sukhada was sitting in the verandah watching the raindrops send up bubbles as they splashed in the open courtyard. The courtyard was set deep and retained some water. The bubbles rose upwards for some distance, like batashas, and then disappeared, providing a most enjoyable spectacle. At times, two bubbles would meet and do a little dance together—just as we try to side step someone that we have accidentally come face to face with. Sukhada had the sudden feeling that the bubbles were alive, as if they were little children wearing round hats and playing in the water.

Just then Naina called, 'Bhabhi, come on, let's race paper boats. I am making some.'

Sukhada replied, staring at the bubbles, 'You play. I don't feel like it.'

But Naina would not take no for an answer. She came with two boats imploring Sukhada to rise, 'Whoever's boat reaches the other side wins. Let's bet five rupees.'

Sukhada was unwilling and replied, 'You race a boat for me. If you win, take the money, but I am telling you they will not be used to buy sweets.'

'Then what shall we buy—medicines?'

'Well, what better use? Thousands of people in the city have a cough and fever. It would help them.'

Suddenly Munna came, snatched both boats, put them in water, and started clapping.

Naina kissed the little boy and said, 'At my in-laws' house I would think of him three or four times everyday and cry. I don't know why I missed him all the time.'

'Achcha, did you ever think of me?'

'Never. But, yes, I missed Bhaiya often but he is so aloof that he did not send even one letter in six months. I have also made up my mind that until I receive a letter from him, I am not going to write to him.'

'Did you really not miss me? And here I thought that you would be anxious about me. But, after all, you are your brother's sister! No sooner out of sight than out of mind.'

'I used to be angry with you. In the last six months, you came only three times and even then without Munna.'

'If he had come with me, he would never have wanted to come back.'

'Then, was I his enemy?'

'I don't really trust your in-laws, so I was uncomfortable taking him with me. I can't imagine how you manage to live there.'

'Yes, but what can I do? Run away? Then the world would laugh at me.'

'Alright, tell me truthfully, does your husband love you?'

'You already know the answer to that one.'

'I wouldn't even talk to such a man.'

'I don't talk to him either.'

'Really! He must be very annoyed. Come, tell me all. What happened on your wedding night? Swear on me that you will tell me the whole truth.'

Naina frowned and said, 'Bhabhi, you hurt me by putting me under oath. Now I am not going to tell you anything.'

'Ok, don't tell me anything. It is not necessary.'

Having said this, she got up to go upstairs. Naina caught her hand and said, 'Now, Bhabhi where are you going? You have put me under oath, so sit down and listen. Up to now, my husband and I have not talked even once.'

Sukhada said, very surprised, 'Really, is that true?'

Naina said with a grieving heart, 'Oh, yes Bhabhi, it is absolutely true. On my wedding night he came to me with a garland around his neck and his eyes red with drink. He was like a peon who had come to collect money on behalf of a lender. Lifting my veil, he said, 'I have not come to see your veil, and I do not like such pretence. Come and sit on this chair.

I am not one of those traditional husbands who play such girlish games. You should have welcomed me with a smile instead of sitting with your veil pulled down as if you don't want to see my face.'

'His touch made my skin crawl. I shivered from head to toe. What right did he have to touch my body? This question rose like a flame in my mind. I started crying; my golden dreams of the previous few days were shattered. Was this the husband I had been worshipping in my dreams: this person who had no grace, no humanity; only a drunken stupidity, pride of possession, and shamelessness? I had been prepared to present to my husband a platter full of offerings—my deepest devotion, happiness, and love. After seeing him for what he was, the platter seemed to fall from my hands scattering the offerings on the ground. His arrogant possessiveness repelled every fibre of my being. All my thoughts of abandoning myself to him disappeared. I felt like saying that my marriage to you does not mean that I am your slave. If you are my master, then I am also your master. I accept no authority except the authority of love, and I expect you to do the same. But I was so distraught that I couldn't even reprove him.

'Immediately I got up and went out into the verandah. He waited for a while in the room; then exasperated, came to me, grabbed my hand and tried to drag me back into the room. I shook my hand free and said harshly, "I won't take this kind of insult from you."

'He said, "Oh, oh, so beautiful and so proud!"

'I was burning with anger. I didn't reply. Even talking to him seemed like an affront to me. I went into the room, locked the doors, and I have not spoken to him since. I pray to God that he marries and leaves me alone. I can't accept as my lord and husband someone to whom only beauty and outward appearances matter in a woman and for whom a woman is only a source of self-gratification.'

Sukhada asked playfully, 'But you didn't give any evidence of your love either! What is there in the institution, "marriage", that dictates that a husband must immediately prostrate himself before his wife?'

Naina said seriously, 'I do think that "marriage" entails just such surrender. One to whom marriage is not a sacred bond, but just a vehicle for sexual gratification, is like an animal.'

Suddenly Shantikumar arrived, dripping wet.

Sukhada asked, 'How did you get so wet, don't you have an umbrella?'

Shantikumar took off his raincoat and putting it on the clothesline, said, 'There was a Board meeting today. There was no transport available to come here.'

'What happened at the Board meeting? Was our proposal presented?'

'What we feared, happened.'

'How many votes did we lose by?'

'Only five. The same five people were against us. Lala Dhaniram did not leave any stone unturned to defeat the proposal.'

Sukhada said, very discouraged, 'So what happens now?'

'We will have to start a campaign through speeches and the newspapers.'

Agitated, Sukhada said, 'Oh, no, I'm not so accommodating. I won't let Lala Dhaniram and his associates sleep peacefully at night. We've been trying to persuade these people for so long, now we have to show them our strength. Perhaps, once again, some people will lose their lives before the eyes of people like Dhaniram are opened. I'll make it difficult for these people to live in the city.'

Shantikumar, who had past grudges against Lala Dhaniram, said, 'This is indeed the doing of Lala Dhaniram.'

Sukhada said angrily, 'I don't care which "Ram" is behind these doings. When the Board makes a decision, the responsibility for that decision rests with the entire Board, not with any one person. I will show these people who live in palaces that the common folk also have some power. Lala Dhaniram will not be able to take possession of those plots of land.'

Shantikumar said helplessly, 'In my opinion, propaganda is enough for the time being, otherwise things might get out of hand.'

Since the Trust had been established, Shantikumar was very reluctant to take any risks. Now he was responsible for an organization and, like other trustees, had come to regard the trust as an end in itself, overlooking its real purpose. He was forever concerned about the reputation of the trust, or its possible demise.

Sukhada rebuked him, 'What are you saying, Doctor sahab! I have had enough of these educated, selfish people. I know now that they only talk bravely. I will show them how the same humble people who have been trodden under their feet become serpents that coil around their legs. Until now, these humble folk have been begging for mercy; now they will demand their rights. They have the right not to be merciful, but who can deprive us of our rights? People don't give their lives for mercy, but everyone knows how to sacrifice his life for his rights. I'll test the mettle of Lala Dhaniram and his sycophants.'

So saying, Sukhada walked out into the rain.

After a few moments, Shantikumar asked Naina, 'Where has she gone? She has a very short temper.'

Naina looked around and asked the servant only to learn that Sukhada had gone out. So she informed Shantikumar.

Shantikumar said, amazed, 'Where would she have gone in this rain? I am afraid that she may have gone out to organize a strike.'

Then turning to Naina, he said, 'You completely forgot me, Naina, when you went to your in-laws. You didn't even write a letter.'

Suddenly, he realized that he had spoken out of turn. He had no right to ask this of Naina. What would she think of him? He was afraid that Naina might have taken offence and would be curt with him. How could he have made such a blunder? He felt as if he were choking and he wanted to run away immediately. His own honour now was in God's hand.

Naina's face was aflame. Without replying she went out of the room, calling for Munna. Shantikumar continued to sit like a statue but, eventually, with head bowed as if he had been beaten with shoes, got up to go. Naina's scarlet face, like a little flame, continued to burn his innermost being.

Naina said kindly, 'Where are you going Doctor sahab, at least wait until it stops raining!'

Shantikumar tried to say something, but instead of words it seemed that a lump of salt was stuck in his throat. Unsteadily and with tears welling in his eyes, he quickly went out.

CHAPTER 37

⁂

Rain was coming down in solid sheets and darkness had fallen before time. Sukhada was sitting in the thakurdwara arranging a strike that would humiliate the Municipal Board and its officers, one that would finally teach them the lesson that their lives depended on the goodwill and service of the very people they considered too lowly to have any rights. A call had gone out for people to assemble at the thakurdwara.

The news of the Board's decision had already spread through the town. On such occasions runners materialize out of nowhere and the air itself becomes electric. The entire town was buzzing with anticipation, as if an enemy had surrounded it. Small assemblies of men—Dhobhis, Chamaars, and sweepers—were gathered here and there. Barbers and Kahaars met in their own panchayats. For months people had been hoping that they would be living in new houses—clean, airy, and well-lit—which would herald a new dawn in their lives. Today the officials of the town had turned their dreams to ashes. The people had become aware of their rights and were no longer in a mood to tolerate any injustice that was heaped on them; they had as much right to a decent life as had the rich; they had tasted the success of collective resistance once. They would no longer tolerate the high-handedness and self-serving ways of the officials. Moreover, this was not a struggle about some vague political ideal which common people have difficulty visualizing. It was about tangible results in their own lives. There was no need to appeal to feelings or imagination. By early evening, there was a substantial gathering at the thakurdwara.

The spokesman for the dhobhis, Chaudhary Maiku, eyes red with drink, said stroking his beard, 'I was washing clothes when I heard the news. I came running. My house has no more room for clothes; where will I dry them in this wet weather?'

To this, Jagannath Kahaar responded caustically, 'Don't tell lies, Maiku, were you really washing clothes just now? You have come here straight from the liquor shop. However much we have tried, you have not renounced your habit.'

Maiku retorted sharply, 'Oh, do be quiet, Chaudhary, you drink bottle after bottle slyly at home, and then you pretend to be so pious.'

The leader of the sweepers, Matai, stood up and said pacifyingly, '*Pancho*, this is no time for squabbles. Deviji has called us for a specific task, we should discuss that and decide on our course of action. Shall we continue to rot in the holes we call our homes, or shall we go and appeal to the officials?'

Sukhada objected, 'Whatever we had to discuss with the officials, we have. They have paid us no heed. These talks have gone on for the last six months with no result, why should there be any change now? We have tried entreaties and requests but they haven't worked. Straight dealing will not work. The more we bend the more these powerful people put pressure on us. Today, you have to decide whether you are prepared to fight for your rights or not.'

The leader of the Chamaar was Sumer—toothless, wearing thick glasses, and leaning on a stick. He spoke up, 'What else can we do apart from making entreaties and requests? We are powerless.'

Murli Khatik thoughtfully responded, stroking his luxuriant moustache, 'What do you mean we are powerless? Aren't we men, don't we have children? Why do the rich live in palaces and bungalows, when we don't even have mud huts? There are five people in my family, four of them have been sick for an entire month. How can one not be sick in that airless hole? You can't even breathe in there.'

Iidu, the vegetable seller, trying to straighten his bent back, said, 'If it had been written in our fates to be comfortable, wouldn't we have been born into rich families. Look at Hafiz Halim. He is now an important person; I remember him when he sold shoes. He made money during the War, now he puts on airs. He wouldn't even deign to recognize me now. There was a time when he used to take radishes and cucumber worth a pice or two on credit. His son is now an officer. Allah's will works in wonderful ways! What can one say.'

The milkman, Jangali, was a big black giant of a man, a famous wrestler. He said, 'I knew from the beginning that nothing much was going to happen. Who listens to us humble folks?'

Amir Beg, thrusting out his long scrawny neck, said, 'One possibility is an appeal against the Board's decision. We should lodge an appeal in the High Court. If the High Court doesn't hear it, then we should appeal to the King.'

Sukhada smiled and said, 'An appeal against the Board's decision is indeed what you have before you. You people are the High Court. You people are the judges. The Board looks after the rich. The settlements of the poor are demolished to make room for the palaces of the rich. The poor are paid five or ten rupees as compensation for the same land that later fetches thousands. That money is used to pay fat salaries to officers. The land that we have laid a claim to has been alloted to Lala Dhaniram. The Board values money above your lives. Give up any hope of justice from these selfish men. But they have no idea of your power. They think— these poor people, what can they do to us. I say to you, everything is in your hands. We don't want a fight, we don't want any trouble. We will only go on a general strike to show that you do not accept the decision of the Board. And this strike will not be just for a day or two; it will continue until the Board rescinds its decision and gives us the land. I realize that it won't be easy. Several among you don't have enough food in your houses for even one day; but I also know that without undergoing hardship one does not get anywhere.'

Sumer had a shoe shop that employed three or four leather workers. Starting as a labourer he was now a businessman, lending money and charging interest to grass cutters and coachmen. Peering short-sightedly from behind his thick glasses, he said, 'Bahuji, I am your servant and know that whatever you do you do for our good; but it is difficult to have a strike in our community. The poor people cut grass all day then sell it in the evening to buy some flour and pulses, only then is the kitchen fire lit. Some tend horses, some are coachmen; they will lose their jobs. Now people from other communities have also taken to tending horses and driving coaches. If others take their jobs, what will they do?'

Sukhada could not bear opposition. She didn't think that these were important concerns. She returned crossly, 'Did you think that you would get comfortable houses to live in without doing anything? In this world, whoever can bear the most hardship is ultimately the victor.'

Matai, the leader of sweepers, said, 'A strike will hurt all of us, without exception; but you cannot light a fire without smoke. If we do not do what Bahuji suggests, rest assured, we will be kicked around throughout our lives. Who else will understand the pain and suffering of us poor? You say you will lose your job; but we are all servants—some serve the government, some serve the wealthy. We will also have to take a communal oath that as long as the strike lasts, nobody will take anyone else's job, even though he or she might die from hunger.'

Sumer admonished Matai, 'You, *jamadaar*, don't understand the argument, but still jump in. Your situation and ours is different. Our work can be done by anyone, but your work can't be done by anyone else.'

Maiku supported Sumer, 'Well said, Sumer Chaudhary. Look at us. Now well-educated people are getting into the laundry business. Laundries have opened at many places. If there is even a day's delay in getting to the customer now, he sends the clothes off to a laundry, and we lose the customer. If the strike lasts five or ten days, our business will be sadly decimated. Now at least we have rotis to eat, then we will pine even for rotis.'

Murli Khatik challenged him, 'If you don't want to go on strike, then how do you intend to fight this? Do you think you will get milk simply by asking for it? Those times are long gone. If you are interested in the well-being of yourself and your children you will have to be ready to shoulder all kinds of trouble and hardship. Otherwise, go home, sit and relax, and die like flies.'

Iidu said with pious gravity, 'Whatever fate decrees will happen. Lamenting will get us nowhere. It was Hafiz Halim's destiny to become a rich man. If Allah so wills, it will not be long before the houses are built.'

Jangali agreed, 'Precisely. What you say, Iidu Miyan is very true. In our milk trade, if the milk is not delivered one day or if it is delivered late, then people begin to threaten—"We will get milk from the dairy, you are always late." If the strike continues for five or ten days, we will go bankrupt. Milk is not a commodity that keeps.'

Iidu said, 'The same goes for vegetables, brother; besides, in this rainy season, what is fresh in the morning is rotten by evening and no one will take it even for free.'

Amir Beg raised his storklike neck, 'Bahuji, I don't know any customs or laws, but I do know this much—that the King is fair to his subjects. At night, disguised, he wanders around among his subjects to find out how they are faring. If we were to prepare an application which bore all our signatures and submitted it to the King, then it will certainly be acted upon.'

Sukhada looked hopefully at Jagannath and said, 'What do you say, Jagannath; these people have given up.'

Jagannath, averting his face, said, 'Then, Bahuji, roasting a single chick pea will not explode the oven. If all these brothers join in, then I am also ready. Our community earns its daily bread through service. Some people have small shops, some carry small palanquins, but most are engaged as servants in rich households. If the women in these big houses become used to doing the housework for two or three days, that would be the end of our trade.'

Sukhada turned away from him and spoke to Matai, 'What do you say, have you also lost heart?'

Matai beat his chest and said, 'To go back on one's word is cowardly. Whatever you order will be done, no matter whether we live or die. Through God's grace, I still have such influence in my community that no one will go against me.'

Sukhada said decidedly, 'Alright, you get your community to go on strike as of tomorrow. All the other chiefs, please go. I myself will go from house to house, door to door, touching everyone's feet, and will not rest till there is a strike. If I fail and there is no strike, then I will blacken my face and drown myself. I had great hopes of you people; your great strength and your pride. You have broken my spirit.'

So saying, she walked out of thakurdwara, getting drenched in the rain. Matai left after her, while the other chiefs continued to sit, looking as if they were criminals.

Jagannath spoke up in admiration, 'Bahuji has the heart of a lion.'

Sumer chewed on his toothless gums and said, 'She is the incarnation of the goddess Laxmi. But, brothers, we can't abandon our business or occupation. Who can tell what the officials may or may not do; they may pay no heed for ten days or fifteen days, and meanwhile, we will all die.'

Iidu thought far ahead, 'We will not die, Pancho; the Chaudharies will all be imprisoned. It is no joke to pick a fight with the officials.'

Jangali assented, 'We have no means to fight the wealthy. Bahuji is different, she has money, she is educated and can talk to the officials. She can bear all kinds of losses. We will all sink in the process.'

But they were all ashamed at heart, like soldiers running away from the battlefield. The soldier's shame in running away far surpasses the joy of saving his life. He may be able to justify his action to other people, but not in his heart.

In a little while the rain stopped. The rest of the people left, their downcast faces, their listlessness, their bowed heads, their silence, clearly reflecting their unhappiness.

CHAPTER 38

❧❧❧

Sukhada reached home, very sad. This was her first experience of defeat in her public life, and her heart, like that of a spirited colt that had been whipped, was anxious to throw off the saddle, bridles and reins, and break away. What could one expect of such cowards! For people who are not prepared to suffer some hardships for lasting gain, there is nothing in this world except sorrow and insults.

Naina was pleased at heart at this defeat. She was a nonentity in her own home and had received nothing but insults there; yet it was there that her future lay. If your eyes hurt, you don't poke a needle through them. Seth Dhaniram had purchased the land for a few thousand rupees, and in a few days it was expected to be sold for hundreds of thousands. She was not in a position to say anything to Sukhada, but she didn't like this movement. She did not have the same feeling of devotion for Sukhada as before because she felt that Sukhada was setting things afire only to appease her desire for revenge! That Sukhada had succumbed to this base instinct had in her view created a gulf between the two.

Naina commented, 'If it had been that easy to unite these people, then why would their condition have been so wretched in the first place.'

Sukhada said sharply, 'There will be a strike, whether the Chaudharies agree or not. The Chaudharies have become prosperous and prosperous people are selfish.'

Naina objected, 'It is only natural for them to be afraid. For those with power and knowledge, their difficulties may appear insignificant. Someone with a plateful of delicacies can afford to throw a piece to a dog, but someone who has only one piece is likely to hang on to it.'

Sukhada seemed not to hear, 'I can't understand how everyone was so brave during the trouble at the temple. I would like to see the same bravery once again.'

Naina shivered and said, 'No, Bhabhi, don't take on such a heavy burden. When the time is right, things happen by themselves. See how the practices of child marriage and untouchability have become less widespread in our own lifetime and literacy has risen considerably. When the time is right, housing for the poor will also be on the public agenda.'

'These are the sentiments of cowards. The strong bend circumstances to suit their will.'

Naina responded, 'It needs propaganda.'

Sukhada said, 'Propaganda means six months at the very least.'

'But it is at least not dangerous.'

'I don't have confidence in the public.'

After a moment she continued, 'Why should people trust me, what service have I rendered so far? Going around in lanes canvassing for three or four hours is not service.'

'I think that whatever little sympathy the public has for the movement now will be lost if you precipitate a strike.'

Sukhada declared, 'If things worked on the basis of sympathy these ills would have been corrected a long time ago. If people willingly acted according to principles, then they wouldn't need laws. As you know, I have been thinking for some time about leaving this house and moving to a smaller one. I think I will have to do that. I cannot command the hearts of the people living in this opulent house.'

The next day there was a sizable strike in the city. Not a single sweeper was working. The Kahaars and ikkawalahs had also stopped work. More than half the vegetable shops were closed. In many homes there was an outcry because their milk was not delivered. The police were trying to have the shops reopened and to encourage sweepers to return to work. The city officials were considering ways to solve the problem and the rich and wealthy in the city were collaborating with them.

It was noon. The clouds were rolling and the sky seemed as if painted yellow. Water had accumulated at various places along roads and lanes and people were rushing here and there through the puddles. There was a big crowd in front of Sukhada's door, when suddenly Shantikumar appeared in the verandah, covered to the knees in mud. He had hesitated to come back today after yesterday's conversation. Naina saw him but did not invite him in. Sukhada was talking to her mother. Shantikumar stood for a moment, then feeling disappointed, was about to leave. Sukhada saw his mournful look, but could not resist saying ironically, 'I hope no one saw you coming here Doctor sahab.'

Shantikumar countered this irony with a light-hearted tone, 'I was very careful. Even if someone sees me here, I'll say I have come to borrow some money.'

Renuka had established a *devar*-bhabhi relationship with Shantikumar. Sukhada had told her what had happened yesterday and provided her with ammunition for tackling Doctor sahab. Renuka realized that she was ultimately responsible for the change in Doctor sahab. She was the one who had burdened him with the Trust and thus made him cautious in his approach. She took him by the hand and, seating him on a chair, said, 'Then, sit here and wear bangles on your wrists; why grow a moustache?'

Shantikumar grinned and said, 'I am ready to wear bangles, but you will have to be ready to marry me. You will have to be the man.'

Renuka clapped her hands and said, 'I am old, but I will find a husband for you who will keep you behind seven veils and abuse you and swear at you. I'll have the jewellery made. You will be veiled and have *sindoor* on your head. You will eat your husband's leftovers and understand, you will eat them as if they were prashad from god! If you show the least bit of annoyance, you will be considered in disgrace. You will massage his feet, and wash his dhoti. When he comes into the house you will wash his feet. You will bear his children. If there are no children, he will marry a second time and you will live in the house like a servant.'

Under this unrelenting onslaught, Shantikumar lost his good humour. He felt ashamed and tongue-tied. Even if he had tried, he could not open his mouth. Renuka had made fun of him three or four times in the past, but today she was literally driving him to tears. Women are pitiless in caustic humour, especially when they are old.

Looking at his watch, he said, 'It is almost one o' clock. The strike was quite a success today.'

Renuka hit again, 'But how would you know, you were lying inside the house?'

Shantikumar described what he had been doing, 'I am not one to sit around relaxing! Every movement needs people behind the scenes. I have changed my approach, but I'm not serving the cause any less having done so. Today, I put ten or twelve young men from the Youth Congress in charge of this strike, otherwise it would not have been even a quarter as successful.'

Renuka thumped his back and said to her daughter, 'Then why were you giving this man a bad name? The poor man endangered his life, even then he gets a bad name. I am beginning to understand his policy. It is not good for everyone to jump into the fire all at once.'

Shantikumar checked the next day's programme and, assuring Sukhada of his support, left.

Evening had fallen. The clouds had broken up and the golden light from the moon was falling like a mother's love on the tear-drenched face of the earth. Sukhada was sitting at her evening meditation. During that deep introspection her weaknesses appeared like the crying of an obstinate child; had Maniram not insulted her so, would she have been so unrelenting about the strike?

Her ego responded—yes, yes, I would have. She had decided on this course of action much earlier. If Dhaniram suffered a loss, so be it. When she was prepared to sacrifice everything for this cause, why should the loss or gain of other people be of concern to her?

Having reassured herself thus, she finished meditating and went downstairs when Lala Samarkant came looking for her. His face was creased with sorrow and his mouth was trembling as if the anguish in his heart was bursting to come forth.

Sukhada asked, 'You seem very troubled Dadaji, what is the matter?'

Samarkant shivered. Desperately trying to keep back his tears, he said, 'A worker in the police force just came to the shop with the news that ...'

His voice choked, nearly drowned in tears.

Anxiously, Sukhada asked, 'So, please, what did he say? Is everything alright in Haridwar?'

Samarkant quickly reassured her, 'No, no, it has nothing to do with that. It concerns you. There is a warrant out for your arrest.'

Sukhada laughed, 'Indeed! So, there is a warrant for my arrest! Why are you so worried about that ? But tell me, what am I charged with?'

Controlling his anguish, Samarkant said, 'It's this strike. Today, the officials had a meeting and decided that you and the Chaudharies should be arrested. Repression is all these people know. They do not address the causes of dissatisfaction, they think that arrest and detention will do the job. It is like a mother beating a child to quieten him when he is crying from hunger.'

Sukhada said calmly, 'The government of a society that is based on injustice knows no remedy other than repression, but it is a mistake to think that that would suppress this movement; just as a ball hitting an obstacle rebounds, the more forceful the hit, the more forceful the reaction.'

Momentarily excited, she continued, 'They may arrest me, but what will they do with those hundreds of thousands of poor people whose sighs are rending the skies. One day those sighs, like an erupting volcano, will destroy the whole of society and, with it its government. If they don't want to open their eyes, they don't have to. I have done my duty.

The day will come when the demi-gods of today will be kicked around like pebbles and stones in the streets. It is possible that following my arrest the official class may still remain oblivious for a few days to the cries and wailing of the people but the day is not far off when these same tears will become the spark that ignites and consumes injustice. From these ashes will arise the conflagration whose flaming peaks will awaken the heavens.'

Samarkant was unmoved by this rhetoric. He was trying to think of a way to avert this disaster. Hesitantly, he said, 'Bahu, I want to say something, please listen to me. The bail ...'

Sukhada's mood changed to one of anger. She said, 'No, absolutely not. Why should I post bail? So I'll keep my eyes blindfolded, so I'll gag my mouth? It would be much better to have my eyes gouged out and my tongue cut off.'

Samarkant's sympathy had reached its limit. He shouted, 'If you can't control your tongue, then have it cut off. While I am alive I can't sit idly by while my bahu is arrested. Why didn't you ask me before organizing this strike? You may not care about family honour, but I do. To protect that honour, I renounced my son; I will not let it be destroyed at your hands.'

From outside came the sound of a car horn. Sukhada listened. Excitedly, she moved towards the door, then, running, took Munna from Naina and hugging him went to her room and started taking off her jewellery. Samarkant's anger was washed away like temporary dye. Quickly he went outside, then came back and said anxiously, 'Bahu, the Deputy has come. I am going to post bail. Please accept this request of mine. I will be around for only a little while longer. When I am dead, you may do as you please.'

Sukhada stood at the doorway and said firmly, 'I will not post bail, nor will I plead this case. I have done nothing wrong.'

Samarkant had never accepted defeat in his life, but today he stood humbled before this proud woman. Her words silenced him. He thought— the world considers women powerless. What folly! What a man considers dearer than life is in a woman's hands.

He said quietly, 'But you have not yet had your dinner. Naina, why do you stand staring, have you eaten *bhang*! Go, get Bahu her dinner. Oh, you, Mahra Kahaar! Where is he? When you need them, not a single servant is in sight. You, Naina, take Bahu to the kitchen; I will go to the market and buy some sweets. After all, she'll have to take some food along with her.'

The servant had been making the beds upstairs. He came running. Samarkant gave him an angry push and said, 'Where have you been? I have been calling out for such a long time; didn't you hear me? Who were you making the bed for? Bahu is leaving. Go, run, bring some sweets from the market. Go to the shop in the Chowk.'

Sukhada said, 'Please, there is no need for sweets; I don't feel like eating anything. I will take a few clothes, that's all.'

A voice called from outside, 'Sethji, please send Deviji quickly, it is getting late.'

Samarkant went outside and stood self-consciously by the door.

The Deputy was a robust, dignified, but humorous man. Having failed to get a good position in other Departments, he had joined the police force. He didn't like to be discourteous and, as far as possible, avoided taking bribes. He asked, 'Well, what is the verdict?'

Samarkant said folding his hands, 'Sir, she won't listen to me. I have tried all arguments. Anyway, what can I advise her, she doesn't understand me. Now I rely on your kindness. I am ready to serve you in any way I can. You must be on good terms with the jailer sahab. Please, do ensure that she does not suffer in any way. She is a woman of delicate temperament.'

The Deputy led Sethji to a chair and said, 'Sethji, what you are saying applies in cases where something has been done with evil intent. Deviji is not doing anything for herself. Her intentions are kind. She is fighting for the rights of our poor brethren. She will not be subjected to any hardship. I am bound by my official capacity; otherwise I would have bowed my head at the feet of a devi such as her. God has given her everything in the world but she has rejected it all and is prepared to undergo any hardship for the sake of what is right. Sahab, this requires extraordinary courage.'

Sethji took out ten gold sovereigns from a box and quietly slipped them in the Deputy's pocket, 'This is just to buy sweets for your children.'

The Deputy took the gold sovereigns out and put them on the table, saying, 'Sethji, do you think that policemen are complete animals? Does placing the red pugree on one's head mean that we are not human? I assure you that Deviji will not be subjected to any hardship. Only those who harm others are treated roughly. If anyone hurts her—a person who has sacrificed her life for the rights of the poor—he would not be human, he would be evil, the devil incarnate. I am not saying we don't have such people in the force; we have them in a goodly number. I am not an angel myself, but in a matter such as this, I would consider taking even a paan a sin. In that temple affair, Deviji faced the bullets with such courage; only she could have done that.'

On the road in front of the house, the crowd was increasing every minute. There were repeated cries of 'Victory, victory'. Women and men were coming to pay homage to Deviji.

Inside the house, a battle was raging between Naina and Sukhada.

Sukhada said, pushing the plate away, 'I said I will not eat anything!'

Naina, reaching out for her hand, said, 'Bhabhi, I beg of you, please eat three or four bites. Who knows when I will see you again.'

Her eyes filled with tears.

Sukhada said hard-heartedly, 'Sister, you are unnecessarily bothering me. I still have lots to do and outside the Deputy is asking me to hurry. Don't you see the vehicle at the doorstep? Who can think of eating at such a time?'

Naina said, overwhelmed with love, 'You keep doing what you have to do, I will feed you with my hands.'

Like a mother running after her playful child to feed him, Naina started feeding her bhabhi. Sukhada would go sometimes to this closet sometimes to that trunk. She would take out a packet of sindoor from one trunk and saris from another and Naina would follow her putting food in her mouth.

Sukhada having eaten five or six bites said, 'Enough, just give me some water to drink.'

Naina said, taking another morsel to her mouth, 'Alright, just this one, my good bhabhi!'

Sukhada opened her mouth, swallowing some tears as well as the morsel.

'Just one more.'

'No, not a single morsel more.'

'For my sake.'

Sukhada took the morsel.

'Will you give me some water or just keep feeding me?'

'Just one last bite in Bhaiya's name.'

'No, certainly not.'

Naina's eyes were filled with tears. Sukhada was holding back her tears. Naina was overwhelmed with grief. Sukhada was keeping her grief under control through willpower. She wanted to protect Naina against the pain of separation by steeling her own heart, by digging, so to speak, a moat around Naina's heart by speaking sharply to her. But Naina's tear-filled eyes, trembling mouth, and pitiable visage kept disarming her.

Naina's suppressed tears erupted like a fountain while offering Sukhada some paan. She covered her face and sobbed, choking with emotion.

Sukhada embraced her and said tenderly, 'Why do you cry, Bibi, we will see each other, of course, while I am in jail. When you come to see me bring some good food. In three or four months I should be home again.'

Naina, feeling as if she were on a sinking boat, lamented, 'I am so unlucky. I am drowning myself but I am also taking you down with me.'

From the moment she had heard about Sukhada's arrest her heart had been troubled by these thoughts, causing her even more suffering because of her love and affection for Sukhada.

Sukhada looked at her surprised, 'What are you saying, Bibi, did you call the police?'

Naina said remorsefully, 'These are the machinations of those who live in the stone mansion. (Seth Dhaniram was known in the city by this epithet.) I am not casting aspersions on anyone, but what he has done will come back to haunt him. A man who can't even give a blessing—his life is without purpose.'

Sukhada said sadly, 'This is not his fault alone Bibi. This is the fault of our entire society, all of us. Come, it's time to part. Promise me that you won't cry while I am gone.'

Her eyes red and swollen, Naina, embraced her and smiled, 'No I won't cry, Bhabhi.'

'If I hear that you have been crying, I'll have my sentence extended.'

'Should we send Bhaiya this news?'

'You do as you wish. Please comfort my mother.'

'Hasn't anyone informed her?'

'Informing her would have meant more delay. She wouldn't have let me go for hours.'

'She'll come running when she hears.'

'Yes, she will come, but she will not cry. Her love is in her eyes, its roots do not extend to her heart.'

They moved towards the door. Naina wanted to take Munna from his mother's arms and kiss him, but he would have none of it. He was very fond of Naina, but today, with uncomprehending eyes, he saw that his mother was going somewhere, and he didn't want to leave her arms. If she left him, what would he do?

Naina reached over and kissed him and said, 'Children can be very cruel.'

Sukhada smiled gently and said, 'After all, whose son is he!'

Reaching the outside door, the two embraced again. Samarkant was already there, standing on the doorstep. Sukhada bowed her head on his feet. With trembling hands, he lifted her up and blessed her; then holding Munna close to his heart, he burst out crying. This was a signal for the entire household to start weeping. Tears were being shed silently earlier, but now it was as if all restraint had been removed. When the calm, collected, and thoughtful elderly become overwhelmed, it is as if the cage has been opened and the birds let loose. When a leader who has been steadfast in life's battles for seventy years lays down his arms, then who can stop the recruits from doing likewise?

Sukhada sat in the car. The crowd was cheering—'Victory! Victory!' And flowers were being showered on the car.

The car started moving.

Thousands of people ran behind the car and Sukhada, raising her folded hands, saluted them. Such devotion, such love, such respect, can wealth command it? Can knowledge command it? It is possible to get such devotion only through one means—serving others. How much time had indeed elapsed since Sukhada entered this arena?

A wall of men and women lined the road on either side and the car was moving, trampling, and crushing their hearts.

In Sukhada's heart there was no pride, no joy, no ill-feeling; there was only pain that the people were in such a pitiful condition that they were grateful for a mere sliver of support when they were drowning.

After a while there was silence on the road. The dark slumberous night of Saavan was putting the world to sleep in its fold and the car was flying like a dream in infinity. Only the touch of cold air on one's body gave an indication of speed. In this darkness, Sukhada's soul was suffused with light, the same light that permeates us in the last moments of our lives when all real and imagined misdeeds, all the knots and pains, and all dark thoughts appear in their true colours. Then we realize that what we had believed in the darkness to be a black demon was only a heap of tiny sticks, what we had believed to be a black snake was only a piece of rope. Today she became aware of her failing, not in matters of truth and justice, but in matters of renunciation and service. For it was a difference of opinion between her husband and her on this question that had ultimately led to their separation.

Although not convinced of the validity of principles of service and renunciation, she had been continually drawn towards them, and today was a follower of her husband's ideals. She remembered the letter Amar had sent Shantikumar and for the first time she thought of forgiving her husband. Not pity but empathy and cooperation tempered this forgiveness. Now they were travellers on the same road, they were devotees of the same ideal. There was no difference between them, no ill-feeling. Today, for the first time, she felt one with her husband. The man she had considered her bad omen was today her devata, the object of her worship.

Suddenly, the car stopped, the Deputy stepped down and said to Sukhada, 'Deviji, we have reached the prison. I'm so sorry.'

Sukhada was happy. She felt as if she had come to get her life's reward.

PART 4

CHAPTER 39

❧❧❧❦❧❧

As soon as Amarkant learned that Salim had been posted as an officer in the district, he went to see him to have a good chat. He was afraid that Salim might have developed the airs of an officer, but his eagerness to meet his old friend was overpowering. It was a twenty to twenty-five mile trek to the city. It was getting quite cold. The sky was a dirty gray with dust and fog, and in that haze it was difficult to find the path. At times it was visible, at other times lost. Amar had started about noon and had hoped to reach the town before sunset, but the day wore on and he didn't know how much farther he still had to go. He had with him only a cotton blanket. If the night fell, he would have to take shelter under a tree. By and by the sun went down and the world was swallowed in darkness. Amar hurried on and when he entered the city it was almost eight o'clock.

Salim had just returned from the club. As soon as Amar was announced he went out, but seeing Amar's rough clothing, he hesitated and, instead of embracing him, he extended his hand. Salim's orderly was standing nearby, and to show any familiarity with this country bumpkin in front of him would have required great courage. He could not even take Amar to his well-appointed drawing room. There was a small garden in the compound. Taking him to it, he said, 'What kind of a regalia is this, since when have you become such a klutz? What a fancy kurta! Looks like a mailbag; and those clodhopper shoes—where on earth did you pick them up? I very much fear you didn't pay for them.'

Amar sat down right there on the ground and said, 'You are not offering any hospitality; instead, you are just rebuking me. I live among villagers, if I dressed like a gentleman how could I live there? Bhai, it is so good that you have come, we will be able to talk once in a while. Now, tell me about your affairs. How come you went into this service? You should have gone into some business; but you could only think of this slavery.'

Salim said proudly, 'Janaab, it is not slavery, it is governance. I will have a car in five or ten days. Then you will see with what grandeur I move about. But I am heartbroken at your condition. You will have to abandon this costume.'

That hurt Amar's self-respect. He said, 'I thought and still do, that clothes are only for protection of the body, and not for impressing others.'

Salim thought—what nonsense. Living with country bumpkins, he has even lost his mind. He said, 'Food is eaten only for the nourishment of the body, then why not munch dried chickpeas? Why not eat dry wheat grains? Why do you relish *halwa* and sweets?'

'I do munch dry chickpeas.'

'You are lying. Dried chickpeas would not make you look so healthy. You have grown to almost one and a half times my size. I probably wouldn't have recognized you.'

'Oh, yes, that is indeed because of chickpeas. Health comes from clean air and self-control. Halwa and *puri* do not give you strength or a broad chest, they give a bulging tummy. I walked twenty-five miles today. I dare you to walk just five miles with me.'

'Excuse me! Someone has said, "Great queen, come and mill the wheat with me." Well, you are welcome to the grinding. Tell me, what are you doing here?'

'Now that you have come, you will see for yourself. I am trying to follow the plan that I had drawn up for my life. Since the arrival of Swami Atmanand, my task has become much easier.'

It was getting quite cold. Salim was forced to take Amarkant to his drawing room.

Amar noticed the cushioned couch, brass vases, carpeted floor, and, round, marble centre table.

He took off his shoes at the entrance and said, 'Shall I close the door? Someone might see us, and you will be ashamed. After all, you are a sahab.'

Salim was embarrassed by this perceptive remark. He said, 'Bhai, that is indeed something to consider, but I am not a slave to custom. I had also wanted to lead a simple life, but I could not go against my father's wishes. Even the Principal at college used to say, "You will never get into the Civil Service;" but they were all astonished at the results. It was with you in mind that I chose this particular district. Tomorrow, I will take you to meet the Collector. You have probably not yet met Mr Ghaznavi. He is a cultured and honest man. In the very first meeting, he became very informal with me. He is close to forty, but he's still a womanizer!

In Amar's view, officers must have high morals. Salim did not believe that being virtuous was required of an officer. The two friends started arguing.

Salim said, 'A dry, staid man can never be a good officer.'

Amar replied, 'To be virtuous, one doesn't have to be dry.'

'I have always found mullahs very dry. It is not enough for officers to just administer the law. In my view, a little weakness in a man is valuable. I respect dry piety from a distance. Yet I have been more successful in life than you. At least I can claim that no one is angry with me. You were not even able to keep your wife happy. You wouldn't survive a day as a district officer; you wouldn't be able to keep anyone happy.

Such discussions used to make Amar quite angry, so he didn't think it wise to continue.

It was time for dinner. Salim took out a shawl and wrapped it around Amar, and gave him a pair of silk slippers to wear. Then they had dinner. For the first time in a long while, Amar had a tasty meal. He did not eat meat, but he relished everything else.

Salim remarked, 'The very thing that was worth eating, you set aside.'

Amir said, feeling slightly guilty, 'I don't have any objection to meat, but I don't want to eat it. Come, tell me the news from home. Has your marriage been fixed yet? That is all that remains for you to do, you should get done with that as well.'

Salim shot back, 'Stop worrying about my marriage, and tell me when are you going to marry Sakina. The poor thing is still waiting for you.'

Amar's face was drained of all colour. This was a question that was the hardest in the world for him to answer. He was no longer in the state of mind in which he had been attracted to Sakina. At that time, Sukhada had stood as a stumbling block in his life. There was no intimate communication between them; each had been looking at life from a different angle, and neither had the ability to bring the other around to his/her viewpoint. But now circumstances had changed. By some grace of God their social bond had been strengthened and their souls entwined. Amar did not know whether Sukhada had forgiven him or not, but now he was devoted to her. He wondered why Sukhada who had been given to a life of luxury and pleasure had renounced those things, and this feeling of wonder kept fuelling his fondness for her day after day. Now he felt that his former unhappiness had stemmed from his own unworthiness. He had not written to Sukhada for two reasons: first, a sense of shame, and second, his feeling that she had accomplished far more than he had. His male ego felt hurt that Sukhada had independently carved a path for herself and that she didn't need him in the least—this hurt appeared to hinder his growing fondness for her. At best, he could now become one of her staunchest supporters. Sukhada would no longer be satisfied to put the *kesariya* tilak on his forehead when he went to do battle, she had jumped into the fray herself, ahead of him. His self-respect was hurt by such a feeling.

Bowing his head he said, 'I now find that I lack the ability to make women happy. I have decided that I will not torment Sakina by marrying her.'

'Then at least, you should write to her telling her of your decision.'

Amar said in a voice heavy with longing and regret, 'That is not as easy to do, Salim, as you think. When I remember her I still lose all self-control. With her my life would have been heaven. When I think of her loyalty I feel like dying, even now ...'

After a moment, Salim said, 'Supposing I persuade her to marry me, would you object?'

Amar felt very relieved. 'No, bhai-jaan, not at all. If you can persuade her then I would think you the most fortunate man in the world. But you are joking, of course. You must be thinking of marrying the daughter of some nawaab.'

When they finished eating, they washed their hands and went to sit in another room.

Salim took a long pull at the hukkah and said, 'Do you think I am kidding? In those days I certainly used to. But lately I have tested her out. If you had not met her then, there is little doubt that today she would be somewhere else. After knowing you she lost the desire to have anyone else. You raised her out of mud and made her a goddess in a temple, and sitting in the seat of a goddess she has in fact become a goddess. If you can marry her, do so with pleasure. I am, after all, carefree and will find some other woman to engage my heart, but if you don't want to marry her, then get out of my way! Now that your wife is on the same path as you, you have no reason to turn away from her.'

Amar dragged the hukkah toward himself and said, 'I'll gladly get out of your way; but do tell me one thing—do you consider Sakina only a flirtation or do you love her from your heart?'

Salim sat up, 'Look, Amar, I have never hidden anything from you and I am not going to hide anything now. Sakina is not an object to love, she is a woman to worship. At least she seems so to me. I cannot swear that after marrying her I will be faithful to her forever, but I know this much, that if I have her I will be able to do something with my life. So far my life has been spent in roaming for pleasure. She will be the anchor for my drifting boat. Without this anchor, I don't know which whirlpool my boat might be sucked into. I need a woman who will govern me, who will continually pull in my reins.'

Amar had found his life unbearable because he could not rule his wife. Salim wanted a wife who would rule him. The irony of it was that they saw in the same woman opposite traits that each desired.

Amar said curiously, 'I think Sakina lacks the qualities that you want.'

Salim said as if emerging from the depths, 'Not for you, but for me she has them. She worships you. I worship her.'

Afterwards they kept talking about various things until two or two-thirty in the morning. Salim referred to the new movement that had begun while he was in Kashi; he also said that the movement was not likely to succeed and that it could lead to bloodshed.

Amar was astonished and said, 'Then Sukhada infused new life in the movement.'

'Your mother-in-law has given away all her wealth to Sevashram.'

'Oh, yes!'

'And your esteemed father has also started taking an interest in community affairs.'

'Then there has been a complete revolution.'

Salim fell asleep, but Amar could not sleep despite being very tired. Things that he could not have even dreamed of Sukhada had accomplished. But whatever it was, it was still the same imperiousness, in a slightly different guise. She craved to make a name for herself, nothing else. But then he rebuked himself—what do you know about anyone's true motives. Today, thousands of people are engaged in serving the Nation. Who can say who is selfish, who is a true servant!

CHAPTER 40

Amarkant had found a new purpose in his life, it seemed as if he were riding a new mount. It had been necessary to use a spur and a whip on his previous horse, but this new horse, with its ears perked up, galloped along on its own. He had arguments with Swami Atmanand, Kashi, Payag, Goodar, all of them. These people were still riding the old horses and had fallen behind. Amar became upset with their slow progress—'That's no way to get things done, Swamiji. Are you doing anything, or is it all a joke! It would have been much better if you had just stayed on in Sevashram.'

Atmanand stuck out his broad chest and said, 'Baba, I can't hurry things any more. If people don't pay attention to the rules of healthy living, they'll be sick, they'll die. I can tell them the rules, but it is up to them to follow them.'

Amarkant thought, 'This man is as fat as he is fatheaded. He eats too much and when it is time to work he is sick. So why did he become a *sanyasi*?'

Reprovingly, he said, 'Your job is not simply to tell them the rules. It is also to ensure that they follow them. You have to infuse such enthusiasm in them that they cannot but follow the rules. I passed through Pichowra today, heaps of garbage were strewn all over the village. You were in the village yesterday, why didn't you arrange to have the garbage picked up? Why didn't you get a shovel and go to it yourself? You think that by simply putting on saffron-coloured robes people will treat your word as gospel.'

Atmanand said in self-defence, 'If I had started cleaning up the garbage myself the entire day would have been spent in Pichowra. I had to tour five or six villages.'

'This is only what you supposed. I had the whole lot removed in half an hour. The minute I took the shovel in my hand the whole village gathered around and in no time, the entire village was cleaned up.'

Then he turned to Goodar Chaudhary, 'You, too, elder brother, are getting lax. Yesterday in the Panchayat of Sautaara I caught some people drinking. I took them by surprise, people were sitting around happily and there were bottles in front of the Headman. As soon as they saw me the bottles disappeared and they assumed grave faces. I do not care for appearances, I want solid work.'

Amar's own perseverance, enthusiasm, willpower, and dedication had sparked a feeling of service among all his associates. He had even started to dictate to them, yet they all accepted his authority and were devoted to him.

Chaudhary said irately, 'Which village did you say, Sautaara? I'll call the Headman. He's Harakhlal, a born drunkard. He has served two terms in the prison. I'm going to call him right away.'

Amar slapped his thigh in frustration, 'Again, talk of admonishment and reprimand! Bhaiya, rebuke and reprimand do not accomplish anything. You have to appeal to the heart. You have to create such an atmosphere that people begin to shun alcohol. If you do your own work all day and sleep peacefully at night then you will never accomplish this goal. You should understand that if our lower caste community takes the lead then the upper castes—Brahmans and Thakurs—will awaken on their own.'

Goodar said, acknowledging defeat, 'Bhaiya, I am no longer able to work all day and run around all night. And if I don't work, then what will we eat?'

Amarkant, seeing that Goodar was feeling discouraged, kidded him, 'How big a stomach do you have elder brother that you have to work all day? If you have such a big stomach, then maybe you should make it smaller.'

Kashi and Payag, seeing that everyone was getting a scolding, quietly slipped away.

It was nearing school time. Amarkant went to his room to get his books and saw Munni standing with a glass of milk. He said, 'I have already told you I will not drink any milk, so why did you bring it?'

For several days now, Munni had been aware of a certain withdrawal in Amar's behaviour. His face wouldn't light up on seeing her nor would he talk to her unless there was a reason. She had begun to feel that he was avoiding her. She could not understand why but it was like a thorn in her side and today she was determined to confront him.

Unruffled she said, 'Why won't you drink it, tell me?'

Picking up a bundle of books, Amar said, 'Because I don't wish to. I don't want to add to your burden.'

Munni looked at him severely, 'Since when has bringing you milk become a great burden to me? And what if I am happy bearing that burden?'

Amar said tiredly, 'Alright, let's not quarrel, give it to me, I will drink it.'

Amar drained the entire glass in one go as if taking a bitter pill, and then started to go out. Munni, stepping aside from the door, said, 'It is not usual to punish someone who has committed no offence.'

Amar hesitated at the door and said, 'I don't know what nonsense you're talking. I am going to be late.'

Munni assumed an air of unconcern, 'I am not stopping you, why don't you go?'

Amar could not leave the room.

Munni spoke again, 'I know very well that I have no claim over you! If you want you could tell me today, "Take care, don't get too close to me." That is what your demeanour has been saying lately. I have noticed it for several days—I will be shameless in speaking to you, in entreating you. Tell me, if you were going to turn away from me why didn't you do so from the beginning? But what nonsense I am talking. You are going to be late, please go.'

As if summoning the strength to break the bond, Amarkant said, 'I don't understand what you are saying, Munni. I am the same as ever. But, yes, lately there has been a lot more work which does not leave much time for talk.'

Munni cast her eyes down and said perceptively, 'I understand what you are feeling, but that's not the issue. You are confused.'

Amarkant was surprised and said, 'Now you are talking in riddles.'

Munni said in the same tone, 'When a man's heart is confused, even straight talk appears like a riddle.'

Then taking the empty milk glass she left quickly.

Amarkant was feeling guilty at heart. He was being drawn to Munni by mutual attraction. 'I understand what you are feeling, but that's not the issue. You are confused!' These words frightened him as if he were facing a deep abyss. His heart trembled at the thought of descending into the abyss, but his path went through that abyss.

He stood transfixed for he knew not how long. Suddenly Atmanand called, 'Is the school going to be closed today?'

CHAPTER 41

A Mahant was landlord in the district where Amar lived. Among Mahantji's followers there was an agent in charge of records and a small court's legal practitioner. Hence collecting the land tax was never a problem. There was always some festivity or other going on at Mahantji's thakurdwara. Sometimes it was for Thakurji's birthday, sometimes a marriage, sometimes a sacred-thread ceremony, or sometimes simply playing on the swings or participating in water-sports. On these occasions, the tenants had to provide free labour; and also, as dictated by custom, gifts, devotional offerings, and many other things. These services and offerings were in the name of religion so how could anyone dispute them? The demands of religion constituted one of the biggest burdens for the poor farmers. The farmers in the region were all lower castes. At the outskirts of the village there were three or four households of Brahmans and Kshatriyas, but their sympathies were not with the tenant farmers but with Mahantji. In one form or another they all served Mahantji. The tenants had to keep him happy. First, they were poor and overburdened with debt; second, they were ignorant, knowing neither custom nor law. Mahantji could levy as much tax as he liked, he could evict people at will; and no one dared say anything. In many cases, the farm tax had risen so high that the entire crop was not sufficient to meet it. But the people, bemoaning their fate, hungry and naked, dying miserable deaths still kept cultivating the farms. What could they do? Many had left and gone to the city to look for work. Many had become labourers. But still there was no shortage of tenant farmers. Farming is not only a means of livelihood in an agricultural country, it is also a status symbol. To be called a farmholder is a matter of pride. A farmer, after losing everything, goes abroad, accumulates money, and returns, to start farming yet again. He seeks esteem and respect just as much as others do. He wants to live a farmholder and die one. Every hair on his body may be mortgaged, but he considers himself fortunate if he has three or four oxen tied at his door. He may live almost the entire year only half fed, he may spend nights trying to keep warm in straw, he may live powerless and die powerless, it doesn't matter, he is a farmholder. His pride enables him to put up with this woeful state of affairs.

But this year, unexpectedly, the prices of commodities fell steeply. They fell to what they had been forty years ago. When the prices were high, a farmer could sell the produce and pay his tax; but what could he do when commodities were being sold for less than half of their usual value. How could he pay the tax, how could he provide the customary services to the landlord, how could he pay his debt? It was an awful situation; and it was not unique to just this region. The depression extended over the whole province, the whole country; indeed, even the whole world. Nobody would buy ten kilos of *gur* even if it were offered for the price of four. Wheat that used to sell for eight kilos a rupee was now considered dear at a rupee and a half per maund—about forty kilos. Cotton that sold for thirty rupees per maund now sold for ten rupees. Flax, which sold for sixteen rupees per maund, now sold for four rupees. The farmers sold off each and every grain, they didn't keep even a bit of straw. But despite it all, they could not pay off more than a quarter of their taxes. And in the thakurdwara the festivities and sports continued. The result was an anguished outcry. Lately, because of the efforts of Swami Atmanand and Amarkant, there had been some spread of literacy in the district, and in several villages people had stopped providing the customary services. This incensed the servants and agents of Mahantji. Although they were unable to do anything about it, the unpaid taxes provided them with an opportunity to relieve their pent-up anger.

One day a panchayat was held on the bank of the Ganges to consider this problem. Women and men from the entire region congregated there as if they had come for a dip on a holy occasion. Swami Atmanand was elected the Chairman.

Bhola Chaudhary stood up first. Formerly, he had been coachman to some officer. Now, with the New Year, he had started farming again. He had a long nose, a dark complexion, a big moustache, and his face was lost in his huge headgear. He said, 'Delegates, the tax rate was levied when prices were high. In this depressed market, it is beyond our capacity to pay those taxes. Even if we pay this time by selling our oxen and harnesses, what shall we do afterwards? This is the only matter for discussion. My suggestion is that we all go together and petition Mahant maharaj. If he does not listen, then we should approach the District Officer. I can't speak for others, but I can swear by Mother Ganges that in my house there is not even an ounce of grain. And if this is the condition in my house, it must be the same in other houses. By contrast, at Mahantji's the same festivities are still going on. Only the day before yesterday there was a mango feast for a thousand sadhus. Several cases of mangoes were brought from Benaras and Lucknow. Today I hear there is a cream feast. We die of starvation, but they gorge on cream! For all this, the blood is being sucked out of our bodies. I've said enough, that's all I have to say to the delegates.'

Opening his deep-set eyes wide, Goodar said, 'Mahantji is our lord and master. He provides us with food, and he is a great man. When he hears of our sorrowful plight, he will surely have pity on us. So we should accept Bhola Chaudhary's advice. Amar bhaiya will speak on our behalf. We do not want anything else. Only that we and our children get a pound per day of grain each. Whatever crop is produced, Mahantji can take it all. We do not ask for anything fancy, like ghee, milk, or cream. We only ask for a pound of coarse grain. If we don't get even that much, then we will stop cultivating. Where will we get any money or seeds? We will abandon the fields, there is no other way.'

Saloni waved her hands and said, 'Why should we abandon the fields? They are our birthright our inheritance. We cannot leave them. I will sacrifice my life for my field. First we give up one field, then another and another. Then what? Will the earth then provide us with gold to survive on?'

Algoo the weaver, with his eyes flashing, exclaimed, 'Bhaiya, I say that nothing will be accomplished by going to Mahantji. He rules with an iron hand. If he gets angry, he'll have us beaten up. We should go to the authorities. The British still have some compassion.'

Atmanand opposed them all, 'I tell you nothing will be accomplished by going to anyone. If the bread on your plate asks you not to eat it, will you agree?'

Voices came from all four sides, 'No, never.'

'Then, why should they agree to help you—you are the bread on their plates.'

Many voices agreed, 'No, they will never agree.'

'Mahant needs money for festive occasions. Officers need big salaries and those will not be reduced. They cannot abandon their grand life-styles. They couldn't care less whether you live or die. Why should they spare you?'

Many voices sounded assent, 'No, they will never spare us.'

Amarkant was sitting behind Swamiji. He was getting nervous seeing Swamiji's mood but how could he stop the Chairman. He knew that Atmanand was short-tempered, but he had not expected that he would get heated so quickly. He wondered what his game plan was.

Atmanand roared, 'Then, what option is open to you? If you people ask my advice and promise to follow it, then I will tell you. If not, then it is up to you.'

Many voices asked, 'Do tell us, Swamiji, tell us.'

People edged closer from all sides. It was evident from their faces that Swamiji was reaching their hearts. The masses are always attracted to extremes.

Atmanand said, 'Let's go then and surround Mahantji's home and thakurdwara, and we will not let any festivities take place until he revokes our taxes completely.'

Several voices shouted, 'We are ready.'

'You must understand very well that you will not be welcomed there with garlands.'

'We don't care. We are dying anyway, why die whimpering!'

'Then, let's go now. We will show them that ...'

Suddenly, Amar stood up, eyes ablaze, and said, 'Wait.'

There was dead silence. People stayed where they were.

Amar beat his chest and said, 'The path you are taking is not the path of redemption; it is the path of total destruction. If your ox is sick, then would you harness it for ploughing?'

No voice was raised from any side.

'You would first try to cure it and until it is well again you would not use it for ploughing. You do not want to kill the ox! If it died your fields would lie fallow.'

Goodar spoke up, 'What you say is very true, Bhaiya.'

'What is our duty if our house is on fire? Should we let the fire spread and add to it those household items that may have been spared?'

Goodar said, 'Never. Never.'

'Why? Because we don't want to burn down the house, we want to save it. We have to live in that house. We have to survive there. This calamity has not fallen on us alone. The entire country is undergoing the same fate. Our leaders are trying to resolve this problem. We have to march in line with them.'

He gave a long speech; but the same public that used to get involved listening to his speeches, today sat listlessly. They all respected him, and so there was no disturbance, no turmoil; but the people were unmoved. For now, Atmanand was their leader.

The meeting dispersed without reaching any conclusion, but it was obvious to everyone where majority opinion lay.

CHAPTER 42

❦

Amar returned home very discouraged. If no way was found to calm the people, there was bound to be a disturbance. He decided to meet Mahantji. He was feeling so despondent that for the first time he felt like abandoning the whole project and going away. He was not yet experienced enough to understand that the masses always follow the more aggressive personality. Despite his arguments about justice and dharma, loss and gain, non-violence and renunciation, the people were still swayed by Atmanand's magic. If he had run into Atmanand at this time, there would surely have been a fight between the two friends; but today Atmanand had disappeared. He had been offered a horse ride and had gone to organize some village.

Amar felt very humiliated. Nobody had paid the least attention to what he had had to say. It was evident from the faces in the crowd that they felt he was talking nonsense and that he was not going to save them. He needed the comfort of tender words—someone who could soothe him and restore his confidence in himself.

Munni came out with rope and a pitcher and, without a glance, went over to the well. He called, 'Listen, Munni.' But Munni ignored him. After a little while she returned with the pitcher, head down, and went past him. Amar called again, 'Munni, please listen, I have something to say.'

Still, she didn't stop. He knew now that she was ignoring him.

Munni came out again and went to see Saloni who was living in a little hut behind the schoolhouse. Saloni was lying on a mat, singing a *bhajan*. Munni asked, 'You didn't cook anything today, auntie, are you going to sleep without eating?'

Saloni sat up saying, 'I have eaten, Beta, there were leftover rotis from lunch.'

Munni looked around the tell-tale clean kitchen, 'Auntie, you are lying. There isn't anything in the house, is there? It hasn't been that long since you returned, how could you have eaten so quickly.'

'You do not believe me, Bahu! I was hungry, and I ate as soon as I came home. I washed and put away all the pots and pans. I wouldn't hide anything from you. If there wasn't anything to eat, wouldn't I have asked you ?'

'Alright, swear on me.'

Saloni laughed and said, 'Yes, I swear on myself, I have eaten.'

Munni was hurt and said, 'You consider me an outsider, auntie, as if I don't care whether you live or die. You just sold the oil seeds, what happened to the money?'

Saloni said, holding her head in her hands, 'My god! How much seed do you think there was? I received a total of one rupee. And Mahantji's servant took that away yesterday. He was going to set fire to the hut. What could I do, I took it out and threw it at him. And now Amar Bhaiya says—"Appeal to Mahantji". He won't listen, beti, that's what I say.'

Munni said, 'Alright, come and eat at my house.'

Saloni said tearfully, 'You will feed me today beti, but there are still four months before the next crop. Right now not even grass is available. I don't know how God will take us through this. There is not a single grain of food in the house. If I were fortunate, then after paying tax there would still be enough to last four months. But it is my rotten luck. Why don't you explain this to Amar Bhaiya, he should let Swamiji go ahead with his plan.'

Looking away, Munni said, 'He is no longer close to me. He doesn't even talk to me. He has no time from his work. One needs some free time to talk to the people at home! When he had nothing, then he had time. Now that he has become well known; an important person, he has no free time!'

Saloni was astonished, 'Are you saying, Bahu, that he is alienated from you? I can't believe that. You must be mistaken. Poor man, he is running night and day; he probably doesn't have any spare time. My blessing will certainly come true, you will see.'

Munni was embarrassed at her unkind words, 'I don't care for anyone, auntie. If he is concerned he will talk; otherwise, he will not. He probably thinks I am chasing after him. I say this truthfully, auntie, such a thought has never crossed my mind. I am not even equal to the dust on his feet. Yes, I do wish this much—that he would talk to me willingly and openly; whatever little I can do for him, that he would accept it willingly. All I want is to love and serve him, and for him to accept my offerings. I want nothing else.'

Suddenly, Amar called from outside. Saloni invited him in, 'Come in, Bhaiya, Bahu just came, I was chatting with her.'

Amar said to Munni sharply, 'I called you twice, Munni, why didn't you answer me?'

Munni said, turning away, 'You have no time to talk to anyone, so why should anyone go near you. You are involved in big things, but others still have their little concerns.'

Amar, overcome with loyalty to his wife, had become somewhat distant with Munni. Earlier, he was on the hill and Sukhada was trying to pull him down; now she was on the top of the hill and, to reach her level, he had to muster all his self-control and determination. His behaviour had to be exemplary. But, try as he might, he was not able to erase Munni's image, that of simplicity and devotion itself, from his heart. He had begun to realize that in his effort to improve his soul, his life had become dry and uninteresting. He had believed that he and Munni understood each other in a way that foreclosed any possibility of misunderstanding. The lamp she had lighted in his heart would never dim whether he was near her or leagues away.

He said with mild reproach, 'I do agree, Munni, that lately I have stayed away from you because of excessive work. I had hoped you would forgive me if in my frustration and worry I said a few harsh things. Now I know that that was my mistake.'

Munni looked at him forlornly and said, 'Yes, Lala, that was your mistake. If you put a poor person on a throne, he will not believe that he is king; he will think that it is a dream. So it is with me, my dream is my lifeline. I don't ever want to wake up—I want to keep dreaming. It is enough for me that you acknowledge me. Can't you even do that much? What happened, why did you and Swamiji have a quarrel today?'

Until now, Saloni had been siding with Atmanand. Now she started to flatter Amar, 'Bhaiya tried to explain to people that we should appeal to Mahantji. People became upset at that. Tell me, what else can you do? If Mahantji decides to have us beaten up, there will be no escape.'

Munni agreed, 'Mahantji is a saintly man. If people surrounded God's temple it would be very inauspicious. The world prays to God by singing hymns to Him, and here we are trying to stop that prayer. How could Swamiji ever think like that and how could people believe him? What abysmal ignorance!'

These words brought Amar some peace of mind. These illiterate women were wiser than Swamiji, and he was supposed to be learned in all the Shastras! His devotees were similar fools.

He said happily, 'In a world ruled by the powerful, who would listen to us humble people, auntie? If people laid siege to the temple, that would be reason enough for martial law to be clapped. These days, officers will order gunfire at the least cause.'

Saloni became frightened and said, 'Bhaiya, it was good that you didn't support them. Otherwise, there would have been bloodshed.'

Munni said tenderly 'I wouldn't have let you go with them, Lala. The British rule the world, will they not listen to the pain and sorrow of their subjects? I will ask Swamiji when he comes.'

These sympathetic and compassionate words, cooled his spirit that was burning like fire. Now Amar would certainly go and pay his respects to Mahantji tomorrow.

CHAPTER 43

The next evening, Amar, together with Goodar, went to Mahant Asharam Giri.

Mahantji was sitting on a golden chair with a velvet cushion. On the clean marble floor around him, was a crowd of devotees, the majority of whom were women. Men were sitting separately. Mahantji was a dignified man, all of six feet tall. He was about thirty-five years of age, with a fair complexion, stout figure, and an energetic countenance. His robes were saffron-coloured but made of silk. He was sitting with his feet dangling above the floor. The devotees would go up to him, touch his feet with their forehead, give him their offerings, and then go back to their places. Goodar could not enter the premises, so Amar went alone but nobody paid any attention to him.

He stood waiting. Finally at eight o'clock he approached Mahantji and said, 'Maharaj, I have come here to make a petition.'

Mahantji looked at him with a pained expression.

A sadhu who was standing next to him looked at Amar with astonishment and asked, 'Where do you come from?'

Amar mentioned the name of the village.

He was told to come after aarti.

Aarti was still three hours away. Amar had never been there before; so he thought he would look around. He started strolling about. To the west was a huge temple. Straight ahead, towards the east was a gate adorned with lions, with two smaller doors to the left and right. Amar entered through the door on the right. He saw wide verandahs on all four sides where preparations for a great feast were underway. Puris and *kachauris* were being fried in large *karahis*; different types of greens and vegetables were being prepared; milk was being boiled, and *malaai* was being taken off the boiling milk. The rooms behind the verandahs were stocked with edibles. It seemed as if they were wholesale markets for grain, greens, vegetables, nuts and fruits, and sweets. One whole room was filled with *parwals*. At this time, *parwals* were very expensive, but here they were piled on top of each other like straw. Ladies from respectable homes were devoutly busy, cooking all the delicacies. It was preparation for Thakurji's dinner. Amar was amazed to see this stockpile. In this season, there were dozens and dozens of baskets full of grapes.

Amar left to enter the gate on the north and came across what looked like a market. There was a long line of dressmakers sewing clothes for Thakurji. Some were doing gold embroidery; others were making embroidered cushions and bolsters. There was a row of goldsmiths making adornments for Thakurji. Some were setting gems, some were polishing, and still others were stringing ornaments in silk and gold thread. In one room, ten or twelve strong young men, their mouths and noses covered with cloth, were grinding sandalwood. One entire room was filled with perfumes, scented oils, and incense sticks. Amar left the marketplace. He walked through the centre court and came out of the main gate thinking how much money was being wasted on Thakurji.

Goodar asked, 'It took you a long time. Were you able to talk to him?'

Amar laughed and said, 'So far I have had only a darshan, I will meet him after aarti.' Then he described in detail all that he had seen.

Goodar said, shaking his head, 'It is God's court. How could He, who nourishes the world, do with anything less? I, too, have heard of the opulence. But I have never gone inside lest somebody should ask me who I was, and then I would be thrown out. Of course, I have seen the stables and the *gaushala*. If you want, you can see them, too.'

As there was still plenty of time left, Amar went to see the gaushala. On the south side of the temple there were animal shelters. First of all, he entered the courtyard where the elephants were kept. Some twenty-five or thirty elephants were standing tied with chains. Some were big as mountains, some as fat as water buffaloes; some were swaying, some were waving their trunk; some were chewing the twigs and leaves of a banyan tree. Their *howdahs*, ropes, canopies, and ornaments were all stacked separately in a storeroom. Each elephant had its own name, its own attendant, and its own enclosure. Some received a maund of food, some received much less. The largest elephant, Thakurji's mount, was worshipped by devotees. Even now there was a pile of garlands around his neck and flowers were scattered beneath his feet.

From here he went to the stables. There were rows of horses, as if a regiment of cavalry was encamped there. There were no less than five hundred horses of all breeds and from all countries. Some were for riding, others were for hunting, some for pulling coaches, some for playing polo. Each horse had two attendants. Mahantji was very fond of horse racing, and there were many racehorses. They were fed on cream and almonds everyday.

The gaushala also had four to five hundred cows and water buffaloes. There were many big urns full of fresh milk. Thakurji would be given a bath in milk before aarti. Five maunds of milk were required for his bath, three times everyday. Additional milk was required for the kitchen.

People were still wandering here and there when aarti started. They hurried in from all sides.

Goodar said, 'If someone were to ask you, "Who are you, brother?"— what would you say?'

Amar smiled and said, 'I will say I am a Vaishya.'

'You may get away with that because very few people know you here, but they see me everyday selling opium. If they recognize me, they won't leave me alive. Now look, aarti is being offered to God and we can't even enter the place. The priests here have most questionable characters and morals. But they are sovereign here, while we cannot even step inside. If you wish to go for aarati, do so. You even look like a Brahman, but my whole appearance announces that I am a Chamaar!'

Amar felt inclined to go and watch the event, but he didn't want to leave Goodar. In another half hour the aarati was finished and the devotees returned to their homes. Then Amar went to see Mahantji and learned that a wealthy rani was visiting him. As he waited, he paced back and forth in the courtyard.

After half an hour he again spoke to the sadhu at the door, then learned that it was impossible to have a darshan at this time. He was told to come the next morning.

Amar was so angry that he felt like confronting Mahantji and rebuking him then and there, but he controlled himself. Embarrassed with his reception, he went outside.

Hearing this, Goodar said, 'Who will listen to our plight in this court?'

'Have you ever had a darshan of Mahantji?'

'Who, I? How could I have had! I have never entered the place.'

It was getting late in the evening, and the trek home was long and tough, across hilly rivers and streams. There was also the danger of wild animals. They decided to spend the night where they were. They went to a dharmshala with the thought of eating and lodging there. Just then two sadhus appeared selling food that had been sanctified by God. All the travellers at the dharmshala ran to get some. Amar purchased four annas' worth of food—a platter of puris, halwa, several types of vegetables, pickles and chutney, cream, and curd; there was so much food that it would have satisfied two good appetites. In this place very few people cooked for themselves. They simply purchased these platters. They both had their fill and, after drinking water, they were preparing to sleep when a sadhu came selling milk for a nightcap. Amar did not want any, but out of curiosity, bought two annas' worth. It was one kilo, thick and creamy, redolent with saffron and musk. He had never in his life had such milk.

Amar said with amazement, 'Is there any end to this extravagance!'

Goodar said piously, 'God provides, what else! It is His glory. A thousand to two thousand pilgrims come every day. Each one of these tycoons offers a purse of ten or twenty thousand rupees. Despite all this extravagance tens of millions of rupees are deposited in the bank.'

'We will see how the meeting goes tomorrow.'

'I think that there will be no darshan even tomorrow.'

The poor men had brought no bedding so they spread half their dhotis like a sheet and lay down.

Both men woke up while it was still dark, bathed, and arrived at Mahantji's doorstep before sunrise. They learned that Mahantji was at puja.

After an hour they went again, only to be informed that Mahantji was at breakfast.

The third time Amar went at nine o'clock. He learned that Mahantji was inspecting the horses. Amar said irritatedly to the gatekeeper, 'Then tell me, when am I going to be able to see him?'

The gatekeeper asked, 'Who are you?'

'I am one of the tenants in his district. I have come to speak to him about his district.'

'Then go to the Agent of Records. He looks after the affairs of the district.'

Amar enquired around and finally reached the Agent's office. Scores of clerks were making entries in long open ledgers. The Agent was reclining on a bolster and smoking a hukkah.

Amar saluted him.

The Agent stroked his beard and said, 'Where is your application?'

Bewildered, Amar said, 'Application? I didn't bring any application.'

'Then why have you come here?'

'I have come to make a petition before Shriman Mahantji.'

'Go and bring a written application.'

'But I want to meet Mahantji.'

'Have you brought any *nazarana*?'

'I am a poor man. How could I offer nazarana?'

'That's why I said to bring a written petition. It will be considered and you will be advised of the decision.'

'When will the decision be given?'

'When Mahantji so wishes.'

'How much nazarana does Mahantji expect?'

'As suits your devotion. At least a gold sovereign.'

'Could you give me a date, please, when I could come to hear the decision? Who could come running here every day?'

'You will be running, who else. It is not possible to give you a date.'

Amar went back into town, wrote an application in detail, and submitted it to the Agent. Then he and Goodar returned home.

The news of their return brought out hundreds of villagers. Amar was in a difficult situation. If he narrated the entire story, he would look foolish. Therefore, he improvised—'I have submitted a petition. It is being considered.'

Kashi said skeptically, 'These deliberations will take months. In the meantime, we will be torn to shreds by their stewards.'

Amar said, embarrassed, 'Why would the deliberations take months? Two to four days should be enough.'

Payag said, 'There are all kinds of ways to procrastinate. Why would anyone willingly give up what he thinks his due?'

Amar went back every morning and returned in the early evening, but the application was not considered. He kept entreating and ingratiating the Agent, the clerks, even the peons; but no one listened. Thoroughly dejected, he returned home at night only to be made fun of by the villagers.

Payag would say, 'Oh, I heard that eight annas out of a rupee have been remitted.'

Kashi would say, 'You are lying. I heard that this year Mahantji has remitted the entire land tax.'

Meanwhile, Atmanand continued to fuel unrest in the district. There were daily reports of large farmer associations being formed from one

place to another. Amar's schoolhouse was also closed down. He had no
free time and there was no one else to teach. When he returned at night
only Munni was able to console him with her tender sympathy.

Finally, on the seventh day after his application, Amar received an order
to appear in person before Mahantji. It was noon when he was taken in.
Mahantji was reclining against a bolster on a hard couch in a room cooled
by khas-khas. On all four sides of the room there were khas-mats, which
were being sprayed with rose water. Electric fans were running. It was
July, but it was so cool indoors that Amar began to feel cold.

Mahantji's face expressed compassion. Drawing a puff from a hukkah,
he spoke soothingly, 'You live in my district, don't you! I am very sad to
hear that my tenants are suffering such hardship. Is their plight really as
bad as you have represented in your petition?'

Amar felt encouraged, 'Maharaj, their condition is even worse than I
have represented; there are many houses where the stove is not even lit
because there is no food.'

Mahantji closed his eyes and said, 'Oh God! What have you done?'
Then, turning to Amar, he said, 'Why did you not inform me earlier, I
would have stopped tax collections for this crop. In God's treasure chest
there is no shortage. I will immediately correspond with the government
on this issue and whatever reply I get will be forwarded to the tenants.
You tell them to be patient. God, what are you doing?'

So saying, Mahantji put on his glasses and started looking at other
applications. Amarkant rose. As he was stepping out, he pleaded, 'Sir, it
would be a great mercy if you would order your stewards not to trouble
the tenants at this time. People don't have anything, but because of their
fear of beatings and abuse they are selling household items to pay the
land tax. Many are abandoning their fields and running away.'

Mahantji's face assumed a severe expression, 'This will not be allowed
to happen. I have given strict instructions to the stewards that no tenant
should be dealt with harshly. I will ask them for an explanation. I don't
like the tenants to be persecuted at all.'

Amar bowed in homage to Mahantji. He came out ecstatic. He wanted
to get back as soon as possible and spread the good news. He was walking
so fast, he seemed to be running. Indeed, he would break into a run at
times, but then realizing what he was doing, he would slow down. There
was no hot breeze, but the sun was strong and his body was burning, yet
he kept hurrying. Now he would ask Swami Atmanand, 'Do you believe

now that not everyone in this world is motivated by selfishness? Some are indeed pious souls who understand others' sorrow and pain.' Now he would also be able to deal with Atmanand's thoughtless associates. If he had had wings, he would have flown.

By evening he reached the village and was greeted by numerous pairs of eyes, eager but unbelieving.

Kashi spoke, 'You seem very happy today, Bhaiya, it seems that you scored a round at kabaddi.'

Sitting down on the cot, Amar said proudly, 'One who is dedicated to his work does eventually score.'

Several people started asking, 'Bhaiya, what was the decision?'

Amar comforted the people as a doctor does his patients, 'You people were unnecessarily condemning Mahantji. I can't describe the graciousness with which he met me. He said, "I was completely unaware, why did you not inform me earlier? I would have stopped the collections." Now he has written to the government. Meanwhile, the stewards have been forbidden to collect any taxes.'

Kashi said sullenly, 'Look, we will believe this when it happens.'

Amar said with pride, 'If you are patient, everything will be accomplished. If you create a disturbance, nothing will happen; on the contrary, you might get beaten up.'

Saloni said, 'It depends on whether or not the fat Swami agrees.'

Goodar donned his mantle of a Chaudhary, 'How could he disagree? He will have to agree.'

A dark youth, one of Swamiji's ardent followers said sheepishly 'Bhaiya, no one can match your zeal.'

The next day the stewards still dealt with people just as harshly, but on the third day they softened their manner. News spread all over the district that Mahantji had written to the government that half the taxes were to be remitted. Meanwhile, Swamiji became the object of derision in whichever village he went to. Swamiji was still singing the same tune— This is all trickery, nothing is going to happen. He had become a captive of his own words—he was not concerned quite as much with the tenants as with proving his own viewpoint. If an order indeed remitting half the taxes were received, he would probably have run away. Now he was busily trying to prove that Mahantji's promise was a sham. Although he did not sway the majority of the public, some people, of course, listened, but with half an ear.

Days went by, but there was no order. Then people again began to doubt. When two weeks had gone by, Amar went to the district headquarters and, together with Salim, met the District Officer, Mr Ghaznavi. Mr Ghaznavi was a tall, slim, fair, elegant man. His nose was so long and his chin was so round that he looked comical. He was also very humorous. He would only do as much work as was necessary or work that would require an explanation if it wasn't completed, but he was an honest man, kind of heart and willing to help others. When Amar narrated to him the condition in the villages he said laughingly, 'Your Mahantji has stated that whatever collection the government foregoes, he will forego the same amount in land tax. That shows a legal disposition.'

Amar said with misgiving, 'What is so unjust about that?'

'The Mahant has tens of millions of rupees deposited in the bank, while the government is in debt for trillions.'

'Then have you issued any order regarding his suggestion?'

'So soon! It will take at least six months. First, we will have to assess the farmers' situation, then a report will be sent, then that report will be deliberated upon, only then will an order be issued.'

'By then, the tenants will all be finished. It wouldn't be surprising if a riot started.'

'Do you wish the government to forego its due? Sir, this is a bureaucratic government, where everything is done according to rules and regulations. You shout abuse at us, we can't do anything to you but we will file a report with the police, who, in turn, will prosecute you. Ultimately, we would achieve our objective, but with due process. Anyway, that was a joke. Your friend, Mr Salim will very soon investigate the district, but, look, don't put up any false evidence that will discredit him here. Mr Salim praises you a lot. But, Bhai, I am afraid of you people, especially that Swami of yours. He is a very mischievous man. Why not have him trapped? I have heard that he goes about maligning you.'

That such a senior officer should be speaking to him so informally was enough to addle Amar's brain. Indeed, Atmanand was setting things aflame. If he were to be arrested, there would be peace in the District. Swami is a courageous man, he speaks the truth, he is a true servant of the country; but at this time it would be better if he were arrested.

Amar replied in such a way that his deeper feelings were not exposed, but nonetheless it was a stab at the Swami. 'I have indeed no grievance against him, he has the right to defame me as much as he wishes.'

Ghaznavi turned to Salim, 'You note this, Mr Salim. Tomorrow, write to the officer commanding the police station in that area to attend to this Swami. Enough. That is the end of official work. I have heard, Mr Amar, that you have some magic over women.'

Amar caught Salim by the throat and said, 'You must have maligned me.'

Salim said, 'You are being maligned by your own antics. I don't need to say anything.'

Ghaznavi said gallantly, 'Bhai, your wife is an astonishingly brave woman! These days she and the municipality are being tested, but I am confident that the Board will have to give in. Bhai, if my wife had been like her, I, too, would have given up everything to become a beggar. I praise her, hear, hear!'

Amar laughed, 'Why? I should have thought you would be happier doing what you are.'

Feigning surprise, Ghaznavi responded, 'Oh, yes! You know that, of course?'

Salim interjected, 'He ran away precisely because he was afraid of her.'

Musingly, Ghaznavi suggested, 'We should plan some festivity and invite her here.'

Salim responded, 'Why make trouble for no reason at all. As soon as she comes the city will be aflame, and we will have to attend to it.'

Ghaznavi said, 'Oh, well, that is bound to happen one day. This country is ruled by the English whose upper class government is going to last only a little while longer. Thus wealthy Indians and those who side with them are happy to join ranks with the poor. Why? Because the poor people respect them, whereas the English do not. I consider myself part of this group.

The three friends kept up this informal chatter late into the night. Salim had sung praises of Amar from the outset, and, hence, despite his rustic appearance, Ghaznavi treated him as an equal. For Salim, governance was still a new thing; like a new pair of shoes he was trying to keep it clean. Ghaznavi was used to governance and knew that feet are a much more precious commodity than new shoes. Conversation about women is his main source of happiness and amusement. The sensuality of bachelors takes a long time to dry up. Their unsatisfied lust often takes the form of sensuality.

Amar asked Ghaznavi, 'Why didn't you marry? One of my friends, Doctor Shantikumar, is also unmarried. You people must be afraid of women.'

Ghaznavi said, thinking back, 'Shantikumar, is he the one I am thinking of—a somewhat handsome, fair, sturdy-looking man? Oh, he was a fellow student with me, yaar. Both of us were at Oxford. I was studying Literature, and he was studying Political Philosophy. I used to tease him. He is at the University, isn't he? I used to think of him often.'

Salim told him about Shantikumar's resignation from the University, his establishment of a trust fund, and his community work.

Ghaznavi nodded his head as if some mystery had been solved. 'Then, in truth, you people are his disciples. We often used to discuss marriage. My doctors, of course, had cautioned me against marriage, because at that time I had some symptoms of tubercolosis. My soul used to shudder at the thought of leaving a young widow. Since then, I live my life on a day-to-day basis. Shantikumar was obsessed with ideas of community service and what not; but I am amazed that he is still pursuing that obsession. I think that now he just doesn't dare quit. I know him; after all, he was my colleague. Give me his address so that I can invite him here.'

Salim shook his head, 'He has no time to spare. I have invited him, but he doesn't come.'

Ghaznavi smiled, 'You must have invited him on your own. You should invite him on behalf of some institution and promise that some funds will be raised, then you will see whether he comes running on all fours or not. The soul of these community workers is fund-raising, their conscience is fund-raising, and perhaps even their God is fund-raising. No matter who it is, they are always crying for funds. I have often tricked these workers. At those times their faces are worth a study. They shout abuse, change postures, and fire verbal cannon balls, while you look on amused. Once I had one leader sahab locked up in the madhouse. They say that they are servants of the community and think that they are its leader.'

Next morning, Mr Ghaznavi had his car take Amar to his village. Amar's pride and happiness knew no bounds. After being in the company of officers he had developed some official airs. Amar mulled over what he would tell the villagers. 'The officer-in-charge of the subdivision is coming to investigate your condition. Be careful, nobody is to give him any false evidence. Whatever he asks, you must reply truthfully and to the best of your ability. Don't either hide your plight or exaggerate it. The investigation has to be based on facts. Mr Salim is a very kind man, a friend of the poor. The investigation will, of necessity, take time; but government dealings do take time. It is such a large district; it will take months to complete a circuit. By that time, you people should have planted your *kharif* crop. You can count on me; you will be forgiven eight annas out of a rupee in taxes. The reward of patience is sweet, understand?'

Swami Atmanand also had now come to believe that justice would prevail. He realized that Amar alone was getting all the accolades and that he was getting nothing but discredit, so he changed his stance. At one event they both spoke from the same podium. Swamiji bent somewhat, Amar extended his hand a little; thus they became fellow workers again.

In the month of Asarh when the rains started, Salim went to the sub-district to investigate. He took down evidence from tenants in three or four villages, but he was bored by the end of a week. It was an ordeal for him to lie alone like a ghost in a *dak* bungalow in the hilly countryside. One day he left, pretending he was sick and kept making excuses for a month. Finally, when pulled up by his superior and warned by Ghaznavi, he returned. By that time the Saavan downpours had started. Rivers and streams were running full, and the weather was somewhat cooler. The hills were verdant, peacocks were calling, and the countryside was aglow with natural beauty.

After several days, there was a break in the clouds and the rains stopped. Mahantji had announced a four anna per rupee relief pending the decision by the government and the stewards had again started collecting the balance. They had come down hard on three or four tenants. To consider this new situation a huge meeting was being held by the bank of the Ganges. Bhola Chaudhary was made Chairman and Swami Atmanand was making a speech.

'Gentlemen, there are very few amongst you who have not already given half the tax. Until now we were worried about paying half the taxes, now we are worried only about paying half of one half, that is four annas per rupee. You people should willingly give another two annas for a total of ten annas per rupee—you should be satisfied with a relief of six annas per rupee. The government will certainly offer some compensation to Mahantji for the relief he has given you for land taxes. If the grain prices stay as they are for the next crop, we are hopeful that the relief will be eight annas per rupee. This is my proposal. You people should consider it. My friend Amarkantji is of the same opinion. If you have anything else to propose, then we are ready to consider it.'

Just then, the postman delivered a letter to Amarkant. The writing showed that it was from Naina. After reading it he seemed intoxicated.

His face lit up like a fire fed with an offering. He looked here and there, his eyes full of pride, his imagination running wild. The letter described Sukhada's arrest and imprisonment. Oh! She had gone to jail and he was still outside! What right did he have to stay free? That tender woman who could not even bear harsh or stern looks, who was used to living in luxury, was today in prison, bearing the hardships of jail! That ideal woman, the icon of the family, the one who spoke for the country, was in prison! At this moment, Amar was ready to sacrifice everything for Sukhada. Sukhada! Sukhada! All around him, he saw the same vision—Sukhada. In his imagination, he saw Sukhada riding the waves of the Ganges glowing red with the evening sun. He saw her rising up into the heavens draped in a saffron-coloured sari. He saw her standing in front of the dusky chain of hills with a garland of dust from cows' feet around her neck. As if demented, Amar ran a few steps forward to touch her feet in respect.

He had no idea who said what at the meeting. He didn't know what he said either. When people returned to their respective villages it was evening and the moon was shedding its glow. Amarkant's soul was permeated with gratitude and he felt a protective mantle spread over him with the same glow. It seemed to him as if there was a mission to his life, some direction, some blessing, some truth; that balanced and saved him at every step. Today for the first time, he experienced a communion with the one noble desire, one noble awakening.

Suddenly Munni called, 'Lala, you really ignited a fire today.'

Amar said, astonished, 'Who, me?'

Then he remembered every single word of his speech. He took Munni's hand and said, 'Yes, Munni, we will now have to do what I said. Until we stop paying the land tax, the government will keep on procrastinating.'

Munni said anxiously, 'You are leaping into fire now!'

Amar laughed heartily and said, 'Leaping into fire will take us to heaven. There is no other way.'

Munni stared at him, surprised. She didn't understand what he found so funny.

CHAPTER 44

Salim was staying in a dak bungalow about seven or eight miles from the village. The police inspector of the region had already informed him about the meeting the night before and had even read to him Amarkant's speech. He had been instructed to report such meetings.

Salim was very surprised. Just the day before he had met Amar, and although Amar had protested against Mahantji's new move it had only been with regret, not anger. How could he have changed his mind so suddenly?

He asked the police inspector, 'Mahantji has not pressed them too hard, has he?'

The inspector, ready to erase such a notion altogether, said, 'Not at all, Sir. He had given strict instructions that the tenants were not to be persecuted in any way. The poor man, on his own, gave a relief of four annas, but, of course, everyone still abused him and called him names.'

'What was the effect of his speech on the meeting?'

'Sir, it was like putting a lighted match to straw. It will now be very difficult to collect the land tax in Mahantji's district.'

Salim looked skyward thoughtfully, and asked, 'Are you prepared to come to Headquarters with me now?'

What objection could the police inspector have? Initially, Salim thought he should meet Amar; but then he changed his mind. He felt that if Amar could have been persuaded by him, he would not have ignited the fire in the first place.

Suddenly, the police inspector asked, 'Sir, you know him, of course?'

Salim said, annoyed, 'Who told you that? I know hundreds of people, so what? Even if my own son were to break the law, I would have to pull him up.'

The inspector said sycophantically, 'I did not mean that, Sir. What I meant was that even though he knows you, Sir, he did not hesitate to cast you in a bad light.'

Salim did not answer, but this presented a new angle to the situation. Amar should not have started this storm in his district; the other officers will think, 'He is a new man; he doesn't have any authority in his district.'

Clouds were gathering and it was a dark night; the road was rough, and rivers had to be crossed, but he felt it was essential that he meet Ghaznavi. An experienced officer would not have become so agitated; but Salim was a new man.

After an all-night ordeal, the two men arrived in the city in the morning. Miyan Salim understood today what official life was all about. He realized that his position meant not only governance and authority, but also trials, tribulations, and danger. During the night whenever he was buffeted by a gust of rain or had to cross a ditch he would resolve to tender his resignation—is this service or suffering! Life was passing pleasantly enough before this all started, but now he was caught in a dogfight. Civil Service be damned! If this car went over a cliff not even their bones would be found. A new car had been totally ruined! Upon reaching the city, Salim went to his bungalow and the inspector went to the police station. Salim changed his clothes, had breakfast, and at eight o'clock arrived at Ghaznavi's. The inspector arrived at the same time.

After hearing about the meeting, Ghaznavi said, 'Has Amarkant gone mad? He seemed such a gentleman; but it is difficult to be a leader! How can the poor man make a name for himself? Perhaps the fellow thinks that we are his friends, so there is nothing to worry about—"My lover has become the police inspector, what is there to fear." There is unrest in other districts as well; possibly instructions came from there. They all think that in striking they are taking the long view, but they fail to realize that, in fact, they are adding to the hardships of the farmer whose condition is already very precarious. Even under normal circumstances the poor devils don't get enough to eat. Now the grain prices have fallen even further; they can't pay even half, let alone the full tax, but the government has to carry on! It is essential for the government to inspire a certain element of fear and respect; otherwise, no one will listen to it. If the government conceded today and relieved taxes by half; the next day the farmers would fight to have three-quarters relief, and the day after that would ask for total relief. I think that you should go and arrest Lala Amarkant. There will be some unrest, there may even be an uprising in three or four villages, but an open revolt is not as difficult to control as inflammatory speeches that incite trouble. When pus appears in a boil, it can be cut open and removed; but, if left inside, it spreads to the heart or brain, and life is finished. You should take the Superintendent of Police with you and arrest Amar under Section 124. Take that Swami also into custody. *Darogaji*, please go and tell the Superintendent to get ready.'

Salim said in a choking voice, 'Had I known that I would be embroiled in this mess the minute I got here I would have tried to get posted to some other district. Can't I be transferred now?'

The inspector asked, 'Sir, won't you give me a letter for the Superintendent?'

Ghaznavi scolded him, 'There is no need for a letter. Can't you just say it?'

The inspector saluted and went away; then Salim remarked, 'You pulled him up very sharply. He almost cried. He is a good man.'

Ghaznavi smiled and said, 'Oh, yes, a very good man! He must be supplying a lot of merchandise to his superiors, but he extracts ten times as much from the public. The minute a subordinate flatters me or offers me more service than necessary, I know that he is a rascal *extraordinaire*. As to his abilities, there are crimes in his region all the time, but no one is ever charged. He doesn't even know how to muster false evidence. He makes his living by sycophancy. If only the government could reform the police, the demand for self-rule would be postponed for fifty years. These days no civilized man wants to have any connection with the police, he turns his face away from the police station, considering it a nest of scoundrels. The Police Department is a black mark on this Raj.'

'If you are not feeling up to arresting your friend, then I could send the Deputy Superintendent of Police. But it is now imperative to arrest him. If you don't want him to be humiliated, then you should go. If for no other reason, you should go because of friendship. I know that you are feeling sad. I myself am sorry. In that short meeting, Amar made a deep impression on me. I respect his kind intentions. But we are in two separate camps. We also want self-rule, but not through rebellion. Although it sometimes seems to me that we may have no recourse other than rebellion. What is the need for maintaining such a large army that takes up half the government's revenues. If the expenses of the army were to be reduced by half, then the land tax on the farmers could easily be cut in half. If I am afraid of self-rule, it is only because the conditions of the Muslims might deteriorate even further. Reading trumped-up histories, the two communities have become enemies of each other. It is possible that Hindus, getting an opportunity, may take revenge against Muslims on specious accusations. What comforts me is the thought that in this twentieth century a community as educated as the Hindus will never resort to religious factionalism. The reign of religion has ended. Only in India it still has some life. This is the time for capitalism. Now in a community, the rich and the poor—those with wealth and property and those dying of hunger—will form their respective organizations. They will be much more narrow-minded, and there will be far more bloodshed among them. Finally, after a century or two, there will be only one regime, one law for all, one magistrate for all. The servants of the community will rule the community, and religion will be a matter of individual belief. There will be no king, no subjects.'

The phone rang. Ghaznavi picked up the receiver and listened, 'When will Mr Salim leave?'

Ghaznavi enquired of Salim, 'How soon will you be ready?'

'I am ready'

'Then please come in an hour.'

Salim took a deep breath and said, 'Then I have to go after all?'

'Undoubtedly! I don't want to hand over our friend to the police.'

'Why can't we get Amar to come here under some pretext?'

'He wouldn't come.'

Salim thought that he would be the most despised person in Kashi, when they heard that it was he who had arrested Amar. Shantikumar would tear him to bits and Sakina would probably not even want to see his face. He trembled at the thought. It was like a golden sickle stuck in the throat, you could neither swallow it nor spit it out.

He got up and said, 'Please send the Deputy Superintendent of Police, I don't want to go.'

Ghaznavi asked seriously, 'Do you want Amar to be brought here by four constables, handcuffed and with a rope around his waist, so that when the police start taking him away they have to fire bullets to disperse the crowd?'

Salim asked nervously, 'Can't you stop the Deputy Superintendent of Police from going to such extremes?'

'Amarkant is your friend, not a friend of the DSP.'

'Then please don't send the DSP with me.'

'Can you bring Amar here?'

'I will have to trick him.'

'Alright, you go, I will stop the DSP.'

'I will not say anything to him there.'

'You have that authority.'

When Salim returned to his field camp, he was very despondent as if someone very dear to him had died. As soon as he arrived, he wrote individual letters to Sakina, Shantikumar, Lala Samarkant, and Naina, expressing his helplessness and grief. He wrote to Sakina, 'I can't describe to you my anguish. Perhaps it would have hurt less had I plunged a dagger through my heart. The good friend for whom I came here is going to be arrested today by my brutal hands. I am weeping, wipe my tears with your veil. I am so grateful to Amar, I should shed blood for every drop of his sweat; instead, I am shedding his blood. I am constrained by the collar around my neck and when the leash is pulled, I have to do what I would otherwise never do. Sakina, for God's sake, don't think of me as being treacherous, insensitive, and selfish. Have pity on me, I am most unfortunate.'

The cook came and said, 'Huzur, dinner is ready.'

His head down, Salim said, 'I am not hungry.'

The cook wanted to ask how huzur was feeling. Seeing many letters lying written on the table he was afraid that there might have been some bad news from home.

Salim raised his head and said emotionally, 'You remember, the other day one of my friends came, the one who looked like a country bumpkin, he and I are friends from childhood. We studied at the same college. His family are millionaires. His father is still alive and he himself has a family. He is so clever that he used to teach me. If he had wanted, he could have obtained any high position. There is nothing lacking in his home either, but he feels so much sympathy for the poor that he has abandoned his home and family and is serving the farmers in a village here. I have been ordered to arrest him.'

The cook came closer and sat down on the floor, 'What offence had this Babu sahab committed, huzur?'

'Offence! No offence whatever, only that he could not see the affliction of the farmers.'

'Huzur, didn't you explain this to the bara sahab?'

'Haneef, I alone know what anguish I am suffering. He is an angel, not a man. But this is government service.'

'Then, huzur will have to go.'

'Yes, right now. This is how we repay the dues of friendship.'

'Then that Babu sahab will be imprisoned, huzur.'

'God knows what will happen. Tell the driver to bring the car. It will be necessary to return by evening.'

In a little while the car arrived. Salim's eyes were wet as he got into the car.

CHAPTER 45

This afternoon, after several days of deep meditation, the Sun god heard the call of the earth—had come out from behind the clouds and was giving his blessing; while the earth, having spread her cloth, seemed to be gathering up that blessing.

Just then, Swami Atmanand and Amarkant arrived at the school from two different directions.

Amarkant said, wiping perspiration from his forehead, 'We had planned so well that we both got back at the same time. There was not a moment's delay. Now we should eat something before going out and return by eight o' clock tonight.'

Atmanand lay down on the ground and said, 'Bhaiya, right now I can't move a muscle. But, yes, if you want to kill me, I will go with you. Running, running, I am all worn out. First, let's have some sharbat. I would like to drink it, cool down, and feel refreshed.

'The work we planned for today was all finished!'

'Yes it was; if not, it can go to hell! I won't sacrifice my life doing any more. If you can do it, do it; but I can't.'

Amar smiled and said, 'Yaar, you are twice my size, but are complaining already. Give me your strength and digestion, then you'll see what I can accomplish.'

Atmanand had thought he would be patted on the back; and instead, his manhood was being mocked. He said, 'You want to die, I want to live.'

'The purpose of living is action, doing something.'

'Yes, the purpose of my life is action. The purpose of your life is untimely death.'

'Alright, you will get your sharbat. Should I have some curd added to it?'

'Yes, add a lot of curd, and have at least two big jugs prepared. We will have dinner after two hours.'

'This is murder. By that time, the day will be all gone.'

Amar called Munni and asked her to prepare the sharbat. Then he lay down on the ground next to Swamiji and enquired, 'How are things in the district?'

'I am afraid we will be betrayed by some people. If non-payment of taxes results in evictions; then many will be shaken in their faith in us.'

'You were never a philosopher. Since when did you get this feeling of doubt.'

'We should not start a thing that ends in shame and disrespect. I tell you honestly, I was very disappointed with the response of some people.'

'This means that you are not cut out to be the leader of this movement. The chief attributes of a leader are self-confidence, courage, and patience.'

Munni brought the sharbat. Atmanand filled up a whole pitcher and drank it down in one breath. Amarkant could not drink more than one cup.

Atmanand made a face and said, 'That's all! And you still call yourself a man?'

Amar replied, 'Eating a lot is the trait of animals.'

'If one doesn't eat, how can one work !'

'No. The less one eats the better one can work. A glutton's biggest job is to digest his food.'

Saloni had been sick since yesterday. Amar was just about to go see her when he saw a car arriving in front of the school. It was probably the first time a car had come to the village. He stopped and was wondering whose car it was when Salim got out. Amar rushed over to shake hands, 'Is it something urgent, why didn't you call me?'

Both men went into the school. Amar brought out a cot, set it down, and said, 'What can I offer you? We are all paupers here. Shall I have some sharbat made?'

Salim said, lighting a cigar, 'No, nothing, thank you. Mr Ghaznavi wants to consult you on some matter. I was going to see him today, so I thought of taking you along. You indeed ignited a fire yesterday. Now what is the good of an investigation. It is now useless.'

Amar said hesitantly, 'Mahantji left us no option, what could I do?'

Salim took cover behind friendship, 'But at least you could have remembered that this was my district, I bear the entire responsibility for it. I have seen crowds of people lining the streets in villages. In some places, even stones were thrown at my car. These are not good signs. I fear that there may even be a riot. I don't consider it a crime if people get agitated about their rights or if they rise against uncalled-for oppression, but I doubt that these people will stay within the law. You have given voice to mute people, awakened those that were asleep; but I don't see even one-tenth of the amount of control and patience that is needed for this particular enterprise.'

Amar heard the government bias in this homily and said, 'Are you sure that you are not making the same mistake that officials keep making? It is easy for those who spend their lives in comfort and leisure to talk of patience and control; but, those to whom every day in life brings a new calamity, can't wait for deliverance to come at a snail's pace. They would like to haul the change in, the sooner the better.'

'But you should remember that before deliverance there will be catastrophe.'

'A long investigative process is in itself a catastrophe for us. If it costs more to produce than the crop is worth, then how is it possible to pay taxes? Even then we were ready to pay eight annas per rupee of tax, but under no circumstances can we pay twelve annas. Why doesn't the government exercise some economy? Why is so much money needlessly spent on the police, the army, and official functions? Farmers are mute, helpless, and weak. Does that justify that the entire burden of taxation should be borne by them?'

Salim said with proud authority, 'Do you realize what the result of this will be? Village after village will be ruined, martial law will be declared, maybe police will be stationed everywhere, crops will be auctioned off, land will be annexed. Catastrophe will confront us.'

Amarkant said calmly, 'Come what may, to die is better than to bow before oppression.'

The crowd in front of the school was getting larger. In order to put an end to the discussion Salim said, 'Let's go. We will discuss this matter on the way. It is getting late.'

Amar hurriedly donned a shirt and after attending to three or four essential matters with Atmanand, was ready to go. Both men got into the car. When the car started, Salim could barely hold back his tears.

Amar became suspicious, 'You are not betraying me, are you?'

Salim embraced Amar and said, 'There was no other way. I did not want you to be humiliated at the hands of the police.'

'Then wait a bit, I should take a few essential things with me.'

'Yes, yes, take them, but if news of your arrest gets out, then I will be a dead man.'

'Then let's go, it is not necessary for me to take anything.'

They had just left the village when they saw Munni coming towards them. Amar had the car stopped and asked, 'Where have you been, Munni? Get my clothes from the Dhobhi and keep them. There is medicine in the alcove in my little room for aunt Saloni, see that she drinks it.'

Munni asked apprehensively, 'Where are you going?'

'I am going to a friend's for a feast.'

The car started. Munni asked, 'When will you return?'

Amar put his head out of the car and saluting her with both hands folded, said, 'When it is destined.'

CHAPTER 46

꧁꧂

Two inseparable friends who had studied together, played together, and laughed together, by force of circumstances were going two separate ways. Both had the same goal, the same purpose; both were patriotic, both wished the farmers well, but one was an officer, the other a prisoner. They were sitting close together in the car, but it was as if there was a wall between them. Amar was happy, as if he were climbing the steps to martyrdom. Salim was dejected, as if he had been thrown out of a meeting hall. He would have felt victorious if he had spoken up at the meeting for the principle of gradual change. But, instead, he had taken shelter behind non-involvement.

Suddenly, trying to smile, Salim asked, 'Amar, are you angry with me?'

Amar said happily 'Not at all. You are still the same old friend you've always been. We have had conflicts regarding ideals all along, and they will continue. That will not affect our friendship.'

Salim said in self-defence, 'Bhai, it is human nature. It is not surprising if there is some malice or bad blood between people in two opposite camps.' Then changing the subject, he continued, 'At first, it was suggested that the DSP should be sent to get you, but I didn't think that was appropriate.'

'For that I am very grateful to you. Will there be a charge filed against me?'

'Yes, there is a report on your speeches and evidence has been collected. What do you think, will this movement be suppressed after your arrest?'

'I don't know. If it is suppressed as a result of my arrest or conviction, then it is better so.'

After a moment he said, 'People know what their rights are. They also know that to preserve those rights, sacrifices have to be made. My duties ended right after making them aware of these things. Now they know and it is up to them. They may give in to strong measures by the government, or they may not. But whether they are suppressed or aroused, they have certainly been hurt. I can also say that to forcibly suppress the people is not a measure of successful governance.'

The truth dawned on Munni as soon as the car left. She shouted excitedly, 'Lala has been arrested!' Then, running after the car, she continued to shout, 'Lala has been arrested!'

In the rainy season, farmers are not very busy in the fields. For the most part, they stay at home. Munni's voice was like a panic alarm. In moments the entire village reverberated with the sound, 'Bhaiya has been arrested!'

Women came out of their houses, 'Bhaiya has been arrested!'

In a trice, the entire village gathered together and started running toward the road. The car was travelling on a winding road, but the footpath was straight. The people thought they could catch up with the car by running along the footpath.

Kashi said, 'We have to die one day anyway.'

Munni said, 'If they arrest anyone, they will have to arrest everybody, take everyone away.'

Payag spoke, 'The government's job is to arrest thieves and culprits, not those who are sacrificing their lives for others. Look, here comes the car. Just stand in the way. Do not move, let them holler.'

Salim said, stopping the car, 'Now what do you say, bhai, shall I take out my pistol?'

Amar caught his hand and said, 'No, no, I will explain it to them.'

'I should have brought three or four police constables with me.'

'Don't be nervous. I would die before I let anyone lay his hands on you.'

Amar put his head out of the car and said, 'Sisters and brothers, now bid me farewell. I will never forget the love and happiness that you have given me. I was a stranger. You gave me a place to live, your respect and love. Whatever service I could have provided in return I have done. If I have made any mistakes or omissions, please forgive me. My only request to you is that you do not abandon the work you have undertaken. And the greatest gift you can give me is that the whole work be done and be done well. Dear friends, I am leaving, but my blessings will be always with you.'

Kashi said, 'Bhaiya, we are all ready to go with you.'

Amar said smilingly, 'The invitation is for me alone, how can you go?'

No one had an answer for that. Bhaiya argued in such a way that nobody could formulate an answer easily.

Munni was standing at the back, crying. How could she face Amar in that condition? The lamp that was lighted in her heart with the dream of illuminating her dark life, was being extinguished. How would she be able to bear that dreary darkness?

Agitatedly, she said, 'So many of you are standing there just staring! Get him out of the car!'

The crowd was stirred up. They looked at each other confused, but no one spoke.

Munni exhorted again, 'Why are you standing and staring, don't you have any compassion! When the police and army colour the whole district red, then ...'

Amar stepped out of the car and said, 'Munni, you are so wise, how can you say such things. Please don't humiliate me.'

Munni said hysterically, 'I am not wise, I am an ignorant countrywoman. Men sacrifice their lives for the smallest things, do you expect us to just keep staring while you are taken away? You are not a thief, you are not a robber!'

Several men moved aggressively towards the car, but hesitated when they heard Amarkant's rebuke, 'What are you doing! Get back! If this is the result of all my service and teaching, all this time, then I say that all my labour has been wasted. This is our *dharmayuddha* and our victory depends on renunciation, sacrifice, and truth.'

The effect was magical. People moved aside. Amar stepped back into the car and Salim slowly drove away.

Munni, feeling both regret and anger, saluted Amar with folded hands. It was as if her life was leaving in the car.

PART 5

CHAPTER 47

The central jail in Lucknow is in an open area outside the city. Sukhada was standing under a tree in the women's ward in the jail and watching a horse race among the clouds. The monsoon season was over. Clouds still occasionally covered the skies with great splendour, but only a drizzle came down. The donor still had kindness in his heart, but his hands were empty; whatever he had, he had already given away.

Whenever someone visited and the main gates would open, Sukhada would go stand in front of the gate. The gates were open only a moment, but in order to have a fleeting view of the outside world she would stand for hours under the tree in front of the gate. She felt suffocated within the confines of the mile-long perimeter. She had not yet been there two full months; but it seemed that there were many changes in the world that she did not know about. A traveller derives a strange pleasure in watching the road. The outside world had never been so attractive.

Sometimes she thought that if she had pleaded her case she would perhaps have been acquitted; but how could she have known how she would feel. Feelings that she would not have entertained even accidentally before were now agitating her like the misguided strivings of a sick person. She had never had any desire to go on a swing; but today, repeatedly, she wished—if there were a rope, I would put it on this tree and make a swing. In the yard, milkmen's daughters were eating the boiled pits of raw mangoes while tending water buffaloes. Sukhada had tasted a pit during her childhood. At that time, it had tasted sour and she had not repeated the experience, but now she craved those pits. The feel of their hardness, their contours, and their fragrance had never seemed so dear to her. She had mellowed considerably, just as a fruit wrapped in straw becomes juicier, tastier, sweeter, and softer. She did not let Munna out of her sight even for a moment. He was the anchor of her life. Several times a day she would prepare milk, halwa, and other things for him. She would run around and play with him, and even cry herself when he would cry for his aunt or grandfather. Now she thought of Amar constantly and longed to read the letter she thought he must have written when he received news of her arrest and sentence.

The matron came and said, 'Sukhada Devi, your father-in-law has come to visit you. Please get ready; the Superintendent has allowed only twenty minutes.'

Sukhada immediately washed Munna's face and dressed him in new clothes, which she had sewn a few days earlier. She picked him up and went with the matron, as if she had been ready all the while.

The meeting room was in the central section of the jail and to get there one had to go outside. Coming out of the jail after more than a month, Sukhada's joy was like that of a sick man who gets out of his bed. She felt like skipping in the field, and Munna, of course, was running after the birds.

Lala Samarkant had been sitting there a while. He was overwhelmed seeing Munna, and picking him up in his arms, hugged and kissed him. He had brought a whole bagful of sweets, toys, fruits, and clothes for him. Sukhada was overcome with tender regard and devotion; she bowed her head at his feet and started crying—not because a calamity had befallen her, but out of happiness.

Samarkant blessed her and said, 'If you have any trouble here, speak to the matron. She is very kind to me. From now on Munna will be allowed to play outside each evening. There are no other problems, are there?'

Sukhada noticed that Samarkant had become thinner. She was touched with affection. She said, 'I am very comfortable here; but why have you become so thin?'

'Don't ask me that, ask how I am still alive. Naina has gone to her in-laws, and the house has become like a haunted house. I hear Lala Maniram is going to live separately from his father and is going to marry a second time. Your mother has gone on a pilgrimage. The movement is carrying on in the city. There is a crowd of people everyday on that piece of land. Some people sleep there at night. Hundreds of huts were put up there one night, but the next day the police set them on fire and arrested the Chaudharies.'

Sukhada was delighted and asked, 'Why did they do these foolish things? By now, I suppose mansions are going up there?'

Samarkant said, 'Yes, bricks and mortar were stock-piled; but one night they all just disappeared. The bricks were scattered around and the mortar was mixed with dirt. Since then, one can't get any labourers to work there—neither mortar mixer nor mason. At night there is a police patrol.

That old Pathanin is behind it all now. It is amazing what an organization she has set up.'

The fact that an ignorant old woman had done so well where she herself had been unsuccessful was a blow to her vanity. She said, 'That old woman, she wasn't even able to walk!'

'Yes, the old woman has baffled many a smart people. I can't tell you how well she has managed people. Pulling the strings behind her is Shantikumar.'

Sukhada had not asked him or anyone else anything about Amarkant up to now; but now she could not stop herself. 'Has there been a letter from Haridwar?'

Lala Samarkant's demeanour hardened. He said, 'Yes, there was one. It was a letter from that ruffian, Salim. He is the officer in that district. He has started arresting people and putting them in custody. He himself arrested Lalaji. That is how his friends behave. I would have shot such a friend as Salim! Perhaps now Amar's eyes have been opened. Anyway, it's not my problem. He is being punished. Now he is probably grinding a millstone in prison. He went to serve the poor, and that is his reward. What galls me is that he was arrested but he didn't even let me know. He acts as if I am dead. But this old man doesn't die so easily—he eats contentedly and sleeps peacefully; he won't die because someone else wishes it. Just think how stupid Lala is; he didn't even inform anybody else at home. I may be his enemy, but, after all, Naina is not, Shantikumar is not. If someone from here had gone to argue his case then at least he would have been placed in a better-class prison. But, no, he is lodged with ordinary criminals. He may cry, weep, and wail; well that is no skin off my nose.'

Sukhada said in a distressed tone, 'Why don't you go yourself now?'

Samarkant turned up his nose and said, 'Why should I go? He should take the consequences of his actions. That girl, you know, Sakina—there is talk of her marriage to that same rascal Salim, who arrested Lalaji. Now Lala will know what is what.'

Sukhada said gently, 'Dada, you are holding him responsible. Actually it was not his fault; it was totally my mistake. How could an ascetic like him be happy with a comfort-loving woman such as I was? But I think that the fault was neither his nor mine; it was Laxmi, the goddess of wealth, who sowed all the poison. There was no place for him in your household; you were always distant from him. I was also raised in a household where Laxmi reigned, and so I could not understand him. Whatever he did, good or bad, he was opposed at home. He was always insulted and rebuked. No one could be happy under those conditions. I have thought a lot about this during my solitude here and I haven't the least hesitation in accepting my fault. You shouldn't delay even a moment. You should go there and meet with the officials, meet Salim, and do whatever you can for him. We wanted to tie down his great ascetic soul in material bonds of enjoyment; we wanted to cage a bird that flies in sky. I thought it was my misfortune when the bird broke through the cage and flew away. Now I know that it was my extreme good fortune.'

Surprised, Samarkant stared at Sukhada, as if he couldn't believe his ears. This calm forgiveness, like water to a wilting plant, served to revive his affection for his son. He said, 'I, too, have given it great thought; there was really no cause for us to be alienated. I was angry with him, and in that anger I said whatever came into my head. He never had the flaw in his character that he was blamed for, but at the time I was blind. I ask, in all honesty, do all such people in the world suffer this kind of punishment? I know many people of loose morals before whom I bow. Then why should I put all the burden of dharma and good behaviour on someone in my own house from whom there is no danger of retaliation? A human being behaves immorally only when he is not bound by love. A beggar goes from door to door because his hunger can't be satisfied by simply one door. If that is considered a flaw, then why didn't God create a flawless world? If you say that that is not the will of God, then I will ask, if God is omnipotent, then why does he make our minds such that, like a broken-down hut, they require the support of so many props. It is similar to saying to a sick man, why don't you get better? If a sick man was capable of healing himself, why would he have fallen sick in the first place?'

Having poured out all the malaise of his heart in one breath, Lalaji paused to catch a breath. It seemed that he was trying to pull out everything that was still left sticking here or there.

Sukhada asked, 'So, when will you go?'

Lalaji said promptly, 'I will leave today after I go from here. I have heard there is a lot of repression by the government there. Now even the newspapers are reporting the news from there. Several days ago, a woman named Munni was arrested along with several men. More or less the same sort of movement is going on in the entire province, if not the entire country. Everywhere people are being put in custody.'

The child had left the room. When Lalaji called him, he ran towards the road. Samarkant ran after him. The child thought that it was a game and ran faster. How fast could a child two and a half to three years old run? But for an old man such as Samarkant, it was hard work. He caught him with great difficulty.

After a minute, he spoke with the air of someone saying something of deep import, 'I think that we should overlook the faults of those who are prepared to sacrifice their lives for the public good.'

Sukhada opposed this, 'Do not say that, Dada. The character of such people must be ideal, lest their altruistic work be tainted by selfishness and immorality.'

Samarkant said philosophically, 'I feel it is selfishness if you feel good at heart when you obtain something and feel sad when you don't. One who feels neither glad nor sad—he is not human, he is not god, he is inanimate.'

Sukhada smiled, 'Isn't there anyone in the world who is unselfish then?'

'Impossible. If self-serving is petty, it is selfishness, if it is large, it is altruism. In my opinion, even devotion to God is selfishness.'

The permitted meeting time was well past, and the matron could not show any more leniency. Samarkant hugged the boy, blessed his daughter-in-law, and went out.

For the first time in a long while, he felt a deep happiness and enlightenment, as if the cover of clouds had moved away from the face of the Moon god.

CHAPTER 48

When Sukhada returned to her room, she saw a young woman in prisoner's garb sweeping her room. A female guard was scolding her.

The guard kicked the prisoner and said, 'Harlot, you don't even know how to sweep! Why are you making dust? Press the broom down.'

The prisoner threw the broom down and face aflame said angrily, 'I have not come here to be anyone's servant.'

'Then have you come here to be a rani?'

'Yes, I have come here to be a queen. It is not my job to serve anyone.'

'Will you sweep or not?'

'If you speak civilly, then I will even sweep the house of your sweeper, but if you threaten me with a beating, you will not get me to sweep even the house of the raja. Understand that.'

'Will you not sweep?'

'No.'

The guard caught hold of the prisoner by her hair and pulling her and slapping her, led her out of the room.

'Move, we are going to Jailer sahab.'

'Yes, take me. I will say the same thing to him. I have not come here to be beaten and abused.'

Sukhada had been provided with this attendant after a long exchange of letters. This incident depressed her so much that she felt badly even about entering her room.

The prisoner looked at her tearfully and said, 'You are my witness, see how this guard is battering me.'

Sukhada came closer, and taking the prisoner's hand from the guard, led her into the room.

The guard said threateningly, 'You have to be here every morning and do what this lady tells you. Otherwise you will be beaten with a stick.'

The prisoner was trembling with rage, 'I am not anybody's maid and will not do this work. I have not come here to tend to any rani-maharani. In prison everybody is equal.'

Sukhada saw that the young woman was self-respecting. Embarassed, she said, 'Sister, there is no rani-maharani here. I asked for you because I was nervous being alone. We will live here like sisters. What is your name?'

The young woman's face softened. She said, 'My name is Munni, I have come from Haridwar.'

Sukhada was taken aback. Lala Samarkant had just spoken of the events there.

She asked, 'What offence were you sentenced for?'

'What offence! The government was not prepared to reduce the land tax. There was a relief of four annas. The produce didn't fetch even half the usual price. How could we pay the tax? We filed an appeal on the matter. That was it, the government started arresting and sentencing people.'

Sukhada had seen Munni several times in the courthouse in former times. Since then, her face had changed considerably. She asked, 'Do you know babu Amarkant? Wasn't he also arrested in the same connection?'

Munni was thrilled, 'How could I not know him? He used to live in my house. How do you know him? He is our leader.'

Sukhada said, 'Like him, I also come from Kashi. His house is in the same locality. Are you a Brahman?'

'Actually I used to be a Thakur, but now I am nothing. Caste, community, son, husband—I have lost them all.'

'Did Amar babu ever talk about his home?'

'Never. There was no one coming or going; no letters, no exchange of news.'

Glancing at her slyly, Sukhada said, 'But of course, he is a passionate man. Didn't he get attached to anyone in the village there?'

Munni pressed her tongue between her teeth, 'Never, Bahuji, never. I never saw him looking at a woman or passing the time of day with one. I don't know why he was alienated from his wife. You might know.'

Sukhada laughed mirthlessly, 'Alienated? He abandoned the woman. He ran away from home clandestinely. The poor woman is still sitting at home. You probably don't know, but he must have given his heart to someone.'

Munni shook her head and said, 'No, Bahuji, anything like that couldn't be kept secret in the village. I used to see him three or four times a day. He would never even look at me. Besides, who would have attracted him in that village? There was no one with education, or talent, or manners.'

Sukhada probed further, 'Men don't look for talent or manners in a woman, or for education. They go for physical beauty, and that God has indeed given you. You are young too.'

Munni said, turning away, 'You are maligning me, Bahuji. Why would he ever look at me, one who is not his equal in any way; but Bahuji, who are you, how did you happen to come here?'

'In the same way as you did.'

'So the same agitation is going on here as well?'

'Yes, it is on similar lines.'

Munni was surprised that educated ladies like Sukhada were also being sent to prison. What would cause such a lady to become involved in the agitation?'

She asked curiously, 'Was your husband also arrested?'

'Yes, that's why I came.'

Munni blessed her, 'May God fulfil your aspirations, Bahuji. When ranis who are used to sitting on cushions start doing penance, then God will soon bestow his gift on us. How long is your sentence? I have been given six months.'

Sukhada told her how long her sentence was, and said, 'They must be taking very harsh measures in your district. What do you think, will the people bend before repression?'

Munni tried to explain, 'While I was there, people used to say that even if they were hanged they would not pay any more than half the land tax. But you can imagine for yourself—when bullocks and ploughs are being seized, when police enter the houses, when the dead are hit with sticks and bullets, how much will a man bear. A whole detachment came to arrest me, probably no less than fifty men; they were ready to shoot at the slightest provocation. Hundreds of people had gathered. I entreated them—"Brothers, go home, let me go;" but no one would listen. They left only when I put them under oath, otherwise many people would have lost their lives that day. I don't know where God is that he sees so much injustice and yet does nothing. For half of the year, the poor get to eat just once a day, and they wear rags; but look at the government, it is still dealing so harshly with them! The officials all want bungalows cars, every delicacy to eat, travel, and entertainment, but no one can bear to see the poor have even a little bit of happiness. Whoever you look at, is ready to suck the blood of the poor. We are not asking for riches, nor do we wish for luxury and comfort, but surely some bread for the stomach and cloth to cover the body are not too much to ask for. They can have whatever else is left. But who listens to the poor!'

Sukhada realized that this countrywoman was unusually aware and symapthetic to the cause of community service. Her praise of Amar's renunciation and service had washed away all of Sukhada's anguish and doubts and worries and cleansed her soul. She saw Amarkant before her eyes—in prisoner's garb, with long, overgrown hair, and a sad face, he was grinding the mill stone with other prisoners. She trembled with sadness and longing. She had never felt so tenderhearted.

The matron came and said, 'Now you have a servant, Sukhada Devi. You should make sure she works hard.'

Sukhada said in a low voice, 'I don't want a servant any more, mem sahab. I don't even want to be in this ward. You should lodge me with the ordinary prisoners.'

The matron was a short Anglo-Indian lady with a broad face, small eyes, and bobbed hair. She was wearing a skirt that came up above her knees. She said, astonished, 'What are you saying, Sukhada Devi! Now you have a servant. Please tell me whatever else you need and I will speak to the jailer sahab.'

Sukhada said politely, 'Thank you for your kindness. I don't wish for any kind of leniency. I want to be like an ordinary prisoner.'

'You will have to live with base women and eat coarse food.'

'That is just what I wish to do.'

'You will have to do the same kind of work. You may even have to grind the millstone.'

'I have no problem with that.'

'You will be able to see your family members only once every three months.'

'I know that.'

Lala Samarkant had been responsible for ingratiating Sukhada with the matron. She was sorry to see such a prize slipping out of her hands. She kept trying to dissuade her, but went away regretfully when Sukhada wouldn't change her mind.

Munni asked, 'What was the mem sahab saying?'

Sukhada looked at Munni affectionately, 'Now I will live with you.'

Munni folded her hands on her chest in horror and said, 'What are you doing, Bahu? You can't live in my ward.'

Sukhada smiled and said, 'Where you can live, I too can live.'

An hour later, as Sukhada was leaving her ward to go with Munni, her heart was trembling with hope as well as fear. She felt like a child, who having passed the examination, had moved to a higher grade.

CHAPTER 49

❦

Police had surrounded the hilly district where Amar had been arrested. Constables and mounted police patrolled the area twenty-four hours a day. No more than five people were allowed to congregate at any one place. No one could leave his house after eight in the evening. It was forbidden to have any house guests without informing the police. Martial law was in force. Many houses had been burned down and their residents, like nomads, took shelter with their children under trees. The school had been torched and its half-blackened walls seemed like grieving women with their hair falling down. Swami Atmanand was still stationed under a bamboo canopy near the school. At the least opportunity ten or twenty people from various places would assemble there, but would disappear as soon as they saw the mounted police coming.

One day Lala Samarkant, with his bedding on his back, arrived at the school. Atmanand ran and relieved him of the bedding and hurried to find a cot. The news electrified the village—Bhaiya's father had come! He was old, but he still appeared fit. He looked like a well-to-do businessman. Quickly many people gathered around him; some had their heads bandaged, some had bandages on their arms, and some were hobbling.

Evening came. The police had been running night and day and, using batons, had established peace in the whole district. Now, sensing that everything was quiet, they were resting, exhausted.

Goodar, supporting himself on his cane, came and touched Samarkant's feet. He said, 'You must have received news of Amar Bhaiya. Nowadays we have police rule. The officials say, "There will be a charge of twelve annas;" we say, "We have no money, how can we pay it." Many people have abandoned the village and run away. You are witnessing the condition of those who have remained. Munni bahu was arrested and thrown in prison. I regret that you have come at a time when we can't even entertain you.'

Samarkant sat down on the raised dais by the school and holding his head in his hands started thinking—'how do I help these poor people.'

He was consumed by anger and demanded, 'Isn't there an officer here?'

Goodar said, 'Yes, sir, there is not one officer, but twenty-five. The senior officer is the Muslim gentleman who is Amar bhaiya's friend.'

'Didn't you people ask that freeloader—'Why do you beat people, is that legal?"

Goodar said, looking toward Saloni's hut, 'Bhaiya, we asked him everything, but who listens. Salim sahab used a crop himself. Even the policemen were astonished at his heartlessness. Saloni, who is like my sister-in-law, spat in his face. She shouldn't have done that, it was sheer lunacy. Miyan sahab was so enraged that he hit the old woman with his crop so many times that now only God can save her. But she was also obstinate; every time he hit her, she retorted with an insult. Only when she fell senseless did she stop yelling. Bhaiya used to call her *Kaki*. No matter where he had been, when he returned he would go see Kaki first. If she had been able to, she would certainly have come to greet you.'

Atmanand was annoyed and said, 'Alright, that's enough, you don't have to tell him everything today. Let him rest a bit. He is exhausted. Send for some water. Turning to Samarkant, he said, 'You have a wash... Look, Saloni has heard, she is coming leaning on her crutches.'

Saloni said, coming nearer, 'Where have you been devarji? If you had come in the month of Saavan we could have sat on the swing together, but you have come in Kartik! Anyone who has a son like Amar, who is such a leader, can't be afraid or worry about anything. Looking at you, devarji, I have forgotten all my pain!'

Samarkant saw that Saloni's whole body was inflamed and her face was swollen. The bloodstains on her sari had dried to a reddish brown. How could Salim have been so cruel with an old and feeble woman! And he claimed to be a scholar! Samarkant's eyes became red with anger and the thought of violence dominated his mind. We may not accomplish anything in impotent rage, but certainly we berate God. 'You are omniscient, omnipotent, You are the protector of the weak and yet such inequity before Your eyes! It seems that no one is running this world. If there had been a kind God looking after this creation, then this atrocity would not have occurred! You are omnipotent! Why don't You dwell in the heart of these animal-like humans, or is it that they are beyond Your reach! It is said that this is all "Bhagwaan ki lila", divine play. What play it is! If You get joy out of it, then You are even worse than an animal; if You are ignorant of these deeds, then why are You called omniscient?'

Samarkant was a man of religious disposition. He had studied religious texts, and read from the Bhagavad Gita every day; but now all his religious knowledge seemed farcical.

He got up without washing and asked, 'Salim would be at the headquarters, wouldn't he?'

Atmanand replied, 'These days he is camped here. He is staying at the dak bungalow.'

'I will go and see him.'

'He is still very angry; what will you accomplish by seeing him? He might even be rude to you.'

'That is precisely what I want to find out, how low can a human being get.'

'Then let's go, I'll come with you.'

Goodar spoke up, 'No, no, you mustn't go, Swamiji! Bhaiya, although Swamiji has renounced the world and is kindness personified, when he gets angry, his anger is like that of Durvasa muni. When the officer sahab was whipping Saloni four people had to hold him down otherwise he would have killed him right there, even though he may have been hanged afterwards. We can't afford to loose him, he provides medical help to the entire village.'

Saloni took Samarkant's hand, 'I will come with you, devarji. I will persecute him morally which will be worse than his physical torture. If he is a murderer, there is One who is bigger than him who is the Saviour. Till He orders, no one can die.'

Samarkant's eyes filled up seeing her boundless faith in God. He thought—these ignorant people are better than I that, inspite of so much pain and sorrow, they still invoke His name. He said, 'No, Bhabhi, let me go alone. I will soon return.'

Samarkant moved away while Saloni was still trying to balance her crutch. Teja and Durjan led the way to the dak bungalow.

Teja asked, 'Dada, when Amar bhaiya was little, he was quite naughty, wasn't he?'

Samarkant replied, puzzled, 'No, no, he was very civil even as a child.'

Durjan clapped his hands and said, 'Now, what do you say, Teju, have you lost or not? Dada, we had this argument, he said that boys who are very naughty as children grow up to be polite; and I said that those who are well-behaved grow up to be civil. How can something that is not in a man from the beginning appear out of nowhere?'

Teja objected, 'A boy doesn't have wisdom, where does he get it from when he becomes a young man? A seedling has only two leaves, how does it get branches and leaves? Your example is no argument. I can give examples of so many famous people who were rascals in childhood but became saints later on.'

Samarkant was enjoying this argument between the children and, becoming a mediator, supported both sides. The road was very muddy at one spot; Samarkant's shoes got stuck and came off his feet, causing everyone much laughter.

They saw five riders coming towards them. Teja picked up a stone and threw it at one of the riders. His pugree fell to the ground. He jumped off his horse to pick up his pugree while the other four galloped towards Samarkant.

Teja ran and climbed up a tree. Two riders went after him and started yelling at him. The other three riders surrounded Samarkant; one raised his crop when, suddenly taken aback, he said, 'Oh, it is you Sethji! What are you doing here?'

Sethji, recognized Salim, 'Yes, yes, use the crop, why are you stopping? When will you ever have such chance to show your authority. If you don't use your crop on poor people, what kind of an officer would you be?'

Salim was ashamed, 'You witnessed their mischief, yet you blame me. The brat threw a stone which knocked off this inspector's pugree, it was lucky that it didn't hit his eye.'

Samarkant got carried away in his agitation, 'It's alright. Why shouldn't our officer, who is the fount of wisdom, use a crop when this ignorant boy throws a stone at him? You should ask two of your people to climb up the tree and throw the boy down. If he dies, so what; he will at least have been punished for being disrespectful to the officer.'

Salim protested, 'You have just arrived. You wouldn't know how troublesome these people are. One old woman spat in my face; I controlled myself, otherwise the entire village would have been in prison.'

Even this terrible 'revelation' did not daunt Samarkant, 'Son, I have just seen the results of your self-control. Now, don't make me say anything. She was an illiterate, ignorant woman; but you, who are so educated and urbane, what was your response? Her entire body is bloodied and broken! She may not even live. Do you know how many people's limbs were broken? All this because of you! If taxes could not be realized from them, you could have dispossessed them, auctioned off their crops. Since when has it become legal to beat and maim?'

'There is no point in dispossessing, who is there to purchase the land? In the final analysis, how can the government's revenue be realized?'

'Then go ahead, wipe out the entire village, see how much money you collect. I didn't expect such behaviour from you; but perhaps being in government intoxicates one with power.'

'You do not yet know the misdeeds of these people. Come with me and I will tell you the whole story. Where are you coming from?'

Samarkant told him about his visit to Lucknow and his meeting with Sukhada. Then he came to the point, 'Amar must be here. I have heard that he has been put in the third class ward.'

It had become dark and it was getting cold. The four policemen rode off towards the village, while Salim, holding his horse's reins, walked on foot with Samarkant towards the dak bungalow.

After walking a short distance, Samarkant said sarcastically, 'You have served your friend well! You sent him to prison, that might be acceptable; but at least you could have had him lodged in a better class. But you are an officer, how could you have recommended leniency for your friend.'

Salim was hurt, 'Lalaji, you are taking out all your anger on me. I did put him in the second-class ward, but Amar insisted on staying with ordinary prisoners, so what could I do. It is my misfortune that from the moment I came here I have had to do things that I dislike.'

When they reached the dak bungalow, Sethji reclined on a lounge chair and said, 'Then my coming here was useless. If he is in the third class of his own choice, then there is nothing one can do. Will it be possible to see him?'

Salim replied, 'I'll come with you. No date has yet been set for him to receive visitors; the jail officials might oblige, but the problem may be Amarkant himself. He doesn't want any favours.'

Then, with a slight smile he asked, 'I hear you have also started participating in this social movement now?'

Sethji said politely, 'At my age what can I do, where will this old heart find the enthusiasm of youth? My daughter-in-law is in jail, my son is in jail. Possibly, my daughter will also go to jail. And here I eat and drink contentedly and sleep comfortably. My children are paying for my sins. I have sucked the blood of the poor for so long and destroyed so many homes, that I am ashamed even to think about it. If I had understood anything when I was young, I might have reformed myself to some extent. What can I do now? The father is his children's mentor, his children follow him. I have had to follow my children. Without understanding the truth behind religion, I considered the outward symbols of religion as the whole of religion. That was the biggest mistake of my life. It seems to me that the ways of the world have gone wrong. As long as we are dedicated to accumulating wealth, we will be miles away from dharma. I do not understand why God has created the world in this fashion. The world will have to rid itself of its love for money, only then will men be men, and sin will be eradicated from the earth.'

Salim did not want to get embroiled in discussing these lofty ideas. He thought that after he had enjoyed the pleasures of life as Sethji had, then on his deathbed he would also become a philosopher. They were both silent for a few minutes. Then Lalaji said affectionately, 'When one is a servant, he has to obey the orders of his superior. I do not doubt that. But I will say one thing. You should try to wipe away the tears of those you have oppressed. These poor people can be easily controlled with a little gentle treatment. You can't change the policy of the government, but you can exercise discretion and not be unduly harsh with anyone.'

Salim said apologetically, 'I don't want to be harsh with anyone, but I get angry at the impertinence of people. I have a big responsibility on my shoulders. If the land tax is not collected, I will be considered totally incompetent.'

Samarkant said sharply, 'Beta, the land tax won't be collected, but you could certainly have the blood of the people on your hands.'

'That remains to be seen.'

'Yes, we will see. My hair hasn't turned grey without learning something. Farmers in my times used to tremble in front of officers. But times have changed. Now they, too, are very conscious of respect and disrespect. You are unnecessarily acquiring a bad name.'

'If doing one's duty gives one a bad name, I don't care.'

Samarkant was secretly amused at this vanity of officials. He said, 'If a duty is tempered with a little sweetness, it doesn't do anyone harm but can be very constructive. These farmers are so poor and pitiable that with a little bit of sympathy we can make them our slaves. They have borne a lot of arrogance from government officials. Now they want civil treatment. The woman you beat with the crop would have done anything for you if you had just addressed her as Mata. Don't think that you have come to

rule over them, think that you have come to serve them! I realize that
you get your salary from the government; but ultimately it does come
from these people's labour. I might have to explain this to someone who
is stupid, but you, through God's grace, are learned and know better. Why
should I need to explain it to you. You have been taken in by the stories
policemen tell you. Isn't that right?'

Salim could not agree.

But Samarkant held his ground, 'I don't believe you. You may not
accept a bribe yourself, but have been taken in by others who live on
bribes. Your face belies you, you are sorry for what you have done. I don't
think that you should collect a penny more than eight annas, but if you
exercise empathy you could collect more. It is unjust to forcibly collect
even one paisa from people who are suffering and starving and who wear
rags and sleep on straw. You and I, working just three or four hours a day
consider comfort, luxury, and wealth our birthright; but when these poor
souls, working eighteen hours a day with their wives and children, want
just bread and clothing, we consider it unreasonable. They are poor and
mute and cannot organize themselves; and, for that reason, everyone, big
and small, lords over them. But it is sad that a person as kind-hearted and
educated as you is going the route of common officials. Don't bring
anyone with you, just come with me. I will ensure that no one is insolent.
All I want is for you to put some balm on their wounds. They will
remember you as long as they live. Graciousness is like magic, it attracts
people.'

Salim's heart was not hardened to the extent that it could not be
changed. He said hesitantly, 'You will have to speak on my behalf.'

'Yes, yes, I will do that; but I trust that when I leave you won't start
using the crop again.'

'Please don't embarrass me any more.'

'Why don't you suggest that an enquiry be held into the condition of
the tenant farmers. You are not supposed to obey orders blindly, first you
have to satisfy yourself that you are not doing anything unjust. Why don't
you make a report to this effect? The senior officers may not like it, but,
if doing the right thing means some hardship, you should bear it stoically.'

Salim was convinced, 'I am very grateful to you for your wise advice
and I will try to act on it.'

It was now dinner-time. Salim asked, 'Shall I have some dinner made
for you?'

'As you wish, but remember that I am a traditional Hindu. I still observe the customary taboos regarding who touches the food.'

Salim responded, 'Do you consider these taboos right?'

'No, I don't, but I still observe them.'

'Why?'

Samarkant responded, 'Because it is difficult to eradicate something that you were raised with. If it is necessary, I will clean up your waste and throw it away, but I won't ever be able to eat off the same platter as you.'

'Today you will have dinner sitting with me.'

'You eat onions, meat, and eggs. I won't be able to eat food cooked in the same utensils.'

'You won't have to; but you will have to sit with me. I soap myself and bathe everyday.'

'Do have your utensils scoured thoroughly.'

'Sahab, your food will be cooked by a Hindu. We will only sit and eat at the same table.'

'Alright bhai, I will eat. I drink a lot of milk and have my food cooked in ghee.'

Sethji sat down for his evening meditation and afterwards started reading from a holy text. Meanwhile, a Hindu constable who worked for Salim made puri, kachauri, halwa, and *khir*. Curd was already set. Out of deference to Samarkant, Salim would eat the same food. When Sethji returned after his evening rituals he saw two durries spread, each with a platter of food on it.

Sethji was delighted and said, 'You have arranged this very well.'

Salim laughed and said, 'I thought I wouldn't defile your religion, otherwise I would have had only one durrie spread.'

'You shouldn't think that way. Move over to my durrie. No, better still, I'll come to yours.

Taking his platter, he went and sat on Salim's durrie. He thought that he had made the biggest concession of his life today. Even if he had given away all his wealth, he would not have felt so proud.

Salim quipped, 'Now you have become a Muslim.'

Sethji said, 'I have not become a Muslim, you have become a Hindu.'

CHAPTER 50

At dawn, Samarkant and Salim left the dak bungalow for the village. A blue haze was rising from the hills and the day was misty as if with some unspoken burden. It was quiet all around. The earth, like a sick person, was shivering under the fog. Some people, perched like monkeys on top of the thatched roofs, were repairing them and, here and there, women were making cow dung cakes for fuel.

The two men went to Saloni's house. Saloni was feverish and her entire body was aching like a boil, but she sang stoically:

> Saints watch while the world goes rabid.
> Comes after you murderously if you tell the truth,
> falsehood prevails in the world,
> Saints watch …

When the pain in the heart is unbearable when it finds no solace anywhere, when it doesn't find refuge in crying and wailing, then it prostrates itself on the feet of music.

Samarkant called, 'Bhabhi, just come out for a minute.'

Saloni got up at once and, hiding her grey hair under her veil and blushing like a young woman, she went out and asked, 'Where have you been, devarji?'

Suddenly, seeing Salim, she moved back a step and said contemptuously, 'This is the officer!'

Then she rushed like a lioness and pushed Salim so hard that he nearly fell. Before Samarkant could get her off, she caught hold of Salim's neck and squeezed it, trying to strangle him.

Sethji pulled her off, saying 'Have you gone mad, Bhabhi? Just move, do you hear?'

Saloni stared at Salim, her eyes burning with hatred, 'He needs to be punished. You, my warrior, are here now. Trample on his head.'

Samarkant reproved her, 'You are staining the face of this warrior black, nothing else. You are old, you are close to death, and you still act like a child. Is this your dharma that you insult an officer when he comes to your door?'

Saloni thought to herself, 'This Lala is a yes-man also. He is acting like this because his son was arrested, isn't he.' Then malevolently she said, 'Ask him, didn't he beat everyone?'

Sethji said angrily, 'If you were an officer and as soon as the villagers saw you they came out with their lathis, what would you do? When the public is bent on fighting, should the officer worship them? Had Amar been there, he would not have been so free with his lathi. The villagers should have made the officer conversant with their pitiable condition; they should have petitioned him with respect and politeness; they shouldn't have rushed to hit him the moment they saw him, as if he were their enemy. I brought him here after much explanation and argument to effect a peace, to begin again with a clean slate; and, here you are, ready to pick a fight with him again.'

Hearing all the commotion, several people from the village gathered around, but no one greeted Salim. They all looked angry.

Samarkant appealed to them all, 'Think, you people. This sahab is your officer. When the public is impertinent to him, it is not surprising if he gets angry. This poor man does not even consider himself an officer, but we all want respect. No man can tolerate being insulted. Goodar, tell me, am I saying anything wrong?'

Goodar bowed his head and said, 'No, sir, you speak the truth. But of course she is crazy. Don't take to heart anything she says. She is embarrassing everyone, that's all.'

Samarkant continued, 'This officer is like a son to me. He studied with Amar, played with him. You saw with your own eyes that he came alone to arrest Amar. Why? Couldn't he have sent the police to make the arrest? As soon as they had received the order the constables would have come shoving and pushing, and would have tied him up and taken him away. Because of his good breeding he came himself and did not bring any police with him. Amar also did what was his dharma. If he had wanted to, it wouldn't have been difficult to insult a single man. This officer is sorry for whatever has happened, although you people were also at fault. Now you should forget the past. From now on, there will be no harshness in his dealings with you. If he is ordered to auction off your possessions, he will auction them; if he is ordered to arrest anyone, he will arrest him; that should not provoke you. You are fighting a battle of dharma. No, it is not a battle, it is your *tapasya*, your penance. If you feel anger or malice while doing penance, you have lost.

Swami Atmanand spoke up, 'Dharma can't be defended from only one side. The government formulates a code of behaviour and it has to defend that code. When government employees trample the code under their feet, how can the public be expected to stand by it?'

Samarkant rebuked him, 'Swamiji, you a sanyasi, how can you say such a thing! We have to bring our rulers to observe the code by our steady adherence to it. If our rulers had been observing the code, then why would we have to do tapasya? You can attain victory over unethical behaviour, not by being unethical, but by being ethical.'

Swamiji felt humbled and went quiet.

Saloni's aggrieved heart, like a bird that has left its home, was looking for a refuge. This reproach, filled with civility and good intent, was like scattered grain for her. The bird bobbed its head three or four times, looked watchfully, and then hearing the beckoning call from its protector, spread its wings and came down to feed.

Her hands folded and eyes brimming with tears, she stood before Salim, 'Sir, I have made a grievous error. Please forgive me. Have me beaten with shoes ...'

Sethji said, 'Don't say "Sir", say "beta".'

'Beta, I have committed a grave offence. I am ignorant and crazy. Punish me however you want.'

Salim's youthful eyes were filled with tears. He forgot the glory of governance and arrogance of authority, and said, 'Mataji, do not shame me. All you people who are here, and those who are not here, please forgive me for my misdeeds.'

Goodar said, 'Bhaiya, we are your slaves, but we are not ignorant; if we had recognized your civility and good intent, all this would have been avoided.'

Swamiji whispered in Samarkant's ear, 'I am afraid that he will betray us.'

Sethji assured him, 'Never. He may lose his job, but he will not oppress you. He is a cultured man.'

'Then will we have to pay the full land tax?'

'If you don't have anything, how can you pay it?'

When Swamiji moved away, Salim came and whispered something in Sethji's ear.

Sethji smiled and said, 'This gentleman is offering you people one hundred rupees for medical treatment. I am adding nine hundred rupees to that. Swamiji, come with me to the dak bungalow and I'll give you my money.'

Goodar, suppressing gratefulness, started to say, 'Bhaiya ...' but no more words came out of his mouth.

Samarkant said, 'Don't think that this is my money. I didn't inherit it from my father. I got it by squeezing people like you. Now I will return it to you.'

The village that had been overcast by sorrow now appeared festive, as if there was music in the air.

CHAPTER 51

꧁꧂

Amarkant was able to get the daily news in jail by one means or another. The day he heard of the beatings and burnings his anger knew no bounds, but just as a fire spending itself turns to ashes so, after a little while, his anger turned to despair. The painful lament of the people seemed to ring in his ears. The flames of burning houses seemed to be scorching him. In his imagination that terrible scene was one of almost total destruction. And who was responsible for it? If he had not given that speech, which had inflamed the people, there wouldn't have been such repression; the government would have exercised some leniency, and the tax would have been collected one way or another. But after such a revolt, how could the government have taken a gentler approach? Being unable to pay taxes is nobody's fault! Who knew where this plague of falling prices had come from? But it seemed as if the government was punishing someone whose thatched roof had flown away in a storm! What was the purpose of this government, who did it benefit?

Such thoughts tore at his heart and he hid his face in despair. 'There was oppression, so be it. What should I do? What can I do? Who am I! What concern is it of mine? If the weak are destined to, they will be beaten; I am in no great comfort either. What can I do if everybody in the world behaves like an animal? Whatever will be, will be. This is God's lila! Bravo for Your lila! If You find pleasure in such lila, then why do You pretend to be kind? The powerful rule with disdain, is that also ordained by God?'

Faced with a difficult problem, he turned agnostic. The entire universe seemed to him to be mysterious, without order and without purpose.

Absentmindedly, he was braiding thread; but another scene was being re-enacted in his imagination—there was Saloni, half-naked, her hair loose, being beaten, and he was hearing her pitiable cries. Then Munni's image appeared. She has been arrested and the constables were dragging her along. Involuntarily, he called out—'Hey, hey, what are you doing?' All of a sudden his mind cleared, and he again began braiding the thread.

During the night these scenes would plague him unceasingly and the lament would ring in his ears. Having taken on the entire blame for the calamity, he was feeling overburdened; but he had no means to lighten his load. He had turned away from God, and it seemed that he had abandoned the boat and was drowning in bottomless waters. His pursuit of a particular course of action would not let him reach out for even a straw to save himself. Where was he headed, where was he taking these hundreds of thousands of helpless creatures, and where will it all end? Was there any silver lining in these dark clouds? He wished there would be an encouraging ray of hope from somewhere—'Keep going! Keep going! This is the correct path;' but deep, dense darkness surrounded him. There was no sound from anywhere, no light, no guidance, and no direction. When he was himself in darkness, when he didn't know whether the cooling shades of heaven or the annihilating flames of total destruction lay ahead, what right did he have to endanger the lives of so many human beings. In this state of mental paralysis his soul cried out—'God, enlighten me, save me.' And he started crying.

It was morning and the prisoners had had their roll call. Amar was somewhat at peace. His extreme emotional state had subsided and the fog in his mind had cleared. He was seeing things more realistically. He was analysing the incidents of the recent past in his mind. While trying to link the threads of cause and action, he suddenly realized why he had become so agitated—it was that letter from Naina about Sukhada's arrest. That was why he had left the correct and attainable path of compromise and had turned towards an untenable path. He was taken aback as if kicked, and the kick opened his eyes. He realized that it had been his desire for personal fame and glory, coupled with arrogance disguised as service, that had led him to abandon the correct path. What other consequence could such thoughtless and emotional action have had?

A prisoner sitting next to Amar was braiding thread. Amar asked him, 'Why are you here, bhai?'

He looked at him curiously and said, 'First, you tell me.'

'I was bent on making a name for myself.'

'I was bent on making money.'

Just then the jailer came up to Amar and said, 'You have been transferred to Lucknow. Your father had come and wanted to visit you. But your visiting dates had not yet been fixed. The chief officer refused.'

Amar asked with surprise, 'My father came here?'

'Yes, yes. What is there to be astonished about! Mr Salim was also with him.'

'Is there any fresh news from the district?'

'It appears that your father has mediated and struck an accord between Salim sahab and the village people. He is a civilized man. He has donated almost a thousand rupees for the treatment and general care of the villagers.'

Amar smiled.

'You are being transferred because of his efforts. Your wife is in Lucknow prison as well. She has been sentenced to around six months.'

Amar stood up, 'Sukhada is also in Lucknow?'

'Why else would you be transferred?'

Amar experienced an unusual peace in his heart. Where did that feeling of hopelessness go? Where did that weakness go?

He sat down and started braiding thread again. His hands were extraordinarily dexterous. Such transformation! Such auspicious change! How could anyone doubt God's mercy? He had sown thorns, and they had all turned into blossoms!

Today Sukhada is in jail. She who was devoted to luxury and comfort, is finding meaning in her life through service to the poor. My father, who was such a miser, is busy being charitable. If there is no godly power, then who is instigating all this!

He made obeisance before God with absolute devotion in his heart. The weight of the burden, that was pressing him down had been taken off his shoulders. His body felt light, his heart was light, and the struggle that was still ahead welcomed him.

CHAPTER 52

❧

Amarkant had been in the Lucknow jail for three days. There he had been given the task of grinding flour. The jail officials were aware that he was the son of a rich man; consequently, even though he had been assigned hard labour, he was treated leniently.

There were rows of grinding mills under a thatched roof. Two prisoners were standing at each mill grinding the flour. In the evening the flour would be weighed; if it was less than expected, they would be punished.

Amar said to his companion, 'Stop a bit, bhai, let me catch my breath, my hands can't move anymore. What's your name? I seem to have seen you somewhere.'

His companion was a man of stocky build, dark-complexioned, with red eyes, and stern appearance. Hard work did not seem to tire him. He smiled and said, 'I am Kaale Khan who once came to sell you a pair of gold bracelets. Remember? But what surprises me is how you came to be here. I have been meaning to ask since you came, but kept thinking that maybe I was mistaken.'

Amar gave a brief account of himself and asked, 'How did you come here?'

Kaale Khan laughed and said, 'Lala, what are you asking? If I stay six months outside the jail, then I stay six years inside. Now I pray that Allah will call me from here. It is very difficult for me to live outside. I feel resentful when I see everyone dressed well and eating well. But where would I get all that? I have no talent, no education. If I don't steal or rob, then how will I eat? Here in prison there is no one to resent. I don't see anyone dressing well or eating well. All are like me, so why should there be any envy or jealousy? For that reason I pray to Allah that He calls me from here. I have no wish to be released.

'If your hands hurt, let go. I will do the grinding by myself. Why have the jail officials assigned you labour at all? People like you are kept in comfort, separate from us. Why have they left you here? Move aside.'

Amar held on to the mill's handle more firmly and said, 'No, no, I am not tired. I'll get used to it in three or four days, then I'll be able to work as much as you.'

Kaale Khan pushed him away, 'But it is not right that you should grind the mill with me. You have not committed any crime. You have fought against the government on behalf of the public; I will not let you do the grinding. It seems that God has sent me here for you. He is very enterprising. It is impossible to understand His Nature. He makes a man do a misdeed, then He Himself sentences him, and He Himself pardons him.'

Amar objected, 'God does not make us commit misdeeds, we commit them ourselves.'

Kaale Khan looked at him with eyes that seemed to hold a wisdom beyond Amar's understanding. 'No, no, I won't accept that. You must have heard, "Not even a leaf shakes without His bidding." How can one commit a misdeed then? His hand is behind everything that happens, and then He pardons as well. I tell you—all evil will end the day this tenet is accepted in our belief. You yourself taught me this lesson that day when I had come to sell you jewellery. I consider you my mentor. You didn't accept even for thirty rupees an article that was worth two hundred rupees. That day I understood how evil I was. Now I wonder how I will show my face to Allah. I have committed so many sins in my life that when I remember them my hair stands on end. His mercy is my only hope now. Bhaiya, what is written in your religion? Does Allah pardon the sinful?'

Kaale Khan's harsh face was alight with his deep and simple faith. His eyes became soft and his voice was so poignant that Amar's heart thrilled with joy, 'I hear, Khan sahab, that He is very merciful.'

Kaale Khan, grinding the millstone twice as fast, said, 'He is very kind, Bhaiya. He provides nourishment to a child in the mother's womb. This world is a mirror of His mercy. Wherever you lift your eyes there are examples of His mercy. There are many murderous dacoits imprisoned here. They are looked after in comfort. He gives you opportunities, repeated opportunities, to get back in line. Who can endure His anger? The day He becomes indignant, this world will go to hell, why would He get angry with the likes of you and me? If we see an ant in our way, we step aside. We take pity and do not tread on it. The Allah that created us, who nurtures us, can He ever be angry with us? Never.'

Amar felt a wave of faith rise inside him. He had never heard anyone speak on this subject with such unshakable belief and simple devotion. He heard these words everyday from the mouths of the weak and the powerful, but faith had made them come alive.

After a little while Kaale Khan spoke again, 'Bhaiya, you have a troubled spirit. To force you to grind the mill is like killing a bird with a sword. You should have been in hospital. Medicine does not cure as much as sympathetic talk does. I've seen many prisoners fall ill in this prison, but not one was cured. Why? Because the prisoner is just indifferently handed medicine—he may drink it or throw it away.'

Amar saw a heart of gold shining through that dark face. He said with a smile, 'But how could I be in the hospital and do my grinding at the same time?'

'I'll grind the mill by myself and have all the flour weighed.'

'Then you'll get all the credit.'

Kaale Khan spoke with humble wisdom, 'Bhaiya, no work should be undertaken with the idea of reward. One should condition oneself in such a way that one gets the same pleasure out of working as one gets from a song or a play. To work with the idea of profit is merely business. What can I tell you! You understand these things better than I do. I'm not even qualified to take care of a patient. I get angry very quickly. How I wish that I would not get cross, but if someone disagrees with me once too often, I lose my temper.'

The rogue that Amar had once found contemptible had now achieved saintliness. It seemed as if a beam of light was shining from his soul and lighting up Amar's soul.

He said, 'But it seems wrong that you do all the hard work and I ...'

Kaale Khan interrupted, 'Bhaiya, what is the point of talking like that! Your work must be far more demanding than grinding this mill. You will not have the leisure even to talk to anyone. I will have a sweet night's sleep. You will spend nights awake. Even your life is threatened. What is there in this mill? Even a donkey or a machine can grind it. But the work you do only very few people can do.'

The sun was setting. Kaale Khan had milled all his allotted share and was going across to the other prisoners to check how much each was left to do. Several prisoners had not yet finished their quota and the jail official would be coming by shortly to weigh the flour. These poor souls would be in trouble and might even be beaten up. Kaale Khan started helping the other prisoners one by one. People were amazed at his diligence and speed. In half an hour he made up the deficiency of all the laggards. Amar, standing next to his mill, looked on at this paragon of service devotedly as if he were seeing a deity.

Kaale Khan, having finished everything, performed his invocation, spread out his blanket on the ground, and started praying. Just then, the jailer accompanied by four warders, came to weigh the flour. The prisoners put their flour in gunny sacks and came to stand by the balance. The warders began weighing the flour.

The jailer asked Amar, 'Where did your partner go?'

Amar replied, 'He is at his prayer.'

'Call him. He should have his flour weighed first, and then say his prayers. He has become very keen on prayer. Where has he gone to pray?'

Amar pointed to the back of the shed and said, 'Please, let him pray, you go ahead and weigh the flour.'

The jailer could not tolerate it that a prisoner should be at prayer when the master of the prison had arrived! He went to the back and said, 'Hey, you! You praying slave, why don't you get your flour weighed? You have munched away the wheat and now you are pretending to be at prayer. Come at once, otherwise I will use my whip to skin you alive.'

Kaale Khan was in another world.

The jailer approached him and, prodding his back with his stick, said, 'Hey you, have you gone deaf? Are you asking for trouble?'

Kaale Khan was engrossed in prayer. He did not turn around to see.

Exasperated, the jailer kicked him. Kaale Khan was bent low in homage. With the kick, he fell flat on his face, but immediately regaining balance he again bowed in homage.

The jailer was now determined to stop him from praying. Possibly, Kaale Khan was also determined not to get up without finishing his prayer. He kept on with his obeisance. The jailer started to kick him with his boot. One warder hurriedly called two soldiers from the garrison. Another rushed to the jailer sahab's aid. Kaale Khan was being administered kicks from one side, and sticks from the other, but he would not raise his bowed head. With every blow, there came from his mouth the call of 'Allah-ho-Akbar!' Meanwhile, the aggressors got more and more frenzied. What greater insult could there be to Jailer sahab than that a prisoner in his jail should choose to pay homage to his own God rather than to the god of the prison? Blood started to flow from Kaale Khan's head. Amarkant moved to protect him, but a warder held him back firmly. The blows kept falling and Kaale Khan kept up the litany of 'Allah-ho-Akbar'. Finally, the voice, getting feebler and feebler, became quiet and Kaale Khan, having lost so much blood, lay still. But his lips were still parting to soundlessly utter 'Allah-ho-Akbar'.

The jailer said shamefacedly, 'Let the rascal lie there! Tomorrow, he will be given standing leg-irons and confinement as well. If that doesn't straighten him out, then he will be hanged upside down. I'll be damned if I don't rid him of this prayer fetish.'

In a minute, the warders, jailer, and soldiers had all left. It was mealtime for prisoners and all went and sat for their meals. But Kaale Khan still lay face down where he was. Blood was coming out of his head, nose, and ears. Amarkant was sitting next to him washing his wounds and trying to stop the flow of the blood. His understanding of the physical world was shattered by this unimaginable display of spiritual strength. Would he himself have sat so still and self-controlled under these circumstances? Probably with the first blow he would either have retaliated or abandoned the prayer. There is no dearth of sacrifices at the altars of science, morality, or patriotism. But such calm fortitude could come only from faith in God.

The prisoners returned from their meal. Kaale Khan was still lying in the same spot. They lifted him and took him to the barracks and notified the doctor, but he didn't want to be disturbed at night; furthermore, there was no medicine available, not even hot water could be obtained in the jail.

In the barracks, the prisoners sat up the entire night. Several were determined to go after Jailer sahab the next morning. The worst that could happen to them would be that their sentences would be increased by another year. They did not care! Amarkant was a peaceful man, but now he was in agreement with these people. All night a battle had raged inside him between his animal nature and his human nature. He knew that fire is not quenched by fire, but by water. No matter how brutish a man may become, he still retains some humanity. If that humanity is to be awakened, it can only be through repentance or atonement. Had Amar been alone he would not have been shaken in his belief; but mob rage had unsettled him. People in a crowd are able to do good or bad deeds that they would never be able to do if they were acting alone. And the more Kaale Khan's condition deteriorated, the more intense became the flame of revenge against the jailer.

A prisoner who had been sentenced for armed robbery said, 'I will drink his blood, yes his blood! Who does he think he is? The worst that can happen to me is that I will be hanged.'

Amarkant said, 'They didn't think they were killing him when they did this.'

Quietly a scheme was made. The attackers were selected, their action-plan was decided upon. The arguments for their defence were thought through.

Suddenly a dwarfish prisoner said, 'Don't you people realize that by morning the jailer will have been informed?'

Amar asked, 'How will he be informed! Who will inform on us here?'

The dwarfish prisoner looked left and right and said, 'Bhaiya, we don't know where the informers come from. Nobody has that written on his forehead. Who knows who amongst us might go and tell? Everyday you see people turning informers. Given the opportunity, leaders become witnesses for the government. If you want to do something, do it now. If you wait until dawn, all of you will be caught and you will be punished with a five-year sentence each.'

Amar responded suspiciously, 'By now he is probably asleep in his quarters.'

The dwarf said, 'Bhaiya, that is our job, you wouldn't know how to do it.'

They all turned aside and talked in whispers, then five men got up.

The dwarf said, 'Whoever amongst us is a traitor will be guilty of the heinous crime of slaughtering a cow.'

Having said that, he started wailing loudly. Several other men also started crying and screaming. In a moment, a warder appeared at the door and asked, 'Why are you people making so much noise? What is the matter?'

The dwarf said, 'What is the matter? Kaale Khan's condition is very serious. Go and fetch Jailer sahab. At once.'

The warder said, 'Who do you think you are? Be quiet! Stop ordering me around!'

'We are telling you, go and get him, otherwise there'll be trouble.'

Kaale Khan opened his eyes and spoke in a feeble voice, 'Why are you shouting, friends, I am not dead yet. It seems that my backbone is injured.'

The dwarf said, 'Pathan, we are preparing to avenge that.'

Kaale Khan said reproachfully, 'Brother, against whom will you take revenge, against Allah? If this is the will of Allah then how can anyone interfere with it? Can even a leaf stir without Allah's will? Just give me some water to drink. And look, when I am dead all of you brothers pray to God for me. Who else is there in this world to pray for me? Perhaps your prayers will redeem me.'

Amar cradled him in his arms and tried to get him to drink some water, but he could not swallow. He gave a deep sigh and lay down again.

The dwarf prisoner said angrily, 'Such a fiend deserves to have his throat cut with a blunt knife.'

Kaale Khan said haltingly, 'Why do you shut the door on my redemption, brother! This life was ruined; do you want to ruin my afterlife as well? Pray to Allah that He is merciful to everyone. Have I not committed enough sins in my life that even after death my legs should be tethered! Yea, Allah, have mercy!'

These words seemed to signal his death. They were words that one heard everyday, but this time they had such a moving quality that they were all touched. Coming from a man so close to death, the words served to calm their anger.

At dawn, when Kaale Khan breathed his last, there was not a single prisoner whose eyes were not wet with tears. But while others were crying from sorrow, Amar was crying out of happiness. Others were sad at having lost someone dear to them, but Amar felt much closer to Kaale Khan. He had found this jewel among men before whom he could bow his head in veneration and when separated from him feel as if he had received a blessing.

From now on this enlightenment was to give his life a new direction where, instead of uncertainty, there was confidence and, instead of doubt, there was truth personified.

CHAPTER 53

After Lala Samarkant had left, Salim went on a tour of every village to enquire into the financial situation of the tenant farmers. He discovered that their condition was far worse than he had thought. The value of the crop was much less than either the cost of producing it, or the rent. There was not enough money for food and clothing, let alone other expenses. It was a rare farmer who was not overburdened with debt. Salim had studied economics in college and he knew that the condition of the farmers here was bad. But now he understood that the difference between bookish knowledge and practical experience was the same as the difference between a man and his photograph. The more he knew of their real condition the more he felt sympathetic towards the tenant farmers. How unjust it was that full rent should be collected from those who were desperate for bread and had nothing but rags to cover their body, who could not afford even a paisa worth of medicine when sick, or to light a small oil lamp in their house. Somehow they had been able to manage bread once a day when the price of the grain was high. In these depressed times their condition was indescribable. To demand full rent from the farmers whose children started labouring by the age of five or six gathering cow dung for fuel, was like sucking blood from a stone.

Once Salim understood the true state of affairs, he determined on a course of action for himself. He was not one of those men who were motivated for selfish reasons to follow every order of his superior officer. He was not prepared to sacrifice his soul to the civil service. For several days he sat alone and wrote a detailed report and sent it to Mr Ghaznavi.

Mr Ghaznavi responded immediately by letter, 'Come and see me.'

Salim was reluctant to meet him. He was afraid that he might be asked to suppress his report. But then he thought there was no harm in going. If he convinces me, then it doesn't really matter. But he would not let his report be suppressed because of fear of the authorities. That same evening, he reached the headquarters.

Mr Ghaznavi extended his hand with alacrity and said, 'You have discharged your obligations of friendship with Mr Amarkant very well. He could probably not have written such a detailed report himself, but don't you think that the government knows these things?'

Salim said, 'No, I don't think so. The reports they get are from flattering officials who are intent on filling the government's coffers at the sacrifice of the tenants. My report is based on facts.'

The two officers began a discussion. Ghaznavi said , 'Our job is to obey orders from above. They have ordered us to collect the rent. We have to collect it. If the public is hurt in the process, so be it. It is not our concern. We ourselves are hurt when we pay our income tax, but helplessly we pay. No one pays tax happily.'

Ghaznavi thought it wrong and against his duty to oppose the order. He was not satisfied simply to administer the law, but was prepared to enforce the order at any cost. Salim was of the opinion that officers were employees of the government and their sole purpose was to serve the people, to improve their condition, and to help them achieve a higher standard of living. If an order of the government was an obstacle in fulfilling these goals, then it must not be enforced. Ghaznavi said with a long face, 'I am afraid that the government will transfer you out of here.'

'They may transfer me, I don't care about that, but they have to promise that they will seriously consider my report. If they wish to transfer me from here and also file away my report, then I will resign.'

Ghaznavi stared at him in astonishment, 'You don't seem to understand the difficulties of the government. If it gave in so easily do you realize how bold the tenants would become! There would be a storm brewing over every small issue. This is not simply a problem in this district; it affects the whole country. If the government was lenient toward eighty per cent of the farmers, then it would be almost impossible to govern the country.'

Salim objected, ' The government is for the people, people are not for the government. If the government wishes to survive by oppressing the farmers, by killing them with hunger, then at least I will opt out of it. If there is a shortfall in revenue the government must reduce its expenses, not make the public face hardship.'

Ghaznavi tried to reason at length, but Salim was unshakable. He would not agree to collection of tax by force. Finally, left with no choice, Ghaznavi sent his report to his superior. Within a week the government dismissed Salim. How could it trust such a dangerous rebel?

The day he handed over his post to the new officer and prepared to leave the district, a crowd of men and women surrounded his quarters. All started pleading with him not to leave them to their fate. Salim wanted to stay. He could not return home for fear of his father. Also, he had developed an affection for these poor people. It was partly pity and partly the affront to his dignity that made him their leader. The officer who had just a few days previously been full of official arrogance, had now become a servant of the people. To bear oppression, rather than to oppress, seemed so much nobler.

The people took courage again when Salim took over the reins of the movement. Salim was now rushing from village to village with Atmanand, just as Amarkant had previously done. Salim, who had been fiercely hated by the people, was now the uncrowned king of the district. They were ready to give up their lives for him.

One evening when Salim and Atmanand had returned after a hard day's work, Mr Ghosh, the new Bengali Civil Officer, arrived suddenly with police. He announced that all the livestock in the village was to be auctioned. Some butchers had been called in and they were looking forward to a bargain. In a few moments the constables unleashed the animals and assembled them in front of the schoolhouse. Goodar, Bhola, Algoo, all the village chiefs had already been arrested. The crop had been auctioned off earlier, but as little had been realized the authorities had decided to auction off the livestock. They believed that the farmers would be so afraid of the auction that they would be prepared to save the animals at any cost, even if they had to go into debt or sell their women's jewellery. Oxen are a farmer's arms.

When the farmers heard this announcement, they lost all heart. They had been under the impression that whatever the government might do it would not auction their livestock. Surely, the government would not destroy the farmers!

At first they thought it was only a threat. However, when the animals had been herded in front of the school and the butchers started examining them, the situation had reached the point where violence could break out any time.

By the time the little earthen lamps were lighted, the cattle market was in full swing. The officers had decided to collect all the monies at once. They thought that the villagers would fight amongst themselves but then settle their tax with them individually.

Salim came up to Mr Ghosh and said, 'Do you know that you do not have the authority to auction the livestock?'

Mr Ghosh responded with hostility, 'That policy is not meant for occasions like this. There are special policies for special occasions. The policy during times of rebellion will be different from the policy during times of peace.'

Before Salim could reply, news came that the police were using lathis to disperse a crowd in the milkmen's locality. Mr Ghosh rushed to that area. The soldiers also fixed their bayonets and followed him. Kashi, Payag, and Atmanand all rushed in the same direction. Only Salim continued to stand where he was. When they were alone he stepped up to the chief of the butchers, greeted him, and said, 'My dear brother, do you know that by purchasing these animals you are gravely injuring these poor tenants?'

The chief was named Tegh Muhammad. He was a short, stocky, powerful man, dressed in a loose shirt and a checkered *tahmad*, with a silver amulet around his neck and a heavy stick in his hand. He said politely, 'Sahab, I have come only to purchase goods. It is no concern of mine whose goods they are or in what circumstances. A man goes wherever he can make a profit of a few rupees.'

'But do at least consider why the cattle are being auctioned off. You should have sympathy for the tenants.'

Tegh Muhammad was unmoved, 'Whoever has a quarrel with the government may have it. We have no quarrel.'

'I am saddened that you, a Muslim, can say such things. Islam has always defended the helpless. But you are putting a knife to the throats of the helpless.'

Tegh replied, 'When the government is nurturing us we can't wish it ill.'

'If the government were to seize your property and give it to someone else, then wouldn't you feel badly?'

Tegh said, 'To fight the government is against our creed.'

'Why don't you say that you are unfeeling.'

Tegh returned, 'You are a Muslim. Is it not your duty to help the Emperor?'

'If to be a Muslim means that one should suck the blood of the poor, then I am an infidel.'

Tegh Muhammad was an educated man. He was ready to debate and discuss, but Salim tried to make light of him. Salim thought that sectarianism was a blot on the world; that it had divided the human race into opposing camps and made them enemies of each other. Tegh Muhammad observed the fasts and prayers and was a devout Muslim. He could not tolerate anybody ridiculing religion.

Elsewhere, the police and the milkmen were fighting each other with lathis. Here these two men started to push and shove one another The butcher was a wrestler, Salim was quick and fit and was an expert at kickboxing. The wrestler attempted to grab and smother him, but Salim kept on kicking, one kick after another. The wrestler fell down against his fusillade of kicks and started swearing. At first, his two companions had been watching this show from a distance, but when Tegh Muhammad fell down, they both tightened their belts and joined in. Both were young stalwarts, equal to Salim in agility and fitness. Salim kept backing off, and the other two kept pushing him. Saloni was out with her stick searching for her cow which had been let loose from her doorstep by the police. Seeing the fight, she tucked the end of her sari into her waist and, balancing the stick, started to hit the two butchers from the rear. One of them turned around and pushed the old woman so hard that she fell back three or four steps. This interruption gave Salim the chance to box the youth in front of him so hard that his nose started to bleed, and he sat down holding his head. Now there was only one man left. Seeing the condition of his two warrior friends, he ran off to appeal to the police. Tegh Muhammad had lost the use of both his knees. He could not get up. Seeing no opposition, Salim quickly untied the cattle and, clapping his hands, made them disperse. The poor cattle had been standing apprehensively, partly aware of the impending disaster. As soon as they were untied, they raised their tails and took off towards the pasture.

Just then Atmanand arrived, running breathlessly. He said, 'Could you please give me your revolver?'

Salim was stupefied, 'What's the matter? Tell me.'

'The police have killed many people. We can't sit idly by. I want to give Ghosh a taste of his own medicine.'

'Are you out of your mind? Is this the time to use a revolver?'

'If you don't give it to me, I will snatch it from you. That wicked man has ordered the police to fire into the crowd; four or five people have lost their lives. Ten or twelve people are badly injured. He must be taught a lesson. One has to die sooner or later, anyway.'

'My revolver is not to be used for this purpose.'

Atmanand was an impetuous man by nature, and these murders had pushed him over the edge. He said, 'Those oppressors are shedding the blood of innocent men, and you say that the revolver is not to be used for this purpose. For what purpose is it to be used then? Bhaiya, I beg of you. Please give it to me for a moment. I must avenge the dead. It makes my blood boil to see these murderers killing such brave men.'

Without replying, Salim quickly headed towards the milkmen's locality. Along the way all the doors were shut, even the street dogs had gone into hiding.

Suddenly the door to a house was pushed open and a young woman, bare-headed and clothes soaked in blood, ran towards him like a distressed fawn, threw herself at his feet, and breathed with a frightened glance backwards at the door, 'Sir, these policemen are killing me.'

Salim comforted her, 'Don't be afraid. What's the matter?'

The young woman said falteringly that several policemen had forced their way into the house; then she could not continue.

'Is there no man in the house?'

'He has gone to graze the buffalo.'

'Where have you been injured?'

'I am not injured. I have wounded two men.'

Then, two constables with guns came out of the house. Seeing the young woman standing next to Salim, they rushed towards her, caught her by her hair, and started dragging her toward the door.

Salim stood in their way and said, 'Let her go or else you will regret it. I will shoot the two of you.'

One constable said angrily, 'How can we release her. She has to be taken to our officer. She has seriously wounded two of our men with an axe; they are writhing in pain.'

'Why did you go into her house?'

'We went in to set the cattle free. She attacked us with her axe.'

The young woman objected, 'You lie. You grabbed my arm.'

Salim pushed at the constable angrily and said, 'Let go of her hair.'

'We are taking her to our officer.'

'You will not take her.'

The constables had known Salim as an officer. They had been his minions. Some remnants of that authority still persisted in their hearts. They did not dare use force against him. They went and appealed to Mr Ghosh, who was envious of Salim. He believed that Salim was behind the entire movement and, if he were to be removed, even though it might not to be quelled at once, its roots would be cut. Accordingly, no sooner had the constables reported to him than he mounted his horse, rode to where Salim was, and started spouting the law in English. Salim was also proficient in English. At first the two discussed the legal aspects of the case, followed by religious and moral issues. This degenerated into metaphysics and sophistry, finally ending in a shower of personal abuse. Very soon words were followed by action. Mr Ghosh struck out with his whip, which left a broad, blue welt on Salim's face. His eyes were saved by a hair's breadth. Salim also lost control. Grabbing Mr Ghosh by his legs, he pulled him off the horse, sat on his chest and boxed him on his nose. Mr Ghosh fainted. The constables stopped Salim from giving a second blow. Four men held on to Salim, while four others lifted up Mr Ghosh and revived him.

Darkness had fallen. Panic had gripped the entire village like a demon. People, sad, quiet, and afraid of persecution, were removing the bodies of the dead. No one whimpered. The injuries were fresh; so there was no throbbing pain. Weeping was a sign of defeat. These people were proud. They did not want to show their vulnerability by weeping. It was as if even the children had forgotten to cry.

Mr Ghosh went to the official quarters riding his horse. Salim, accompanied by a sub-inspector and several constables, was sent to the city headquarters of the district, in a lorry. The young woman from the milkmen class was also sent in the lorry. As the night progressed, four shrouded biers made their way toward the Ganges. Saloni with her stick tapping the way walked ahead singing—'God has deserted us, oh, my friend, ...'

CHAPTER 54

Kaale Khan's sacrifice proved to be an anchor in Amarkant's life. Previously his life had had no direction and had lacked ideals or commitment, but Kaale Khan's death had enlightened his soul. His memory was like a secret well from which he drew peace and strength. He wanted to fulfil Kaale Khan's bequest in such a manner that his soul would find peace in heaven. He threw himself into work, getting up at night to check with the prisoners how they were faring, writing letters to their homes to arrange medicine for the sick, listening to their complaints, and meeting officials to make sure that the complaints were acted upon. He performed these tasks with so much courtesy and compassion that even the officers, instead of being suspicious, trusted him. He had the trust of both prisoners and officials.

Until now he had believed in a kind of utilitarianism, and that philosophy, though unconsciously, had directed his course of action. There was no place in his life for reflections on cause and effect, and the unfathomable depths that lie beneath the surface held no meaning for him. He thought there was nothing there. Kaale Khan's death, as if taking him by the hand, immersed him in those depths. He saw his entire life like a blade of grass floating on the surface of water, sometimes moving forward with the waves, sometimes being pushed backwards by gusts of wind, sometimes going around in circles in a whirlpool. He had no stability, no self-control, and no willpower. Even his idea of service had been tinged with arrogance, egotism, and malice. In his arrogance he had slighted Sukhada. He had made no effort to understand the reality that lay beneath her love of luxurious living; instead, he had cast her off. But what effort could he have made? At that time he did not even know what effort was. His perception had not gone beyond the superficial.

In his egotism, he had played the farce of being in love with Sakina. Was there even a semblance of love in that passion? At the time it had seemed that he was deeply in love, he was ready to give his whole life to her; but now he could see nothing but lust in that love. Not only lust, but meanness. He had wanted to satisfy his lust by taking advantage of the poverty of that simple woman.

Then Munni came into his life; she was broken by disappointments but was full of life's desires. His treatment of that good woman had been wicked. He would console himself with the thought that in his relationship with her there was no lewdness. But now, on self-examination, it was clear to him that even in their jests, their affection, there had been an element of lust. Then did it mean that he was indeed a depraved man? His self-examination gave him an answer that was not at all complimentary. He had blamed Sukhada for being a pleasure seeker, but he had himself been absorbed in sordid and contemptible pleasure seeking. He had an overpowering desire to put his head down at the feet of Sakina and Munni and say, 'Ladies, I have been perfidious with you and have deceived you; I am petty and depraved, my head is on your feet, punish me as you wish.'

Amarkant also had developed a new feeling of reverence for his father. A man he had once considered a slave of materialism, one who was easily tempted and incapable of any kind of sacrifice, he now saw as saintly. Absorbed in the superficial aspects of life, he had never accepted the existence of a just and kind God, but now, seeing these miracles, there had risen in him a wave of belief and devotion. He began to discern God's will in the least of his actions. His life had now acquired a new assurance, a new awakening; every fibre of his being was pulsating with a joyous optimism. The future was not dark anymore. There was no room for doubt in God's will!

It was evening and Amarkant was standing in the parade ground when he saw Salim coming toward him. He had heard that Salim had undergone profound changes, but he had no idea of their extent. He rushed to embrace him and said, 'Welcome, friend. Now I believe that God is indeed with us. Sukhada is here in the women's ward; so is Munni. You were missing, now that lacuna is filled. I had been hoping that you would come here one of these days, but I did not expect you so soon. What is the latest news from outside? No major upheaval, I hope?'

Salim said ironically, 'No, no, not at all. Not even a whisper of trouble. People are happy, well-fed, and singing *phag*. You are quite comfortable here, aren't you?'

Then, in a few words he described the situation outside—the auctioning of cattle, the arrival of butchers, and the firing in the village of cowherds. He took special delight in talking about the thrashing he had given Ghosh.

Amarkant's face fell, 'That was pretty stupid of you.'

'And did you think that it was a village assembly where, with drinks and hookah, everything would be resolved equitably?'

'But that is no way to lodge an appeal.'

'We were not asking for any favours.'

'There is favour involved alright. If there is a condition attached to accepting the land, then justice dictates that you fulfil that condition. The farmers were not tilling the land on the condition of produce but on the condition of annual tax. The landlord or the government is not concerned with the lack or abundance of produce.'

'But if the tax is increased when the produce fetches a higher price, there is no reason that it should not be reduced if the price of the produce falls. It is sheer injustice to be charging a higher tax in times of depression.'

'But tax is not raised on the basis of armed might. It is done following due process of law.'

Salim was astonished that Amar could stay so calm after hearing such disturbing news. If, under the same conditions, he had heard such news, his blood would have boiled and he would have lost control. It must be that imprisonment had made Amar passive. Thus he thought it better not to divulge the various preparations that were going on to counter the oppression.

Amar waited for an answer. When Salim did not respond, he asked, 'So, who is in charge these days, is it Swamiji?'

Salim said hesitantly, 'Swamiji was probably taken into custody. Along with me, Sakina was there.'

'Oh, good. So, Sakina has also emerged from her veil and entered public life. I was not hopeful that she would do so.'

'Why, had you thought that after lighting the fire, you would be able to circumscribe her activities?'

Amar said worriedly, 'I had hoped that we had renounced all thoughts of violence and thus would be able to control it.'

'You want freedom, but you don't want to pay its price.'

'That is not the price for freedom. Its price is the strength to remain steadfast in pursuit of right and truth.'

Salim got agitated, 'This is useless talk. Whatever is based on self-control is not affected by ideas of right or justice.'

Amar asked, 'Don't you think that the world order is based on right and justice, and that deep in every man's heart there is a chord that resonates to all sacrifices?'

Salim said, 'No, I don't. The world order is based on selfishness and might, and there are very few individuals who have that generous chord in the depths of their hearts.'

Amar smiled and said, 'You were a civil servant devoted to the well-being of the government. How did you happen to land in prison?'

Salim laughed, 'For the love of you.'

'Who was my father in love with?'

'His son.'

'And Sukhada?'

'Her husband.'

'And Sakina? And Munni? And those hundreds of people who are bearing various types of hardships?'

'Alright, I agree that there is a chord in the hearts of some people, but how many such individuals are there?'

'I would say that there is not a single individual who does not have the chord of human sympathy. True, some are affected early, some later, and some others who are bound to their own ego, perhaps never.'

Conceding, Salim said, 'Alright, what would you want? We can't pay the tax. The government says they will not forego it. So what can we do? Should we let everything we own be auctioned off? If we protest we are fired upon; if we stay quiet, we are destroyed. What other recourse is there? The more we suppress ourselves the more aggressive they become. The man who dies undoubtedly earns our sympathy; but the man who kills engenders fear, which is far more effective than sympathy.'

Amar had thought over this question for months. He acknowledged that brute force was dominant in the world. But brute force also depended upon the force of justice. These days the mightiest of mighty nations would not dare to launch an open attack against any of the weak nations declaring: 'We want to rule you; therefore you should become our subjects.' They had to find one excuse or another to show that their cause was just. He said, 'If you think that bloodletting and killing will lead to the freedom of any nation you are completely mistaken. I don't call it freedom when power is wrested from one community to be taken up by another, which then rules by armed force. I call it freedom when humans are humanitarian and humanitarianism is the enemy of injustice and selfishness.'

Salim felt that this statement lacked any logic. Pulling a face, he said, 'Your lordship should understand that humans inhabit this world, not angels.'

Amar replied calmly and collectedly, 'But don't you see that humanity, after floundering for centuries in bloodletting and massacre, is now set on the true path? From where did it get such strength? That divine force was already there. No one can destroy it. The mightiest armed power cannot crush it. Just as parched ground appears bare, but no sooner does it rain, than the roots become alive and the whole field becomes lush with grass; similarly, in this period of technology, weapons, and self-seeking, the divine force is secretly active within us. The time has come when the voice of what is just and right will be more effective than the clash of a sword or the roar of a cannon. The big nations are reducing the strength of their armies and navies. Can't you see what the future holds? We are a subject nation because we ourselves have put the chains of slavery around our feet. Do you know what these chains are? Distrust of each other. We will remain slaves until we cut these chains and learn to love each other and see God in service to others. I don't say that we will not be free until every individual in India has so changed. That may never happen, but at least the leaders of the community must be enlightened. But how many amongst us are there, whose hearts are enlightened with love. We are still full of thoughts of high and low rank, self-seeking, and conceit.'

It was getting cold outside. The two friends retired to their own rooms. Salim was anxious to respond, but the warder hastened them on and they had to leave.

When the doors were shut, Amarkant took a deep breath and looked up beseechingly. So much responsibility rested on his shoulders. His hands were stained with the blood of many innocent people. So many orphaned children and feeble widows were dependent on his actions. Why had he acted so hastily? Was there only this one avenue for the farmers' appeal? Was there no other way to voice their appeal? Was this cure not worse than the disease? This turmoil caused Amarkant to lose track of his path. In this troubled state, Kaale Khan's image rose before his eyes. He felt that it was saying—throw yourself at God's mercy, you shall be enlightened.

Then and there Amarkant bowed his head and with a pure heart sought guidance—'My Lord, I am floundering in darkness. Show me the right path.' This calm, submissive prayer gave him peace; it was as if a lamp had been lighted and in its wide beam he could see his path clearly.

CHAPTER 55

❧

Pathanin's arrest caused an upheaval in the city that no one had expected. Such severe penalty for one who was feeble and old seemed to bring the dead to life and the timid and self-seeking onto the field of action. But there were still many shameless people who said—'What had she left in this life, only death. What does it matter where she dies, outside or inside the prison? I still have a long life in front of me, I have many things to do, why should I put myself at risk?'

It was evening. Labourers had left their jobs and small shopkeepers had shuttered their shops. All were rushing to the field of action. Pathanin was not there anymore; she must have been taken to prison. There were armed police on duty; no festivities were allowed, no speeches either, and large assemblies of people were deemed dangerous. But on this occasion no one was thinking or noticing anything; all were being carried forward as in a rapid current. In moments the entire field was filled with people.

Suddenly, people noticed a man who was standing on a pile of bricks and saying something. People crowded in from all sides. A whole sea of humanity had burst forth. Who was this man? It was Lala Samarkant, whose daughter-in-law and son were both in prison.

'Well, now, this Lala! If God made anyone prudent, it was him. The wealth he sinfully accumulated is now being lavished on virtuous deeds.'

'He is a great saint.'

'Had he not been a saint, how could he have won such accolades in his old age?'

'Listen, listen!'

Samarkant was saying, 'The day will come when houses for the poor will be constructed at this very place. A square will be built at the place where our mother was arrested and in the centre of that square a statue of Mother will be erected. Say victory to Mother Pathanin!'

Ten thousand voices, restless, eager, and sombre, rose, 'Victory to Mother!' It was as if the lament of the poor having found no sanctuary in this world was appealing to the angels in heaven.

'Listen, listen!'

'Mother sacrificed her life for her children. You and I also have children. Today, we will have to decide what you and I want to do for our children.'

There were shouts of 'Strike, strike!'

'Yes, go on strike. But the strike will not be for just one or two days. It will continue until the time that those who control the destiny of this town listen to our voices. We are poor, humble, distressed; but if the powers that be think calmly, they will realize it is the same humble people who have made them powerful. Who risks their life to construct these big palaces? Who provides labour in the textile factories? Who calls at the door with milk and butter in the morning? Who serves fruit and sweets to the powerful at breakfast time? Who does the cleaning? Who washes their clothes? Who brings the newspaper and mail in the morning? Three-quarters of the people in the city are toiling for one-quarter of the people. Their reward is that they have no place to live. One bungalow requires several hectares of land. Our important people want open, clean, and airy places. They are not aware that they are not safe and secure living in open bungalows when countless people live in rank and dark quarters, dying of perilous diseases and spreading the germs of those diseases. Whose responsibility is it to ensure that all people in a city, small and big, rich and poor, lead a healthy life? If the Municipal government cannot discharge this basic function, then it should be disbanded. Why is land given so generously for the residences of the rich and wealthy, for their gardens, for their palaces? It is because our Municipal government does not value the lives of the poor people. It needs money to pay huge salaries to its higher officials. It wants to decorate the city with big palaces, wants it to be as beautiful as heaven. But what good are these huge palaces when the general public is moaning in dark fetid lanes? It is like a man who swaggers out after covering the sores of leprosy with silk fabric. Gentle people, to tolerate injustice is just as great a sin as committing it. You must decide today that you will not tolerate this miserable situation. These palaces and bungalows are sores on the tender body of the city, they are excrescences, which must be excised. The land we are standing on is enough to build at least two thousand small pleasant houses where at least ten thousand people can live in comfort. But all this land is being sold to build four or five bungalows, for which the Municipality is getting one million rupees. How can they resist that money? The lives of ten thousand labourers in the city are not equal to one million rupees.'

Suddenly, people at the back shouted, 'Police! The police have come!' Some people fled, others converged and moved forward.

Lala Samarkant said, 'Don't panic, don't run. The police will arrest me. They consider me guilty. And not only me—my entire household is held guilty. My son is in jail; my daughter-in-law and grandson are in jail. What other place is there for me except jail? I am going willingly.'

He said to the police, 'Please stay where you are, sir, I am coming. I will go with you, but this I will say: if, on my return, I do not see here rows of houses flourishing like flowers for my poor brethren, this place will be my death bed.'

Lala Samarkant jumped down from the mound of bricks and, cutting through the crowd, stood near the police captain. The lorry was ready. The captain seated him and the lorry left.

A cry of 'Victory to Lala Samarkant' rose upwards. It was full of deep emotional pain, like that of a trapped animal struggling to break loose the bonds of subservience.

One group of people ran after the lorry, not to rescue their leader but out of devotion, expecting simply to receive some word, some blessing. When the lorry disappeared in a cloud of dust, they fell back.

'Who is standing there talking?'

'It seems to be a woman.'

'She seems to come from a good family.'

'Oh, don't you know? She is Renuka Devi, mother-in-law of Lalaji's son.'

'Oh, yes. The one who donated all her money and belongings to the school.'

'Listen, listen!'

'Dear brothers, when a yogi like Lala Samarkant is moved to pursue happiness in jail, it has to be a big happiness; but I am, after all, a woman. As the scriptures and holy books say, women are subject to temptation. Then how can I resist that temptation? I was the daughter-in-law of a wealthy man, wife of a wealthy man. I lived in indulgence and luxury, devoted to song and music, what would I know of the pain and suffering of the poor? But this city has snatched away my daughter, taken away my belongings, and now I am also poor like you. Now my only desire is to have a thatched hut constructed in this city of Vishwanath. I have no one else but you to beg from. This city is yours. Every inch of its land is yours. You are its rulers. But like true rulers, you are also hermits—ready to renounce your worldly possessions. Like Raja Harishchandra, having given away all your possessions to others, having made beggars wealthy, you have now become beggars. Do you know how you will regain that land that was lost through trickery? Like Raja Harishchandra, you have been sold by the sweeper Dom, and will have to renounce your dear ones.[4] Only then will the gods smile on you. My heart tells me that among the gods there is talk of restoring your possessions. If not today, then tomorrow you will take possession of your land. At that time, don't forget me. I am putting in my application in your court.'

Suddenly, voices broke out in the rear, 'The police have come again.'

'Let them come. Their job is to catch lawbreakers. We are guilty. If we are not arrested, we may commit robberies in the city, steal, or plot some heinous crimes. I say to you that any organization that controls the populace not by the rule of law, but by brute force, is an organization of robbers. People who have become wealthy by robbing the rights of the poor, and who have become officials by seizing the claims of others, they are the true plunderers. Brothers, I am leaving, but my application is in front of you. You must teach a lesson to this plundering Municipality so that it does not dare to trample on the poor. If anyone treads on you, become a thorn and prick him in his foot. Your strike tomorrow must be such that it makes the wealthy citizens and the city officials realize your strength. They should understand that without your cooperation they could neither enjoy their wealth nor their authority. You must show them that you are their arms and legs, without you they have no limbs.'

As she got off the mound and walked towards the policemen, the entire assembly stared at her, like the tears that well up in the heart but are arrested in the eyes. They do not cross the bounds of propriety by rolling out. Tears of the brave do not roll out to dry; instead, like the sap of a tree, they stay within to nourish the tree and allow it to grow and bloom. It was a very large assembly, but not a single voice could utter the victory cry. The energy for action was internalized. But when Renuka was seated in the car and the car started moving away a wave of respect, breaking the bounds of propriety, emerged from their throats like a narrow, deep, and swift current.

An old man chided, 'Enough of victory shouts. Now go home and store flour and pulses, for tomorrow begins a long strike.'

[4] Reference is to Rohitas and Shaivya, the son and wife of Raja Harishchandra, respectively.

Another man said in support, 'And remember! It shouldn't so happen that we shout ourselves hoarse here; and then in the morning everyone goes to their respective jobs.'

'Now, who is this?'

'Hey, don't you recognize him? It is Doctor sahab.'

'Now that Doctor sahab is also with us, victory is assured.'

'Such refined and cultured people are fighting on our behalf. Just think, what does this poor soul get in return for abandoning his life of peace and quiet, and for incurring the enmity of his peers and endangering his life.'

'Allah has been merciful to us. Doctor sahab served the poor so gallantly during the last plague epidemic. He fearlessly visited people who were abandoned even by their own kith and kin and helped them in every way with medicine, care, and money. Our Hafizji used to say he is an angel sent by Allah.'

'Listen, listen! You have the whole night for such ramblings.'

'Brothers! What was the result of the last strike? If this strike is conducted along similar lines, then we alone will suffer. Some of our people will be picked up; the remainder, because of differences of opinion, will fight against each other forgetting the real goal. As soon as the leaders are gone, old vendettas will start surfacing and dead and buried issues will be exhumed. No unified organization will remain nor any thought of responsible action. Everybody will be terrified. For these reasons, search your hearts carefully. If there is any doubt, give up the thought of a strike. To die in dirt and squalor is far easier than undertaking such a strike. If you believe that you are capable of suffering hardship, dying of starvation, and enduring pain, only then should you go on strike. Take an oath that as long as the strike lasts you will forget private vendettas, and that you will have no thought of profit or loss.

'You must have played the game of kabaddi. It often happens in kabaddi that one side loses all its players except one, and that single player continues to play by the rules of the game. He keeps on hoping to the end that he will be able to resurrect all his fallen playmates and then, together in full strength, they will win the round. Every player has only one aim—to win the territory for that round. He has nothing else on his mind. He does not remember petty squabbles with his playmates: which one had abused him some time, which one had torn his kite, and which one had hit him. You will have to steel your hearts the same way. I cannot promise that victory will be yours. Victory is possible, so is defeat. But we should not be concerned with either. A hungry child cries because he is hungry. He does not think that crying will get him food. It is possible the mother has no money, or she is ill, but it is in the nature of the child to cry when hungry. We are also crying in the same way. Whether after crying a child will tire and fall asleep or, compelled by affection for the child, the mother will feed him, no one knows. We bear no animosity towards anyone; we are servants of the community, what would we know about bearing animosity ...'

On the far side of the field the police captain was chiding the *thanedar* of a police station, 'Get us a lorry quickly. You were saying there are no leaders left; then where did this one come from?'

The thanedar said shamefacedly, 'Sir, Doctor sahab has appeared at the forefront of the movement for the first time. We could never have guessed that he would assume leadership. If you say so, we will arrest him and take him on a tonga.'

'On a tonga! People will surround the tonga. We will have to open fire. Run and quickly get a taxi.'

Doctor Shantikumar continued, 'We have no grudge against anyone. A society that has no place for its poor is like a house without any foundation. The slightest push can make it fall down. I ask my brothers who are rich, learned, and resourceful, is it just that one brother lives in a bungalow, while the other does not deserve even a hut? Aren't you ashamed to see men, the same as you, living in such abject poverty? You might argue that you have earned your wealth through the pursuit of knowledge, so why shouldn't you enjoy it? Such knowledge is called selfish knowledge. When a society is based on selfish knowledge instead of just knowledge, then you must understand that society faces an impending revolution.' A rise in temperature is soon followed by a storm. Humanity cannot be trampled upon forever. Balance is the key to life. That is the only condition that brings stability to a society. A few rich people do not have the right to deprive other people of their God-given right to light and air. This large assembly of people is simply the angry wailing of that deprivation and injustice. If the wealthy do not open their eyes now they will regret it later. This is the age of awareness. Awareness does not tolerate injustice. Thieves and robbers do not target the house of an awakened man ...'

Meanwhile, the taxi arrived. The police captain, accompanied by the thanedar and several constables, marched towards the assembly.

The thanedar shouted, 'Doctor sahab, your speech must be over now. Now you should come to us, why make us go to you?'

Shantikumar, standing on the platform of bricks, said, 'I will not surrender on my own accord, you can arrest me by force.' And he resumed his speech: 'Who is the power behind our rich people? The police. We ask the police, we ask this question of our constable brothers, 'Are you not poor? Don't you and your children live in dark, dank, disease-infested holes? But it is a strange time indeed that you should be ready to strangle your own children in defence of injustice ...'

The captain waded into the crowd, caught hold of Shantikumar's hand, and moved back with him. Suddenly Naina stood in front of them.

An astonished Shantikumar asked, 'Why are you here, Naina? Sethji and Deviji have been arrested. Now it is my turn.'

Naina said smilingly, 'And after you it will be mine.'

'No, you must not do such a senseless thing. Everything is dependent on you.'

Naina did not reply. The captain moved away with the doctor. On the far side, the crowd was getting restless. Now they could not decide on their course of action. They were like molten metal. They could be moulded any which way. Any effective person assuming leadership could have swung them in the direction he wished, but with greatest ease towards hooliganism. Since the series of arrests was turning them away from the peaceful path, they could quite easily have started throwing stones at the police or looting shops.

Just then, Naina came and stood before them. She had gone in her carriage for an outing. On the way she had heard of the arrests of Lala Samarkant and Renuka Devi. She immediately asked the coachman to hurry towards the field. Up to this point she had observed all the proprieties due to her husband and father-in-law. She was inclined to distance herself from the movement so her in-laws might have no cause to feel dissatisfied, but after hearing of these arrests she could not restrain herself. She would no longer be sorry if Maniram lost his temper, or Lala Dhaniram pounded his chest. Indeed, if anyone had attempted to stop her she might even have committed suicide. By nature she was shy and self-effacing. Sitting alone at home she might die of starvation, but to go out and question anyone was impossible for her. Frequently there were festive occasions, but she had never been courageous enough to give a speech. It was not because she lacked ideas or that she could not express her ideas, but only that she was too diffident to stand in front of the public. Or one could say that her inner voice had never been strong enough to break the bonds of shyness and inertia. There are some animals who have a special spot. You may kill them, and they would not move a step, but you touch their sensitive spot, and a new enthusiasm, a new life shines through. Lala Samarkant's arrest touched that sensitive spot in Naina's heart. For the first time in her life she stood before the public without any misgivings, resolute and bathed in a new glow, a new grace. In the light of the full moon, standing on a mound of bricks, when she addressed the public in a soft husky voice, it was as if the entire world had come to a standstill.

'Gentle people, I am the daughter of Lala Samarkant and daughter-in-law of Lala Dhaniram. My beloved brother is in jail. My dear sister-in-law is in jail, my golden boy of a nephew is in jail, and today my father also has been imprisoned.'

A shout rose from the crowd, 'Renuka Devi as well.'

'Yes, Renuka Devi, who is like a mother to me, also. For a daughter, the only parental home is one where her father, mother, brother, and sister-in-law reside, and the parental home is dearer to the daughter than her in-laws' home. My father-in-law has purchased several parcels of this land, gentle people. I believe that if I insist, instead of building bungalows for the rich, he would have houses for the poor constructed. But that is not our aim. Our battle is to show that a city where more than half the population lives in filthy holes, has no right to sell land for palaces and bungalows. You know that there were several prosperous villages here. The Municipality created the office of city development. The land belonging to the farmers of the village was grabbed for a pittance, and today the same land is being sold at a premium so that bungalows for the powerful and the rich can be built. We ask the architects of our city, is it only the rich who are alive? Are the poor not living beings? Is it only the rich that have a right to a healthy life? Do the poor not need good health? The people are no longer prepared to die like that. If one has to die it is much better to die under the open skies of this field in the cool glow of the moon, than to die in holes. But first, you must ask the powers that be in our city once again whether they will accept our request, whether they will accept this principle even now? If they are arrogant enough to think that they can use force to trample on the poor and silence them, they are mistaken. For every drop of blood of the poor that is shed, a new person is born. If the architects of the city listen to the voices of the poor now, they will be lauded like saints, because the poor will not remain poor for long; those times are not far away when the poor will hold power in their hands. "Do not tease the beast of revolution to awake. The more he is teased, the more he will be provoked, and awakened he will yawn and let out a big roar so that you will have no escape." We must give this warning to the Board members. Now is a great opportunity. Brothers, let us all proceed to the Municipal Office, let us not delay any longer, because the members will shortly be leaving for their homes. There is always the danger of rioting in a strike. And hence a strike should be called only when all else has failed.'

Naina took the flag and started marching toward the Municipal Office. A sea of twenty to twenty-five thousand people swelled after her. This crowd was not like the disorganized crowd of a fair, but like the organized columns of an army. Eight columns of men in countless rows were marching gravely, aware of the inner strength that comes from a unity of thought, purpose, and aim. And its continuity was unbroken, as if it were emanating from the womb of the earth. On both sides of the road, onlookers were crowded on balconies and roofs. Everyone was astonished. Oh, Oh! So many men! They still keep coming!

Naina broke into the song which these days was on the lips of every child,

We also are bearers of a human body...'

Thousands of throats sang in unison, their voices resounding in heaven— 'We also are bearers of a human body!'

Naina continued, 'Why do you consider us inferior?'

Many thousand throats accompanied, 'Why do you consider us inferior?'

Naina sang, 'Why upon your true servants?'

The crowd repeated, 'Why upon your true servants?'

'Do you such injustice administer!'

And the crowd sang, 'Do you such injustice administer!'

Away, in the Municipal Board office, the same question was being debated.

Hafiz Halim said, putting down the telephone receiver, 'Dr Shantikumar has also been arrested.'

Mr Sen said heartlessly, 'Now this movement has been cut off at its roots. Doctor sahab was its vital force.'

Pundit Onkarnath foretold, 'That block will not see any bungalows constructed. So the omens say.'

Mr Sen had purchased a parcel of that block in the name of his son. He was touched to the quick, 'If the Board does not have the fortitude to stick to the resolutions it has passed, then it should resign.'

Mr Shafiq, a university professor and a friend of Dr Shantikumar, responded, 'The Board's decisions are not decisions made by God. Some time ago, indeed, the Board had decided to auction that block in small parcels, but what was the result? You people stored a lot of building materials there; no one knows what happened to those materials. More than a thousand people sleep there every night. I am sure that not a single labourer would consent to work there. I am cautioning the Board that if we do not change our policy, there will be grave trouble in the city. The support of Seth Samarkant and Shantikumar shows that this is not an affair to be taken casually. The resistance has deep roots, which it would be nearly impossible to dig out. The Board will have to rescind its decision, whether now or after fifty or a hundred lives have been lost. To date the hard line taken by the Board has not quelled resistance at all, rather it has had the opposite effect. The strike that will take place will be so horrific that the very thought of it is hair raising. The Board is taking far too great a responsibility on its head.'

Mr Haamid Ali was the manager of a cloth mill. His mill was operating at a loss. A long strike would be tantamount to a death knell. He was very fat, but also very industrious. He said, 'I can't understand why the Board is so hesitant to acknowledge what is right. Perhaps it is because its pride would be wounded. But to bend before what is right is not weakness, it is strength. If this matter were to be discussed today, I can guarantee that this resolution of the Board would be erased like a typographical error. If the Board has to suffer a loss of ten or twelve lakh rupees and five to ten members have to suffer heartburn for the improvement and welfare of twenty to twenty-five thousand people, then it ...'

The telephone rang again. Hafiz Halim listened carefully, and said, 'An army of twenty-five thousand people is marching toward us. Lala Samarkant's daughter, who is also Seth Dhaniram's daughter-in-law, is at its head. The Deputy Superintendent of Police is asking for our advice. He has also said that that the procession is not likely to withdraw without police firing. I would like to have the opinion of the Board on this matter. It would be better if a vote were taken. There is not enough time to observe the formalities. You can raise your hands— For?'

Twelve hands were raised.

'Against?'

Ten hands were raised. Lala Dhaniram remained neutral.

'Then the Board is of the opinion that the procession be stopped even if there has to be police firing.'

Sen said, 'Is there any doubt now?'

The telephone rang again. Hafizji listened. The Deputy Superintendent of Police was saying, 'A terrible thing has happened. Lala Maniram has just shot his wife.'

Shocked, Hafizji asked, 'What happened?'

'We still don't know. It seems Mr Maniram stopped the procession in great anger and asked his wife to come away. She refused, which led to an exchange of words. Mr Maniram had a pistol in his hand and he shot her. If he had not run away he would have been skinned alive. The procession, bearing the dead body of its leader, is marching towards the Municipal Board.'

When Hafizji communicated this news to the members, the entire Board was stunned, as if the whole assembly had been turned to stone.

Suddenly Lala Dhaniram stood up and said in a choked voice, 'Gentlemen, the edifice that I had been building for the last fifty years, putting one stone up after another, has been demolished today in one moment; even its foundation has disappeared. We used the best of materials, employed the best of artisans, the best of designs, and the palace was ready; the only thing remaining was to put the finishing touches. Just then, a tornado hit; the immense edifice is blown away as if it were a pile of straw. Now I understand that that edifice was only a dream. You may say a golden dream or a black dream, but a dream nonetheless. That dream has been shattered—has been shattered.'

So saying, he walked towards the door.

Hafiz Halim said sadly, 'Sethji. I personally and, I trust, the Board have all sympathy for you.'

Turning around, Sethji said, 'If the Board has sympathy for me then it should authorize me immediately to go and tell the people that the Board has given the land to them. Otherwise this fire will consume many other houses, shatter many dreams.'

Several members of the Board spoke simultaneously, 'Come on, we'll all go with you.'

Twenty members of the Board stood up. Sen, noticing that only four persons remained seated, also stood up, and with him his three allies. Hafiz Halim followed suit.

The procession was marching with Naina's dead body. Where had all the people come from? The line was miles long, calm, solemn, united, prepared to die. Naina's sacrifice had made them unconquerable, indivisible.

Just then, the twenty-five members of the Board stepped forward showering flowers on the dead body, and Hafiz Halim taking the lead said in a resounding voice, 'Brothers! You were going to see the members of the Municipal Board; but the members have themselves come to greet you. The Board has today unanimously agreed to give the entire plot of land to you people. For this, my congratulations go to the Board and also to you. Today the Board has acknowledged that the health, comfort, and needs of the poor are matters of greater concern than the pleasures, desires, and greed of the rich. The Board has recognized that the poor have greater rights over these things than do the rich. We admit that the Board held money in greater esteem than the lives of the people. Now it recognizes that the glory of the city lies not in grand palaces and bungalows, but in small comfortable houses in which labourers and people of small income can live. I, myself, was one of those who had not recognized this principle. The majority of the Board was of the same opinion as myself. But your sacrifices and the eloquence of your leaders have won over the Board and today I congratulate you on that victory, and the credit for this victory goes to that lady whose bier you shoulder.

'Lala Samarkant is an old friend of mine. My son is a good friend of his noble son. I have not seen any young man as courteous as Amarkant. It is the effect of his company that my son left the Civil Service and now sits in jail. You and I cannot even guess at the struggle that was going through the mind of Naina Devi. On the one hand her father and sister-in-law were imprisoned in a jail, on the other hand, her husband and father-in-law were devoted to the pursuit of wealth and property. Lala Dhaniram will excuse me. I am not casting any aspersions on him. He was a captive of the same desire that you, we, the entire world were captives of. But his heart has been struck a blow which cannot be exceeded in severity by any other anguish. We and, I believe, you as well, are fully compassionate towards him. We all share in his grief. Perhaps in the heart of Naina devi the conflict between the claims of her father's and her father-in-law's houses started at the same time as this movement and today it has come to this dreadful end. I am confident that the memory of this holy sacrifice will last in our city until such time as its charter lasts. I am not an idol worshipper but, first and foremost, I would propose that in the middle of the neighbourhood that is going to be built, there be a monument to her so that the memory of her splendid sacrifice is fresh for all coming generations.

'Friends, I am not putting forth any argument before you. This is an occasion neither to make an argument nor to listen to one. Light is accompanied by darkness, victory goes with defeat, and joy goes with sorrow. The blending of darkness and light gives blissful dawn, and the blending of victory and defeat gives peace. The blending of this happiness and tragedy is the voice of a new order. I pray to God that this order is with us always, and that pure souls prepared to give their lives for a righteous cause keep being born among us because the stability of the world depends on such souls. My request to you is that after this victory you give the vanquished the same treatment as should be meted out to a valiant enemy. In this holy land of ours, defeated enemies have been considered as friends. With the end of battle, resentment and anger have been cast out of our minds and the enemy embraced with an open heart. Come, you and I will embrace each other to please the soul of that devi, who is our true guide, who, in darkness brought radiance, the message of dawn. God give us grace that we may learn the lesson of selflessness and service from this true martyr.'

As Hafizji became quiet, a resounding cry, 'Victory to Naina Devi' rose, so drenched with devotion that it shook the heavens. 'Victory to Hafiz Halim' also followed, after which the procession moved towards the Ganges. All members of the Board were in the procession. Only Hafiz Halim went back to the Municipal office and started discussions with police authorities on ways to effect the release of prisoners. The battle that had been started six months previously by one devi had come to an end today with the self-sacrifice of another devi.

CHAPTER 56

Sakina's arrival at the women's jail coincided with the delivery of the order of release for Sukhada and Pathanin. It also coincided with the news of Naina's assassination. Sukhada sat, head bowed, like a statue, as if unconscious. How costly the victory!

Sighing deeply, Renuka said, 'Indeed, there are people in this world who for selfish reasons will murder their wives.'

Sukhada said heatedly, 'Mother, he did not kill Naina; this victory is a gift from that devi's life.'

Pathanin said, wiping her tears, 'I can't help crying because Bhaiya will be so hurt. I have never seen such affection between a brother and sister.'

The jailer came to inform them that they should all get ready, 'The ladies, Sukhada, Renuka, and Pathanin, will be leaving by the evening train. Please forgive us for any oversights on our part that may have occurred.'

No one responded. It was as if they had not heard. There was little pleasure in going home. The joy of victory was overshadowed by their grief.

Sakina whispered in Sukhada's ear, 'Please see Babuji [Amarkant] before leaving. I don't know what will happen when he hears this news. I am afraid.'

Sukhada's child, Renukant, had slipped on mud in the prison courtyard. He was stamping the ground for being bad while crying at the same time. Sakina and Sukhada both rushed to pick him up, and, standing under a tree started to calm him. Sakina had arrived the previous morning but until now, except for common pleasantries, there had been no conversation between her and Sukhada. Sakina was shy to open a conversation because she was afraid that the subject of Amarkant might come up. And Sukhada was avoiding her because she felt that she might not have atoned enough.

Sakina's empathetic understanding overwhelmed Sukhada. She said, 'Yes, I am thinking of doing so. Do you have any message for him?'

Eyes brimming with tears, Sakina said, 'What message will I have, Sukhadaji! Just let him know—'Naina Devi is gone but while Sakina is alive, you can consider her Naina.'

Sukhada said with a pitiless smile, 'You have had a different relationship with him.'

Sakina countered humbly, 'Then he needed a woman, now there is need for a sister.'

Sukhada said sharply, 'I was still alive at the time.'

Sakina knew that the time she was dreading had come. She was now bound to explain herself.

She asked, 'You won't mind if I say something?'

'Not at all.'

'Then listen. You turned him out of the house at that time. You were headed east; he was headed west. Now you and he are of the same mind, the same way of life. You have accomplished the things that he held in greatest esteem. If you were together now, he would kiss your feet.'

Hearing this, Sukhada felt the joy that a poet feels when another poet compliments him, and the doubt she had in her heart about her atonement also vanished.

'Sakina, this is what you think. Who knows what is in his heart? I have lost faith in men. It is possible that he now has some respect for me—even then he had no disrespect for me—but I don't think that he can get you out of his system. You may be married to Mr Salim, but he will continue to worship you in his heart.'

Sakina's face turned sombre. She was frightened, as if an enemy was trying to put a noose around her neck. She said, trying to save her neck, 'Sister, you are again being unjust to him. He is not one of those men who would do something because he is afraid of the world. He arranged all the paperwork regarding Salim and I. I understood his intention. I knew that you had won over your estranged husband. I was afraid how an ignorant woman like myself would be able to keep him happy. My situation was like that of the destitute man who, having found a treasure, knows not where to hide it in his hut, how to keep it safe. When I understood his intention, the weight on my heart was lifted. A god is an object of worship. If he comes to our house, where shall we seat him and bed him down, what shall we feed him? When we go to the temple, we become benevolent and temperate for a while. If God comes to our house and sees our real selves, then he may perhaps find us repulsive. Salim, I can take care of. He is a man of this world, and I can understand him.'

Just then, the doors of the women's ward opened and three prisoners were brought in. All three were wearing knee-length shorts and short-sleeved shirts. One had a bamboo ladder on his shoulder, one had a sack of lime on his head, and the third was carrying clay pots for lime, brushes, and buckets. White-washing of the women's jail was to start today. The time for annual clean up and repair had come.

Seeing the prisoners, Sakina jumped up saying, 'The one carrying the pots and rope seems to be Babuji. Salim is holding the ladder.'

Saying this, she lifted the child in her arms and hugging him leapt towards the door. She kept kissing him, saying, 'Come, your babuji is here.'

Sukhada was also moving, but at a gentler pace. She felt like crying—'We meet today after such a long time, and in this condition.'

Suddenly Munni came running and, seizing the bucket and rope from Amar's hand, said, 'Oh Lala, what shape you are in, you have lost so much weight. You sit down and rest, I will draw the water.'

Amar held on to the bucket firmly and said, 'No, no, you won't. Let go of the bucket. If the jailer sees, he will berate me.'

Munni snatched away the bucket and said, 'I'll answer the jailer. You are the same as ever.'

Sakina and Sukhada then arrived from one direction, Pathanin and Renuka from the other, but nobody could utter a word. They all had tears in their eyes and their throats were choked. Everything had started happily, but with each step they had got into deeper and deeper water until it was over their heads.

Seeing them, Amar was filled with amazement and pride. He felt so small and negligible in front of them. What words could he use to praise them, what offerings could he make? In his most optimistic mood he had never visualized such a bright future for the nation. He was shaken from top to toe by a current of national pride while tears of respect started in his eyes.

He had heard that they were in prison, but seeing Renuka he lost control and fell at her feet.

Renuka, placed her hand on his head and blessed him, 'It is good to see you, son, though we are just departing. May God grant you your heart's desire. It has been just five days since I came, but the order for our release has been issued. Naina has set us free.'

With palpitating heart, Amar asked, 'Is she also here? Her in-laws must be very upset.'

His question crushed the women and they could not restrain their tears. Amar looked at everyone in surprise. He was shaken by an ominous doubt. Their faces did not have the flush of victory; rather they were darkened by the shadow of tragedy. Anxiously he asked, 'Where is Naina, why is she not here? Is she not well today?'

Renuka said, controlling her grief, 'Son, you will see Naina in the city square in Kashi, where her statue is being erected. Naina is the queen of that city. Everybody is paying her homage.'

Amar was thunderstruck. He sat down on the ground and, covering his face with both hands, started crying. He thought that life in this world was futile and that Naina, resplendent with ornaments, was standing in heaven beckoning him.

Renuka said, placing her hand on his head, 'Son, why do you grieve for her? She has not died; she has become immortal. Her life was the last sacrifice in this *yagya*.'

Salim asked, clearing his throat, 'What happened? Was she hit by gunfire?'

Renuka answered, 'No, Bhaiya, what gunfire! There was no fight with anyone. When she was marching from the field to the Municipal office with the procession—there were no less than a hundred thousand men—Maniram came and fired a bullet at her. She fell on the spot. Her brother was foremost in her mind even them. She has gone to heaven, but we have been left behind to grieve.

As the events of Naina's life flashed before Amar's eyes, a new wave of regret swept over him. The thought that he had not observed any of his obligations toward his sister filled him with remorse. If he had not run away from the house, would Lalaji have married her to that greedy Maniram! And then would she have met this tragic end?

But suddenly, drowning in this sea of sorrow, he found the raft of a divine plan. Without divine encouragement, how could anyone have developed such a longing for service! What better use could a life be put to? Most human beings die performing the chores of a householder, or in the pursuit of self-aggrandizement. Only the chosen ones are fortunate enough to die in the service of others. Amar's despondent soul saw the magic of divine grace all around him—all pervading, infinite, and boundless!

Salim asked again, 'Poor Lalaji must have been devastated.'

Renuka said proudly, 'He was arrested earlier on, and Shantikumar as well.'

Amar felt that his insight and strength had increased tremendously. He bowed his head to God and the tears that fell from his eyes were not those of anguish, but of rapture and pride. He had experienced such an awakening of faith in God that it seemed that he himself was nothing. Whatever was, was due to God's will; whatever happened, happened because of Him; He was the giver of all bliss and knowledge. Sakina and Munni both were standing in front of him. In the past, when he saw their beauty, a storm of lust would rage in his heart. Today, the same beauty evoked serene love, which calms the affliction of the soul and fills it with the gentle radiance of truth, with renunciation in place of desire, with spirituality in place of sensuality. He felt as if he were a worshipper and these beautiful women, goddesses, and to apply the dust of their feet on his forehead was his life's justification.

Renuka took the child from Sakina's arms and lifting him to Amar said, 'He is your father, son, go to him.'

The child, seeing Amar's prisoner's garb, shrieked and clung to Renuka. Then, hiding his face in Renuka's arms, he kept glancing shyly at him, as if wanting to be friendly but afraid lest the police should catch him—-he had doubts in his heart that a man so dressed could be his father.

Sukhada was getting cross with the child for being diffident, as if Amar would eat him. She wished that this crowd would go away, so she could talk privately to Amar. Who knew when they would meet again?

Amar said, looking at Sukhada, 'You people have outclassed me even here. You have completed the work that you undertook, but I am still where I was. Who knows whether we will succeed? Whatever little progress has been made, the credit for that goes to sisters Munni and Sakina. The affection for the country and the dedication to duty that these two sisters have displayed makes us hold our heads high. You all know better than I do what Sukhada has done. It is almost three years since I rebelled and ran away from home. I thought then that with her my life would be destroyed, but today I will consider myself fortunate if I am able to put the dust of her feet on my forehead. I ask for her forgiveness in front of all of you, mothers and sisters.'

Salim said smilingly, 'Words alone won't do. You will have to hold your ears and do one lakh sit-ups.'

Amar glanced at him and said, 'You forget, Bhai, you are no longer a magistrate. You cannot mete out such punishments.'

Again mischievous, Salim asked Sakina, 'Why are you standing quietly?

You also have something to say to him, or are you waiting for a suitable occasion?'

Then he said to Amar, 'Janab, you cannot go back on your word! You will have to fulfil the promise you have made.'

Sakina's face turned red with embarrassment. She felt like pinching Salim. Her face was so suffused with rapture and triumph that she could not hide it. It was as if the blame that had tarnished her for so long had been washed away and she could trumpet her innocence before the world. She looked at Pathanin with reproachful eyes, which seemed to say— 'Now you know how grave an inequity you had committed!' In her own eyes, her self-esteem had never been so high. She had never in her life imagined that she would receive such devotion and esteem.

Sukhada's countenance was no less proud and joyful. Her face used to be harsh and stern, but was now graceful and serene. She had found a treasure today, which she had been unaware that she was missing, but nonetheless there had been a niggling of emptiness and incompleteness in her life. Today it seemed that the void had been filled with honey, that she had been made whole. Today, she had found in a man's love her own womanhood. She was dying to lose herself in his arms. Today, her penance seemed to have borne fruit.

As to Munni, she stood alone and aloof. A bird flying in from some unknown place had come and rested on her life's lonely fence. Seeing it, she had filled her apron with grain and stepping softly had hastened to catch it. She had spread the grain on the ground. The bird had pecked on grain and gazed at her, as if asking—will you keep me with affection or, after dallying with me for a few days and clipping my wings, you will abandon me? But as soon as she extended her hand to catch the bird, the bird flew away. Sitting on a distant branch, it kept looking at her with eyes full of detachment, as if saying—I belong to the heavens, your cage does not hold anything but dried grain and a sipping bowl!

Salim put the painting lime in the trough. Sakina and Munni each took a bucket and prepared to draw water.

Amar said, 'Please give me the bucket, I'll fill it.'

Munni said, 'You'll draw water, and we will sit watching?'

Amar laughed and said, 'Or else you will draw water and I will watch?'

Munni ran with the bucket. Sakina also ran after her.

Renuka had gone to prepare some food for her son-in-law who she thought would have been getting nothing but roti and daal in prison. She wanted to prepare hundreds of dishes and feed him with ceremony. While she had been in prison Renuka had all the comforts of home. The lady jailer, the watchman, and other workers all did her bidding. Pathanin, getting tired of standing, had gone away to lie down. Munni and Sakina had gone to draw water. Salim wanted to share several things with Sakina, so he also went to the water pump. Only Amar and Sukhada remained.

Amar moved toward Sukhada and embracing the child in her arms, said, 'This jail has turned into paradise for me, Sukhada! The gift I have received is much greater than the penance I have done, whatever it was. If it were possible to show my heart, you would see how much I have missed you. I kept regretting my mistakes all the time.'

Sukhada interrupted him, 'Oh ho, so now you have learned the art of sweet-talking as well. I also know a little about the state of your heart. From top to bottom, it is full of anger only. Forgiveness and kindness have no place in it. I may be self-indulgent, but for that fault you gave me such harsh punishment! And that too while you knew that it was not my fault but that of my upbringing.'

Amar said ashamed, 'This is unjust of you, Sukhada!'

Sukhada raising his chin upward said, 'Look at me. Am I being unjust; and are you justice incarnate? All right. You sent me hundreds of letters and I did not reply to any of them. Why? How could you be so angry? Man develops affection even for animals. I was after all a human being. You were so provoked that you forgot me, as if I was dead.'

Amar could not reply to this charge, but still said, 'You didn't write any letters; and if I had written, would you have responded? Tell me the truth.'

'So you wanted to teach me a lesson?'

Amarkant quickly refuted this charge, 'No, that is not so Sukhada. I must have wanted to write you a letter thousands of times, but...'

Sukhada completed, 'But was afraid that probably I would not even touch your letters. If that is all you know about a woman's heart, then I would say that you don't understand it at all.'

Amar admitted defeat, 'So, when did I claim to understand woman's heart.'

He may not have claimed so, but Sukhada had already assumed that he had laid such a claim. She said in a sweetly chiding tone, 'A man's gallantry does not lie in getting a woman to fall at his feet. If I did not write you a letter it was because I thought that you had been unfair to me, you had insulted me; but let us drop this subject. Tell me, whose was the victory, yours or mine?'

Amar said, 'Mine.'

'And I say—mine.'

'How so?'

'You had revolted. I quelled your revolt.'

'No, you fulfilled all my demands.'

Just then, Lala Dhaniram entered the ward accompanied by prison officials and workers. People stared at them curiously. The Seth had become much weaker. He was leaning on a stick and walking with great difficulty and coughing at every step.

Amar stepped forward and greeted the Sethji respectfully. Seeing him, all the ill-feelings he had in his heart towards him melted away.

Sethji blessed him and said, 'You must be surprised to see me here son. You must be thinking—"This old man is still living, why doesn't death claim him?" It is my misfortune that the world has always looked at me with distrust and put everything I did down to selfishness. That I, too, have some honour, some humanity, has never been recognized by anyone. In the eyes of the world, I am simply an animal because I believe that there is an appropriate time for every action. An immature fruit does not ripen in storage alone. It ripens only if all conditions are right. When I look around, I see darkness which can be removed only by sunrise. Go to any office, you will find that nothing gets done without bribery. Go to any house, you will see animosity reign. Avarice, ignorance, and laziness have a tight hold over us. They will be removed only by God's will. We have forgotten our cultural heritage. That culture placed the human soul above all else. Until God is merciful, there will be no resurgence of that culture, and until its resurgence, we will not be able to do anything. I have no faith in movements of the type you were engaged in. Instead of goodwill, they increase animosity. As long as the ailment is not diagnosed correctly, it cannot be treated correctly; external patchwork alone will not cure the disease.'

Hearing this, Amar said with a disdainful smile, 'Then should we sit with folded hands and wait for the arrival of that auspicious moment?'

A warder hurriedly brought out several chairs. Sethji and two of the prison officials sat down. Sethji took out paans and had one, meanwhile thinking of an appropriate response. Then he said pleasantly, 'No, I don't say that. That is what lazy people with no work ethic do. We should continue to raise awareness and a sense of character in the public. All our strength should be devoted to awakening the community's soul. I don't accept that people would have been satisfied even if the tax had been cut by half. The public suffers from such social and mental flaws that, never mind half, even if the entire tax had been excused, it wouldn't have been happy. I also don't believe that the strategy of appeal and the manner in which it was carried out were the only possible avenues.'

Amar said excitedly, 'We kept begging them to the end. Ultimately, we had no recourse other than to launch this resistance.'

Then, immediately regaining his composure, he said politely, 'It is possible that we made a mistake, but at that time we couldn't think of anything else.'

Sethji said calmly, 'Yes, it was a mistake, indeed it was a blunder. Nothing came of it except the destruction of hundreds of households. I have had a talk with Governor sahab on this subject, and he also is of the opinion that not enough thought went into the resolution of this complex issue. You know, of course, that Governor sahab and I don't stand on much ceremony with each other. He sent a telegram of condolence on Naina's death. But you may not know that Governor sahab himself toured the district and met the inhabitants. At first, no one came near him. Sahab said that he had never seen such empty bluster. Not enough clothes to cover the body, but a temperament that disdains talking to anyone. With great difficulty, a few people were assembled. When the Governor comforted them and said, "You people should not be frightened, we have no wish to be unjust to you," then the poor souls started crying. Governor sahab wants to bring this strife to an early conclusion. Accordingly, he has ordered that all prisoners are to be released and a committee set up to determine the future course of action. That committee will, of course, have you and your friend Mr Salim on it; you will also have the power to select three other members. From the government's side there will be only two members. That is all that I had come to say. I hope that you will have no objection to this arrangement.'

Sakina and Munni started whispering to each other. Salim's face lighted up. Only Amar remained immersed in thought.

Salim asked eagerly, 'We will have the authority to choose anyone we want?'

'Absolutely.'

'The committee's decision will be final?'

Sethji said, hesitantly, 'Such is my belief.'

'Your belief won't do. We need a guarantee that it will be so.'

'And if a guarantee is not forthcoming?'

'Then we do not accept the offer.'

'With the result that you will be left here and the populace will continue to suffer.'

'Whatever it is.'

'You do not suffer any particular hardships, but think of what the poor are going through.'

'We have thought enough about it.'

'You have not thought at all.'

'We have thought it through very well, indeed.'

'If you had thought, you would not be saying such things.'

'We have thought, that is precisely why we are saying this.'

Amar said harshly, 'What are you saying, Salim? Why are you getting into an argument? To what purpose?'

Salim said agitatedly, 'I am arguing? I am amazed at your perception! Sethji is rich and used to giving orders, therefore, he does not get into an argument. I am poor, I am a prisoner, hence I argue!'

'Sethji is an elder.'

'I have heard only today that to be argumentative is a privilege of age.'

Amar could not contain his laughter. He said, 'This is not like composing verse, Bhai-jaan, that you speak whatever comes into your head. These issues affect the lives of hundreds of thousands of people. Respected Sethji, as is his obligation, is trying to help us in resolving this problem. And for that we should be grateful to him. We don't want anything except that the poor farmers be treated in a just manner. And now when a committee is being planned to fulfil that goal, a committee that is not expected to be unjust to farmers, it is our duty to welcome it.'

Sethji said admiringly, 'What analysis! The Viceroy himself was impressed by you.'

A motor horn sounded at the jail gate. The jailer said, 'The car has come for the ladies. Come, let us go, the ladies have to prepare for their departure. Sisters, please forgive me for whatever mistakes I may have made. I had no intentions of giving you any discomfort, but I was bound by government rules.'

At Renuka Devi's insistence, it was decided that they would all go in one vehicle. The ladies started their preparations. Amar and Salim's clothes were also brought there. In half an hour, they were all ready to leave the jail.

Suddenly, a second car arrived and Lala Samarkant, Hafiz Halim, Dr Shantikumar, and Swami Atmanand stepped out of it. Amar, his heart full of respect ran and bowed at his father's feet. He felt as if Naina, eyes brimming with tears, was imploring him—Bhaiya, don't ever hurt Dada; even if you don't like his ways, don't utter a word. He was washing his father's feet with his tears and Sethji was shedding tears of joy.

Salim also embraced his father. Hafizji blessed him and said, 'Thank God hundreds of thousand times that your sacrifices have been fruitful. Where is Sakina? Let me see her, so my heart can find peace.'

Sakina, head bowed, came forward and saluted him. Hafizji looked at her once and said to Samarkant, 'Salim's choice doesn't seem to be bad at all!'

Smiling, Samarkant said, 'Along with her face, she also brings womanly heroism for her dowry.'

On joyful occasions we forget our sorrows. Hafizji's sorrow on Salim's discharge from the Civil Service; Samarkant's at Naina's death, and Seth Dhaniram's at the loss of his son had not lessened, but at this moment they were all happy. After a victorious battle, warriors do not sit weeping for the dead. Instead, they indulge in celebrations, drums are beaten, soirees are held, and greetings are exchanged. For crying we seek solitude, for laughter company.

Everyone was happy. Only Amarkant was holding back and pensive. When they all arrived at the station, Sukhada asked him, 'Why are you sad?'

Amar said, as if waking up, 'Me! I am not sad.'

'Is sadness ever hidden by hiding it?'

Amar said somberely, 'I am not sad, only thinking that because of me there has been loss of life and belongings for no great reason. Could the same approach that is being taken now not have been taken earlier? The weight of that burden is oppressing me.'

Sukhada said in a calm tender voice, 'I think that whatever has happened has been for good. Work that is done with good intentions is God's doing, whatever the consequences are. If a devotional ceremony does not yield any fruit, at least it is a pious act. But I consider this decision a victory, a unique victory. Our sacrifices pale in comparison with the awareness that has been created in the people. Do you think that such awareness could have been achieved without these sacrifices; and that, without this awareness, this compromise could have been reached? I clearly see God's hand in all this.'

Amar looked at Sukhada with affection. He felt as if God Himself was speaking through her. His sorrow and regret had fused to give him meaning in the same way as a pile of dirt and debris catching a spark of fire is converted to radiance and light. He had never experienced such enlightened peace.

He whispered, choking with affection, 'Sukhada, you are indeed the light of my life.'

Just then, Lala Samarkant, with the child sitting on his shoulder, came and said, 'Aren't we thinking of going to Kashi now?'

Amar said, 'I have to go to Haridwar.'

Sukhada said, 'Then we will all go there.'

Amarkant, somewhat taken aback, said, 'Alright. Can I go to the market to buy some saris for Saloni?'

Sukhada smiled and said, 'Why only Saloni? There is Munni also.'

Munni was coming their way. Hearing her name she asked curiously, 'Are you talking to me, Sukhadaji?'

Sukhada putting an arm around her said, 'I was saying that now Munni Devi will also live with us in Kashi.'

Munni said alarmed, 'Then are you people going to Kashi?'

Sukhada laughed, 'And what did you think?'

'I will go to my village.'

'Won't you come and live with us?'

'Then is Lala also going to Kashi?'

'Where else, what do you want him to do?'

Munni's face fell.

'Nothing, I was only curious.'

Amar reasssured her, 'No Munni, she is only teasing you. We are all going to Haridwar.'

Munni's face lighted up.

'Then there will be a great celebration. Auntie Saloni will sound the drums.'

Amar asked, 'So, do you understand what this decision means?'

'Why wouldn't I understand? A committee of five people will be formed. The government will accept whatever it decides. You and Salim will both be on the committee. How could anything be better than that?'

'We will choose the remaining three persons as well.'

'Then it is even better.'

'It is due to the civility and kindheartedness of Governor sahab.'

'Then people were unnecessarily calling him names.'

'Completely so.'

'We are going to our village after such a long time. Other people have been released as well.'

'I hope so. We will have to write some letters for those that have not yet been released.'

'Achcha, who will the other three be?'

'Whoever may or may not be, you will certainly be one of them.'

'You see, Sukhadaji, he keeps teasing me so.'

Saying this, she turned away. Her eyes were filled with tears.

GLOSSARY

aarati:	religious ceremony performed in the worship of gods with a rotatory motion of a platter of small lighted lamps before the idol (or image) of a god
abba (abba-jaan):	father (father, dear as life) in Urdu
achcha:	alright!, is that so?, okay!
achkan:	long coat, usually worn buttoned up to the chin
Allah:	God, the Supreme Being
amma:	mother (or grandmother) in Hindi and Urdu
angithi:	small coal-burning, hibachi-like stove, a brazier
anna:	unit of currency, 1/16 of a rupee (sixteen annas make a rupee)
arre:	exclamation expressing surprise
Asarh:	fourth month of the Hindu calendar, corresponding to June-July
baba:	exclamation meaning giving up in disgust; Anglo-Indian term for son
babu:	often used to address a clerk
babuji:	respectful form of address, used for father, or an older man
bahu (bahuji):	daughter-in-law of the house, also used to address the woman in charge of the house.
bai:	suffix used after a woman's name signifying respect
Baniya:	caste of tradesmen; often used derogatively to signify the mentality of tradespeople
bara:	senior, older (Bara sahab = senior officer)
batasha: (pl. —e)	type of puffed sweet made from ground rice and sugar, often used on festive occasions
beta/beti:	son/daughter, often used in a general sense and lovingly to address someone young enough to be a son/daughter

bhabhi:	wife of an older brother, so addressed by younger brother or sister; also used for a woman who is unrelated
bhai:	Hindustani (spoken language which is mixture of Hindi and Urdu) word meaning brother, used among friends and relatives, (bhai jaan = brother, dear as life)
bhaiya:	young man
bhajan:	devotional song
bhang:	cannabis
Bharat:	ancient name of India
bigha:	measure of land, five-eighth of an acre; [1 hectare = 2.96 acres]
bira (of paan):	bundle (of paan)
brahmachari:	religious student who observes celibacy
Brahman:	the priestly caste
Chamaar:	man engaged in leatherwork, a low caste
chapatti:	same as roti
chaprasi:	peon, orderly (the lowest functionary of the government)
charpai:	four-poster frame with woven string mesh for bed
Chaudhary:	leader, usually the headman in a village
chaupal:	meeting place in the village, usually in a landlord's house
chausar:	a board game played by two
daal:	lentils, thick soup-like dish made of lentils
dada:	elder brother, also used in a general sense to address someone older with respect; also used for grandfather.
dak bungalow:	residence provided by the government for officers travelling on duty
darshan:	viewing of a deity or an idol thereof; often used for viewing of a saintly person, a devata or a devi
devar:	younger brother of husband, a relationship that allows risque jokes between devar and bhabhi
devata (m) and: devi (f)	deity, god/goddess, divinity; in common parlance, however, they mean a good or a noble man/woman, a virtuous woman, or a person of unusual generosity or kindness.
dharma:	depending on context, dharma means religion, duty, morality, moral principles, obligation, righteousness.

When a specific meaning is clear I have translated 'dharma' in that meaning; otherwise, I have left it as 'dharma'

dharmshala:	lodge where pilgrims can stay for nominal room and board, a hospice
dharmayuddha:	battle fought for dharma
dhela:	a coin worth half of one paisa, an infinitesimal amount of money
dhobhi:	washerman
dhoti:	a long piece of cloth that is wrapped around the lower half of the body; men and women wrap it differently
Dom-Chamaars:	lower caste, workers at cremation places
Durga:	Hindu goddess of power
durrie:	cotton carpet
Ekadashi:	eleventh day of a lunar fortnight
gaushala:	cowshed
ghat:	bank of a river or pond, a place where dhobis wash clothes
ghazal:	a form of Urdu poetry generally dealing with love; derived from a Persian lyric form of the eighth century
ghee:	clarified butter
ghuyian:	roots of *Arum calocasia*
gilauri of paan:	prepared and folded betel leaf
gur:	jaggery
hafizji:	a Mohammedan who learns the complete Quran by heart
halwa:	a sweet dish
howdah:	an enclosed platform tied to the back of an elephant for people to ride in
hukkah:	a water pipe for smoking tobacco
huzur:	Urdu word for Venerable Sir, my Master
ikka and tonga:	horse-drawn carriages; ikka is smaller and one-horse-drawn, tonga is bigger and more respectable
Inshallah razeoon:	Muslim chant when taking a coffin for burial. Literally means, 'from God we come, to God we return'.

jamadaar:	chief of sweepers
-ji:	a suffix denoting respect
kachauri:	type of puri with some filling and deep fried
Kahaar:	caste of workers who draw water (from a well)
kaki:	aunt
karahi:	wok
karma:	act, deed, work, occupation, business, fate, destiny
Karmabhumi:	place of action, where work is worship
katha:	recital, reading usually of a religious texts or epics
Kartik:	the eighth month of the Hindu calendar, corresponding to October–November
kauri:	small shell, an insignificant amount
kesariya tilak:	saffron-coloured tika applied on the forehead of a warrior going to battle
khaddar:	homespun cloth
kharif:	crop which is harvested in Autumn
khas:	type of grass that is woven in the form of a thick mat to cover doors and windows. When wet, it exudes a very fine fragrance and is used widely in north India to cool rooms and houses in hot summer months.
Khatik:	Hindu butcher, an untouchable
khir:	sweet dish prepared from milk
khurpee:	tool for weeding, scraping, or reaping grass
kirtan:	devotional song
Kshatriyas:	one of the four major castes, the warrior caste
kurta:	loose shirt, worn as an upper garment
lahanga:	a loose, embroidered petticoat skirt worn by women on special occasions
lakh:	one hundred thousand
lala:	form of addressing people, sometimes used sarcastically
lalaji:	respectful form of address
lathi:	length of hard bamboo, a common means of defence and offence, often used as a stick by police to disperse crowds
Laxmi:	goddess of wealth
lila:	play (divine play/frolic) (e.g., bhagwaan ki lila)

lorry:	motorized bus used to transport passengers or goods
Magh:	eleventh month of the Hindu calendar, corresponding to January–February
Maharaj:	respectful form of address, e.g., your eminence
malaai:	rich cream
mata or mataji:	mother, often used in a general sense and with respect to address someone old enough to be a mother
maulvi:	learned Mohammedan, specially versed in Arabic and Persian literature
maund:	a measure of weight, equal to ca. 40 kg
maya:	Hindu concept that the world is an illusion (make-believe)
mem:	a form of address for a western woman, probably derived from 'madam'
miyan:	Urdu word for Mister, sometimes used in a derogatory sense
moh:	illusionary love or affection, tied up with the concept of the world as maya; also means ignorance, delusion, spiritual ignorance
morha:	a comfortable chair or stool made of reeds
nawaab:	Muslim potentate; in Mughal period, a provincial ruler
nazarana:	the practice of offering gifts or presents to a superior or overlord
ojha:	sooth-sayer
paan:	folded betel leaf with lime and katechu and small pieces of areca nut; presented to guests as a welcome gesture
pancho:	community leaders
panchayat:	council of elders that governs the village
pakori:	savoury made of vegetables coated in batter and deep-fried
parwal:	a small, zucchini-like vegetable
Phag:	a song sung collectively at Holi in the month of Phagun
Phagun:	twelfth month of the Hindu calendar, corresponding to February–March

Poos:	tenth month of the Hindu calendar, corresponding to December–January
prashad:	food offered to an idol and hence blessed or sanctified, leavings of food partaken by an eminent person
pucca:	staunch, true blue
pugree:	turban (red pugree = symbolic of police constables)
puja:	act of worship
pundit:	learned man, often of the Brahman caste
purdah:	curtain, seclusion (especially of a Muslim women)
puri:	type of bread, rolled and deep-fried in hot ghee or oil
Rajput:	Kshatriya people of Rajasthan, famous for their valour
Ramayan:	the epic story of Rama, the Hindu god
Ram-nam: satya hai	the Hindu chant when biers are taken for cremation. Literally means, 'God's name is the truth', similar to 'Inshallah razeoon'
rani:	queen, colloquially a wealthy woman
roti:	bread made from wheat which is rolled out like a tortilla and cooked on open fire
sadhu:	holy man, an ascetic
sahab:	suffix often used to denote respect , e.g. bhai sahab; sometimes used by itself to mean respected sir
sahgaamini:	woman associate of the husband
sanyasi:	one who enters the path of renunciation, an ascetic
sari:	traditional form of women's wear, about 5–6 yards long which is wrapped around the waist
Saavan:	fifth month of the Hindu calender corresponding to July–August, monsoon season in north India
seth (sethji):	wealthy businessman
Sevashram:	place/institution devoted to service (from seva = to serve, to be of service, and ashram = place/abode), a house of community service
sharbat:	cool drink
shastra:	scripture, code of law, science, knowledge, a sacred book
shastri, –ji:	versed in the shastras
sindoor:	red powder applied where hair is parted, signifies a married woman

tahsil: a sub-district

tahmad: garment made of a single piece of cloth tied around
                     waist, usually worn by Muslim men

tapasya: self-mortification, austerity, penance, steadfast devotion
                     to a cause

Thakur: man of high caste, a Brahmin, often a ruling class

Thakurji: expression meaning God or His image

thakurdwara: abode of God, an idol, a temple

thanedar: officer-in-charge of a police station

tola: unit of weight, about 12 grams, 10 tolas is about a quarter
                     pound

tulsi-dal: paste made of ground leaves of tulsi, a holy herb, holy
                     basil

Vaishya: one of the four castes, that of business people

wah: an exclamation which signifies wonderment, curiosity,
                     praise as in hurray

walah: suffix denoting a class or occupation, e.g., paan walah,
                     police walah

yaar: friend

yagya: a devotional sacrifice, a religious sacrifice